DEAD LETTERS

Also available from Conrad Williams and Titan Books

THE JOEL SORRELL SERIES

Dust and Desire
Sonata of the Dead
Hell is Empty (November 2016)

DEAD LETTERS

AN ANTHOLOGY OF
THE UNDELIVERED, THE MISSING, THE RETURNED...

EDITED BY

CONRAD WILLIAMS

TITAN BOOKS

Dead Letters
Print edition ISBN: 9781783294503
E-book edition ISBN: 9781783294510

Published by Titan Books
A division of Titan Publishing Group Ltd
144 Southwark Street, London SE1 0UP

First edition: April 2016
1 3 5 7 9 10 8 6 4 2

To the memory of Joel Lane
(1963–2013)

CONTENTS

INTRODUCTION

There are many different ways, these days, of getting your message across. Quick tweet. Fire off an email. Too busy for words? Click on the thumbs-up button. As the world gets smaller so do our missives. I've yet to receive a *kthxbai*, but I've seen them out there. The steady dismantling of considered inked pages. A Boolean transmogrification of Dear/Yours into so many (or rather, so few) 0s and 1s.

But everyone likes receiving mail, don't they? Physical mail, that is. I know I do. And I love writing it too. Long, meandering mind-burps committed to textured paper with a fountain pen. A handwritten letter complete with smudges and creases and crossings out. You can appraise the effort that has gone into such a thing without reading a single word. Maybe a parcel, if you're lucky. Books, perhaps. An item of clothing. You can forgive any brief note that accompanies such things – *I saw this and I thought of you* – because the subtext speaks volumes.

You might detect, in the breath of air that rises from the unsealed flap, notes from the room in which it was penned, or the person who held the pen. It's a tangible memorial. A palpable moment that can be held and read and referred to in the way that the ephemeral email or tweet cannot. In time all of that will be lost.

And yet… we've all sent things in the post that never arrived. We've all been promised items that were never delivered. The price we pay for eschewing digital postboxes is the risk of undeliverables.

In the UK, lost or misdirected post ends up at a massive warehouse, the Royal Mail's national return centre in Belfast. If these items haven't reached their intended location within four months much of it is put up for auction. Some things take an age to arrive. Some things never make it.

I recently received a parcel that had been sent to me from America. It had been dispatched, erroneously, to an old address. Then it had been returned to sender. Eventually it found its way to my door. But it had taken a year to get here. What dark corners had shrouded it in the meantime? How many hands had held it? How many chances did it get to become truly lost, to slip into the netherworld where so many millions of other items have passed? Such thoughts inspired the book you now hold in your hands.

But I thought there was the opportunity to play around with the theme a little bit and actually make the idea of misdirected/lost/returned mail a physical part of how the writers would put together their stories. So instead of just asking for submissions dealing with lost post, I sent the writers an actual parcel that was constructed to look like an item of mail that had done the rounds and accidentally landed on their doorstep. Inside was the prompt they would then use as a trigger for their own story. The one stipulation was that they incorporate the concept of dead letters, however tangential, into their fiction.

They all delivered.

CONRAD WILLIAMS

Manchester, September 2015

ABOUT THE EDITOR

Conrad Williams is the author of the novels *Head Injuries*, *London Revenant*, *The Unblemished*, *One*, *Decay Inevitable*, *Loss of Separation*, *Dust and Desire* and, forthcoming, *Sonata of the Dead* and *Hell is Empty*. He has also written four novellas, *Rain*, *The Scalding Rooms*, *Game* and *Nearly People*, and has two collections of short stories to his name: *Use Once then Destroy* and *Born with Teeth*. His work has won the British Fantasy Award and the International Horror Guild Award. His previous anthology, *Gutshot*, was a finalist for the World Fantasy Award. He lives in Manchester with his wife, three sons and a Maine Coon. For more information, visit www.conradwilliams.net, or follow him on Twitter @salavaria.

THE GREEN LETTER

STEVEN HALL

The green letter always arrives between 10.25 a.m. and 10.27 a.m. It's true that a small percentage of the recipients believe that theirs arrived later, as late as 3 p.m. in one instance, but Research and Analysis have attributed these anomalies to the letter simply having gone unnoticed until that point. Likewise, the previously puzzling fact that some recipients claim to have received the letter as part of a regular postal delivery is now entirely dismissible, as in every case analysis of postal data shows that a standard delivery also occurred in or around the 10.25 a.m.–10.27 a.m. window, making it appear as if the green letter had been delivered with the regular mail. In fact, the green letter always arrives alone. From available CCTV data – which at this point is considerable – we may now add a further assertion, incredible as it might seem – the green letter is not delivered at all.

To be clear, this means that not only is there no footage of a green letter being posted to a recipient, it means the green letters have no poster in any conventional sense. CCTV shows empty streets, unopened garden gates, no one whatsoever approaching, and nothing whatsoever passing into the letterbox during the 10.25 a.m.–10.27 a.m. window when the green letter will inevitably land (it does land, there are audio recordings of the letter falling, and – even more curiously – the sounds of the letterbox opening internally, even as it remains undisturbed externally) on the recipient's porch or hallway floor.

In line with protocol, Research and Analysis have proposed the full spectrum of explanations to account for this disparity. These range from the mundane but highly improbable (hoaxing, or some persistent, somehow unrecognised fault in our data-gathering processes and systems) to a range of wild, yet apparently more statistically likely causes (temporal displacement, a many worlds/quantum reality anomaly or communication attempt, a data error/smoking gun which may prove the simulation hypothesis). At present, analysis indicates that the letter does drop through the recipient's letterbox internally, despite nothing being posted into the same letterbox externally at that time, though we are no closer to being able to select a 'why' from the several exotic options identified by Research and Analysis (and – as Dr Blakeson, head of R&A has postulated – from an unknown number of additional exotic options as yet unidentified by science). In the face of this, we must simply note this disparity and move forward. The green letter phenomenon is of unparalleled scientific interest, but we must also accept that we are woefully unequipped at the present time to draw even the most rudimentary conclusions.

Outwardly – and certainly by comparison to the process of its arrival and other attributes (see later) – the green letter is a fairly mundane object. The envelope is unusual, though by no means remarkable. At 216mm across it is the perfect width to accommodate a standard A4 paper sheet, but it is not very tall, with a height of only 78mm – about the height one might expect for the envelope of a small Christmas card. The envelope then, is best suited to posting perhaps one or two sheets of A4 paper that have been folded top to bottom many times. Its usefulness beyond this seems very limited. It's fair, I think, to say it is an odd shape. It's also bright green.

The envelope is always addressed to 'Ethan', the word handwritten with a sharp, B2 pencil according to R&A. Below and to the right of this name, 'NO ADDRESS' is written and underlined in black permanent marker. In the top right corner, the words 'Postage unpaid' appear in a hand-drawn circle, again in B2 pencil. All three sections of text appear to have been written by the same individual. On the reverse, in fountain pen, and the same handwriting – 'no return address'.

So far, we have identified 674 green envelopes and their recipients through police and government referral over the last four years, and through other means, though we must imagine that the true number is significantly higher than this.

This brings us to the second phenomena: they are all the same.

We have 176 surviving green envelopes and they are all exactly the same. Actually, this statement is somewhat inaccurate. Let me be more specific, by quoting Dr Blakeson directly: '…these are not 176 very similar green envelopes as was initially supposed, but 176 instances of the exact same envelope'.

Not only does the handwritten text match perfectly across

all the specimens, but all display identical postal damage and wear and tear. This includes what R&A refer to as 'the anchor rip', a small, curved, T-shaped tear on the front left of every envelope, and the same number and random pattern of white 'rub marks' along the envelope's bottom edge, where the green printing has given way to the white paper stock beneath. To be clear, each envelope also contains unique damage, but this can almost always be shown to have derived from the recipient's opening and subsequent treatment of their iteration of the envelope. At the present time, our team feel confident in stating that, at the time of arrival, every green envelope looked exactly the same because, somehow, they are all the same envelope. Research and Analysis have extracted robust data on many fronts – paper stock, inks, dyes, fibre identification and fibre displacement in the various reoccurring rips, etc. – and concluded that all specimens must somehow be one and the same specimen, or that an original was somehow copied and reproduced at a molecular level many times, to create this series of perfect 'clones'. Again, for now we can only note this remarkable information and proceed, in the hope that our future investigations may reveal insights into how and why this should be the case.

Now we'll progress to the contents. Every green envelope contains a single item we refer to as the List. We have only succeeded in acquiring one 'unused' List thus far, so have been unable to make the sort of material comparisons that had been possible with green envelope samples. That said, our tests on the List have been extensive, culminating in an experiment named Investigation Number One, the results of which you are probably aware, even if you have not been briefed on the context of the experiment or the green envelope phenomenon previously. As I have the luxury of speaking more candidly than my superiors to you in this capacity, I will not sugar coat this information and report simply that Investigation Number One was an unmitigated disaster, and responsibility for the loss of Captain Michael Wayne rests squarely with this department.

I'd like to warn you that the attached footage is very distressing. As you'll see for yourself, Captain Wayne made fourteen requests for the test to be aborted, which were not observed despite clear and increasing levels of distress. I consider this inexcusable and will implement whatever reprimand you consider appropriate without hesitation, including my own resignation from the project and the department, if you feel this to be appropriate.

But, as time is of the essence, back to the subject at hand:

The List is exactly what its name implies – a simple list written on what is, to all intents and purposes, an ordinary yellow Post-it note. Written in black biro, in the same hand as the envelope, the list reads:

1. TO BE SUCCESSFUL
2. BE HAPPY
3. AND FOR OTHERS AROUND ME
4. PROGRESSION
5. MONEY
6. xxx   A LOWERCASE 'P' AND 'R' SCRIBBLED OUT   PRAISE
7. REWARDS FOR U
8. MUSIC
9. SECURITY
10. BLANK

On the day of the green envelope's arrival, most usually around 1.40 p.m.–2.30 p.m., the recipient typically succumbs to an absentminded urge to draw a circle around one of the first nine points on the list, the selection varying from recipient to recipient (from interview data it seems that the recipient does not make a conscious choice to select one point over another, although our data suggests that the choice is not random, selection probabilities forming loose clusters in line with a number of demographic markers – see attached).

What happens next depends on the point selected. What we call the 'List Outcome' is solidly linked to the recipient's selection – the same selection will always result in the same outcome 100% of the time. The List Outcomes are bizarre in many instances, but thousands of hours of interview footage along with substantial medical and site investigation work has convinced us that the below – though outlandish – are all accurately presented, and a direct result of point selection on the List. Here are the outcomes:

1. TO BE SUCCESSFUL

Outcome: Typically within 24 hours, recipients who circle this item will find that babies and small children (usually under the age of five) in close proximity to them become extremely frightened, often degenerating into outright hysteria if forced to make any sort of physical contact. The children exhibit what seems to be a panic-stricken terror that endures as long as the recipient is in the child's sightline, and typically for some 20–30 minutes afterwards, with nightmares following an encounter in around 65% of cases (and 90% of 'touching' cases). The child will always outright refuse to explain their extreme reaction at the sight of a number one recipient, and even mentioning the experience is likely to cause considerable distress. There are no exceptions to the effect – we have observed a newborn baby react to her own mother in this fashion. The effect also appears to be permanent. As an addition, several recipients in this group have reported occasional feelings of deep uneasiness when catching sight of their own reflection out of the corner of their eye, though none have yet been able to put this experience into clearer terms. Physically, the recipient appears to be completely normal, and Research and Analysis can identify no physiological changes of any kind.

2. BE HAPPY
Outcome: Recipient will find a mug with the slogan 'No. 1 Dad' at the back of a cupboard. [Note: this outcome has only recently been discovered by our investigators, after following up this seemingly 'blank' outcome.]

3. AND FOR OTHERS AROUND ME
Outcome: A recipient who circles number three will have sex with a relative within 100 hours. In most instances, extreme distress and revulsion will follow, with recipients reporting a disturbing 'coming to my senses' moment following intercourse. Relatives are generally older than the recipient, with grandparents or aged parents being the most common partner. We are running therapy sessions with additional data mining for all known number threes. But – with the exception of number sixes – this outcome is reported least according to our records, perhaps unsurprisingly.

4. PROGRESSION

Outcome: Number fours vanish within 60 seconds of circling this point, leaving a pile of whatever clothing they were wearing behind. Where they go is unknown, as no number four has ever been seen or heard from again. Whether this disappearance relates in some way to the word 'progression' or is as unrelated an outcome as most of the other numbers is unknown, but relatives have been known to find some comfort in this notion, and current protocol for field officers is not to dissuade them of it.

5. MONEY

Outcome: An illness manifests in number fives within three to six weeks. Often these are withering diseases, or diseases that cause a severe reduction in brain function.

6. PRAISE

Outcome: As far as we know, no recipient has ever circled number six. This would suggest either (a) an inactive portion of the List, (b) a positive outcome that 100% of recipients would wish to keep secret from the world at large, or (c) a negative outcome which would likewise cause 100% of recipients not to contact the authorities.

7. REWARDS FOR U

Outcome: [REDACTED FOR REASONS OF NATIONAL SECURITY]

8. MUSIC

Outcome: A rare instance of the selected word on the list

having some relation to the outcome itself. Number eights develop a constant, melodic tinnitus which has been proven to accurately predict the next-but-one song on any tuned radio within thirteen metres. Research is ongoing, but early results suggest number eights are capable of developing some wider capacity for precognition if supplied with extensive training and favourable conditions.

9. SECURITY

Outcome: The next time a number nine returns home after an absence of over one hour, they will discover a pet, spouse or child living in the property who did not exist previously. The newcomer and other members of the family (if any) will believe that everything is as it has always been. Reported responses to this have been widespread, with many number nines submitting themselves for psychological evaluation in the weeks following the discovery. Some families split when the nine cannot accept the interloper, but in a few cases, the result is extremely positive. We have records of a female number nine who could not have children returning home to discover her husband and nine-year-old daughter cooking dinner. After a period of adjustment, the woman felt very happy with her altered circumstances. It may be supposed that more of these 'happy outcomes' occur, but few are reported.

10.

The blank. As you will see from the attached footage, Captain Wayne had been instructed to write 'Are you trying to communicate with us?' in this space. I repeat, I am fully prepared to submit to whatever reprimand you feel is appropriate for this experiment and the tragic loss of life, however I must state in closing – it is entirely possible that what happened to Captain Wayne might be considered to be some form of response.

STEVEN HALL

Steven Hall was born in Derbyshire in 1975. His first novel, *The Raw Shark Texts*, has been translated into twenty-eight languages, though it stubbornly refuses to be adapted for screen. In 2013, he was named as one of Granta's Best of Young British Novelists.

OVER TO YOU

MICHAEL MARSHALL SMITH

I didn't go to the mailbox in expectation of finding anything worth the trip. I never do these days. There will be bills from the utility company, of course, clothes catalogues for my wife, direct mail from Comcast excitably pimping some new cable TV/Internet/home security package in which I would have no interest even if I could comprehend how it differs from their previous offering. All more meaningful forms of communication now arrive on my computer or phone. Gone are the days when you made a choice over when to encounter a missive from the universe: now they get right up in your face and ping at you. Somebody — I can't recall who — once said that each letter is an uninvited guest, turning up on your doorstep without warning, armed with the potential to make or ruin your day. Emails can certainly do that. The stuff in the mailbox, once an iconic symbol of community and far horizons? It's just recycling waiting to happen.

I didn't even go to look for mail, if the truth be told. Walking down the path was cover for having a sneaky cigarette. Smoking is bad for you, it would appear. I long ago made an internal accommodation over this — by ignoring the fact — but my son, now ten, has different views. When I was his age, lots of people smoked. Now nobody does (at least amongst the middle classes) and the media and schools are full of dire warnings on the subject. Scott is extremely keen that I give up, and manifests this position in a strident campaign that includes destroying my packs whenever he finds them.

I'm working on it, kind of. I smoke less than I want to, certainly. And in secret. An occasional walk to the mailbox has become a ruse for grabbing a morning nicotine hit in relative safety, during what was beginning to feel like a somewhat endless school summer vacation.

I stubbed the butt out and rolled it into a discreet ball which I slipped in my pocket for later disposal. Then, because I might as well, I checked the mailbox. There wasn't much inside, as I'd done the same a couple of days before. Supermarket coupons. Credit card companies urging me once again to consider getting further into debt. A small padded envelope.

I shoved all the junk under my arm — remembering once again my idea of moving the recycling container so it was right next to the mailbox, a notion I'd again forget as soon as I started walking back to the house — and examined the envelope. It was four inches by six, a buff color. The most notable thing about it was the NOT KNOWN AT THIS ADDRESS scrawled across the front. It'd been sent to someone called Patrick Brice, who lived — or was supposed to live — in Rockford, Illinois.

My name is Matt, and I live in California.

I flipped it over. Someone had written 'Return to sender' on the reverse, in a different hand and colour. In a third hue

— and different handwriting once again — someone else had further written 'NO FORWARDING ADDRESS'.

None of which explained what it was doing in my mailbox. I considered putting it back, but realised it'd likely been sitting there a couple of days already, and the mail person hadn't taken it away, having discovered their error. So instead I carried it and the other stuff back to the house, where I dropped the whole bundle on the kitchen table and forgot about it.

Late morning found me back in the kitchen, making coffee. Karen had taken Scott out for a few hours, giving me an opportunity to work in peace and, coincidentally, have a smoke or two without being given a hard time. As I headed toward the back door, coffee in hand, I noticed the envelope on the table and grabbed it in passing.

Outside, I looked at the package again for a few minutes without learning anything new. The only way to do that would be, of course, to open it. It wasn't for me, self-evidently. It was to this Patrick Brice person. But — equally obviously — it wasn't going to get to him. I could put it back in the box or take it down to the post office, but it had clearly done the rounds already without finding a home. So what should I do? Drop it in the trash? That felt wrong. Someone had sent something to somebody else. An engagement had been commenced, a baton proffered. To simply dispose of it, be a stranger summarily curtailing that journey, didn't seem right.

I could at least find out what was inside, and make a judgment as to how important it was. If it seemed like some big deal, there might be something I could do. Plus if I took my time over the process, I'd be outside long enough to legitimate having another cigarette.

Sounded good.

The envelope had been securely sealed with brown duct tape. I circumvented this by tearing it open at the other end, fairly neatly. Inside was an object wrapped in a small piece of white paper, secured in place with a piece of scotch tape. I used my thumbnail to slice through this — again, fairly neatly — and unwrapped something that was immediately recognizable.

A chess piece. A bishop, to be precise, about an inch and a half high, quite nicely made out of a darkish wood. On the base was a thin pad of dark red/brown felt. The piece was in good condition, but a little worn, as if it had been used many times.

So?

Realizing that there was something on the paper wrapping, I took a closer look. A short sentence, three words, ending with a period — all of it in Courier, or some near equivalent, as if produced on a typewriter.

`'Over to you.'`

'Huh,' I said. I lit my second cigarette, and tried to make a mystery out of what I'd found. Most likely there wasn't one. Two guys playing long distance, I guessed, and this a notification of a move, presumably one in which the bishop had been taken. Though… instead of 'Over to you', or even 'Your move', shouldn't the message have been 'Knight to King 4 x Bishop', or however it was they indicated those things? I'd never been a player, finding the game both hard and boring, and couldn't remember the exact terms. Plus you wouldn't actually send someone a piece, would you, even if you'd taken it? You both needed to retain full sets in order to keep playing the game.

Whatever. I could imagine it'd be annoying for the move to have gone astray, but if the guy was no longer at that address, and had left no forwarding information, there wasn't a lot that could be done about it.

At that moment I heard the sound of a car turning in off the street, and swore, and rapidly stubbed out my cigarette, and scurried inside.

'What's this?'

I was sitting at my desk, Scott standing beside me. He was bored, and had come in to say hi, hang out, and generally avoid doing the book report that was supposed to be his mission for the afternoon/week/summer.

'Chess piece,' I said. I'd put it and the other bits on my desk when I hurried back in. He picked it up.

'Why's it here?'

'I found it,' I said, to avoid explaining at length. I was in the middle of working, he wasn't supposed to come in while I was busy, and though it made me feel a heel to be distant toward him, Karen would be pissed at me if I wasn't, as it made her job of keeping him out of my hair during the summer days even harder.

'What kind?'

'A bishop.'

'Is that the type that…'

'Diagonally,' I said.

'Oh, okay. What's the smell?'

I stiffened, thinking he'd caught a hint of cigarette smoke on me from earlier. He raised the chess piece to his face, however, and sniffed. 'It's on this.'

I took it from him. The odour was faint, but Scott has a keen nose. 'Don't know,' I said.

'Smells like disinfectant. The kind they use in big buildings.'

'You're right,' I said. 'Could be something like that.'

'Why's it wet?'

'It's not.'

'Yes it is. The base.'

I turned it upside down and gently touched the felt. It was a little damp. 'Huh,' I said. 'It wasn't earlier. I mean, before.'

I looked at the part of the desk where the piece had been, but Scott was ahead of me, wiping his finger across it. 'It's not wet here.'

At that moment his mother hollered from the kitchen, expressing a hope that Scott wasn't bugging his father and how was he doing with that book report, hey? Scott made a face like a frightened frog.

'You're fine,' I said, winking. 'But go.'

He smiled, and slipped out of the room.

Just before bedtime I wandered down the path toward the road. Our neighborhood is on the edge of town, in fact a little past it, and the houses are widely spread on heavily wooded lots. It's kind of like being out in the country, except you're not, which is my preferred combination.

'Still on the old cancer sticks, huh.'

Our neighbor, Gerry, was standing at the head of his

own path. He's in his mid-sixties and the previous year, in the aftermath of his wife leaving him for some guy, had laboriously curtailed his own two-pack-a-day habit, on the grounds life couldn't feel any worse.

'Yeah,' I said, annoyed at having been caught, especially as Scott was asleep and so I'd believed myself safe from censure. 'Cutting down, though.'

'Don't work,' Gerry said. 'You'll still be cutting down when those things cut *you* down. Clean break. Only way to get that job done.'

'Worked for you, I guess.'

'Sure did. Hurt like crap for a couple months, but I stuck with it. And you should, too. You've got a son. And that kid loves you.'

'I know.' Gerry and his wife never had children, a fact he has spoken of with regret several times.

'Just saying.'

He nodded goodnight, and ambled back toward his own house, where he now lived alone, and drank.

I went for a run the following morning, but cut it short after 5k. Our area is home to just about every variety of tree known to man, which makes it very attractive but something of an allergy motherlode. There are few months of the year when something airborne isn't wafting out of the branches to irritate the membranes.

I came out of the shower still coughing and sniffing.

'The regime's evidently doing you a power of good,' Karen said.

'And you last exercised… when?'

'I exercise restraint on a daily basis, darling. Be grateful for that.'

Thus bested, I went to my study.

As anyone who works at home, and alone, knows, there are times when your focus drops. You can either beat yourself up over this — as I used to — or accept it as part of the ebb and flow of the creative process.

Put another way, mid-afternoon I found myself sitting staring into space. I long ago set up a system on my computer that disbars any interaction with the Internet during working hours, except for email, so that wasn't a temptation. It would, of course, have been an ideal moment for a contemplative and focus-recharging cigarette, except Scott was home, up in his room, ostensibly doing his book report but more likely involved in covert work on his Minecraft empire. I could probably get away with it, as he'd be keeping his head down in case his mother checked on progress, but I don't actually enjoy misleading my son. I could last out a couple more hours.

I could — and possibly should — call my mother. It had been a few days. I like my mother, and since my father died a couple years ago we've spoken twice a week. It's a serious undertaking, however. My dad's passing revealed my mother to be a more anxiety-prone person than I'd realised, something he'd been adept — consciously or otherwise — at diffusing. Without his buffer her energy coursed in scattershot directions, especially over the phone, an hour of which could derail my work mojo for the rest of the afternoon.

Eventually my eye happened upon the chess piece, still in position near the base of my computer monitor. I picked up my phone — not subject to the same Internet sanctions as the desktop machine — and googled 'Patrick Brice'. The first several pages of results related to some up-and-coming movie director of that name. It seemed unlikely he'd be the intended recipient, or that he lived or had lived in Illinois. Wikipedia indicated he'd been born in California. After this were screeds of other randomers who happened to have the name, all doubtless leading perfectly decent albeit unremarkable lives. None were self-evidently long-distance chess players.

I put the phone down and picked up the bishop. As with any small object whose purpose inherently involves being touched, it was hard not to roll it around in the fingers, and to wonder who else had done so. What with me not being psychic, no answers were forthcoming.

When I touched my finger to the base, it was at least as damp as the day before. Which seemed odd, as the ambient temperature was reasonably high. I raised it to my nose, and thought the smell was a little stronger, too.

I closed my eyes and tried to get closer than Scott's pretty decent summation. I couldn't be sure, but it seemed to me to have something of hospital corridors about it. Disinfectant of a type both fusty and clinical, designed to do its job reliably rather than beguile the senses. This made me wonder whether one of the chess players — still assuming that's what was going on — was mired in some kind of long-term hospital sojourn.

If so, there was all the more reason to try to get it back on its journey. I still had no way of doing this, however. Unless...

I opened the drawer where I'd stuffed the envelope, and

took another look. This showed me something I should have noticed before. No stamps on it. No franking. To judge from the number of times it had failed to find a home, it should have had two or three pieces of evidence of passing through the mail system.

It had none.

That evening, when Scott was in bed and Karen was sleepily scrolling through Facebook on her phone, I took a walk down the path again. I enjoyed a cigarette in peace, though actually I'd been semi-hoping Gerry would be around, and when I'd finished, I stood at the road for a moment, making a decision.

It took a couple minutes for him to answer his doorbell. He was wearing old sweats and a T-shirt that had seen better days, probably the late 1970s.

'Hey.'

He stood aside. I shook my head regretfully. 'Just wanted to check something.'

'Sure.'

'I found something in my mailbox yesterday. Small envelope, looks like it's been around the block a few times — and addressed to someone in Illinois.'

He frowned. 'Okay.'

There were a few empty beer bottles on the table in the room behind him. 'Weird thing, there's no postmark. I just wondered… you didn't put it there, right?'

'Why would I do that?'

I smiled. 'No idea. Just trying to solve a minor mystery.'

He nodded affably. 'Sure I can't tempt you, Matt? Got a box

of Boont Amber open. Nice and cold.'

'Some other night, okay? Soon.'

'I'll hold you to it.'

When I got back indoors Karen had taken herself upstairs. I could hear preparations for bed. The kettle was boiling. We've both long been in the habit of taking a cup of chamomile tea to bed, made by me.

While I waited for the water to boil I walked through into my study and stood at my desk. I hadn't expected Gerry to be behind the envelope. He has, so far as I can tell, no sense of humour whatsoever, assuming that's the quality you require for a practical joke of this type. I could ask our mail person tomorrow, if I caught her, but Marie is a stolid person of middle age and approximately pyramidal shape and I couldn't imagine her playing a prank on me either. The mystery the bishop presented was therefore unsolvable, and frankly not terribly interesting.

I picked it up and examined it again.

The base was still wet. It still smelled a little weird. That's all there was to be said about it. I carried it out to the kitchen, where I poured water onto the waiting teabags. Then I went out the back door.

I still didn't want to put the piece in the trash. It deserved to continue on a journey of some kind, but I was bored of it, and I really didn't like the smell, which was now beginning to pervade the study.

So I walked a few yards toward the woods, and threw the piece into the trees.

* * *

Next morning Scott had a dental appointment, which — for reasons too tedious to relate — meant going to a town twenty miles away, and thus — given the practice's playful way of pretending they've never, ever seen you before, and making you fill in more forms and then jump hoops through dental nurses and assistants and senior assistants before you got to the maestro himself — at least three lost hours. I'd assumed I'd be in the frame for this adventure, but Karen volunteered.

I got a lot of work done, as is often the case when the house is empty and you're free to work to your own rhythms. Which meant, in my case, a fresh cup of coffee and a cigarette about once an hour. I was on one of these breaks when my phone vibrated in my pocket.

I pulled it out quickly, assuming it would be Karen wanting my say-so on some unusually outrageous dental charge — or, I dared hope, her giving me news that they were going to make a day of it and come back the slow way.

The screen said no, it was my mother.

I winced. Partly because she'd called me, which meant it had been too long since I'd called her. Also because, goodbye productivity. But… she's my mother.

She was in good form, generally, and spent the first twenty minutes on a free-form catch-up on the ins-and-outs of the tiny Midwestern town where she lives, delivered in a style that Garrison Keillor might be proud of, were he a little bitchier in nature (and presently without an editor). This segued into a list of the tasks she was currently undertaking around the house. In the last six months she'd acquired the decluttering bug, and while I feared this might eventually see her living in a house with a single chair, her phone, and no other possessions, it seemed more positive than how she'd spent the period immediately after my father's death, restlessly going from room to room, weepily sifting through old photo albums and mementos, repeatedly, trying to arrange them into an order which no one — including her, I'd been confident — would ever comprehend.

'One thing, though,' she said. My attention had been wandering a little, I'll confess, but this re-focused me. Over the last two years I'd come to realize these three words often signaled whatever her current low-key obsession had become. 'Something's missing.'

'What?' I asked, keeping my tone light. I had plenty of practice in deflecting these minor manias, at reassuring her that not being able to find the store receipt from when they bought the new dishwasher in 2008 was not a huge deal in the scheme of things.

'The bishop,' she said.

My mind spent half a second wondering which of the clerics in her town she was referring to, but my body was quicker. My heart beat hard, once. 'What?'

'Your father's chess set.'

'Dad had a chess set?'

'Of course he did. You must remember it.'

I did not. 'What do you mean, it's missing?'

'The bishop,' she said, patiently. 'I hoped I'd been reasonably clear about that. By saying… "the bishop".'

It's as well to remember that your parents remain potent individuals, however batty they may appear from time to time. 'Sure, okay, sorry. But missing how?'

'I was clearing through the drawers in his den, and found

the set. I can't get rid of it, of course. He never played much, well, he didn't have the opportunity at home… I can't play, and you never showed any interest, but I remember him buying it, not long after you were born. Lovely brown wood. You *sure* you don't remember it?'

I felt short of breath. 'No. The bishop, Mom?'

'Oh yes. Well, it's gone. One of them. All the other pieces are there — well I assume they are, I'm not sure how many of those pawn things there are supposed to be, but the others all come in pairs or fours. Quartets. Or quads. Or whatever the word is. Except the bishops. There's only three of them. That can't be right, can it?'

I had no recollection of my father owning a chess set. That didn't prove anything — you don't remember everything from childhood. But it seemed very odd to me that we should be having this conversation today.

'It's probably in another drawer somewhere.'

'Nope,' she replied, smartly. 'Checked them all.'

Of course you did, I thought. 'What about…'

'It's nowhere in the house.'

'Well, I guess it just got lost at some point,' I said. 'He figured maybe it'd turn up, and anyway no big deal, as he never used it.'

'I'm sure you're right, Matt,' she said, sounding relieved, as though what I'd said constituted a statement on the subject from a higher and more reliable authority than she felt herself to be. We spoke for another ten minutes, but I can't remember what was said.

When I walked back into my study, the first thing I noticed was the smell.

The chess piece was standing on the desk.

I heard our car pulling into the drive, and reached into the drawer to get a breath mint.

Toward the end of the afternoon, Scott came in. Instead of heading straight to my desk, as he usually did, he lurked in the background. He seemed subdued.

'Everything okay?'

'I guess.'

'I wanted to ask you something, actually,' I said.

'What?'

I nodded toward the chess piece. 'Did you put that there?'

'No. It was here when I came in yesterday. I asked you about it, remember?'

'I know. I meant... did you put it there today? This morning? Before you went to the dentist?'

He looked confused. 'No. It was already there, right?'

'Right.' I knew it had been extremely unlikely that he'd gone wandering into the woods, happened to find the piece where it had landed somewhere in the bracken and leaves, and brought it back. It was the best idea I'd been able to come up with, however. I'd spent a long time trying to produce a rational explanation for the piece's reappearance. That had been my only shot.

Now I had nothing, except for the hollow feeling in my stomach.

'Never mind. How's the book report coming along?'

'You've been coughing all afternoon,' Scott said. 'I can hear you from my room.'

'Seriously?'

'Yes. It's not that far.'

That wasn't what I'd meant. I hadn't been aware of coughing at all. 'Sorry. Allergies.'

'No, it isn't.'

I turned to look at him. 'What?'

'You've been smoking, haven't you?'

'No,' I said.

'You're a liar. I know you have.'

'Scott, I…' I stopped. 'Yes, okay. I've had a couple today. I'm sorry.'

He nodded distantly. This was far worse than his usual tactic of shouting. 'I really am,' I added.

'So stop.'

'It's really not that easy.'

I expected him to launch into another iteration of his well-worn analysis of how incredibly simple it was to stop putting a dumb burning thing into your mouth, but instead he sniffed. 'I don't like that smell.'

'What smell?'

He indicated the bishop. 'From that thing.'

'I don't like it either.'

'It smells like dying.'

I didn't know what to say to this.

'You should get rid of it,' he said.

I've tried, I thought. *It's harder than you'd think.*

Suddenly he came over and hugged me. 'I love you,' he said, very quietly, arms tight around my shoulders, face buried into my neck.

* * *

After dinner, when Scott was up in his room and in the downward spiral toward sleep, I told Karen that I was going to take a walk, maybe stop in next door, see how our neighbor was doing.

'You're nice,' she said. 'See you in bed.'

I stopped by the study, put something in my left and right trouser pockets, and left the house.

'True to your word,' Gerry said, gratefully, as I walked up his path. He was sitting out on his deck, a short line of empties on the side table. "Fraid I'm done with the Boonts, though. Anchor Steam work for you?'

'Plenty good enough.'

We sat and talked a while. I drank a beer slowly, and accepted a second. By then, Gerry must have been on his sixth or seventh.

'So how come you never had kids?'

He shrugged. 'Darlene never wanted any. Figure she looked at the mess her parents made of it, decided she didn't want a part of that scene.'

'Not such a great childhood?'

'Kind of fucked up. And eventually her dad walked out. Darlene never forgave him for that, though from the few times I met her mom, I could kind of see his point. Family like that, I guess it was always a long shot she'd be able to make a marriage stick forever.'

I'd heard all this before. I'd just needed to hear it again. 'I suppose it's hard when a parent leaves you. Casts a long shadow.'

'It does that. Another beer?'

'One more, maybe.'

When the next bottle was opened, I reached in my pocket and pulled out my cigarettes. If you're a smoker, you'll know: they go together with beer far too well.

'You mind?'

Gerry shook his head. When I put the pack on the table, I saw his eyes drift toward it.

We talked some more, about this and that. Halfway through the beer, I lit another cigarette. This time it was pretty clear that Gerry was looking at the pack.

'I'm not going to offer,' I said.

He held out until we started the next beer.

By then we were having a whale of a time, and it was a foregone conclusion.

A couple hours later, and by now pretty drunk, I finally stood.

'I really better go.'

Gerry smiled blearily up at me, around his fifth or sixth cigarette. 'Glad you dropped by, Matt. It's been a blast.'

'We'll do it again soon.'

I put a hand out for the pack of cigarettes on the table, saw his eyes flick toward them.

'Heck, keep 'em,' I said.

'You sure?'

'Got more at home.'

'Awesome.'

He pushed himself laboriously to his feet, we shook hands and clapped each other on the shoulder, like men, and I walked away up his path.

I glanced back as I turned the corner around the short section of fence that led onto my own property. Gerry was sitting in his chair on the porch, feet up, looking like king of the world.

Fresh bottle in one hand, cigarette in the other.

I've tried throwing my pack away before, putting it in the trash, brushing my hands of the whole sorry business and declaring I'm done with it. That doesn't work. You can easily go buy more. You can't just halt the journey, any journey. Dad becomes dead, son becomes dad. The path goes on. And what you can never do to a child is leave, especially via corridors that smell of disinfectant.

I stopped and pulled out the thing in my other pocket. The chess piece was back inside, rewrapped in the scrap of paper, resealed with tape. I'd used a Sharpie to write GONE AWAY across one corner of the envelope. I put it in my mailbox, then walked back up the path to our house.

Gerry glimpsed me through the trees, and raised a hand in cheery goodnight. The tip of his cigarette glowed in the dark.

I waved back.

'Over to you,' I said, quietly. 'I'm sorry.'

Next morning the envelope was gone.

I don't smoke any more.

MICHAEL MARSHALL SMITH

Michael Marshall Smith is a novelist and screenwriter. Under this name he has published over eighty short stories, and four novels — *Only Forward, Spares, One of Us* and *The Servants* — winning the Philip K. Dick, International Horror Guild, and August Derleth Awards, along with the Prix Bob Morane in France. He has won the British Fantasy Award for Best Short Fiction four times, more than any other author.

Writing as MICHAEL MARSHALL he has published seven internationally bestselling thrillers including *The Straw Men* series, *The Intruders* — recently a BBC series starring John Simm and Mira Sorvino — and *Killer Move*. His most recent novel is *We Are Here*.

He lives in Santa Cruz, California, with his wife, son, and two cats. For more information visit www.michaelmarshallsmith.com

IN MEMORIAM

JOANNE HARRIS

Imagine a warehouse in Belfast. Over five hundred miles of shelves, running from floor to ceiling. Red-draped yorks; plastic crates; sorting tables and boxes and bins all filled with weird ephemera.

This is the National Returns Centre for the UK – in other words, the dead letter office.

This is where Her Majesty washes her hands of the Royal Mail. Letters that have travelled across the world, and found no destination. Parcels returned, only to find that the sender has moved away, or died. Letters to fictional places, fictional people, or to the dead. In these cases, Her Majesty graciously allows us to open the mail; to seek out hidden identities; to divide the gold from the garbage.

I am a CEW. Customer Experience Worker. I've been here for twenty years, and I've seen it all, let me tell you. Two hundred million pieces of mail a year, give or take, pass through our hands. Begging letters, death threats, photographs of lost loves, keepsakes, unopened Christmas cards, undelivered manuscripts. There's a forgotten Picasso in there, somewhere along the thirtieth stack, plus enough pieces of jewellery to send off a dead infanta in style. And still they keep coming, every day: the undelivered letters, the ones with no return address; the parcels with torn-off labels, inscriptions that are illegible; mail refused by the addressee, or sent to weedy, deserted plots and old abandoned buildings. There are letters here addressed to God, though He has never claimed them. Lots more addressed to Santa Claus, or Superman, or Wolverine. I sometimes wonder how many kids sat waiting for their heroes to call, until, one day, they realised that no one was coming to save them. Or how many desperate lovers, bottle of poison or dagger in hand, waited in vain for their loved one's reply. So many dreams end up in here. So many everyday tragedies. Messages in bottles, sent in hope across the sea, only to wash up here at last, at the foot of a cliff of paper.

The paper-cuts are the worst thing. I get dozens of those a day. I even tried wearing gloves for a while, but it didn't seem right, somehow. These letters have already been through so much. They deserve the touch of a human hand. They deserve to be read, and understood, and acknowledged, before we burn them. The black-edged notes of condolence; the tearful declarations of love; the dutiful letters from boarding school; the last words from the battlefield. It feels as if, by reading them, I can put them at rest, somehow; these strangers, whose words have travelled so far, and never been delivered. What I do is so much more than simply cataloguing mail. I am the one who lays them out; the one who delivers the last rites. I am the embalmer of memories; the custodian of the last word.

First I open, and read, and sort the letters containing valuables. Cheques and cash we return, if we can. Sometimes you can find an address if you open the envelope. Things of intermediate value – clothes, trinkets, toys, books – we keep for six months, then dispose of. Watches, jewellery, artwork, we tend to try to keep longer. Perishable items we get rid of at once. Birthday cakes; live bait; garden plants; groceries; and once a box of soft, pale moths, drowsy in their wrapping of banana leaves and rice paper, which, slipping through my fingers like dusty old transparencies, came back to life in the clear, cold air, and flew up into the overhead lights, where they remained until they died, dropping one by one to the floor in clusters of brownish blossom.

Who on earth sends moths through the post? What were they supposed to mean? Sometimes I still find their wings on the ground like torn-off pieces of paper. The fallen wings are intricate, patterned with tea-coloured hieroglyphs. If you laid them side by side, and looked at them from a great height, then perhaps they might spell out a message. I try not to think too hard about the messages I could have passed on, if only I'd known where to send them. It keeps me awake at night if I do. It's too much responsibility.

I never, ever send letters myself. That may be something to do with the job. I read so many love letters here, so many messages of hate. I don't want to put my thoughts on the page; to risk some stranger reading them. Maybe that's also the reason that I never married. Maybe I know that world too well to dare to be a part of it.

But, last week, something happened. I was going through a load of undeliverable mail. Letters like spent tennis balls, bouncing back and forth for so long that all momentum has been lost. I was about to take a break, when for some reason, a letter at the edge of the pile caught my eye. The address was handwritten, in faded blue ink.

Carey Loewe,
89 Manor Oaks Rd,
Sheffield, S2 5ED

The name and address had been crossed out. On the back, in the same faded script, was the name of the sender:

Liesel Blau,
29 Sevington Drive, Didsbury,
Manchester, M20 5JJ

More recently, someone had added: NOT KNOWN AT THIS ADDRESS. It was postmarked Scarborough. The date stamp read 1st June, 1971.

Sometimes that happens. It isn't so strange. A letter gets lost in transit. Perhaps it falls through the floorboards, or down the back of the sorting machine. With so many letters in the mail, that's bound to happen sometimes. It's no one's fault. It's not even all that unusual. But this time something was different. The letter was addressed to *me*.

Of course, it was a coincidence. Yes, we'd once lived in England. We'd had lots of different addresses. And after all, among so many names, I was bound to see mine one day. But it gave me a chill, nevertheless. Like seeing myself on a gravestone.

I opened up the envelope, taking care not to damage it, and looked inside.

It was empty. No, not quite – here was a square of red plastic, tipped with a nub of metal. A memory stick. And a photograph of two children on a beach. A little girl of five or six, with pigtails and a yellow dress. And a boy of about the same age, wearing a swimsuit and carrying a plastic bucket. His fringe was a little over-long, and he was squinting – not at the sun, but because he needed glasses. I knew this at once, just as I knew that the air had smelt of salt and fried fish; and that the sky had been mackerel-blue, all patterned with little scales of cloud. I knew all this, because I was the boy. I was the boy in the photograph.

For a moment, I was stunned. My head was like a hive of bees. Where had that memory come from? And how could a picture of me as a child have found its way into an envelope dated 1971, along with a piece of technology that wouldn't be available for another thirty years?

I looked around. There are security cameras here, to safeguard anything valuable that might be found in the dead mail. But I know where the cameras are. And I know how to fool them. I slipped the opened envelope, the memory stick and the photograph into my overall pocket. Then I went for my lunch break, although I was no longer hungry. I finished my shift. I went home. Once more I looked at the photograph. Then I sat at my computer with the memory stick in my hand, wondering if I was going mad. I'd stolen mail from the sorting room. I could be fired for doing that. My job is a position of trust, and I'd risked it all – for what?

The photograph of the children was lying on the keyboard. An almost generic picture; a beach that could have been anywhere. The children were playing by the water's edge, not looking at the camera. A shadow in the foreground was probably the photographer.

I told myself it wasn't me. That little boy could be anyone. A five- or six-year-old boy with brown hair, squinting in the sunshine. But that was my name on the envelope. My face in the photograph. And, though I'd heard the ocean, smelt the scent of frying fat, felt the sun and seen the sky mackerel-blue above me, why did I have no memory of that little girl on the beach, or even of being on a beach at all?

The memory stick was a cheap thing; unmarked and unlabelled. It might contain a virus, or a malicious program that would download illegal porn onto my laptop. I ought to throw it away, I thought. It will be bad for my peace of mind. And yet I couldn't help myself. I had to see what was on there.

Whatever it was took some time to download. I waited, and looked at the photograph. It wasn't a very good photograph, with that shadow in the foreground. You'd have thought the photographer would have noticed something like that. Instead, they'd framed the photograph so that half of it was in shadow, and the children looked like an afterthought in the top half of the picture.

Where was the beach? Who was the girl? Was the little boy really me? I have so few photographs of myself as a child. But the one that stood on the mantelpiece in my mother's old house was of that little boy with the fringe and the National Health glasses. Of course, that picture was lost in the fire. But I remember it so well, and I could have sworn the face was the same.

Poor Mother. It can't have been easy, bringing up a child alone. Especially in Belfast, at the height of the Troubles. Not that the fire was deliberate, of course – just a silly accident that might have happened to anyone. But it left me all alone in a hostile country – an English boy with a German name and nothing much else to sustain me. I took a job as a postman, and thirty years later, here I am, here in the dead letter office, doing whatever it is that I do.

The laptop made a chiming sound to announce that the download was complete. I looked at what it had brought me. Pictures – half a dozen of them. No porn, thank goodness. Only a handful of snapshots. My mother was there in black and white. She was wearing a coat with a fur collar, and her hair was loose. She looked young, maybe twenty-five; pretty; impossibly slender. Next, there was a door, under a peeling sign that read: SUNSET VIEW; PRIVATE HOTEL. It could have been almost anywhere. And yet I knew it wasn't. There was a number on the door. 87. I knew that. Just as I knew that the door was green, although it looked black in the picture, and that the steps were yellow tile, and that it smelt of something like cabbage, and worse, and that it was often damp and cold.

How did I know that? How could I know? A moth flew into the table lamp. I checked the window; it was shut. I turned back to the laptop. There she was again, my ma, wearing a yellow raincoat and a multicoloured dress. She had gained weight when we moved to Belfast, and here she was already obese, caught in an unguarded moment, eating a sandwich in a crowd. Was this a wedding? A parade? Her colourful clothing suggested as much. But her face was lined and sour. For a woman who ate so much, she never seemed to enjoy it.

And then I remembered the Orange walk; the sashes and the marching bands; the cordons of police; the man riding on the white horse. My hands began to shake. It was cold. It smelt of cigarette smoke and fish. I hated tuna sandwiches. That was all my mother had brought.

When can we go home? I said.

She shook her head. *When I say so.*

And when she started to heckle and shout at the Orangemen in their bowler hats, I felt myself cringe and shrivel inside at the sound of her voice, broken by drink, shouting hoarsely above me. And when the people around her started to laugh, then got angry, saying: *Shut it, you drunken hoor,* and worse, I wanted to die – no, not quite. I wanted *her* to die.

Another moth came to join the first on the side of the lampshade. The lampshade was blue, and I recalled someone telling me insects were especially drawn to the colour. Another moth, a darker one, fluttered underneath the shade. It made a surprising thudding sound – soft, and yet oddly sinister. I've never liked moths. Even butterflies, if you look at them closely, are ugly in spite of their brilliant wings. My mother's dress in the picture was white, with large spots in orange and fuchsia-pink. Ugly. Like a butterfly.

What's the difference between a butterfly and a moth? I asked.

She told me: *Moths come out at night. They come at night and eat your clothes.*

After that I was always afraid that moths would come and eat my clothes. Why they would want to, I didn't know. But they always frightened me, with their fat, furry bodies and their dusty, thumping wings. That's why I don't open windows at night. And yet, they'd managed to enter, bringing with them those memories.

I turned back to my laptop and saw another photograph appear. Another black-and-white photograph, showing me and the little girl standing on the side of the pier at Scarborough, looking out to sea. I was wearing my glasses this time. The little girl's face was turned away.

Who was she? I knew so much, and still I didn't know her name. I knew we were in Scarborough; I knew that we were six years old. I knew my mother was at the hotel, conducting grown-up business. My mother's grown-up business often involved meeting strange men. It sometimes involved drinking, too; and the little room in which we slept often smelt of vodka. There was a record player there, and a small pile of records. One of them made my mother cry. Its name was *Madam Butterfly*.

There. Another moth. I swiped at it as it blundered through the dusty air towards the lamp, where already a dozen more were crawling plumply on the shade. Brown moths; white moths; moths like torn-up newsprint. Where the hell were they coming from? What were they trying to tell me?

Moths come out at night, replied my mother's voice from beyond the grave. *Moths come out at night*, she said. *Moths come out—*

In Scarborough, we shared her room in the hotel. Sometimes people knocked at the door. My mother always ignored them. During the day, if it was fine, I went off to the beach to play. I had a yellow bucket and spade. Sometimes I took sandwiches. My mother had told me never to go any further than the pier, but I liked to stand on the walkway, pretending to be an adventurer. If I took my glasses off, I could see America, rising up out of the sea like a castle in the clouds.

Another moth. I could hear them, thudding around in the lampshade. I pulled the electrical plug out of the wall, but with the screen of the laptop glowing so invitingly, they started to move towards the light; crawling on the carpet; moving onto the edge of the desk; one of them settling onto the screen, its soft and plushy wings spread out like a swatch of velvet.

I went into the kitchen and checked all of the windows. I left the main light on in there, so that the moths would be drawn away. The air was filled with moths now; pointillistic brushstrokes that dabbed their colours on to my face.

Moths come out at night, she said. *Moths come out at—*

I thought of my mother's powder-puff, and the way she would sit at the window, doing her makeup with the help of a tiny pocket-mirror. I didn't like her makeup. It felt both greasy and powdery, like sugar on a doughnut. Then there was the scent she wore to cover the smell of vodka and smoke; a scent that was sweetly dangerous, like burning rope and Bonfire Night.

There. The moths would fly away, and later I would spray them. Close the kitchen door and wait for them to fall like blossom. I turned back to my laptop, swept aside a dozen moths and saw myself and the little girl, hand in hand on the pavement. Another shot in black and white, our faces turned away, and yet I knew she was wearing a pale-pink dress, with thin grey stripes, and that my shoes had been full of sand, and that we had decided to run away. Maybe to America; or maybe we'd just stay on the pier, living on ice-cream and candy floss, and fish and chips wrapped in newspaper.

Why had we wanted to run away? I couldn't quite remember now. My mother was inside the hotel, with one of her business partners; a man in a suit, with a handsome face, who called her by another name that wasn't the one she went by.

Liesel Blau. It's right there, right there on the envelope. How could I have forgotten that? It was staring me in the face. And it had sounded familiar, even then, though I didn't know why. Of course, it's also a German name, although we didn't speak German any more. By then, even Oma Loewe had receded into a bright point of memory, like the dot on a rented TV when you've turned the picture off.

Oma. It's been so long since I even remembered her. I've forgotten all my German, of course – I lost it many years ago, along with most of my memories – but now I could almost hear her voice, and the songs she used to sing to me.

Another moth settled onto the screen. It gave shadow-wings to the little girl. The photograph was over-exposed, and she and I were luminous, filled with a dangerous clarity. I brushed the moth away – it left a smear of powder across the screen. And then I was there; with Liesel Blau, and Oma, that day by the sea, with the sound of the gulls and the scent of the spray and the feel of the little stones under my feet and the mackerel sky above me.

And Izzy. There was Izzy. That was her name; my little friend with the ponytail and the stripy dress. Izzy Loewe, whom Oma had brought from Germany to see me, travelling across the sea, from town to town, in search of us. We'd played together for more than three weeks while Ma was with her businessmen, and Oma had watched from the boardwalk, with her knitting on her knees, and her sandwiches in a plastic bag – German sausage and *Schwarzbrot*.

The moths were back. I could hear their wings. The kitchen door must have opened again. In the glow of the neon strip, the air was a growing maelstrom. The tube was old and flickering, and their bodies fluttered against the light with stupid, awful persistence, buzzing and burning their wings on the light and falling like bunches of rags on the floor. I turned back to the laptop screen, and there was the sky, that mackerel sky that hung above us all summer like a ragged curtain, and Oma, still sitting there on the steps of the private hotel, waiting for Ma to notice.

She called me Karlin. That was my name. Carey was American. My mother liked American names. She thought they were modern; sophisticated. She'd changed the Liesel to Lisa when we moved. Now we were Gail and Carey Loewe. She pronounced it Low, though actually it was something like Ler-vah. But Ma didn't want to remember that. The less German we sounded, the better. If I happened to let something slip – a word, a name, a story – she used to get angry. Sometimes she'd cry. And so I soon learnt to be English, as later, I learnt to be Irish. After all, what did it matter? Names on an envelope, forwarded from a dozen different addresses. Snapshots on a memory stick; postcards from the distant past.

Izzy didn't speak English at all. That was okay; I understood. Although Ma wouldn't speak German, I still knew a lot of words. And Izzy and I could understand each other without even having to say things aloud. I know that sounds crazy. But when you're so young, anything is possible. Izzy had blue eyes like mine, although she could see to the end of the world. And her hair was brown like mine, and when she smiled, she was pretty.

She always had the best ideas. She always took the lead in our games. Izzy was smart, and she never cried when the big kids jumped on our sandcastle. Instead, she put stones in the turrets, and pointed sticks in the sides of the moat, and when the big kids came again, they hurt their feet, and limped away, and never came back. And so, that summer, while Ma was inside, we played together on the beach. We played at being adventurers, looking out from the end of the pier. We looked for starfish, and pieces of jet, and buried pirate treasure.

And then came the day when the businessman with the handsome face came along, speaking to Ma in German and calling her by her vanished name. We didn't hear much, but the shouting told us something must be wrong. Oma gave us pieces of cake from her sandwich box and told us it would be all right – that it was grown-up business. But then the man with the handsome face came running out onto the beach, shouting in guttural German:

"*Wo is Karlin? Wo ist mein Sohn?*"

That was when we realised that it had all been a trap. You see, Oma had called my father. The man from whom my mother had fled, long ago, in Germany, taking her little son with her. Ma told me the story herself, years later, when I was grown – how she'd had to make a choice between her two young children, and how she'd chosen the weaker twin, the little boy who needed her most, leaving Isabella in the care of her paternal grandmother.

By then, we'd been living in Belfast for years. I'd completely forgotten Oma, and Izzy, and that day by the sea in Scarborough. In fact, until she mentioned it, I'd even forgotten I had a twin; but Ma was drunk, and when she drank, she sometimes let the truth slip.

They come out at night, she used to say. Moths, and sometimes, memories. Memories of our old life, and of the sister I'd left there. Izzy Blau, with whom I'd spent the happiest summer of my life, and who had died when Oma agreed to let her son – after a year of therapy, anger management and remorse – take his daughter, unsupervised, for a day by the seaside.

She was six. Ma didn't know what had made him so angry.

He was always angry, she said. *That was why I ran away*. But this time, his anger had found a special kind of focus. Perhaps my sister had tried to fight back. She was tougher than I was. Anyway, he'd tried to make out that it had been an accident – that someone else had done the deed – but no one had believed him. Konrad Blau had made the news. My mother went back to her maiden name. And I grew up angry, without knowing why, until my mother told me:

You look so like him, she used to say. *You always did. It's frightening.*

She must have seen the look on my face, because she turned away, lit a cigarette, and said, "Don't be like that, Carey."

I said: "Why did you leave her behind? When you knew what he was like?"

She shrugged her helpless shoulders. Years of indulgence had made her fat; if I struck her, the blows would make ripples in the pallid flesh. I remembered smacking a jellyfish with the side of my spade – her skin was just the same shade of white – dead and helpless on the sand.

"I did it for you, Carey," she said. "Izzy was the strong one. Izzy wouldn't have grown up like him."

"Izzy didn't grow up at all."

She started to cry, as I'd known she would, and reached for the bottle at her side. And afterwards, there was a fire – always a risk, when smoking in bed – and I was alone in the world, at eighteen, with nowhere to go but to the place where everything returns, in the end.

The last of the photographs came onto the screen. It looked more modern than the rest – it could have been taken yesterday. A group of people, looking up, some holding digital cameras. I thought it might be another parade; but this was something different. The faces here were pinched with concern, and looking beyond them, I could see the palisade of the National Returns Centre, reflected with a hellish light—

The laptop screen was covered with moths. I tried to brush them aside with my hand. Their sooty wings left a residue that blurred my mother's face from view. And yet here she was, looking older now, her hair gone from bleached-blonde hair to white, tied up in an old woman's ponytail. Over twenty years after her death, thinner than I remembered her, watching, camera in hand, from the scene of an incident.

That was a week ago. What now? The moths – the moths are everywhere. The sound of their wings is like the sound of flames against the window. I haven't been to work all week. I know the moths will be there too; clustering in the overhead lights; casting their giant shadows. Their acrid dust is on everything: my skin, my clothes, my possessions. Their plump and furry bodies hang from the ceiling in luxy swags; the sound of them is the grazing of sheep in a field of white noise.

Moths come out at night, she said. In this case, they are hungry for more than the contents of my wardrobe. They crawl into my ears; my hair; they spill from drawers and suitcases. I have tried to run. But the moths always manage to follow me. Even in this boarding house, the moths are already everywhere; teeming with those memories that only dare come out at night.

I'd thought myself safe in the mail room. It was quiet and peaceful there. There I laid the dead to rest, away from the ghost of my mother. But mothers, like moths, come out at night; and now my mother is everywhere. In my bed, my clothes, my head – eating me from the inside.

Imagine a warehouse in Belfast. Imagine the dead letter office. Miles and miles of memories, safely cocooned in envelopes. Continents of paper, waiting to be discovered. And those moths are in them all; pressed between the pages; hungry for more than just revenge. Cut me open after this and there will be nothing but dust inside me; dust, and the wings of a million moths, a million vanished memories. Imagine setting a match to it all, in the dark, at midnight. Imagine typing in the code; coming in through a side door. Imagine the silence of the place, like a mausoleum. Imagine my mother standing there, all in dust and velvet. *Moths come out at night,* she says. But the night is endless.

As I strike the match, she comes towards me like a cumulus. As I try to turn and run, the moths descend upon me. And as we fly towards the flame, she holds me in her soft embrace, and whispers:

Darling. Mother's here.

JOANNE HARRIS

Joanne Harris is the best-selling author of fifteen novels, three cookbooks, two collections of short stories, two short musicals and a *Doctor Who* novella. She has judged a number of literary awards, including the Orange and the Whitbread Prizes, and in 2014 was awarded an MBE by the Queen. In spite of this thin veneer of sophistication, she also tweets compulsively as @joannechocolat, plays regularly with the #Storytime band – which was formed when its members were still at school – and dreams of being marooned on the *Lost* island.

AUSLAND

ALISON MOORE

"The past is a foreign country"
L.P. Hartley, *The Go-Between*

Karla had known Lukas when they were children. Lukas had wanted to be an inventor, to make things with buttons to press and levers to pull, machines fizzing with electricity. They were still very young when they lost touch. She thought of him often over the years, and always imagined him building something in a garden shed or working at an experiment in a laboratory or standing in front of a blackboard that was covered in almost impossible mathematics, though Lukas himself, in her imagination, was always a boy, frozen in time, in the 1940s.

Anyone whistling or cracking their knuckles made her think of Lukas, as did cap guns and fireworks, whose sulphurous smell lingered in the cold air.

She supposed that he was still in Germany, while she had moved to London with her English mother. One summer, in her teens, she had sent him a postcard, but she never received a reply. Nowadays, she could have typed 'Lukas Birchler' into a search engine and let it find him for her, but in those days there was no such thing. By the time computers were replacing the typewriters in the office in which she worked, she was retiring.

She was in her seventies before she saw Lukas again, in the lobby of a Spanish hotel. She was there on holiday, and had noticed the arrival of this elderly man wearing a trilby and walking with a stick. Despite his age, when he put down his suitcase and cracked his knuckles, Karla was sure that it was him, even before she heard him say 'Birchler' to the receptionist.

Over dinner, Karla told Lukas about her life in London, her secretarial career and her late husband, and Lukas told Karla about his work as a physicist, the research he had done, the papers he had published in scientific journals. 'I knew it!' she said. 'Please tell me you have an inventing shed!' and he told her that he did. 'I remember all the things you wanted to invent,' she said. 'You wanted to make a robot that would do your homework for you.' Lukas laughed, nodding. 'You had plans to build all sorts of machines.'

'I've had some success,' he said.

'Yes,' she said. 'My goodness, it sounds like you've done very well for yourself. We have so much catching up to do. How long are you here for?'

'For two weeks,' said Lukas. 'I've been told I have to take it easy.'

'You do that,' said Karla, patting his hand. She suspected that Lukas was one of those people who never quite manage a holiday even when they've made it as far as the beach; his head, she thought, would still be back in the lab or the inventing shed.

They talked about their home town. It turned out that Lukas and his mother had left there not long after Karla and her mother. Both their fathers had already gone missing by then.

'I found some curious old photographs,' said Karla, 'in amongst my mother's effects, after she died. There are half a dozen of them, black and white, in an envelope marked "Lucerne, 1941".' One, she said, showed some men outside the Hotel Schlüssel in Lucerne. In another, there were men and cars gathered on a mountain road, and on the back of this one, someone had written, 'WHERE IT WAS DECIDED'. 'I assume that my father took the photographs, and I wondered if one of the men might be your father, but I didn't remember him well enough to be sure. Now I've seen you, though, I swear that one of them must be either your father or your grandfather. There is a man – seen walking away from the Hotel Schlüssel, and in the gathering on the mountain road – who is the spit of you, right down to the trilby and the walking stick.'

'Is that right?' said Lukas. 'That's very interesting.'

'The photographs are at my house in London,' said Karla. 'I could send you a copy when I get home, but I'd very much like to look at them with you. Are you ever in England?'

Lukas said that he had no plans to come to England in the foreseeable future.

'Never mind,' said Karla. 'I'll send them in the post.'

Lukas came to Karla's room that night. Sitting on the edge of her bed in the lamplight, he asked her about the photographs. Having studied them many times, she could tell him all manner of details, such as, outside the hotel and on the mountain road, it was raining – the men were wearing overcoats and carrying big black umbrellas; and one picture showed an incoming ferry whose name was *Rigi*; and it was possible to read the time on the clock at the ferry terminal, and the name of a street, Löwengraben, and the number plate of one of the Volkswagen Beetles on the mountain road.

When Karla had told him everything she could, Lukas said goodnight and returned to his room.

In the morning, Karla phoned her daughter, told her where she might find these photographs and asked her to send them to the hotel so that she and Lukas could look at them together. The post should only take a few days.

Karla looked for Lukas in the breakfast room, so that she could tell him, but he wasn't there; she didn't see him anywhere that day, or the next. By the time the photographs arrived – found and posted promptly, with a note on the envelope to say 'They were where you said they would be' – Karla had discovered that Lukas had gone. His luggage, she had learnt from the reception desk, had been sent on to the Hotel Schlüssel in Lucerne.

Karla asked the receptionist to find and dial the number of the hotel. Lukas could not at first be reached – he did not appear to have arrived – but some hours later the Hotel Schlüssel returned her call, putting Lukas on the line. Karla said to him, 'What are you doing there?'

'I looked online,' he said, 'and saw that the hotel was still here. It has a good rating on TripAdvisor.'

Karla could hear some commotion going on around him. 'What's going on?' she asked.

'It's my luggage coming in,' he said. 'I've only just got here. I went via home to collect a few things. I have rather a lot of luggage, including a few awkward items.'

'Well, I've just received the photos. I asked my daughter to send them here. Are you coming back?'

'I'm not entirely sure,' said Lukas.

'Well, how long will you be in Lucerne for?'

'Indefinitely,' he said.

He was exasperating. Karla put the phone down and looked at the packet of photographs in her hand. She would send them on to him.

In her room, she made use of the hotel stationery, addressing an envelope to Lukas at the Hotel Schlüssel and enclosing the packet of photographs. She went to the post office before lunch.

When she did not hear from Lukas, she called the Hotel Schlüssel again and was told that Mr Birchler had gone.

'Gone?' she said. 'Gone where?'

'I don't know exactly,' the receptionist said, 'but he said that you might call. I didn't personally see him leave but he has gone, although he left behind many of his belongings.' Amongst these abandoned belongings were some unwieldy items of equipment and some books: *Germans Against Hitler: The Stauffenberg Plot and Resistance Under the Third Reich* and *The Plots to Kill Hitler: The Account of Fabian von Schlabrendorff*. For now, the hotel had put these things into their lost property.

'And you've no idea where he went?' asked Karla.

'I think somewhere far from here,' said the receptionist. 'I think somewhere he knew when he was small.'

'Perhaps Germany, then,' said Karla. 'Was he expecting to return?'

'I really couldn't say,' said the receptionist. 'But we won't keep his things in lost property forever.'

Karla asked about the photographs, whether they had arrived in time for Mr Birchler to see them, but the receptionist could not be sure what Mr Birchler had or had not received before leaving. Karla left her contact details with the receptionist and with the desk of her own hotel in Spain so that Lukas would be able to get in touch and so that she might get the photographs back at some point.

In fact, this package had not yet been delivered to the Hotel Schlüssel; it was still in transit. When it did arrive, the receptionist, seeing that Lukas Birchler was not a guest of the hotel, wrote on the envelope '*Unbekannt!*' and '*NACHSENDEN*', before recognising the name, remembering him and adding '*INS AUSLAND VERZOGEN*'. She put it back in the post, to be returned to the Spanish hotel whose address was printed on the envelope.

Karla, meanwhile, was aboard the aeroplane that would take her back to London. She had not heard from Lukas again, but she was very pleased to have encountered him after so many years and to have had the chance to catch up. She had been so tickled to discover that he really did have an inventing shed in which to build those machines he had always talked about – everything from the homework robot to what he had always called his big project: a machine that could travel through time. He used to talk about that a lot. Karla had said that if she could go back in time she would like to be Jean Harlow kissing Clark Gable but Lukas had said it would not work like that. What he had been interested in was whether one could go back and change the past. And if not, he had said, at least one might learn something by being there.

Karla, strapping herself into her seat on the plane, recalled hearing someone say on the radio that most people, if they could travel back in time, would want to go and kill Hitler. She pictured Lukas, with his trilby and his walking stick, leaving the Hotel Schlüssel, looking precisely like the man in the photograph. She wondered whether she would ever see Lukas again and it occurred to her that she would not.

ALISON MOORE

Alison Moore's short fiction has been included in various anthologies including *Best British Short Stories*, *Best British Horror* and *The Spectral Book of Horror Stories*. A selection from her debut collection, *The Pre-War House and Other Stories*, has been broadcast on BBC Radio 4 Extra, and the title story won the New Writer Novella Prize. Her first novel, *The Lighthouse*, was published in 2012 and shortlisted for the Man Booker Prize and the National Book Awards, winning the McKitterick Prize. Her second novel, *He Wants*, was published in 2014. Both *The Lighthouse* and *He Wants* were *Observer* Books of the Year. Her third novel, *Death and the Seaside*, will be published in August 2016. www.alison-moore.com

WONDERS TO COME

CHRISTOPHER FOWLER

Roy Brook spent his life in meetings.

For this one he sat in the seventeenth-floor boardroom of the Atlantica Hotel and shook with air-conditioned cold. With him were five senior engineers, seated around the walnut conference table, clutching dead Starbucks cups. The session had been called to determine why the hotel construction had missed its deadline. A Skype link had been set up with the consortium heads in Guangzhou.

'Let's put this problem in perspective,' said McEvoy, a soft-featured engineer from Leicester whose soporific tone slowed any urgent meeting to a crawl. 'In the past three months we've had over thirteen hundred fails. Mostly circuit breaks, burn-outs, shorts and blown transformers. Our margin for error is set at four hundred a month. I'm trying to explain the shortfall, and the best I can come up with is human error.'

'It's an electrical problem, pure and simple,' said Jim Davenport, one of the hotel's most senior engineers. 'Something big is shorting. That means it's either in the main substation, which is unlikely, or wrongly installed wiring below ground level.'

It was the worst news he could possibly have delivered; close to a million pounds' worth of marble flooring had been laid over the electrical circuits and fibre-optic lines, which had been buried deep on the supposition that no one would have to touch them for at least a decade.

The arguments ran back and forth for over an hour. Roy rarely spoke, but when he did everyone listened. 'You aren't going to increase staff and you won't delay the launch, so we have to take everything up, and that'll mean imposing longer working periods. Do you think you can drive that through?'

McEvoy looked at the calculations on his tablet. 'It'll play right into the hands of the unions.'

Finally it was suggested that they break for more coffee. His back aching with cold from the air-con units, Roy rose and walked over to the vast windows that looked onto the site. He thought about the resort's launch tomorrow night, and how much they could hide from public view. The smaller cosmetic elements like the exterior lights and the planting could be carried out hours before the opening, even though the big stuff would have to wait. The innovative wall-wash techniques involved geo-mapping the buildings, and the arboculturalists would require notice to airlift fully mature date palms into the humidity-controlled plant beds.

Yet he could still imagine these events roughly dovetailing. There would be further panics and slipped deadlines, but it was feasible that they might get everything locked down a week after the launch, providing there were no more outages.

'Hey, Roy,' Davenport called from the doorway. His grey,

cadaverous appearance made him the living embodiment of deadline-stress. 'The boys ran a pressure test on a section of pipe three millimetres thicker than the ones we've installed,' he said, 'blasted it the whole weekend and nothing, not so much as a hairline fracture. The trouble has to be somewhere else.'

'Suppose it's not a pipe at all?' said Roy.

'Then how would the sewage have reached the outfall?'

'The tests showed it was untreated, right? That means it hadn't passed through the primary or secondary clarifiers, the aeration tanks or the dryers, so the fault has to be way back, before contaminant removal even starts. The only junction there is the separator between the runoff and domestic channels.'

The Atlantica's sewage control system was designed to be one of the most efficient in the world, with eight separate treatment processes in place, including solar-powered microfiltration and aerobic procedures in which bacteria and protozoa consumed biodegradable material. Ultimately, they would use an ultraviolet peroxide process to break down organic contaminants and destroy microbes. It meant that the hotel would be able to recycle previously used water with virtually no wastage. A model for all resorts to follow, not that the guests would ever know. When you sell people a dream, he thought, they don't want to know how the dream works.

'Have you got time to come down to the treatment station?' Roy asked.

Davenport looked reluctant. 'You know I mostly firefight PR these days, Roy. I'm not even cleared for that part of the installation.' Davenport had trained as a structural engineer, but had found the job's responsibilities too much to bear. 'I could get into trouble just being there.'

'I didn't think of that. I guess I'll have to figure this out for myself.' Roy watched as Davenport loped off along the breezeblock service corridor, then aimed for the basement control room, descending the fire stairs and pushing open a steel door in the building's first icy sub-level.

Raj Jayaraman was sitting alone in the gloom with a leaky taco in his left hand, tapping out code with his right. His plaited pigtail hung down over the back of his chair, and ended in a cluster of coloured wooden beads. 'Hey, Roy. Pull up a chair if you can find one. Welcome to the downsized unit.'

'Where is everyone?'

'They were let go.' The heavyset young environmentalist had trained in ecological resource management at Bangkok University, but now found himself staring at computer screens monitoring hotel waste all day. 'You missed a couple of our friends from Guangzhou. They brought an efficiency team with them and decided we were overstaffed.'

'So who's left?'

'Just me, bro.'

'That's crazy. What do you do when your shift ends?'

'The program takes over. It even kicks in when I go for a piss. There'll come a point when I'm not needed here at all.'

Except in situations like this, Roy thought. 'You get any problems with the separator? We're still trying to figure out why we had raw sewage hitting the ocean. Kids are going to be swimming in a lot of dead fish tomorrow.'

'Tell me about it,' said Raj. 'I ran diagnostics on every square centimetre of the thing and found nothing. Actually, that's not true. I found this.' He extricated himself from his mesh chair and shook out a plastic envelope. 'Any guesses?'

On the table lay a small irregular sphere of pocked beige material, aerated like a solidified chunk of latte foam.

'Igneous rock,' said Roy. 'Cooled lava. Except this isn't a volcanic area. Can't imagine what else it would be. Maybe an old meteorite. This whole coastline is littered with them.'

'Could be the problem.'

'There's no way that could have beaten the filtration system and split a pipe.'

Raj set down his taco and wiped his fingers on his T-shirt. 'True, unless it was organic and flexible and sentient. Touch it.'

Roy reached out his index finger, expecting to encounter the rock's hard surface. His nail sank in up to the cuticle. He hastily withdrew his hand. 'What the fuck?'

'Your guess is as good as mine. It smells of ammonia, but that may just be absorption. It's not the only one. They're all over the place, immediately beneath the Atlantica's pipework. First time the mappers picked them up I thought I was just seeing gravel. Then I ran an expanded view and found millions of them. I mean, millions.'

'They couldn't have been there before.'

'What I said.'

'What do they do?'

'I don't know. Nothing. If they can move I've missed it. All I know is they're wet to the touch, they stink and a few hours after you leave them out from the ground they go hard. I posted a sample to Liz Peabody at the Marine Biology and Ecology Research Centre, Plymouth University, but I haven't heard anything back.'

'Tell me you didn't use Royal Mail.'

'I know, I'm a douche. It was late.'

'Two billion euros' worth of tech here and you used a Victorian postal service.'

'What else was I gonna do? It had to physically get there. She's the only person I know who could tell us if it's natural or man-made.'

'What do you mean, man-made?'

'I thought maybe a leaked by-product.'

'You didn't say anything to the Guangzhou team about this, did you?'

'No, man. I want to keep my job for as long as possible.'

'Did you see the pipe fracture happen?'

'No, I told you, I was sitting right here in front of the screens, and nothing. If it had been something as simple as a sticky valve it would have shown on this.' He tapped the monitor. 'Then it would have rerouted itself. But it didn't, so there must have been two errors.'

'What do you mean?'

'A physical issue with one of the outfall pipes, and a simultaneous glitch that prevented it from showing in the diagnostic.'

'That's kind of unlikely, isn't it?'

'Unless there's a problem with the program that we're not picking up on, so when a malfunction actually does occur we're not seeing it. Because of that thing.'

'You mean some fucking Quatermass-style piece of space rock that can get itself inside a hair crack and simultaneously interfere with the electronic output? Jesus, Raj, can we go back to the real world? The whole system could go down without you seeing it. Have you talked to anyone internally?'

'They say they're going to put someone on it, but no sign

yet. I thought it was weird that nothing – and I mean nothing – showed up as a fault, but this is beyond my field.'

Considering the hotel was primarily controlled by a complex web of overlapping computer programs, Roy had always been surprised by how few technicians they had on hand. The company's faith in technology was touching but, in his opinion, hardly deserved.

'If a foreign object gets into the soil pipe – and it happens if there's a temperature fail, because this stuff starts to solidify if it falls a few degrees – it should show up on here, but yesterday...' Raj faltered, suddenly aware that he was speaking to someone in a different department.

'I'm not going to say anything, Raj. It stays in this room, okay? I'm assuming it hasn't escaped your attention that the launch is less than twenty-four hours away. You have to call Elizabeth right now and get a diagnostic, assuming she got the package.'

'I tried calling but it went to voicemail, so in the meantime I looked at the regulators in the primary sedimentation treatment tanks. If one of those fails the entire resort will be ankle-deep in shit. The point is that it won't show up here. If there is a problem, it's invisible. The screens show everything clear and normal. So I ran a deliberate fail I could pinpoint.' He tapped the corresponding monitor. 'Nothing. Now, that's not right.'

Roy studied the diagrammatic representation of pipework and cabling, laid in a 3D matrix of blues, greens and yellows, but he couldn't see what Raj saw. 'Nothing unusual came up here at all?'

'If I had to take a guess,' said Raj, 'I'd say that thing managed to freeze the program and overwrite it, but I can't see how. It's a fucking rock.'

'All right, all right, let's try to look at it logically.' Roy breathed out slowly, pressing his hand against his chest, and started again. 'For the three years that this hotel complex was being constructed, nobody came across anything geologically unusual.'

'No, that's the point,' said Raj. 'I don't think they were there.'

'Then where the hell did they come from?'

Raj raised a hesitant index finger at the ceiling, then lowered it to the ground.

'Great, so we have a lump of lava with bio-electrical sentience burrowing under the biggest hotel resort ever to open in this country. It's got good timing, I'll give it that.' He looked back at the spongiform rock doubtfully. 'I'll get someone to come and take a look, off the record. That way nobody gets in trouble. But really? I mean, really? If you're fucking with me and that turns out to be a dried mushroom from your pizza, you're a dead man.'

'I'm not, Roy, and I'd appreciate it. But you'd better make it soon because I can't tell what's going on out there. Everything looks straight.'

Roy left Raj staring at the immobile screen, a lone figure in charge of the biggest waste management resort project in the country, and its most lethal potential hazard.

The red chrysanthemums were already beginning to wilt in the early evening heat. The main stage of the Atlantica had been sewn with sixty thousand of them, imported from Amsterdam and arranged in an immense ziggurat by a florist from London. Ice-water misters sprayed the seated guests every twenty seconds. The Minister of Culture's speech had been followed by a few mystifying English phrases learned by rote from the Chairman, Mr Lau. The Sheikh's representative for business development talked about Middle Eastern finance leading the way in eco-tourism, and the Russian head of the International Finance Group for Advanced Technology spoke about an epoch-defining moment for computer-designed architecture. The Russian delegation vigorously applauded as instructed.

The international press were impatient for the spectacle to begin. Waiting in the wings were the evening's hosts, two fading Hollywood stars who had been lured to the event with the promise of support for their favourite pet charities. The line-up of acts had not been confirmed until the day before, when the level of security risk surrounding the opening could be officially confirmed and communicated to the PR chiefs who controlled their stars' movements. The actors and singers who had got cold feet and pulled out were said to have undergone scheduling clashes.

Roy was anxious for the event to be over. As he waited in one of the many hospitality suites with the other engineers and architects he forced himself not to think about what could be going wrong just beneath the surface of the resort.

The geologist had duly appeared and registered mystification. If the igneous particle had once been alive, it was not now, and had hardened solid in the temperature-controlled air. Raj chose not to come up to the hospitality suite. Someone else had smoothly slipped into his empty space. No gaps could be allowed to show in the organisational structure.

An Arabic singer had taken centre stage in a flowing silver diamanté dress and hijab, and had just started miming to her most popular hit when the power went out.

At first Roy thought that the outage had only affected the stage, but when he looked around he realised that the entire resort was in darkness. The crowds remained silent, expecting some grand display, fireworks or computer-choreographed fountains, but as the seconds passed it grew incrementally warmer and quieter. The ice-mists were no longer working. Somebody tapped him on the back.

'Roy, come with me.'

'What's happened?'

'It's better we talk where we can't be overheard.'

Raj Jayaraman led the way back into a makeshift service corridor that connected with the side of the hotel. 'The power is out through the entire fucking complex. I mean everywhere. You understand what this means?'

Roy realised the implication at once. Different sectors within the resort had their own generators in case the main power grid should fail, so it was impossible for two areas to lose power at the same time. There was only one thing that united them: they shared the same computer operating system. The network was still being patched after a number of security flaws had been discovered, and the upgrade wouldn't be finished until several hours after the opening.

'It feels like the OS has been attacked, and the power killed from a point inside the resort,' said Raj.

'Has anyone been out to Unit Two?' asked Roy. The Atlantica's secondary IT resources were handled from a secure unit further along the coastal highway.

'There's a team on its way there right now, but I don't think they'll find anything. The problem's here.'

Raj ushered Roy into a bare-walled concrete operations office and closed the door. 'This is not just electricity,' he said. 'All of the resort's utilities have been shut down.'

'How is that possible? I thought the system was foolproof.'

'There'll be time to discover how this happened later. Right now we have a serious problem developing. There are two hundred VIP guests inside the hotel on the mid-level viewing floor. The lights are still on inside because there's an emergency generator on the roof.'

'I didn't think they were opening that viewing floor to anyone,' said Roy. 'There are still some windows missing. H&S must have had a shit-fit.'

'The guest invitations were increased at the last minute. They had nowhere else to put them.' He indicated the blank closed-circuit screens. 'The atrium doors have sealed and the air-conditioning has shut down.'

'The air-con was never designed to be turned off, only to go down to its lowest setting,' said Roy. 'You know the ground-floor windows can't be opened. Anyone left in there will run out of air.' The hotel atrium was hermetically sealed to prevent cold air from escaping. All the floors were sealed off from one another, except for a series of service airlocks.'

'How long do they have?'

'I can give you a rough estimate. Have the emergency services been called?'

'Mr Lau is anxious to avoid creating a public disturbance. He has all of the directors here from Guangzhou, and can't lose face in front of them.'

'He'll lose more than face when those people start passing out. You need to call in the fire service now. You don't have to tell them everything.'

'You know I can't do that without Mr Lau's approval.'

'Then you need to call him, Raj.'

'There must be something you can do.' Raj was sweating pints. 'I cannot trust anyone else to handle this problem.'

'Let me go over there,' said Roy. 'If the OS is down I can only do the same as anyone else – try and break the doors in.'

'Yes, but you need to do this without—'

'Without any fuss? I don't know, Raj. Somebody has to keep the crowd from suspecting anything. There's a very expensive PR team out there waiting to be told what to do.' He called Davenport.

'What can we say?' asked Davenport when Roy had finished explaining the problem.

'Get them to make an announcement. Use an American, they always sound more formal. Don't try to make light of it, but don't tell them any more than they need to know. There are candles – get every performer to carry two each on stage and continue the show acoustically. Make it look like a deliberate fallback plan.'

'We can't do that. The whole thing's on playback. They can't sing.'

'Jesus, they must be able to do something – what the fuck were they employed for? You have a lot of people out there standing in the dark and any minute now they're going to start getting antsy.'

Roy left the office and headed for the Atlantica. He could see dark figures moving behind the smoked glass of the hotel's upper windows, but had no way of getting to them. He rang Davenport back. 'Who do we know who's on the viewing platform? I need a list of mobile numbers.'

Although the ground-floor doors could be released from outside, the fail-safe system relied on swipe-cards that needed to be reset, and the screens were still a scramble of static. An engineer called Darroll Jones was working inside the only IT suite that remained on-site. Roy called him.

'Darroll, why isn't the override generator program responding? Is it just a crash and reboot?' He was waiting for Davenport to contact those employees trapped inside the building, and felt powerless to take action.

'The attack isn't on any single part of the resort's access protocols,' the stocky Welsh IT engineer explained. 'It's on the system as a whole.'

'That's not possible, is it? There must be hundreds of separate components.' He knew it would take a small army to sabotage the mainframe, all armed with the right codes. A single mistake anywhere would trigger warnings.

'This hasn't been carried out by a single person,' Jones replied. 'It's the work of a very large group with a lot of inside knowledge. Has to be. But that doesn't make sense. The information is way too protected for any outsider to get hold of it.'

The words 'large group' triggered a response. He thought of the Atlantica built on a bedrock of stone that somehow wasn't stone at all, that could liquefy and become something else, all the while emitting electrical pulses.

'How much air do they have in there?' He looked up at the darkened windows.

'I'd have to work out the building's cubic capacity but—'

'Take a guess.'

'With so many people inside, maybe two hours. The heat will make a difference.'

One of the senior engineers had found him. 'Roy, there's a flaw in the glass near the ground-floor reception area,' he explained. 'One of the seals came down a couple of nights ago and we replaced it with a temporary plastic resin. There's about three metres of it.'

'Are any of the JCBs still on-site?'

'There's a loader and a couple of speed tractors nearby.'

'Can you get someone to bring over whatever's the heaviest?'

The yellow steel tractor had trouble making it through the milling crowds. With the exit signs no longer illuminated, some spectators were starting to search for ways out of the grounds. A swell of raised voices was washing through the site now.

'Come with me,' Roy told the engineer, hopping into the tractor cab and throwing its lights on high-beam. 'Can I see the replacement resin?'

'No, it's the same colour as the normal seals.'

'Then I need you to point it out to me.'

The glass angles of the Atlantica's grand lobby were picked up by the tractor beams. People moved out of the way, puzzled by the appearance of the tractor. 'There,' said the engineer, 'to your right.'

Roy could make out a thin grey strip connecting the panels. He pumped the tractor into high gear.

'You're just going to ram it?' asked the engineer, disturbed.

'Only to push the plates far enough apart to admit air. There'll be bigger problems starting in a few minutes if this place doesn't get back online fast.'

They buckled up as the tractor shot forward, slamming into the join. The plastic strip gave slightly but refused to break. He put the tractor in reverse and tried again. He could feel the crowd shifting apprehensively behind him. This time, the tractor punched the seal out. Roy looked up and saw that one of the glass panels had been separated from its surround.

He span the tractor and raced it back as the sheet fell, exploding around him in a million iridescent shards, like crystal rainfall. The spectators at his back were agitated now and seeking to move away, animals sensing their journey to the abattoir. There were shouts. Hundreds of mobile phone screens wavered in the dark, like the audience at a rock concert. Roy parked the tractor and ran back to the security stand, where he found Raj.

'We have to evacuate the entire park right now,' Raj warned.

'We can't do that. You won't be able to get the gates open.'

'Then we'll need to find a way. What about manual overrides?'

Roy shrugged. 'Your guess is as good as mine. Could the aquarium blow out?' A vast marineland of sharks, rays and thousands of tropical fish ran along the rear wall of the viewing deck, extending three floors up.

'The glass will hold. It's a foot thick. But the tank doors aren't up to spec. They'll punch out first and the cubic capacity of that thing – without operational limiters, the water pressure will just keep building. By now it will already be way into red. And the gardens—'

'What about them?'

'There are two hundred and seventy thousand submerged water jets out there getting ready to burst.'

'Can't the city cut the supply?'

'The separate main water management systems are in the basement. We didn't want to risk human error so they're controlled and co-ordinated by the system—'

'—that's down. You're telling me you have no other fail-safes.'

'Why would we need them? The system is—'

'Don't say it's fucking foolproof, Raj, okay?'

'It could only be attacked from multiple locations and we know that level of co-ordination is impossible without the right codes all being inputted at the same time. We never allowed for a mass blackout.'

Davenport leaned down from the scaffolded press platform and stopped Roy as he passed. 'We have a team of engineers working on the gates,' he said. 'Nobody can get out. The Sheikh just called, asking when power would be restored. He was very upset.'

'You'll have to physically cut the barriers open.'

Davenport rarely betrayed any emotion, but now he looked horrified. 'How would that look?' he asked. 'There are cameras filming this everywhere. The press booth has its own portable generator. Everything is going out live.'

'I don't know, how would it look to have hundreds of people trampled to death in the dark? Look at them! At the moment they're just confused, but it won't take much to start a stampede. The power's not coming back on. Turn off the generator in the press booth. Then get a team down there and do it the old-fashioned way; cut down the service truck barriers with rotary saws, anything that runs on diesel. Those who want to leave the resort area will try to do so in a hurry. If something else panics them, you'll need to cut down the perimeter fences fast.'

'We cannot do that!'

'We have no choice.'

'But the press—'

'Do what you have to do and mop up afterwards. Firefight the big stuff. There'll be plenty of time later to worry about what the world thinks.'

Defeat stained Davenport's melancholy features. He knew that whatever happened now, his career was finished. Below them, the crowd milled and eddied in the gloom, waiting for instructions that would not come.

Roy turned and looked back at the darkened hotel, at the crowd of photographers, press agents and journalists who were surging out of the shattered wall and buffeting up against the crowds between the stands. He was filled with the sensation of having missed something obvious.

It has to be them, he told himself. *Say these things actually managed to short out the entire place. The timing is as exact as a terrorist attack. It's like they can think. That's just fucking ridiculous. How would they move, roll themselves along the walkways like hairballs or tumbleweed?*

He looked around the darkened arena, the manicured emerald grounds dotted with chairs and tables. He began walking toward one of the hotel's service-entrance doors, where an attractive young woman in a floor-length blue gown was struggling to release the latch.

'Can I help you?' he asked. Her head lifted and she turned to look at him, stepping into the light. As she opened her mouth he saw one of the beige lava-sponges entirely blocking her breathing passage. She stared and stared, then returned to the door.

Suddenly it all made sense: they needed the warmth and moisture of human tissue to reactivate themselves. It was how they moved about. In human hosts. They interfered with the electrical impulses of the brain, encouraged people to pick them up and ingest them, the simple and effective technique developed by all parasites.

Once the young woman had managed to open the serviced door, he followed her inside. She didn't seem aggressive, just motivated to follow a path. He wasn't used to climbing stairs, and stopped on Level 5 to catch his breath. His heart was pounding. Below him, the line between calm and panic was quickly eroding. He could hear shouting even from here.

There were no open areas above the viewing floor. Guards had been placed in the stairwells earlier, but they had all left. The young woman had continued upward without him. He presumed she was going up to the angled concrete outcrop of the observation deck. There were three situated at different heights in the building. The middle one was another seven levels above him. He carried on after her.

When he looked down from the glass stairwell wall he saw that the stage had been vacated. At its back, the immense high-definition screens were black and dead. The movement of the crowd was increasing as those at the back started to push forward. The security teams were trying to herd them toward the service exits, but instinctively the guests were trying to return to the electronic gates through which they had entered.

He felt the plate glass reverberate from an explosion. Running to the next stairwell window, he followed the direction of everyone's turning heads. The first of the fountains, a great concentric circuit of pipework set in the baroque concrete turrets of an artificial lake, had blown itself apart under the unregulated pressure. Shards of stone and steel were raining down on those caught at the back of the crowd.

As a second network of jets blew, the screams spread from one quarter to the next, and the great mass of bodies ploughed forward. Another of the main fountain's spiral water turrets twisted on its base and crumbled, sliding over into the writhing morass of guests like a collapsing cake. The first of the gas pipes, designed to blast spears of flame into the centres of the pulsing fountains, ruptured and caught fire. The elemental displays were arranged around the entire perimeter of the park, and would soon engulf the resort in a ring of flame.

There was nothing anyone could do at ground level now. The guards had left it too late to start taking down the fences. Roy continued grimly up toward the deck, his thighs shaking and burning. When he reached it, he was able to enter through the airlock that sealed the kitchens. He found the open-plan floor deserted. It looked as if they had found the way down through one of the other service airlocks. *Journalists with initiative*, he thought, *that's a first.*

It was only as he made his way back to the stairs that he discovered the woman in the blue gown. It looked as if she was lying on the floor laughing at something. Then he saw that her jaw had been wrenched down until its muscles tore. The thing in her throat had gone, leaving behind a ragged red hole. There was very little blood. Most of it had already oxidised.

It dries out the host, he thought, intrigued. *So it has to keep moving on.*

He had not formulated any further plan beyond coming here. He felt disconnected from everything that was happening below. There was no rational way of accounting for it. Rather, it seemed inconceivable, dream-like, that anything could do this.

He needed to concentrate on solving problems minute by minute instead. Ten flights further up there was a smaller deck, off limits to the press. Here were the unfinished floors without walls. He could check that the rest of the hotel was clear, see the scale of the event from above, then leave when it was quieter.

It took him a while to reach the upper observation platform, sixty-five levels above the unfolding horror. The leeward walls of the deck had yet to be fitted with replacement glass, and wind moaned through the concrete shell, distorting the sound of the fire-truck sirens far below. The entrance to the resort was barricaded by a bottleneck of police vehicles, their red and blue lights strobing the crowd like some kind of militia-inspired discotheque. The town beyond the resort had patches of total darkness where there should have been street lights.

'Kinda wild, isn't it?'

Roy turned to find Jim Davenport leaning against the platform balustrade. At his feet was an open laptop with some kind of live streaming application open.

'It's better to learn the most sophisticated technology first,' he explained. He sounded as if he was speaking through a mouthful of food. Whenever his teeth parted, Roy saw the pocked thing sitting in the back of his throat. 'I never understood that old idea. You know, when a new lifeform reaches us it'll first be seen by a couple of hillbillies in a pick-up truck. Makes no sense, does it? You start at the top and the rest is easier.' He bent over, coughed and spat red. 'It must be strange for you, suddenly realising that it's coming to an end. You must wonder what it was all for.'

'Just me?' Roy took a step forward. 'If this place goes up, you're not going to get out of here. What happened, you draw the short straw?'

'I don't need to get anywhere, my cycle is different to yours. Anyway, it's out of my hands. We started here, but soon we'll be everywhere. Global economic collapse. They'll all blame each other. The last thing we want is to draw attention to ourselves. We're doing something that everyone secretly wants to happen.' He bent down and folded his laptop shut, sliding it into his backpack. 'I'm done. Want to come and see the end of empire?'

Roy threw himself at Davenport, tearing the backpack from his hands. Spinning, he hurled the laptop bag as far as he could. It flew through one of the unfinished window panels, out into the night.

'It doesn't matter,' said the engineer, watching the bag fall. 'I finished my part.'

Roy slammed himself into Davenport's bony chest. He did not even try to move out of the way, and was knocked from his feet. He landed on his back and slid across the polished marble floor with Roy on top of him. Kicking down, he carried on pushing, the rubber soles of his trainers finding purchase so that he propelled them to the edge of the deck.

Roy struck out at Davenport's face, but only succeeded in landing a glancing blow. Grabbing the rim of the steel balustrade, Davenport dispassionately kicked at Roy's back and legs, moving him closer to the edge.

Below, the crowd screamed as the remaining gas jets ruptured and ignited, popping from one nozzle to the next, spraying flames across the gardens.

Roy landed a punch, knocking the breath from his opponent. Davenport was stronger and back on his feet in seconds, stamping him down.

Neither of them would give way. Davenport was blocking Roy's return to the floor, keeping him at the windy edge of the platform. He dropped his jaw, and Roy saw that the thing inside had come forward, ready to be spat into a new host.

Below, a massive explosion shook through the resort, blowing out most of the lower windows. The tethered raft housing the firework display had ignited, sending a peacock display of sapphire, emerald and ruby comets into the assembly. Gold plumes sprouted from the running figures below, crimson and indigo cartwheels of fire appearing about them, turning them into fabulous beasts. The rainbow of fire spiralled and burrowed its way through the howling crowd.

An updraft caught the building, bringing with it the reek of burning copper, aluminium, sodium chloride, scorched flesh. Another explosion, this time from within the hotel. Glittering shards of glass cascaded from the Atlantica like the contents of an upended jewel box. It was an appropriately tasteless spectacle, the end of the world repainted in Day-Glo colours.

Roy barrelled at Davenport with human hatred in his eyes. The slick marble floor of the platform functioned as an ice rink, and the impact sent them both over the edge.

Davenport climbed up easily. He leaned on his haunches, catching his breath, watching and waiting.

'Pull me up,' Roy asked. 'My arms.' He was still hanging in the dark windswept space above the screaming mob.

Davenport considered the consequences of doing so and decided against it. He was in no rush. He sat motionless and waited until the man suspended below him could hold on no longer, and was forced to release his grip.

Roy Brook did not fall in silence, and was not heard above the greater cacophony of the crowd.

The thing that had once been Davenport decided to remain on the deck and watch the unfolding disaster for a few more minutes. Then, his lifecycle ending without another host, he simply dropped himself discreetly over the side of the building.

Roy saw the engineer fall. Lying across the raft of scaffolding poles on the floor below the viewing deck, he wondered if it was worse to have survived. The wind shear had punched him back in. He eased himself painfully off the poles and back through the floor's shattered picture window. There was something badly wrong with his left leg. It shot a lightning bolt of pain when he tried to stand on it.

He sat watching the fire trucks, the ARVs and ambulances eddying around the entrance gates as the police attempted to redirect the public and clear the resort. The surrounding pavements were still filled with orderly panic and chaotic attempts at control. The sealed-off roads had created bottlenecks of stalled vehicles. Something rare and unthinkable happened: authority began to fail as crushed pedestrians pushed down barriers and ignored directions. Fighting broke out, and the crowds began to thin, dispersing into the dark.

Roy found a piece of steel lintel to lean on. He made his way down and out through an alley at the back of the site, the one used as a shortcut by its workers. Resting up in a café lit by hurricane lamps, overlooking the smouldering shoreline, he watched in fascination as the blackened buildings pulsed with muffled explosions and fires. The resort's greatest flaw had been its paranoid level of security; the management team had refused to allow its staff to make decisions, and had been brought down by the technology in which it had placed its trust. A lesson to be learned there, he thought, although it's too late for lessons now. He wondered what might have happened if Raj's letter had got through. It might have changed everything.

As expected, there were no cabs to be found, but he was able to hitch a ride heading away from the resort. His leg was grinding at the joint and bleeding badly. The truck dropped him at the edge of the compound where he lived.

If any neighbours were watching events unfold at the coast, they continued to do so behind drawn curtains. He was halfway down his street when its lamps winked out.

He let himself into his apartment and lay on the bed, bruised and exhausted. When he closed his eyes he saw the rotating red and blue lights of the emergency vehicles. He saw the windows of the Atlantica bulging and shattering. He saw chunks of pediment and pilaster being blown into the night air by the force of water. He saw the thing in Davenport's bulging throat, using the manager as a puppet. He saw millions of them hard at work, remaking the world for themselves.

We're not so different, he thought. *Everybody works, and for what?*

He saw himself falling away from the viewing platform, his eyes and mouth wide, his arms as limp as if he was floating in water.

The dream ended and he awoke. He sensed someone at the end of the bed, standing over him. The familiar, comforting figure of his wife.

'You're awake,' she said, her voice thick with emotion. She looked as if she might fall down at any moment.

'I thought you'd gone,' he said uselessly.

'I have to tell you something.'

Roy winced as he pushed himself up on one elbow.

'The children.'

'What about them?'

'They couldn't sleep with all the noise so I gave them sleeping pills. They ate them all.'

'Why would they do that?'

'I think they saw the news.'

'What are you doing?'

'It's for you.'

She wasn't holding the gun correctly, the military service revolver he had brought home after finding it in the resort's security storeroom. She had probably never held a gun before. Her left hand clasped the barrel to steady it. The trigger was tighter than she had expected it to be. She fired four shots into his body, hitting his stomach, his heart, his throat, his face.

Somebody must have heard the noise, seen the flashes of light in the bedroom. Nobody opened their front door. Nobody called the police.

'It's better if you're dead to start with,' she said. 'Now you'll find there are wonders to come.'

Hunching over him, she pulled down his ruined jaw and spat red.

CHRISTOPHER FOWLER

Christopher Fowler is the author of more than forty novels and short-story collections, including the *Bryant & May* mysteries, which record the adventures of two Golden Age detectives in modern London. He is the recipient of the 2015 CWA Dagger In The Library. His latest books are the thriller *The Sand Men* and *Bryant & May: Strange Tide*. Other works include video games, graphic novels and plays. He writes a weekly column in *The Independent on Sunday* and lives in King's Cross, London, and Barcelona.

"When I wrote *The Sand Men*, about the owners of a futuristic resort trying to impose order on a chaotic world, I didn't get to go into wholesale apocalypse mode, so when Conrad's letter arrived it gave me the world-trashing opportunity I'd been looking for – or rather it nearly didn't, because I'd forgotten he was sending it and dismissed it as junk mail, which got emptied into a six-foot high waste container that I had to climb inside after realising who the letter was from. So, as in the story, my ordered world also became a place of chaos."

CANCER DANCER

PAT CADIGAN

Weird shit happens to you when your life turns into liminal space.

Actually, I thought it was a perceptual shift. When the oncologist tells you that the uterine cancer they thought was gone has come back and you're looking at a life-expectancy of maybe two years, the personal paradigm shift is like nothing you've ever been through before.

I can't speak to anyone else's experience but here's mine: when you have a baby, you find out what's important and that, my friend, is the fucking secret of life. I'm sure there are other ways to get clued up about that; this is how I learned it. And I figured that was the Big One; I'd never do anything more profound than become someone's mother. It never occurred to me that Big Things aren't only things you do – they also happen to you.

The Macmillan Cancer Centre in London is a pretty nice place. They've made it look like a hotel lounge, or maybe a casual reading space in a library. I've been to the Google Office Space or whatever it's called in east London, where you can go work on your start-up or find somebody else's, and the Macmillan Centre is nicer than that. It would be a great place to hang out if you wished you didn't have to go there.

I knew it was cancer. I'd had a brush with uterine cancer the year before and they'd taken care of it with a hysterectomy. I just didn't know whether this was the same thing or something new. I was thinking things like, *Will I go bald* and *Is there a special place to buy those I-have-cancer head scarves* and *Am I going to puke so much that I actually lose some weight*, shit like that. And then the oncologist, this nice lady in a tasteful wool dress, even more tastefully accessorised with a print scarf, a gold brooch, and plain black pumps with low but authoritative heels, tells me I'm looking at two years. Then she adds, "It could be less."

My Macmillan nurse phones while I'm on my way home on the bus. She's great, my Macmillan nurse, but I tell her I'll call her back later because I don't feel like subjecting the strangers sitting nearby to my tale of woe. But after she hangs up, I consider talking aloud to the dead phone as if she were still there just to get it out of my system: *The oncologist said this and I said that and now I feel blah blah blah. So you think you're having a bad day? Cheer up, pilgrim, it could be worse by a fuck-ton!*

But I don't. I am very short on luck and what little I have ain't good. The phone would probably ring in the middle of my soliloquy of sorrow. I'd go from tragic heroine to the punchline of a real-life anecdote, which would probably go viral on YouTube, courtesy of someone else's cell phone. Life is ready to kill you without provocation; why tempt fate into humiliating you before you go?

My downstairs neighbour Tim was outside puttering around in the front yard when I got home. He's a nice young man, not even half my age and half again as tall. Normally I'd stop to talk to him but not today. I know what's going to come pouring out if I open my mouth and we do not know each other well enough for that kind of disclosure. Being a nice guy, he'd probably invite me for a cup of tea and listen sympathetically but I can't handle that right now. Plus like I said, he's half my age – he probably thinks sixty-two is old. So I smile, try to look like I've got too much to do to stop and chat and zip through my front door as fast as I can work the locks.

The postman has come and gone, leaving me a single yellow envelope on the carpet at the foot of the stairs. Two thick blue lines are drawn through the address and in black marker, the word *Deceased?*

"Not yet, thanks very much," I tell the envelope, picking it up. There's a number written in pencil, like a serial number; it means nothing to me. In black ink, a different hand has printed, *No longer at this address*, and underneath, what could be a name or initials – *J e p.*

"Hey, don't assume someone died," I scold the envelope and turn on the overhead light so I can see who this was addressed to.

Detective Sergeant Michael Parris (ret'd)
The Oak House

Station Road
Fishponds
Bristol

One of the lines goes through the postcode so I can't read it but it doesn't matter. I don't know anyone in Bristol. Nor do I know any cops, ret'd or otherwise. I turn the envelope over but there's nothing except *Return to Sender* in the same blue as the lines through the address.

"Wrong sender," I say. I'm about to tell myself to stop talking out loud like some crazy old lady when I notice that the envelope's been opened, cut open, and the stamp or franking removed. Jeez, how blind am I, I wonder. Shoulda gone to watchamacallit.

Even as I'm thinking I should ask Tim if this is his, I'm emptying the contents into my hand. Fuck it, I had a rough day, I'm in the mood for the cheap thrill of reading someone else's mail.

I have no idea what I might have been expecting – a birthday card with five quid in it or a love letter or a note from Detective Sergeant Michael Parris (ret'd)'s kid asking for money. What I did get:

I laid it all out on my kitchen table. There wasn't much. Two pieces of paper, one a torn half-sheet with a note:

Mike
Please help
K
xx
Don't call me

I held the paper up to the light but there was no watermark and no indentations indicating something written on a sheet covering it.

The other piece was from a notepad. The logo in the upper right corner said Four Pillars Hotels. Not a chain I'd ever heard of but there are lots of things I've never heard of. There was an elaborate doodle in the lower left-hand corner – all abstract but whoever had done it had genuine artistic ability. I put on my reading glasses for a closer look and discovered that it wasn't completely abstract after all. In the very densest part of all those lines and squiggles and lattices was a single word: *MURDER*. The doodler had gone over each letter several times to make it stand out.

Below the doodle, like the paper had been turned sideways so the doodle was at the top:

WEDS
6:00 pm
"Stella" -- 47
30756

The third item took me from puzzled to what-the-fuck: a plastic card, plain black except for a circle printed on it in shimmery metallic silver – that's a circle, not a solid dot – about an inch in diameter. The other side was brick red – or maybe drying blood red – with a black magnetised strip and tiny print setting out Terms and Conditions. Whose T&C's, however, had been thoroughly scratched out and blacked over. And as if that wasn't enough, someone had punched a tiny hole through the card and attached an old-fashioned property ticket with a bit of cord. On the ticket, someone had hand-printed:

Room 47

Below that, in smaller letters: *NOT a hotel... belongs to THE ETERNITY CLUB.*

The Eternity Club? I'd never heard of that either but given what I had heard today, it definitely sounded like my kind of place.

Now, London is lousy with private clubs, the most well-known being the Groucho Club, named for the Marx Brother who so famously proclaimed he didn't want to join any club that would have someone like him as a member. There are lots more and all of them charge a fortune for membership so no one has to suffer the indignity of belonging to one that would have anyone with a bank account like mine (or yours) for a member. Most are so exclusive that civilians like me have never heard of them. That's okay – it's not like I ever think about exclusive clubs anyway. Although a friend took me to the Groucho once as her guest and if I were going to join one, I'd pick that one; they're a classy bunch.

But after a doctor says you might have only two years to live, a place called the Eternity Club will definitely pique your interest.

Not that I had any idea what it really was. The black card reminded me of the uber American Express card, the one that's several levels above platinum and so exclusive it's just plain black, like it's the Little Black Dress of credit cards. But this one wasn't blank.

I looked from the note to Mike to the doodle and then to

the card with its property tag. I rearranged them on the table in front of me, as if that would tell me anything. And son of a gun, it actually did.

I'd left the envelope on the table; placing the note from the hotel just below it showed me that *No longer at this address/ J e p* and *WEDS / 6:00 pm / "Stella" –– 47 / 30756* had been printed by the same hand.

Just like the tag attached to the card. Except for *Room 47*. That had been written by a different person... the same one who had put *Deceased?* on the front of the envelope. And *Return to Sender* on the back.

This had to be some kind of joke, I told myself, a prank on Mike Parris (ret'd). Maybe a bunch of his fellow detectives decided to punk him on his last day at work by putting together a bunch of fake clues to a fake case. *Mike please help K xx Don't call me.* Only TV detectives get notes like that. Truth is duller than fiction because fiction has to be entertaining. So do jokes. Ergo, this had to be a prank.

But why include a card supposedly from this Eternity Club? An in-joke? Or maybe a jab at his age: Mike's so old, the only club he qualifies for is the Eternity Club.

Nope; it sounded flat even just in my head.

I was about to put everything back in the envelope; instead, I found myself picking up my cell phone and dialling information. I didn't expect to get Michael Parris's number. He could have gone anywhere after retiring – Brighton, the south of France. The north of France, even. Or Paris. But surprisingly, he still had a number in Bristol. I called it and a woman answered.

"I'm trying to reach a Michael Parris," I said after a moment of hesitation. "He was a detective?"

"This is his daughter," the woman said with formal cordiality. "Can I help you?"

"Uh… is Detective Parris available?"

"My father passed away several weeks ago," she said in a quiet, I'm-tolerating-you-because-I-have-manners tone. I waited for her to ask how she could help me again but apparently she wasn't that tolerant. Not that I could blame her.

"I'm sorry for your loss," I said. "I didn't mean to bother you at such a difficult time."

"Did you know my father?" she asked, not quite as stiff.

"Oh, no, I'm not a cop – uh, detective."

"Are you some other kind of associate?"

"You mean like a snitch?" I wanted to bite my tongue off as soon as I said it. "No, it's nothing like that. I'm… uh, this is going to sound kind of strange but please bear with me."

"All right," she said. "I'm listening."

"I have a piece of mail that was meant for your father," I said, holding the envelope in my other hand. "Someone tried to send it to him and it was returned. Only it went to the wrong address."

"I see. Did you want me to come get it?"

"Oh, no, you can't," I said. "Well, technically, you could, it's not impossible. But I'm calling from London."

Suddenly that changed everything. "Is this you, Karen?" she snapped. "Don't you know when to give up?"

"I don't know any Karen," I said. "My name is—"

"Then you're stooging for Karen. I don't really care. It's over. My father's dead, find some other mark."

"Please, Ms Parris, I'm not Karen, I don't know what you're talking about, honest. I just got this piece of mail and it looks like it might be important. There's this black card—"

"Yeah, sure. Send it to the Avon and Somerset cop shop," she said. "Or if you're really in London, you can take it to Scotland Yard for all I care. Now fuck off and don't call here again." There was a click as she hung up, which seemed anticlimactic. There are whole generations who will never know the pleasure of slamming the phone down.

I picked up the note to "Mike". So K probably stood for Karen. Big deal; as facts went, it was pretty anaemic. Even knowing that she was someone who made Michael Parris's daughter very angry didn't tell me much. Hell, I didn't even know Michael Parris's daughter's name. I'd have made a lousy detective, I thought.

And then again, maybe I could improve. I fetched my laptop from the other room.

Googling Michael Parris Bristol sans quotes got me a seemingly endless list of links to stories that included the words Michael, Parris, and Bristol, all listed under the question, *Did you mean Paris?* Then I tried Bristol Police and discovered that you can't just get a list of law enforcement officers on request – unless they're on Twitter, that is. Then you can even see thumbnail photos. But there were no detectives among them. I followed a few, thinking I could ask them about Michael Parris in a Direct Message, only to find you can't DM anyone who isn't following you back.

I kept searching and eventually I found Michael Parris's obit. It was frustratingly short. He'd died two months ago, aged fifty-six, and would be missed by his husband Mark Ramirez and his brother Arthur Parris and that was all; no children. Cremation had been at the South Bristol Crematorium. In lieu of flowers, people could make a donation to Macmillan Cancer Support or to Ballboys, a testicular cancer charity.

Ballboys for testicular cancer. Save the Ta-tas for breast cancer. Uterine cancer didn't lend itself to that kind of whimsy. But then, neither did rectal cancer – although it could have. They were missing an opportunity to give out ribbons saying *Assholes need love, too.*

You think a lot of crazy shit when you get cancer.

I was still thinking when the phone rang, startling me so I nearly jumped out of my skin. I looked at the screen; it was the number I'd called an hour ago. Didn't see that coming, I thought, pressing the answer button. "Hello?" I said, a bit nervous.

"This is Michael Parris's daughter. Is this the person who called me earlier?" Not a bit angry now; in fact, she was practically oozing concern.

"Why?" I asked.

"I just wanted to apologise for how I spoke to you. I'm still grieving for my father. I still can't believe he's gone. We were very close."

"Yeah," I said. "So close you're not even mentioned in the obituary."

Long moment of silence; I could practically hear the wheels turning as she tried to think up an answer for that. "My father was a complicated man. It wasn't always very easy to be his daughter. We were estranged for a long time and then at the end of last year, we finally reconnected."

"Uh-huh," I said.

Another briefer silence. "When you called, I was going through some of our family things and I was feeling very emotional. I'm afraid I took it out on you."

"Apology accepted," I told her. "Anything else?"

"You said you had some mail that looked important, including a black card? You see, that card should have been in with my father's papers, but after you called I checked and it's missing. You seem to have found it—"

"Yeah, I took your advice."

"Pardon?"

"I mailed it to the Bristol Police Department. You'll have to talk to them—"

"Liar." Just like that, the growl was back in her voice.

"Sounds like you're getting emotional again," I said breezily. "We all handle grief in our own way. Don't bother calling back to apologise, I'll forgive you now—"

"I know you've still got it."

I chuckled. "I don't know what your deal is but it's not my circus and not my monkeys."

"Oh, it most certainly is your circus. Keep screwing around and it'll make a monkey out of you. Save yourself a hell of a lot of time and trouble and send me Mike's mail. I'll give you an address."

"Okay," I said, "let me get a pencil and something to write on." I put the phone down, counted to five, and picked it up again. "Go ahead."

"M. Parris, 89 Sixth Avenue…"

As she spoke, I typed the address into Google Maps, enlarged it, then pressed for street view.

"Could you repeat that back to me, so we can be sure you have it right?" She was trying not to be impatient now.

"No," I said. "Street view shows nothing on Sixth Avenue except warehouses and garages."

"You think you're funny?" she barked. "We can use Google, too. We've got your phone number and we know you're in London. You want the circus? Well, the circus is coming to town and when we're through with you—"

I hung up and shut my phone off. Then I sat staring at the blank screen, wondering if I should take out the battery and break the sim card in half like in the movies.

No, I should turn my phone back on and call the police. Better yet, take this misdirected piece of mail to the nearest police station and make a report. I reached for the envelope and stopped. *Officer, I want to report that a woman called me on the phone and threatened to take me to the circus.*

I burst out laughing. Talk about thinking crazy shit when you get cancer. Speaking of which: *Yes, officer, I was diagnosed today. Two years, they said. Yes, I'll be having chemo but it hasn't started yet. Scared? To be honest, I don't think it's really sunk in yet. Would I say I'm in shock? No, not exactly. Drugs? Ibuprofen and antacids. Oh, you mean drug-drugs…*

That was assuming they'd even take that much time with me.

I picked up the card again. The Eternity Club. Room 47. My gaze fell on the sheet from the hotel notepad.

"Stella" -- 47.

WEDS

6:00 pm

I looked at my laptop screen, just to make sure. Yeah, it was almost two pm on a Wednesday.

Maybe this was the craziest shit I'd ever thought in my life but I couldn't believe it was just a coincidence.

* * *

Like anyone else, I can over-think things. I spent most of my adult life analysing data for insurance companies until I took early retirement. My first brush with cancer felt like a wake-up call; you know, time to smell the roses. I don't think I over-thought that. All told, I'd say I'm thorough but not obsessive... usually. But today wasn't exactly usual.

In my whole life, I've never had anyone threaten me, on the phone, in person, whatever. Even when my son's father and I got divorced, there wasn't a whole lot of drama. Things got heated sometimes but not to the point of circus metaphors.

That thought didn't make me laugh. I grabbed the magnifying glass from the silverware drawer (okay, where do you keep yours?) and studied the black card, which was apparently at the centre of the issue. The front really was featureless except for a few scratches. Fingerprints finally occurred to me. Far too late to be useful, of course; I'd handled the thing too much. I really was a crap detective.

Even as I was thinking that, however, something else occurred to me. I'd been living in the UK for twenty years, long enough that I have to stop and think as to whether someone has a British or North American accent. Things can become so familiar that they're completely transparent. Which is why it hadn't registered on me right away that Michael Parris's so-called daughter was from Massachusetts. I hadn't noticed right away because I'd grown up in Massachusetts myself.

One more for the not-a-coincidence file?

The question of what to do – or if I should do anything at all – remained. Then my gaze fell on the hotel notepaper again and I realised I actually had decided what to do.

"Google, don't fail me now," I muttered, turning to the laptop.

A minute later, I was fuming as I scrolled through a multitude of links to church groups and fellowships. When you're not religious yourself, it doesn't occur to you that words like eternal make some people want to pray.

So should I take that as a hint? Since we were filing things under not-a-coincidence, and I'd just been told what I'd been told.

I took time to consider it and decided that there was nothing even remotely liturgical about this card or the tag attached to it, or the two pieces of paper that had come with it. All the Eternity Clubs on my laptop screen were groups of people. This Eternity Club had rooms, at least forty-seven, maybe even more.

Yahoo gave me the same results; so did all the others. Disappointed, I went to my homepage just to have something other than a list of prayer groups in front of me. I smiled at the cute animal of the day but I didn't feel it. Maybe if I changed the background to a lighter colour, I thought, it might lift my spirits. But as I was about to move the cursor, I saw something I'd used more times than I could count.

I clicked on the box under *Search For Things To Do In London Today/Tonight* and typed *The Eternity Club*.

The image that appeared on my screen didn't last even five seconds before it flipped to 404: Page Not Found. But that was okay. It had lasted long enough for me to see the address was in Soho. Not surprising; most private clubs were.

I slipped my laptop and, after a moment's thought, the power lead, into a shoulder bag and made sure all the windows were locked before I left the house. Tim was still puttering around in the front yard. I considered asking him to let me know if any angry strangers came around asking for me and then decided against it. I'd have to come up with a reason and I don't like telling stupid lies; worse, the truth sounded like a stupid lie. So I just tried to look busy as I hurried off to the bus stop.

But since there wasn't really any hurry, I took the number 29 bus southbound toward central London. Depending on the time of day, it can take anywhere between forty minutes to something over an hour to get from my neighbourhood to the edge of Soho. I sat on the upper level and stared out the window at nothing in particular. And then for no reason at all, I remembered I hadn't called my Macmillan nurse back.

I fished my phone out of my pocket and turned it back on. As soon as I did, it rang, and it was that number. Reject? No, Michael Parris's fake daughter had probably already left a dozen messages on my voicemail. Maybe I could get rid of her once and for all.

"What," I said, trying to sound both bored and badass.

"Look, you're holding property that just doesn't belong to you," she said, doing her best impression of a reasonable person. "Suppose I had something that belonged to you. Wouldn't you want to get it back?"

"I don't know that I've got anything that belongs to you," I said. "I don't even know your name. Your real name," I add as she starts to say something.

"It's Michaela. My friends call me Mike."

I caught a very slight hesitation between the first two words. Maybe that means nothing or maybe she had to stop and think of something that would go with the nickname

Mike. "Nice try," I told her and hung up. Immediately, I dialled my Macmillan nurse. Naturally, I got her voicemail. I left a message. The moment I hung up, the phone rang again.

"What's the matter with you?" she demanded before I could even say hello. "That card means nothing to you. You can't use it for anything."

"But you can?" I said.

She stumbled and stuttered.

"Tell me what it's for and I'll consider mailing it to you," I said.

"It's – it's private," she said. "I can't divulge that information. You're not – it's not—"

"Okay, let's try something easier," I said. "Who's Karen?"

"Why are you being such an asshole?" she demanded.

I hung up again, not because I was offended but because it was a good question and I didn't have an answer.

I turned my phone off so I could think undisturbed. Why was I being such an asshole?

It didn't take very long for the answer to come to me: cancer, of course. This was a weird little episode in which I had randomly acquired some measure of control and it was completely unrelated to cancer or my suddenly foreshortened lifespan.

Okay, I was taking my problems out on someone else. But it served her right; she was lying about who she was to get her hands on the late Michael Parris's mail. And let's not forget she had threatened me. With the circus, but still. She could have offered me a reward instead. A hundred pounds – even just fifty – and I'd have sent the goddam envelope to her by overnight mail.

Well... after I found out what the Eternity Club was. And that would depend on what it was.

I found a table in a cafe near a power outlet and plugged in my laptop so I could enjoy free electricity along with the free Wi-Fi. But it was hard to concentrate. I kept double-checking the Eternity Club's address on Google Maps, and then worrying that I might have misread it. I was tempted to go there now just to make sure and then return at six but I told myself to wait. It wasn't just that it seemed like the right thing to do; it was all I could do not to put my head down on the table and nap. Part of it was cancer fatigue – that fucker tires you out. But another part was the drama I'd stepped in with this strange woman. I made a mental note to get a new cell phone number.

Meanwhile, I was in a coffee shop; if I was tired, I could caffeinate myself.

By the time I packed up and headed out into the heart of Soho, I couldn't have slept on a dare. I left my cell phone off.

The thing about London is, it has no grid. Streets wind and wander; you can start out thinking you're going one place and end up somewhere completely different, with no idea how to get back. It's part of London's charm and it can drive visitors crazy, particularly those from the US. After twenty years, I was used to it. I still got lost, I just didn't stress about it.

I thought for sure I'd get lost looking for the Eternity Club. It was in a nookish cranny called a close (as in close by, not close the door), the kind of place you could walk past dozens of times and never notice. But I went right to it, as if I'd been there a thousand times before. The outside of the building was painted dark brown, with equally dark windows too high up for me to try peeking through. No street number, no doorbell, not even so much as a discreet "Members Only" sign. Just a door with an old-fashioned lever-type handgrip instead of a knob, also painted dark brown.

I tried the door; it wasn't locked.

The reception area decor was also done in shades of brown. It was softly lit by wall sconces. Pleasant, but I was going to need my reading glasses if I wanted to see anything.

"Oh!" said a voice. I blinked and realised I was standing in front of a reception counter. The young guy behind it looked surprised for a moment, then quickly covered it with a professionally warm smile. I thought he must have been standing on something because the surface was about six inches too high for me to lean on comfortably. "Welcome to the Eternity Club."

I'd expected to be politely thrown out, not welcomed. "Thanks," I said, feeling awkward.

"Your card?" he said.

"Of course," I said and took my time getting it out of my shoulder bag. "Say, you don't have a step-stool or something, do you? I'm having trouble seeing over the top."

He surprised me by bringing me a tall white leather barstool. "Will this do?"

"Sure," I said as I struggled to get up on it. I hate barstools but I finally managed to get comfortable. Only now the counter was about three inches too low. Apparently awkward was mandatory.

"You mean this?" I said, putting my card down on the counter, tag and all. I thought the hole would get some kind of reaction – *I'm sorry, this card is no longer valid* or just *What the hell did you do that for?* But he didn't bat an eye. I mean he really didn't – he had kind of stare-y eyes, although he didn't look weird or anything. He was quite attractive, fairly tall with olive skin and some artful gold highlights in his short, dark hair.

He reached over to take the card but I didn't let go. "What are you going to do?" I asked him.

"Pardon?"

"I'd rather not let that out of my possession."

"I just need to check you in and, if necessary, update the provenance."

Whatever that meant. "You'll give it right back?"

He nodded and I let go, watching as he swiped it through something next to the keyboard on his desk. "Here you go," he said, handing it back to me. I made it disappear quickly, in case he changed his mind.

"Now what?" I asked.

"You can go through," he said, tilting his head at a door to his right.

"Go through to where?"

Now he did bat an eye, both of them in fact. "To your room." He looked at a screen I couldn't see. "Number 47."

"That's my room?"

"That's what it says here."

I don't know how I got the nerve – cancer, probably – but I lunged forward, grabbed the flat monitor, and twisted it around so I could see the screen. I only saw my own picture before he grabbed it back and put it out of my reach. "Excuse me," he said a bit huffily.

"How'd you get my picture?" I demanded.

Abruptly, the door to his right opened and a tall woman with dark brown skin and a headful of short dreadlocks appeared. "You're early," she told me. It was like an accusation.

"Who are you?" I asked but as soon as I did, I knew.

"Stella," we said in unison. "Come along," she added, a bit sternly, and I obeyed. I had a hunch it would have been foolish not to.

She took me down a carpeted hall to an old-fashioned brass open-cage elevator, which we rode down, getting off at -4. I followed her through a series of hallways until we came to a rich-looking door marked 47.

"You're new, aren't you?" she said, although it wasn't a question.

"I'm glad somebody figured that out," I huffed. "Is that guy at the desk a new hire?"

She sighed. "His name is Nico and without him, this place would fall apart."

I resisted the urge to tell her that was some rather heavy credit for somebody who just swiped cards. Unless updating the provenance was code for saving the world. Instead, I decided to come clean. "Look," I said, "the truth is, that's not really my card."

She raised a skeptical eyebrow at me and produced what looked like a smartphone from her blazer pocket. "Well, let's just see whose it is then." She held out her hand and I gave her the card. She touched it to the phone screen, waited a second, then gave it back to me. "Yes, it is," she said and showed me the screen. "Not having an identity crisis, are you?"

I saw the same photo I'd seen on the receptionist's screen. It was a head-and-shoulders shot taken outdoors but I couldn't tell where. The clothing was familiar but I'd gotten rid of that shirt a long time ago, and I couldn't remember my hair ever being that long. But it was definitely me. Below the picture all in caps was the legend: CANCER DANCER.

"What kind of a sick joke is that?" I said angrily.

Stella rolled her eyes. "Do you or do you not have cancer?"

"Yes, but—"

"It's just a designation, you don't have to tell anybody what it is if you don't want to. At least it's easy to remember and it might even help you with the process."

"What process?" I said.

"Side-step. It's always a step to the side. Like this." She demonstrated by stepping from one side of the hall to the centre. "Then you go on as long as you want to." She took three steps forward. "And when you come to a place where you want to side-step…" She stepped to the opposite side of the hallway. "See? Easy. Side-step till you find one of the lines where you're in remission. But don't bother trying to find one where you didn't get cancer in the first place. You're locked out of those."

Light was starting to dawn. It shouldn't have because this was nonsense, impossible, total woo-woo. Nonetheless, I was getting it.

"Just remember to look for a swipe," she said, pointing at the one next to the door. "If it doesn't work, just move on. Oh, and don't be stupid and try to take someone with you. The Eternity Club has a strict no-guests policy. The consequences are quite severe. Maybe it's not fair but that's just how it is."

"Is that what happened to Michael Parris?" I asked.

"I don't know anyone by that name," Stella said.

I handed her the envelope. She examined it, then looked at the papers inside. "I couldn't say. But let's suppose, for a moment, that, oh, let's say a woman decided she'd try to side-step someone with her, someone she had grown very fond of. Maybe a man with a heart condition and she wanted to save him, by taking him to a line where, say, he didn't die of a heart attack."

"And?" I said.

"Well, it wouldn't work. As a non-member, he wouldn't have a room. He'd die and her card would be lost. And you know the rule about lost things. Finders keepers," she added when I shook my head. "Congratulations." For some reason, her attitude toward me had softened. "You know, except the ones they know for certain are caused by things like smoking or asbestos, most cancers are just plain old bad luck. But every so often, some small compensatory action happens at random. You got lucky. Exercise care and good judgment and don't break the rules and you just might side-step the endgame for two, even three decades."

"What if I were happy where I was and I wanted to give my card to someone else?" I asked. I was thinking of my son.

"It's not yours to give. It's ours. Read the terms and conditions."

"And if I didn't want to use it?"

Stella's expression was pitying. "You could give it back. But I'd suggest not doing anything rash. Hang onto it for a while, in case you change your mind."

"But—"

"Please," she said wearily, "I've told you as much as I can but I can't spare any more time. I'm trying to quit this damned job and if I don't get going, I might be stuck here for ever." She strode off down the hall and around a corner before I could even say "But" again.

I looked at the door, at the swipe, and at the card in my hand. Everything that woman had just told me was complete and utter nonsense, I thought, so it wouldn't matter if I used the card. So I did it, quick, before I changed my mind.

There was a clunking sound as the lock opened. I pushed through—

—and there I was in the reception area again, looking at What's-His-Name. Nico. I whirled, thinking I could catch the door and go back through. Nope – it was the front door from the outside, not room 47.

"Oh!" Nico said. Same brief look of surprise, quickly covered with a smile. "Welcome to the Eternity Club."

Wouldn't you just fucking know it, I thought. I'd stepped from the frying pan into one of those lifetimes. And I still had cancer.

And then suddenly I understood why Stella was so annoyed with me, what kind of help poor Karen, whoever she was, had really been asking Detective Sergeant Michael Parris (ret'd) for, and why I probably couldn't expect any, either.

PAT CADIGAN

Pat Cadigan has won the Locus Award three times, the Arthur C. Clarke Award twice, and most recently a Hugo Award and Japan's Seiun Award. The author of fifteen books, she emigrated from Kansas City to gritty, urban North London, where she has lived for the past twenty years with her husband, the Original Chris Fowler, and Gentleman Jynx, coolest black cat in town. She can be found on Facebook and tweets as @cadigan, and she really did kick terminal cancer's arse, at least for the time being.

"When Conrad invited me to this project and sent my envelope of goodies, I made several false starts. Then I was diagnosed with terminal cancer and the story wrote itself, with barely any help from me. Now the book has come out and, thanks to medical treatments that worked better than anticipated, I can expect to live somewhat longer than the original estimate of two years (which would have made 2016 my last). So I'll be hanging around indefinitely, checking the mail when I'm not trying to finish a new novel and marvelling at how changeable those crazy winds of change really are."

THE WRONG GAME

RAMSEY CAMPBELL

Conrad, I'd better say at once that I don't think this is for your book. It isn't fiction, even though I've given it that kind of title, and so I don't imagine it will fit in. I hope at least you may feel able to respond to it – perhaps even help me understand what happened to me. Please be aware that I'm not blaming you. Perhaps I should blame myself.

You'll recall that I was one of the writers you invited into an anthology of tales based on items returned to the dead letter office. I liked the idea and was eager to contribute, but by the time the proposal found a publisher I'd been overtaken by several projects of my own, and so I had to let you down. Other work put the anthology out of my mind, and when I received a package a couple of months ago I didn't think of your idea at all.

While I don't generally examine mail before I open it, this item put me on guard. It was a white Jiffy bag – to be precise, a Mail Lite manufactured by Sealed Air – with a price sticker on the back, 39p from Osborne Office. The packaging looked unusually pristine, as if it might be designed to seem innocent. The First Class Large stamp wasn't franked, and my address had been written by more than one person. Most of it was in bold capitals inscribed with a black marker pen, but the postcode had been corrected with a ballpoint. You may understand why I was growing suspicious, unless you think it doesn't take much to rouse my paranoia. The contents might have made you feel that way as well.

Inside I found a small white envelope on which several people appeared to have written. It was addressed to Roland Malleson at 1 Harvell Crescent in London (West Heath, SE2), but all this had been crossed out and marked NOT KNOWN AT THIS ADDRESS. Someone else had written *Postage unpaid* where a stamp should have been. On the back I read NO FORWARD ADDRESS in yet another script, and return to sender in a fifth one, using a pink marker. Was all this meant to confuse me so that I wouldn't think about what I was taking out of the envelope? One point in particular made me cautious. Although the NOT KNOWN message was printed with a blue marker, it was unquestionably in the same hand that had addressed the entire package to me. Roland Malleson's mail hadn't been returned to the post office, though I was meant to think it had.

Other aspects didn't ring true either. The envelope had been roughly opened, but if the addressee was indeed not known, why had the recipient looked inside? At least this let me do so. The envelope contained a pair of cardboard rectangles approximately two and a half inches by four and a half, crudely cut out of a larger piece of card and taped together so closely that there wasn't space between them for much more than a scrap of paper. It occurred to me that in the days of LSD on blotting paper this might have been how people sent it through the mail. Call me paranoid again if you like, Conrad, but I was afraid that somebody had set me up – that if I opened the cardboard packet I would incriminate myself or be accused of having done so. I even wondered if the post office was involved in the operation.

It was a Saturday, the 24th of April, and the sorting office was still open. I spent some time at the bathroom sink – my hands felt grimy, and I remember peering at them to convince myself they weren't – and then I went to the sorting office. It's fifteen minutes' walk from this house, three minutes' drive at my age. A number of women were waiting to collect their post, and I've seen faster queues outside a toilet, since there was just one postman behind the counter. When at last I reached the window I showed him the package but kept hold of it. "Who do I need to speak to about this?"

"Depends what it is. Won't I do?"

His smooth round face looked as if he'd tried to scrub it younger, and I thought I smelled soap through the gap under the window; there might even have been slivers of pink soap beneath some of his fingernails. "Is the supervisor available?" I said.

"She's busy right now." Professionalism didn't entirely disguise his resentment as he added "I can help."

"If you can tell me why I've received this."

He stared at the words on the front of the package I pushed under the window. "Is that you? Then that's why."

As he slid the package back across the counter I thought he was a little too eager to return it. "Have a look inside," I said.

Did I glimpse a hint of reluctance? He poked the padded

bag open with a finger and thumb and squinted inside before shaking out the smaller envelope onto the counter. He read both sides of it and then turned Malleson's address to face me. "Did you send him this?"

"Of course I didn't. I've never even heard of him."

"Well, whoever forwarded it to you must think you have."

"And why should they think I want what's in there?"

The postman looked inside the envelope but left the cardboard packet where it was. "What is it?"

"I think you ought to check. It's still your responsibility, isn't it? Property of Royal Mail."

"Not once it's been delivered," he said and slipped the envelope under the window. "It's yours to do what you want with."

I couldn't help thinking he was as wary as I had every right to feel. Was he trying to pretend he thought the packet could be lethal? "I'll open it here," I said, "if you'll be a witness."

I could have fancied he was trying to compete with me at cautiousness. "A witness to what?" he objected.

"To the fact that I'm only just opening it now."

"You could have done it once and stuck it back together."

"I've done nothing of the kind," I said with far less ire than I was experiencing. "I give you my word."

He stared at that as if it was nowhere to be seen. He rubbed his hands together, apparently feeling they weren't clean enough, while I removed the packet from the envelope. I made sure he saw how fragments of the cardboard stuck to the tape as I peeled it off. I opened up one long side of the packet and a short one, and fished out the contents. If I'd been alone I might have laughed at the anticlimax. My prize was a grubby pair of playing cards, a two of clubs and a six of hearts. "Using the mail for a game?" the postman suggested.

"At my expense, you'd have to mean."

"Some people play chess through the mail, don't they? Maybe someone's having a game of cards."

"I shouldn't think so." In case he meant me I told him "I haven't played cards since I was your age."

"So what do you want to do with those?"

"I'll take them home. As you say, they were sent to me."

Had I begun to wonder if they might give me an idea for your anthology, Conrad? If you're like me you never waste material, however trivial it may seem. I put the cards in the envelope and returned that to the padded bag, and was on my way past the queue that had gathered behind me until the postman called "Don't you want this?"

He was brandishing the empty cardboard packet. "Bin it for me," I said, and now I wonder if I should have taken it with me, though I've no idea what difference it could have made.

I found myself rubbing my thumb and finger together as I headed for the car. It felt like a tic, especially since I could see no reason for it, and it didn't let me think much about Malleson. Was the name wholly unfamiliar? Was it somehow associated with a convention I'd attended long ago? Surely I must have Miles Malleson in mind. He'd been in many of the Hammer horror films I'd sought out as soon as I was able to pass for sixteen, and decades later I'd seen him interviewed at the Festival of Fantastic Films in Manchester. All the same, this didn't help me grasp an impression that was loitering just beyond reach in my mind. It seemed too vague to be related to the actor.

Once I was home I emailed you, Conrad, asking if you'd sent me the package even though I'd had to turn down your invitation. I don't know if you received my message, since I never saw a reply. Of course you did say at the outset that you wouldn't enter into any correspondence about the items you sent your contributors. I didn't wait too long to hear from you before I did what I should have done in the first place. I searched online for Roland Malleson and his address.

I couldn't find his name, and the address didn't exist in the form that was on the envelope. While there is a Harvell Crescent in SE2, West Heath is in Birmingham. That district does include a Horwell Crescent, however. After more research and some expenditure I managed to obtain the names and phone numbers of the occupier of the London house and of 1 Horwell Crescent as well. Neither name was Malleson. The London number didn't answer, and so I tried the one in Birmingham, where the phone rang eight times before a woman said "Yes?"

She sounded less affirmative than the word did. I was about to begin explaining my call when it occurred to me to say just "Malleson."

After a silence she spoke, but not to me. "Someone's saying Malleson."

"I'll speak to them." In a moment the man's voice came as close as my ear and grew sharper. "Hello, what do you want?"

"Whatever you can tell me about Roland Malleson."

"Who wants to know?"

"I believe you sent me a package that was meant for him."

"Right." Though the man seemed reluctant to admit this made any difference, his Midland accent had turned shriller.

"It's, don't tell me," he said to me or his companion. "It's, I'll have it in a sec. Ramsay somebody. Ramsay MacDonald, that's who you are, right?"

"He's dead." It was by no means the first time someone had tried to give me the name; I've even been introduced that way as a speaker. "I'm from the other clan," I said. "Ramsey Campbell."

"So I wasn't too far off, right."

He sounded as if he thought I was being unreasonable, which provoked me to retort "You managed to get it right when you sent the package."

"That was her." Without discovering any enthusiasm he said "So what are you after now?"

"For a start I'd like to know why you sent it to me."

"Roland said he played with you."

My memory had let me down a few times, but for some reason I hoped this wasn't such a case. "When?"

"When he saw some of your books in the shops. That was years back."

I didn't need to be told that, however resigned to the situation I've grown. "I'm asking when I'm meant to have played whatever I'm supposed to have played. I certainly don't remember."

"Cards." If it's possible for triumph to be apathetic, the man brought off the trick by saying "Mally said it was a long time back, before you ever got yourself in the shops."

I seemed to experience the faintest stirring of memory, like a glimpse of movement in a virtually lightless place. I won't pretend it was welcome, but I was going to ask for more detail until another question jumped the queue. "Who opened the envelope? I'm guessing it wasn't him."

"He couldn't have even when he was here." Before I could pursue this the man said "We did, right? We needed to find out why we were still getting post for him."

"And was there anything else in the envelope?"

"Just what you've got. Don't you think we'd have sent you anything there was?"

His tone seemed so inappropriate that I almost laughed. "I still don't understand why you sent it at all."

"Because he said he helped you with the cards."

"Helped me do what with them?"

"No, I'm saying he said they helped you, right?" As I prepared to enquire into this if not simply to deny it the man said "Can we leave it now? She's getting upset with all this talking about her brother."

"I'm sorry, but I'd like this to make more sense. Who sent him the cards? I hope you don't imagine I did."

"You could have." More magnanimously than he had any right to sound the man conceded "If it wasn't you, maybe it was someone who didn't like how Mally played cards."

Something like a memory seemed to loom in my mind, but the man disrupted it. "I'm putting this down now, right," he said. "We've resurrected him enough."

"Don't say that," I heard the woman cry, and that was the end of the call. I sat here at my desk and gazed out at the river, where a stubborn length of fog stood for the condition of my brain. I could only examine the cards once more. Though their backs showed an identical picture, they might not have belonged to the same pack, since the two was red as blood while the heart was a pallid amalgam of blue and green, a colour I don't think I've seen anywhere in life. Each bore a slim female silhouette that was leaning against a palm tree beneath a supine crescent moon. The figure might have been dressed in a grass skirt – the tendrils dangling from one bent leg resembled the tufts that sprouted from the black earth – and she was playing with a necklace. Why should I have thought the object at the end of the necklace was an amulet rather than a locket? The entire image brought a phrase to mind, and I didn't know why. "There's magic underneath."

I hadn't time to ponder it. I'd been overtaken by the nervousness I'm prone to suffer when I have to speak in public on a topic I haven't previously addressed – in this case the generation of ideas and how to develop them. Much of the time I've no idea where they come from, but months earlier I'd agreed to talk on the subject at the Bournemouth Festival of Book and Film, and all of a sudden – that's always how it happens – the date of the booking was tomorrow. As usual I felt disgracefully unprepared, and I still did next morning as I rehearsed some of my speech in the shower. I was leaving the house when I decided to take the Malleson package with me, telling myself I might be able to work it into my talk.

I didn't have much of a chance to think how on the drive down to Bournemouth. That took most of Sunday, starting at dawn. Once I'd checked into my hotel room I had time for just a quick shower before I had to hurry to the evening's venue, a hall with far more seats in it than audience. The organisers delayed the event for several minutes, nearly always an ominous sign, but eventually they put me on for the benefit of a dozen listeners. At least the lady who announced me got my name right and wasn't too inaccurate about my career. I read a couple of extracts from tales of mine and went some way towards analysing how the stories came to be, after which I took half a dozen questions from the audience. Throughout the talk the Malleson business had been loitering in my brain, and the session still had more than ten minutes to run. On an impulse I took the package out of the laptop case that serves me as a briefcase and produced the cards, feeling like a magician who'd neglected to plan a trick. "Sometimes something ought to give you an idea," I said, "but you can't think what it might be. Someone sent me these the other day. What do we think they could mean?"

Everyone looked wary, perhaps just of being singled out. After quite a pause a man said "Did that really happen or are you saying it did?"

"Both. There's no difference." I might have said more to prove I can distinguish reality from my own imaginings if I hadn't been driven to ask "Why would you send anyone a couple of old cards?"

"Maybe—" A woman seemed to wish she hadn't spoken, and cleared her throat twice before saying "Maybe they're meant for your fortune."

"I don't know what that means."

"Maybe they're trying to tell you."

I could have said this was impossible, since they hadn't been sent to me in the first place, but it would have called for too much explanation. More disconcertingly, I felt as if she'd let me glimpse some kind of truth. An impression had lodged in my head – the image of a figure watching me across a table spread with cards. The figure wasn't just indistinct but unstable, as if it was composed of the kind of restless darkness you may see where there's no source of illumination. The idea bewildered me much more than it inspired me; in fact, I couldn't say it appealed to me at all. All the same, I told the woman that there might be a story in it and thanked her, and asked for any last questions. When nobody obliged, the organisers brought the event to an end.

I autographed a handful of books and then dined with some of the festival folk, but had difficulty concentrating on the table talk or even savouring the Cantonese banquet. The image of a figure at a table surrounded by oppressive darkness had begun to feel like a memory or a distortion of one, but did this simply mean I was recalling the moment when it had entered my mind at the festival event? As soon as I politely could I said goodnight to my hosts and went back to the hotel, where I felt the need for yet another shower. After that I would have gone to bed if I hadn't been troubled by wondering where to put the Malleson package. I stowed it in the drawer that contained the obligatory Bible, in a chest some distance from the bed.

I must have dozed despite the image that wouldn't leave my mind or grow clearer, because I awoke at a few minutes past two. I had a sense that I'd heard something not especially substantial on the move in the dark. The only light came from the scrawny digits of the bedside clock, which aggravated the darkness. As I groped for the cord above the bed I felt as if the gloom was gathering like soot on my fingers. By the time I located the cord I'd begun rubbing them together. The light showed that I hadn't closed the drawer of the chest as tight as I'd imagined, since it displayed a shadow like a thin strip of earth. Surely it was just because I hadn't fully wakened that the sliver of blackness looked restive. Lurching out of bed, I slammed the drawer and found myself staring at the room. What should it remind me of? Then I knew, and rather more than that. It brought to mind the first time I'd stayed by myself at a hotel.

I'd been in Harrogate, at a science fiction convention more than half a century ago. For decades I'd gone almost every Easter, wherever in Britain the annual convention might be. I would pass these weekends listening to programme items and meeting increasingly old friends, usually in the bar. After the programme was done for the day there would be parties in the bedrooms and often a card game somewhere in the hotel. Recalling this unlocked my memory, and with a shock that felt as if a dark part of my mind had given way I realised I had indeed met Malleson at one such Easter weekend. The people I'd phoned about him had been right after all.

He didn't go by that name at the convention. When he turned up at the poker game he was Malleficus on his badge. "Just call me Mally," he said, having peered at everybody else's badges, and shouldn't I have recognised the nickname when I heard it over the phone? Perhaps the memory was blurred by how he'd seemed to feel I should appreciate the word on his badge. As he sat opposite me across the large round table he caught my eye and indicated the name with his left little finger, which was as pale and thick as his lips and didn't look much firmer. With its cobweb strands of greying hair his big-eyed long-nosed oval face put me in mind of an egg well past its best. He kept up a loose-lipped grin at me until the dealer began laying out the cards. In those days I was only starting to manufacture the personality I use as armour for shyness, and so I tried to ignore Malleson.

I don't think his playing style went down too well.
Whenever it was his turn to open he would say "What
the prince wears," a joke that soon grew tedious and then
irritating. It meant half a crown, not a negligible amount of
money at the time. When he followed someone else's bid he
would wave his hand over the cards in his left one, a gesture
that might have signified indecision or a silent wish. "Waving
goodbye to your money?" an opponent fell to saying, which
didn't deter Malleson, especially once it became clear that he
was winning many of the pots and losing only the smaller
ones. By midnight several players had thrown in their hands
and gone in search of other diversions, and soon an especially
competitive round gave Malleson his most substantial win
with a full house. This proved too much for the owner of the
pack of cards, who took them and himself off. As the other
players wandered away, Malleson detained me by saying
"Aren't you a writer?"

I hadn't much to show for it compared to the authors on
the convention programme – Moorcock, Brunner, Bulmer,
Tubb. I had just a single book and a few short stories to my
name, and so I couldn't help feeling flattered when Malleson
said "I've been looking for someone like you."

"There's a few here this weekend."

"Not like you." As I prepared to feel more acclaimed he
said "They're here for science fiction, not the occult."

I did feel somewhat outcast at the convention. I'd found
one book dealer who stocked fantasy as well as science fiction
– Sci Fi Fo Fum – but he scarcely touched horror. It would be
years before an Eastercon saw its first dealer in my field, the
Horrid Variorum, sadly short-lived even once it changed its

name to Rarum Scarum. All the same, I was about to establish that I never mistook my fiction for reality when Malleson pointed at his badge. "You know what that means, don't you?"

I wasn't sufficiently sure of myself to tell him the word was misspelled. "Wasn't it some kind of criminal in Latin?"

"That's been dead a long time. I thought you'd know better." Having stared at me as though to give me a chance to redeem myself, he said "What's *malefica* mean?"

In those days it was easy to make me feel I was being quizzed by a schoolteacher, and I was forced to guess. "A witch?"

"That's it, a sorceress. I knew you'd know your occult history. It's where they got the title of that vile book from, the *Malleus Maleficarum*. As you see, I've taken the word back."

All I could produce in the way of an answer was "Well, good."

"I knew you'd think so. Our type need to stick together."

This struck me as ominous, especially in a dimly illuminated lounge late at night with nobody else nearby. "Anyway," I said, "if you'll excuse me—"

"Wait there." Malleson stood up, pushing the table towards me so that it came close to pinning me against the shabby upholstered chair. "I want to do something for you," he said.

His approach shook the floorboards and seemed to do that to his lips, which quivered into an ingratiating smile. "What?" I demanded and caught hold of the edge of the table, ready to shove myself back.

"Only to show you what you ought to see." Malleson rested his hands on the table as he sat next to me, extracting a creak from his chair. He dragged the chair around so that he was facing me and lifted his hands with a flourish. "Those are yours," he said.

He'd revealed a pair of cards lying face down. No doubt leaning on the table had let him plant them unobserved. They must have been hidden in the sleeves of his black turtleneck or of his tweed jacket, which was even more voluminous than he seemed this close. "That's a good trick," I admitted. "You're that kind of magician."

"They were there all the time," he said and unfolded his left hand above the cards. "You see, there's magic underneath."

I thought he meant on the backs of the cards, but now I wonder. Perhaps he was talking about the world. At this remove I've no idea whether the backs showed the sylph beneath the tree. I flipped them over, and I don't need to tell you what I saw, Conrad. I didn't know how useful they might have been to me in the final round of poker, but I said "If these are my cards they're a bit late."

"We aren't playing that game any more. We're concerned with your life."

I found this unnervingly intrusive. "Who is?"

"I hope you are." With a winning smile or rather a triumphant grin Malleson said "You could make your name."

"How are these going to help?"

"They can point the way. They'll be part of you. That's why cards were made in the first place. Once they've been read to you they'll direct you."

Of course I didn't believe any of this – I didn't even think I could get a story out of it – which was why I said "So that's what you'd like to do?"

"To read you? I already am." He'd lowered his voice when

he joined me, and now it grew so muted that it made me strain to grasp it. "Would you like to hear?" he said.

"If I can."

"Oh, you will." This sounded less promissory than ominous, not least since it seemed to have become more audible by creeping inside my head. "The deuce of wands," he said and rested his left forefinger on the two of clubs. "I give you power and boldness and originality."

"Well, thank you," I said with some irony, since I imagined I already had them.

"The six of cups." He transferred the finger to the other card, and I saw a moist print fade from the two like ripples sinking into a pond. "I take innocence and childhood," he said. "I leave nostalgia and the influence of the past."

I didn't learn for years how unlike an ordinary tarot reading this was. Shouldn't that have fixed it in my mind? I'm disturbed to think I could have forgotten all about it until that night in the Bournemouth hotel. Malleson lifted his finger from the six, leaving a second sweaty mark, and I couldn't help asking "Is that all?"

"It will be all you need. It can be your life."

At least this seemed to end the session. "Well, thank you," I found myself repeating like a response in church.

As I pushed back my chair Malleson said "Don't you want to hear the price?"

I felt I should have known there would be something of the sort. "You won all my money," I tried protesting.

"It should never be that kind of price." When he rose to his feet he might have been recoiling in distaste. "The price is no more than an acknowledgement," he said, and the trembling of the floor receded as he moved towards the corridor. "Just remember."

He must have raised his voice, because it didn't grow distant as soon as he did. I felt as though it had taken root in my head, and in the Bournemouth hotel room I fancied I could hear its soft insinuating hiss: "the price…" I left the cards on the table in the lounge and didn't follow Malleson until I was sure of not catching up with him. For fear of encountering him at a party I retreated to my room and went to bed. During the rest of the weekend I kept an eye out for him, but I never saw him again – not at an Easter gathering, at any rate.

Could he have meant that remembering was the acknowledgement – the price? In that case I've paid it here and am liable to carry on. Or if he was asking for an acknowledgement in my work, surely this account fits that bill too. I was already striving for originality and boldness, and I hope those lend my stuff some power, but it's also founded on the traditions of my field; you could say I'm nostalgic for them. I haven't been innocent for a long time, and I trust I'm not childish either. Mustn't saying all this settle whatever debt I owed him? What else could he want of me?

It took me a while to recapture sleep in Bournemouth. I wakened just after six with several ideas in my head. This very often happens – sometimes it's a stray phrase or image, more frequently material for the piece I'm writing – but these words seemed more pointed than usual. *Take what's on offer, friends. Cards let us be shrewd. Symbolic images ("X") offer foresight, however enigmatic and random they seem.* Perhaps you find all that as meaningful as I do, Conrad, or your readers would, though if you interpret an oracle it becomes part of you, just as employing any form of magic is said to do. I didn't spend much time on the sentences, because I'd had another waking notion. I thought it might lead to a story, perhaps for your book. On my way home I could revisit the hotel where I'd met Malleson.

I won't name it, though it isn't listed online. I remembered where it had been, which looked as if it was about half an hour's drive from the motorway. By the time I reached the junction I'd been delayed by several traffic queues, all of which seemed to be caused solely by signs warning of a queue ahead. I considered driving straight on, but it felt too much like cowardice. Perhaps I ought to have wondered why I should be nervous, instead of which I made for the hotel.

I didn't recognise the road. It wound through a couple of elongated villages kept apart by miles of fields, and then it wandered between trees that added to the gloom beneath the sunless April sky. To begin with I drove past a side road, which didn't appear to be signposted. Backing up, I saw there was a post after all, though its top was raggedly rotten. The long grass around the post came close to hiding several fragments of a wooden pointer, but I spotted the remains of a word, OTEL, and gave in to fancying that it sounded like an instruction as I turned along the road.

This wasn't as wide as it used to be. The hedges on both sides had swelled up, stretching out thorny branches. Tufts of grass and weeds were well on the way to reclaiming the road for an older landscape. Beyond the hedges trees elaborately cabled with vines blocked most of the view until the road bent, revealing the hotel, a three-storey crescent composed of twin curves on either side of a straight midsection framing a wide pair of doors above six broad steps. At first I thought it was blackened just by the low unbroken clouds, but as I drove closer I saw that the building couldn't have been cleaned for decades. By the time it hosted Eastercon the hotel had been dilapidated, offering discounts to conventions and the like in an attempt to prolong its life. This obviously hadn't worked, since it was clear that the hotel had been boarded up years ago.

The curving drive in front of the hotel was deserted. The splintered concrete was strewn with rubble, shattered slates from the roof, fragments of brick, a board so rotten it had fallen from the window across which it had been nailed. None of the windows above the ground floor was boarded up, and all of them were encrusted with windblown grime. I parked in front of the main entrance, and as I climbed the cracked steps the ends of the building loomed at the edges of my vision like a claw poised to close around me. I nearly slipped on a patch of moss, and the claw lurched closer. I might have fancied that my approach had been greeted in another way – that the left-hand door had crept open to invite me in. I mustn't have noticed it was ajar.

When I pushed the door it lumbered inwards, grinding debris into the carpet. I had to lean against it to make a gap I could fit through. Beyond it I saw the lobby, or rather a few sooty outlines – the reception counter, a dead chandelier. The flashlight on my phone gradually revealed section after section of the extravagantly large high-ceilinged room, where shadows dodged behind everything that stood in the dark. They brought to life the pale child perched on the end of a stone banister. I was crossing the threshold when I thought better of it; at least, I went back to the car to find the Malleson package in my overnight case. I slipped the cards into my pocket as I returned to the hotel. Perhaps I still thought I was creating a tale for you, Conrad.

The floor of the lobby gave as I trod on it, or at any rate the discoloured carpet did. The heavy fabric was sodden with however many years of rain had leaked through holes in the roof above the stairwell. As I advanced towards the counter I felt boards shift beneath the carpet, blundering sluggishly together like blind creatures under earth. That must have been why the rusty bell on the counter emitted a dull muffled note, and I needn't have felt it was summoning anyone. In response to my approach all the denizens of the pigeonholes behind the counter stirred in unison – just shadows roused by the flashlight, which also made the grime on the counter seem to swarm. I halted under the chandelier, in which the blackened bulbs only served to solidify the dark, and swung the flashlight beam around me while I tried to recall the layout of the hotel.

As the stone child stretched its arms out to the light I saw its eyes were caked with grime. Beyond the wide stairs over which it was standing some kind of guard, a pair of lifts began to inch their doors open. The shadows of the bars were shifting, not the grilles themselves, but the beam also found a collapsed face on the floor of the lift, peering out at me with its crumpled eyes. I had to pace a good deal closer to be certain that the face was on an abandoned poster for some forgotten event at the hotel. At least I was heading in the right direction, because I'd remembered passing the lifts on my way to the poker game.

Are you beginning to wonder what I thought I was doing? I had the ill-defined notion that putting the cards back where

I'd left them might bring some form of resolution, perhaps just to the tale I imagined I was in. As I stepped into the corridor beyond the lifts the walls appeared to lunge towards me, not least because whole sections of the wallpaper were drooping towards the floor, exposing their fungoid undersides. A board shivered underfoot, and I couldn't tell whether its muffled clatter obscured a sound somewhere ahead, a whisper or a faint restlessness. It seemed likely that there would be mice or other vermin in the hotel, and I didn't halt too long while I tried to hear. Staying still for any length of time made me feel as if the grime that constituted a good deal of the dark was settling on my skin.

The floor wasn't holding up well. It felt like treading on planks in a marsh. A doorway gaped on my left, and I saw that both of the doors were held open by the carpet, which appeared to have burgeoned around their lowest edges. Beyond the doorway a cavernous darkness was emphasised more than relieved by glimmers of light through chinks in the boards over the windows, but I glimpsed a crouching shape that looked poised for a leap. It was a chair crippled by a broken leg and discarded in the empty dining-room, and I told myself it was the only reason why I felt awaited in the dark.

As I passed the bar I saw fragments of a figure keeping pace with me, my reflection dodging across a long mirror and visible only where the glass wasn't black. Next to the bar the outer doors of both toilets were caught permanently open by the carpet and whatever had taken root in it. Through one doorway I thought I heard a whisper of water, but it fell silent the instant I paused, and so it could hardly have been the plumbing. Might it have been somewhere ahead, around the curve of the corridor? I did my best to assume I'd heard mice again, although now that I tried to grasp the sound, it seemed to have been unnecessarily surreptitious. In a story I might have made it suggest that the dark was taking on more substance – settling together into a more solid form.

I sent myself along the corridor, since otherwise my detour from the motorway would have been pointless. An oval mirror partly draped with sagging wallpaper blinded me with my own flashlight, and I had to halt again while my eyesight seeped back. My vision hadn't entirely returned when the sensation of gathering grime urged me onwards, and so at first I didn't notice the figure behind me in the mirror. Its face looked not merely black with dirt, as though it had just risen from the earth, but composed of it if not fattened by it. The flashlight beam swung around faster than I did, which meant that it took altogether too long to locate the occupant of the corridor. It was a portrait opposite the mirror, its face masked by a stain that had attracted a good deal of grit. Identifying it might have reassured me more if the beam hadn't illuminated something else. The lounge where I'd encountered Malleson was just along the corridor.

It was on the left: a wide space without doors, where I could see a segment of the edge of the round table. By now I'd decided on my course, whether as an incident in the tale I planned to tell or simply to rid myself of the cards in the way that seemed most appropriate. I believed – still believe – that I'd worked out why they had been sent to Malleson. One of the poker players had found them where I'd left them and assumed they were evidence of cheating, which indeed they could have been; after all, what had Malleson been doing with them before he read them to me? Why the sender had waited so long, I couldn't say. Perhaps, having failed to track Malleson down at the convention, they'd been frustrated all these years until they stumbled on his address or thought to search online. Now I proposed to leave the cards on the table once again. If anybody found them – if rubble hadn't hidden them by the time the hotel was renovated or more likely demolished – they would mean nothing. This felt like a conclusion to me.

I took the cards out of my pocket as I advanced towards the lounge. I wasn't intending to linger, especially since I'd heard the noise in the dark again. It was somewhere in the lounge beyond the table, which was scaly with scraps of fallen plaster. It might have been a furtive movement or a bid to whisper or even an attempt to draw a breath through some suffocating medium, if not a combination of them all. As I came abreast of the lounge I couldn't help lowering the flashlight beam. It showed the near edge of the table, which had been divested of its chairs, unless one had been left on the far side, where part of the darkness seemed more solid. I kept the flashlight low while I made for the table, holding out the cards, which felt unpleasantly slippery and gritty into the bargain. As soon as I was close enough I dropped them on the table, where they landed like part of a poker hand, the club peeking out from behind the heart. The impact seemed too negligible to affect the other contents of the table, and the scraps of plaster didn't stir. All the same, there was another movement in the dark.

I raised the flashlight beam with a good deal of reluctance. The grime on the table scurried away from the light, or shadows did, and came not quite to rest on a pair of objects on the far side of the table. Surely they were just a pair of artificial hands, broken off a statue if not sculpted in that fashion. I couldn't identify the material, since they were caked with grime. In fact they appeared to be at least partly composed of it, and it wasn't as tranquil as it ought to have been. It was shifting almost imperceptibly, which put me in mind of a multitude of insects hatching or otherwise coming to life.

I tried to blame this on the shaky flashlight. The spectacle was so disagreeably fascinating that it distracted me from a movement I should have noticed sooner. Almost too gradually for it to be evident, the hands were creeping across the table towards the cards – towards me. Before I could prevent myself I jerked up the flashlight beam.

What did I see? Not much for long, but far too much. The hands belonged to a shape that occupied all the space on a solitary dilapidated chair. Like the hands, the shape appeared to owe its substance to the grime that was everywhere in the dark. Perhaps the soft insidious sound I heard was demonstrating how restless that substance was, but I had the awful idea that it could be an attempt to breathe. I just had time to glimpse a face – eyes as black and unstable as the rest of the lopsided bulk, nostrils desperately dilating, lips that sagged into a helpless grimace and then struggled to produce another expression if not to speak – before the figure collapsed.

The hands stayed on the table. I could have thought they'd been severed for a crime. I don't know whether they continued to move, but the rest of the presence did. Beyond the table I heard a soft dismayingly widespread mass start to crawl across the floor towards me. In the midst of this I thought I heard another sound or a variation on the same one, as if the crawler had begun to regain something like a voice. I didn't wait to make sure. I fled so fast that the corridor appeared to be caving in as the flashlight beam reeled from wall to wall, and I had the nightmare notion that the hotel might indeed give way around me, trapping me with its denizen. By the time I staggered into the lobby I couldn't tell how fast the soft dogged sounds behind me were, or how close. As I dashed towards the way out of the hotel I risked sending the flashlight beam into the corridor, and thought I glimpsed a disintegrating figure heave itself up to summon me back.

I ran to the car and drove away, not slowing for the overgrown road. The car still bears scratches from the hedge. I didn't stop until I reached the nearest motorway services, where I spent so long washing my hands that several people stared at me. I always keep a bottle of antiseptic gel in the car, but it was used up by the time I arrived home. Besides the crawling sensation of grime on my skin I took with me the word I'd seemed to hear in the abandoned hotel. "Cheat," the voice might have whispered as its source recovered some shape.

Perhaps the speaker meant the accusation for himself, in which case the admission may have brought closure, but I fear it was aimed at me. If neglecting to acknowledge my debt was how I cheated, haven't I repaid the debt now? Or perhaps my career has been the cheat, in which case this account disguised as fiction is the latest proof. Writing it has left me feeling grimy, desperate to clean myself up, and I only hope it hasn't invited anything out of my past, let alone given it more substance. Surely reading it can't make you in any way complicit. I hope you and any other readers won't feel the need to wash your hands now that you've finished it, Conrad.

RAMSEY CAMPBELL

The *Oxford Companion to English Literature* describes Ramsey Campbell as "Britain's most respected living horror writer". He has been given more awards than any other writer in the field, including the Grand Master Award of the World Horror Convention, the Lifetime Achievement Award of the Horror Writers Association, the Living Legend Award of the International Horror Guild and the World Fantasy Lifetime Achievement Award. In 2015 he was made an Honorary Fellow of Liverpool John Moores University for outstanding services to literature. Among his novels are *The Face That Must Die, Incarnate, Midnight Sun, The Count of Eleven, Silent Children, The Darkest Part of the Woods, The Overnight, Secret Story, The Grin of the Dark, Thieving Fear, Creatures of the Pool, The Seven Days of Cain, Ghosts Know, The Kind Folk, Think Yourself Lucky* and *Thirteen Days by Sunset Beach*. He is presently working on a trilogy, *The Three Births of Daoloth. Needing Ghosts, The Last Revelation of Gla'aki, The Pretence* and *The Booking* are novellas. His collections include *Waking*

Nightmares, Alone with the Horrors, Ghosts and Grisly Things, Told by the Dead, Just Behind You and *Holes for Faces*, and his non-fiction is collected as *Ramsey Campbell, Probably*. His novels *The Nameless* and *Pact of the Fathers* have been filmed in Spain. His regular columns appear in *Dead Reckonings* and *Video Watchdog*. He is the President of the Society of Fantastic Films.

Ramsey Campbell lives on Merseyside with his wife Jenny. His pleasures include classical music, good food and wine, and whatever's in that pipe. His website is at www.ramseycampbell.com

IS-AND

CLAIRE DEAN

She was the only one watching – nose against glass – as the ferry navigated the turbines. They swooped noiselessly, churning sea and sky. They looked more delicate and awkward close up, like gargantuan flowers, and they went on for as far as she could see.

Gareth was sitting four rows back flicking through something on his phone. He'd made it clear she was irritating him, making a show of herself for a pointless view. Other passengers watched the news on big screens or dozed. The ordinary breakfast news felt incongruous in this place between places. The island was only sixty miles from the coast she'd lived on all her life, but she'd never seen it. The guidebook talked of the mists of a great magician that kept it hidden.

As they left the turbines behind, the sea and sky settled into mute bands of grey, but she still couldn't see the island. She returned to her seat and rested her head against Gareth's shoulder. He remained intent on his phone. Hers had lost signal and wouldn't get it back until they got home. Gareth had forgotten to tell her before they set off that he used another sim card on the island.

She reached for the guidebook and started to reread the section of walks.

'You don't need that,' Gareth said without looking up from his phone.

'I like reading it,' she said. 'I just like it. I haven't been before. I'm allowed to enjoy it.'

'I'll show you everything.'

She let the book fall closed on her lap and rested her head against him again. 'I'm lucky to have my own walking, talking guidebook.' She took hold of his hand. He continued to thumb his phone.

She dozed and when she opened her eyes again the sky had cleared to a startling blue. People were lined up against the front window. The island was there and she'd missed it appearing. She tried to sidle in between an elderly woman and a couple of middle-aged bikers. The island was small at first but it quickly became too big to be contained by the window. The view shifted with an accelerated zoom. She hadn't taken in everything about one image of the island before it grew closer and there was more to see.

The table filled the back of the room and she caught herself on a corner as she squeezed into the place that had been laid for her. The tablecloth was crocheted and there were napkins in heavy metal rings. There were only two places set. 'Isn't your mum...'

'No.' Gareth piled his plate high with potatoes and peas from china dishes. Gareth's plate held three slices of anaemic-looking ham. She had been given one. There was a bottle of lemonade on the table. No wine. She needed a drink. She could hear the radio from the kitchen, where his mum had hidden herself away.

'If it was a problem us eating here… I mean we could have eaten out.'

'No, Mum wanted to cook for us.' He unscrewed the lemonade. There was no hiss of air. No bubbles in her glass. It must have been at the back of a cupboard for years.

The Anaglypta walls were cluttered with paintings. Each was a swirl of garish colours formed into a landscape. They glinted from some angles, but looked rutted and gouged from others. There were more of them, clearly by the same amateur hand, in Gareth's room. 'Are they places on the island?' she'd asked as they unpacked their bags. 'Did your mum do them?' He'd just shrugged.

His room was frustratingly bland. She'd expected posters, old CDs, plastic figurines, some traces of him having grown up here. There were just the paintings, more crochet and a crooked twig and wool cross above the bed. She'd read about the crosses, *crosh cuirns* they were called, in the guidebook. They used to be put up as protection against fairies. His mum obviously had a thing for them because they were all over the house. On the living-room mantelpiece there was a line-up of family photos including several of his brother and him as children, and also his wedding photo. His ex looked young and elegant. They looked happy. Next to it was one of a newborn baby in a blue hat. 'He's beautiful,' she said. 'Why didn't you tell me you're an uncle?' He'd clattered the plates on to the table and gestured for her to sit.

The lemonade left an acidic coating on her tongue. Gareth dissected his ham into long, thin strips before eating them one by one. The meat was cold and left a film of grease on their plates. The potatoes were still hard beneath their roasted edges. 'We'll go for a long walk tomorrow,' he said.

Perched in a wingback chair by the window she leafed through an old tourist magazine. She was desperate to get out and start exploring, but not comfortable enough to interrupt them talking in the kitchen, or to wander round the house to find where his mum had put her boots. She fiddled with her phone, but there was nothing she could do on it. They were talking too quietly for her to be able to separate many words from the murmur of voices and cooking sounds. She heard him say something about an exchange. 'Way it's done,' his mum said, '…if you want… returned.'

The knock at the door made her jump. She half stood, but Gareth came through to answer it.

'This one must be for you,' a man's voice said. 'I've been keeping it for you.'

'Thanks,' Gareth said, reaching out for it.

'It came in unaddressed. Jack wanted to put it in the back with all the other dead letters. People forget a stamp, or get the wrong address, but I said to myself it's a funny business someone forgetting the address all together. I had a feeling about it so I checked it. I think it must be for you.'

Gareth took the parcel without speaking.

'It took you long enough to come back.'

Gareth pushed the door shut a little too hard. The paintings on the wall quivered. He put the parcel down on the dresser without looking at it and went upstairs. The bathroom door slammed.

The bus was full of locals. The only tourists were a middle-aged couple. They kept passing between them the same guidebook that she had brought. They sat right at the front and almost jumped up at every stop. On a wooded stretch of road the man dropped the guidebook, spilling leaflets everywhere.

'That's what they get,' muttered an elderly woman in front of them.

She nudged Gareth and raised her eyebrows in question.

'They didn't say hello,' he said.

'We went over the fairy bridge? I read about that. You should have told me. I wanted to see it, to get a picture of the sign.'

'Sorry.' He went back to his phone.

'What was that parcel this morning?'

'I didn't get chance to open it. Won't be anything important.'

'It was good of them to keep it for you.' She cuddled into him and glanced at his phone screen.

'Who?'

'The post office. All that stuff the postman said, it sounded like they waited for you to come back. You wouldn't get service like that at home.'

He turned to look out of the window. 'Things are different here.'

* * *

The route described so neatly in the guidebook didn't seem to relate to the landscape at all. Gareth took the lead on barely visible paths that skirted wild grass on one side and sheer drops into glistening bays on the other. Grey rocks erupted from the sea and she tried to attach them to names. 'Is that one Sugar Loaf Rock?' Her voice was snatched away by the wind. She stuffed the guidebook into her rucksack and tried to match his pace. She hadn't anticipated the astonishing blue of the sea, or the violence of movement frozen in the rocks. Grey cliff faces tilted at savage angles and looked as if they might shift again. She wanted to take photo after photo but she wasn't sure Gareth would wait. Besides, she thought, it was better to look with her eyes, not her phone, and try and hold the views in her head.

When they reached the Chasms, he strode out among them.

'The book said we have to keep to the wall here,' she called. 'It's not safe.'

'I could walk the Chasms with my eyes closed.' He shut his eyes and jumped to his left.

The uneven ground was riddled with what looked like rabbit holes, but instead of a fall into the earth there was a vertical drop into the roiling sea. She edged out a little in his direction, but kept one hand on the wall.

'You can't see them properly from there. Come here.'

She hesitated.

'Don't you trust me?' There was worry in his expression, and something else she couldn't quite read. He could be quiet and moody, but she could tell he was carrying a weight of hurt. He hadn't talked much about how his wife had left him, but she could feel the sadness in him. She took his outstretched hand and with her eyes on the ground she wound her way after him on the narrow path between the Chasms.

They stopped to eat the packed lunch his mum had made them at a high point on what Gareth said translated as Raven's Hill, looking down at the Calf of Man.

'There's another island off to the left in the painting in your mum's living room,' she said, 'but it isn't there.'

He shrugged, his mouth full. She needed a dictionary for his shrugs.

As they continued on the thin earth path she tried to keep hold of his hand. There was a deep quiet between the sounds of sea and the wind. She no longer tried to fill it with words, but collected images; bluebells unexpected on the high cliffs, blackened thorns with feathers caught in them, a sleek hare that crossed their path in an instant.

His gaze kept falling not on the path, or out to sea, but inwards towards the fields and a row of small whitewashed houses.

'What is it?' she said.

'I… someone I knew lived there.'

'Do they still?'

'No.'

He looked lost. She reached up and smoothed his hair that was rucked up by the wind. 'I love you,' she said. The words felt heavier once they'd left her mouth. She wasn't even sure if she did yet, or if she'd said it to test what was between them, to call it into being.

He turned back to the path and led the way on.

* * *

Light seeped through the loose brown weave of the curtains. He wasn't beside her in bed. She pulled a cardigan over her pyjamas and crept downstairs. The package remained unopened on the dresser. She'd almost pointed it out to him before they went to bed, but suspected that would mean he wouldn't open it. Perhaps he'd opened it when she'd been out of the room, replaced the contents and resealed it. She checked the kitchen, and peered out of the windows at the front and back of the house. There was no sign of him. The house was in a row tucked between narrow lanes. No one passed by. A lot of the houses were holiday lets. She hadn't seen anyone else on the street since they'd arrived.

The padded envelope looked as if it had been reused many times. The paper was worn thin in places, battered and crumpled, but as the postman had said, there was no address on it. How had the postman known it was for Gareth? There was no sound of movement upstairs. His mum must still be asleep. The weight and solidity of the parcel, the straight edges, told her she was holding a book with hard covers. As she turned it over music started playing, a tinny, lilting tune she didn't recognise. She dropped the parcel on the dresser and stood holding her breath. There was no movement upstairs; the sound mustn't have carried. She picked it up again. The flap lifted easily – so he had checked the contents, or his mum had. She eased the book out. It was a baby's board book of nursery rhymes. There was a panel with three shapes to press for different tunes – 'Twinkle Twinkle Little Star', 'Mary had a Little Lamb', 'Three Blind Mice' – but the tune she'd heard hadn't belonged to one of those. She turned the stiff pages. There were letters that had been blacked out of words here and there. Footsteps on the landing forced her to slip the book carefully back into the envelope. She rushed across the room and picked up the magazine she'd read cover to cover the day before.

His mum just nodded at her as she came down the stairs and then crossed into the kitchen. She could see where he got his communication skills.

He didn't return until mid-afternoon. She flicked through the magazine again and again and again, and drank the weak tea his mum kept placing on the coffee table for her. 'Gareth had to nip out to sort something out. He'll be back soon,' was all she'd say about his whereabouts, and then she sat in silence working on her crochet.

Feeling the day slipping away, she considered going out, but with her phone not working he wouldn't be able to contact her. She kept thinking about the baby book. Why had someone sent it to Gareth? The postman must have been wrong. It was meant for someone else. It had to be, but why were the letters blacked out?

She waited until his mum was making the lunch and then eased the book from the envelope again, taking care not to touch the buttons. She looked for a pattern in the letters that were missing, and tried to make them into words: w…e…w… a…n…t…t…o. The kettle had boiled. Plates clinked against a work surface. She put the book back and sat down just in time.

'Did you do the paintings?' she asked as they both ate their salmon spread sandwiches.

'I was taken away after I had Gareth. It wasn't unpleasant where they took me, but I wanted to come home.' His mum clung to the tiny cross at her neck as she spoke.

Unsure how to respond, she nodded and pushed more of

the sandwich into her mouth. It must have been some kind of art therapy. Gareth hadn't mentioned his mum had ever been unwell like that, but then there was more she didn't know about him than she did.

'Gareth's father took so long about sorting it out I thought he was going to leave me there for good.'

'They're nice paintings,' she said. 'Very vivid.'

'Have you ever held a changeling? They have a cry that could scour the heart from your chest.'

Wishing she'd never mentioned the paintings, she looked down at the magazine as though concentrating on an article about the island's kipper industry.

His mum collected their plates and left the room, but her voice came through from the kitchen, 'Just because a thing's happened once, folk think you'll be safe from it happening again, but life isn't like that. There are old patterns to follow.' She returned with more tea. 'Kaye's such a lovely woman. She knew what she had to do.' Cold, milky water sloshed from the cup as she set it on the table, her hand shaking. 'I'm sorry, I'm not supposed to speak to you. He's a good boy, though, my Gareth, I won't have you thinking otherwise.'

'What if we booked into a hotel as a treat for our last night?' His mum was in the kitchen, but she wasn't trying to keep her voice down.

'What about Mum? She would be devastated.'

'I'm sorry, it's just… this is our first time away together. We've hardly done anything. I've spent most of it in your mum's living room…'

'I told you I'm sorry, the errands took longer than I expected. And you know what, Mum's done everything she can to make you feel welcome.'

'There are photographs of you with your ex all over the place.'

He lowered his voice at the sound of pans clattering in the kitchen. 'You know I was married. I've never hidden that from you.'

'Kaye's your ex. Your mum talks like she's... and where is she anyway? Does she live on the island?'

'She's away.'

'Were you seeing her today? Is that what you were doing?'

'No.' He headed for the kitchen and his mum, forcing her into silence.

He was asleep with his back to her, or feigning sleep. The light through the curtains woke her at dawn. She waited as it brightened a little in intensity and then slipped out of bed. She dressed in yesterday's clothes without washing for fear she'd wake either him or his mum. Taking an apple from the bowl in the kitchen for breakfast she crept out into the empty lane. Giddy with the sudden sense of freedom she half-ran down the street into the next. He would wake and find her gone, just like she had with him the day before. He'd realise how out of order he'd been. He'd try to make it up to her. He'd explain what on earth was going on with his mum. She'd stay out just long enough to make him worry, but return in time for them to spend the afternoon together before the ferry home.

In the window of a grimy-looking cottage a *crosh cuirn* leaned against the glass. There were leaves caught in the old wool that had been used to tie it. She passed an antique shop and a pretty little café, but both were closed. The thick dust on the vases in the antique shop window made her wonder when it had last been open. She wandered the long lanes until the early morning damp started to make her bones ache. Another café she passed was closed, but the door to a quaint-looking bookshop stood ajar.

Inside, the shelves were dense with browning books. An elderly man was half-hidden behind piles of books on the counter. He didn't seem to notice her come in. The titles on the spines of many of the books were too faded to read. She picked out a slim book that was the blue of the sea, *Fairy Tales of Mann*.

'Have you a special interest in...' the man looked up and nodded at her, 'because if so I've a number of titles you might like.'

'Do you mean fairy stories? No thanks, I'm just looking.' She flicked through the volume and stopped halfway. There was a story with blacked-out letters: *he wh-stled a soft tune, and touched her shoulder, so that she would look round -t him, but she knew if she did that he would have powe- over her ever after.*

'Excuse me,' she said. 'I've seen another book with letters blacked out like this. Is it some kind of traditional thing?'

'No, I've only seen it twice before.' He held out his hand to take the book. 'It's a story about a *lhiannan shee too*, apt choice...' Her expression must have shown her ignorance because he went on as if telling a story to a child. 'If you so much as glance at one of Themselves you're under their spell for good. They'll have you dancing off into their fine halls under the hill.' He looked up at her as if considering whether to carry on or not. 'From time to time some of their things turn up. I think they let them slip through for mischief. They look just like our books, our paintings, our records even, but there's always an extra story, or a curve in the hill that you'd swear isn't actually there, or a tune you've never heard before – something not quite as it should be.' He shut the book and put it beside the till. 'I've gone on too much. Forgive me, they're old tales, and I'm an old man who spends far too much time shut up with only books for company. Are you with us on holiday?'

'My partner's from the island. It's the first time I've visited.'

'And have we treated you well?'

'Yes, thanks.' She pulled her coat around herself, readying to go.

'Have you been to see the Laxey Wheel?'

'No. I've not seen as much as I'd wanted to and we leave this evening.'

'Well we'll see you again, I'm sure.' He picked up the book. 'Would you like this wrapping?'

There was no sign of Gareth back at the house. His mum was in the kitchen baking. The parcel remained in place on the dresser. She pulled the book out and worked her way through the pages: w...e...w...a...n...t...t...o...c...o...m...e...h... o...m...e. She shoved the book back into the envelope and dropped it on the dresser, setting off the tune for 'Three Blind Mice'. It had to be some weird trick his wife was playing. And that's where he kept sneaking off to: he was seeing her. She headed upstairs to pack. She pulled open the top drawer. Her clothes had gone. Her bag wasn't under the bed. Her washbag wasn't on the windowsill. His stuff was all still there. His rucksack was in the wardrobe. Had he packed for her?

She ran down the stairs and into the kitchen. 'Where's Gareth?'

His mum didn't look up from her mixing. 'He's just nipped out to finish sorting something.' She stirred faster and faster. The bowl was full of broken eggshells.

Out in the lane there was no sign of him. She didn't know where to begin looking. At the end of the street, just as she was about to turn into the next, she heard whistling behind her. She'd never heard Gareth whistle. It was the same lilting tune she'd heard from the book the first time she'd opened the parcel. She turned, furious, ready to yell at him, but everything within her stopped. The stranger held her there with his gaze. She took his outstretched hand and let him lead her away.

CLAIRE DEAN

Claire Dean's short stories have been widely published and are included in *The Best British Short Stories* (Salt, 2014 & 2011), *Spindles* (Comma Press), *Beta-Life* (Comma Press), *Murmurations: An Anthology of Uncanny Stories About Birds* (Two Ravens Press) and *New Fairy Tales: Essays and Stories* (Unlocking Press). *Marionettes* and *Into the Penny Arcade* are published as chapbooks by Nightjar Press. Claire lives in the north of England with her two sons.

"I still have the book Conrad sent me for this project. It's in its envelope in a box under my bed. I think I made it more unsettling for myself when I wrote about it, so I don't want to see it but I can't get rid of it either..."

BUYER'S REMORSE

ANDREW LANE

Even before the letter arrived I'd been interested in strange place names, lost villages and ambiguous locations. The letter just gave me an excuse to give in to that interest. Looking back, perhaps I should have just stuck to reading about these places and not tried to visit them.

I remember picking the letter up from the mat by the door and looking at it, puzzled. The envelope was covered with greasy stains, but it looked like my address on the front:

THE OCCUPANT,
7 VICARAGE CLOSE,
WINTERBOURNE ABBAS,
ENGLAND

The handwriting was blocky and old-fashioned, and there was no postcode, no county listed. The stamps were American and the postmark appeared to be 'Dunwich', or perhaps 'Dulwich'. The red ink had been blurred by one of the greasy stains and I couldn't be sure.

I turned the letter over. There was no return address on the back.

A smell wafted upwards from the envelope as I handled it: a strange, slightly fishy odour, like a freshly opened packet of smoked salmon. Not unpleasant, but not quite what you expect from a letter on your doormat. Fortunately I don't have cats, otherwise they would have been all over it.

I was about to open it when my fingers brushed against something on the front. I turned the letter over again and looked at the address more closely, realising that the last three letters of 'Abbas' were obscured by some kind of sticky substance and a few fragments of adhering dirt. My brain had just filled in the missing bit without me realising. Automatically I brushed the dirt off with my thumb. Removing the residue made the address clearer. The ink was still blurred by the stains, but it was obvious now that the letter had actually been sent to Winterbourne Abase, rather than Winterbourne Abbas, which is where I happen to live.

As I stared at the words I wondered whether that was a mistake. I'd never heard of the place. 'Abase' also seemed a strange partial name for a town. Perhaps, I thought, as I stood there, it had some devout religious connotation – a bit like those American fundamentalists who used to choose their kids' names by opening the Bible at a random page and letting God guide their finger to an appropriate word, like 'Charity' or 'Perseverance'. There is a town near Winterbourne Abbas named Whitchurch Canonicorum, so I was prepared to believe that 'Abase' was correct. Of course, now that I knew the letter was intended for the occupant of another 7 Vicarage Close in another village, I couldn't really open it, not if I wanted to preserve my moral integrity, but I did wonder how I could get it to its intended recipient. Writing 'Return to Sender' on the front probably wouldn't work – the Post Office was unlikely to send it all the way back to America. I suppose I could have underlined the Abase to make it clearer and just put it back into the nearest postbox, but I was intrigued now. I wanted to find out where Winterbourne Abase actually was.

One of the things I love about England is that you can find so many towns and villages with the same name. Take 'Whitchurch', for instance. There are at least thirteen of them around, just based on a quick look at Google Maps. Most authorities think that the preponderance is due to there having been a clutch of churches built of white stone around the countryside, and the phrase 'the town with the white church' having mutated over the centuries to 'the town of Whitchurch'. An alternative explanation that I have seen suggests that the churches were actually built in honour of St Wite – although nobody seems sure who St Wite actually was. Whatever the explanation, the sheer number of Whitchurches can lead to some confusion. For instance, I was once invited to a wedding in Whitchurch, Shropshire, but accidentally ended up going to Whitchurch, Hampshire instead and wondering where everyone was. The answer was that they were cheerfully quaffing champagne a hundred and sixty miles away, but by the time I discovered that it was too late.

Winterbourne is another good example. A 'winterbourne' is the old name for a stream that's dry in the summer, but comes to life in the winter. That's why there are places called Winterbourne everywhere you look in England, from Winterbourne Abbas to Winterborne Zelston.

My fascination with lost, ignored or otherwise ambiguous places probably started with my parents' place. They owned a terraced house in a town in Cornwall whose garden backed onto the garden of the house in the next road, but there was a little patch of ground separating the two fences, barely six feet across. Most of that space was taken up with the trunks of two large trees whose foliage cast shadows over the ends of both gardens, but nobody had ever cut them down or trimmed them because nobody knew who owned that little strip of land. The local council denied all knowledge, and the title plans were no help at all, so the trees just got larger and larger, the gardens got darker and darker and the lawns became paler and paler thanks to the tree roots that extended beneath them, sucking up moisture from the ground. From that unpromising start I became interested in those little unowned alleys and paths that you can see separating houses in roads everywhere, and from there to the various places that have dropped off the maps over the course of the years, from those villages on Salisbury Plain whose inhabitants had been moved out because the houses had been taken over by the British Army for training purposes to the hamlets on the coast that had been lost to the encroaching waves and whose church bells could, allegedly, still be heard sometimes, pealing beneath the surface of the sea at low tide.

That's why, instead of putting the envelope back into the nearest postbox with some clarifying amendment scrawled on it, I went to my computer and looked up 'Winterbourne Abase' on Google Maps. It wasn't there, of course, which didn't really surprise me. I tried Wikipedia next, but there was no listing for the village there either. After half an hour of browsing I gave up and went back to where I should have started – the library of old books that I had scavenged from second-hand bookshops, car boot sales and jumble sales across the length and breadth of England. I eventually found a mention in one of the forty-six volumes of Pevsner's Buildings of England. Apparently it is, or was, a small hamlet in Devon, right on the coast, that had become absorbed into another nearby village for administrative purposes at some stage in the 1960s, around the same time as the Beeching Report led to the closure of several thousand small stations and the rail lines running through them. Its sole item of appeal seems to have been a rather fine church with an apse which has features – including wooden pegs rather than nails used in the construction – dating back to Saxon times.

I was intrigued, of course. It wasn't so much the church that had caught my attention as the idea of a place that existed once, within living memory, but which appeared to have vanished from modern consideration and modern maps.

Perhaps it should have occurred to me to wonder why a writer in America should expect a postman in England to know the old name for an English village. Perhaps things might have been different if I had.

Devon wasn't that far away from where I lived. I could probably drive there within an hour. I wasn't doing anything that day, so I decided to get my scooter out and head off down the A35 to deliver the letter in person.

I don't drive a car. I don't like the enclosed, bubble-like feel of them. Then again, I don't like motorcycles either – too fast, too brutal. I own an Italjet Velocifero scooter, which is like a Vespa, only bigger and faster. It looks like it was built in the

1950s for Audrey Hepburn's older brother, but it's actually of 1990s construction and just looks classic. It certainly makes heads turn as it buzzes down the road. I like it because I can feel the wind in my hair, and I can smell the fields and the riverbanks and even people's gardens as I pass by. Also silage pits and fertiliser being spread across fields, but you have to take the rough with the smooth.

There was a low cloud base across the south-west as I set out, casting an oddly sombre pall across the landscape. The road rose and fell as it crossed the ridges that extended like fingers towards the coast, and I found myself either driving through the mist where it touched the high ground, with visibility reduced to a few tens of feet, or driving so close underneath it that I felt I could reach up and make a trail in it with my hand.

There were no road signs pointing to the village formerly known as Winterbourne Abase, of course, so I was navigating purely based on what I could remember of the map in Pevsner. Several times I took wrong turnings off the A35 and ended up in places like Seaton and Colyton, or travelling along the banks of rivers with strange names, like the Yarty and the Char, but eventually – and more by luck than judgement – I decided to try a narrow, unmarked track that led off a minor B-road. After twenty minutes of winding around the edges of fields and copses of trees, I discovered an old grey metal sign on a post. It was half-covered in moss, and tilted crazily over, but I could see the words 'Winterbourne Ab---' engraved into it. The last three letters were covered with the moss, and I had to brush it off before I could see the 'ase' at the end.

I set off again, down the winding track. It was barely wide enough to get a car down, and if I came across a car coming towards me then I wasn't sure we could get past each other without scraping our respective paint jobs. The foliage closed in overhead so that the track was mostly in shadow. I had to put my headlamp on so that I could see where I was going. As I slowly navigated the ruts and holes in the road, anticipating the way it twisted without warning, I found myself glancing sideways, trying to identify the large leaves, mottled in red and dark green, which covered the bushes. They were the size of my head, but they looked more like grasping hands: five separate lobes curling together into sharp points that were tipped with crimson, like claws. Beneath them, close to the track, were clusters of gnarled white vegetables, like cauliflowers, that looked like misshapen babies' heads nestled in leaves so dark green they were almost black.

Something ran across the track, startling me. I twisted my head to follow it, but all I could see was something thin and blue-grey, like a shaved greyhound. It turned its head to look at me as it vanished into the bushes, and I caught a brief glimpse of a thin face lined with sharp teeth, and little red eyes that seemed to glow in the light from my headlamp. I felt a shudder run through me, but it was gone before I could do anything.

I was relieved when I finally got to the village of Winterbourne Abase. It was a motley collection of perhaps ten or twelve old houses spread out on either side of the dirt road. The paint on them was peeling, hanging off in dry scabs and scales. I could smell that particular odour that people always say is the smell of ozone, but which is actually rotting seaweed. Past the last houses, I could see that the road finished at a stone jetty which extended out into the grey sea at a shallow angle, so that its far end was hidden by the greasily lapping and scum-covered waves. Its sides were covered in bladderwrack seaweed and barnacles. There was nobody around, but the place didn't feel deserted. I had the strangest feeling that I was being observed from behind the grey lace curtains that hung like cobwebs in every window.

The path of the Winterbourne from which the village took its name was obvious. The houses on the left-hand side were separated from the road by a narrow ditch – dry at the moment, and filled with grass and weeds. A small bridge of stone led across the ditch to the front door of each house. The last building before the jetty was actually a village hall – a single-storey structure that covered about as much ground as six or seven of the houses. In front of it was a gravelled car park with several cars in it – quite expensive ones as well: I saw a Range Rover and a Lexus as well as something that was either a Jaguar or a Rover 75. They seemed a trifle out of character for the area. The sign in front of the hall was covered with old ribbons of paper that had peeled off the board and now hung down like creepers – the sole remnants of generations of parish notices, I presumed.

I wondered if the track I was on was actually Vicarage Close – I couldn't see a vicarage, let alone a church – but I suddenly realised that what I had taken to be a gap between two of the houses was in fact a narrow road heading off at right angles. I hauled my scooter around to navigate down it.

The houses were smaller and darker along this narrow road, and I couldn't see any numbers. At the far end was a church set in a small graveyard of crooked gravestones. More of the knobbly cauliflower-things sprouted in the angle between the graveyard wall and the ground, and even on the graves themselves. The church was constructed from a dark stone which was darkened even more by age and speckled with orange mould. It was set with several dark stained-glass windows, and the walls between the windows were covered with a regular array of metal spikes that had been hammered into the stone until only their ends were visible. The lead tiles on the roof were half-hidden by the low-hanging mist, as was the church's bell tower. I could immediately see that Pevsner was right – this was an interesting church.

I parked my scooter just outside the drystone wall surrounding the cemetery. As the engine died a thick silence rolled in – no birds, no sounds of movement, just the distant sound of the unenthusiastic waves. I could see that the church door – a massive wooden affair, painted green and also covered with those metal bosses – was partially open. I wanted an excuse to look inside anyway, and the idea that someone in there might direct me to number seven was as good an excuse as I was going to get.

It took my eyes a few moments to adjust to the low light inside. The stained-glass windows were dirty, and the glass seemed to be mainly green and blue, which meant that the old wooden pews and the uneven stone floor were cast in a strange watery light. Just past the transept, in front of the choir stalls, was a stone pulpit. It was several steps up from the church floor so that its occupant could look down on the parishioners as they preached their sermons. Standing in the pulpit was the church's vicar.

Her head was bowed over a thick book on the lectern in front of her, and it took a few moments for her to register my presence. She looked up slowly. She was probably middle-aged, with red hair that had dulled and was streaked with grey. Her blue eyes glistened in the meagre illumination.

'Good afternoon,' I said.

She hesitated for a few moments. 'You shouldn't be here,' she said. 'It's wrong.'

I assumed that she meant either that I was interrupting her prayers or that this was an isolated church run by religious zealots who didn't want unbelievers contaminating their ceremonies. That meant I wavered between wanting to feel apologetic and wanting to be irritated. I pulled the envelope out from my jacket pocket. 'I was sent this by mistake,' I said. 'It should have come here, to number seven Vicarage Close. I don't live too far away, so I thought I'd just drop it off and take a look around the village.'

She frowned. 'Number seven? That's... Ben and Maureen Cheadler. They won't be in at the moment. Nobody's in, I'm afraid. They'll all be at the village hall for the bring-and-buy.'

'Bring-and-buy' is one of those phrases, along with 'jumble sale', 'flea market', 'garage sale', and 'boot sale', which gets me excited. I've found so many old books in those settings that I knew I had to take a look. Just the smell of old paper makes my pulse speed up.

'The village hall – is that the place down by the quay?'

She nodded, but she was looking at me strangely, frowning and squinting slightly. Maybe, I thought, it was the fact that it was so dim in the church. Maybe she was short-sighted, and had left her glasses back in the vicarage. 'Are you sure that the letter is for number seven?' she asked. 'It's just that I was expecting...'

'It's definitely for number seven,' I said, filling the gap after her voice trailed off into silence. 'You know,' I went on when it became clear she wasn't going to say anything else, 'I saw some very expensive-looking cars parked outside the village hall. It's obviously an exclusive area around here. I'm guessing there'll be some great bargains on the tables.'

She laughed, although it sounded more like a cough. 'Ah, those cars belong to visitors,' she said. 'People come from a long way away to see what's on offer.' She hesitated again. 'Are you sure you're in the right place? Some of the things on offer are very… specialised. You won't find the usual chutneys and jams and knitted tea cosies, you know?'

'What about old books?'

She nodded slowly. I might have been mistaken, but I thought a look of disappointment crossed her face. 'Oh yes, they certainly have old books. Some very old books.' Her hand caressed the Bible on the lectern in front of her. 'Even older than this,' she said sadly.

'But nowhere near as important or influential,' I said, trying to cheer her up.

'I thought so,' she replied, 'when I first arrived here.'

I had been going to ask if I could take a look at the Saxon apse, but she didn't seem to want to come down from the pulpit to show me, and I got the impression that she would rather be left in peace. The following silence grew longer, until I said: 'Well, I'd better go and drop this letter off, then. Am I okay leaving my scooter outside, or would you like me to move it?'

'Please, feel free to leave it,' she said. 'It will be perfectly safe.'

Looking back now, with the benefit of hindsight, I think she may have emphasised the word 'It' very slightly, but at the time I didn't notice. I just nodded to her, took a few steps backwards and then turned to walk towards the door.

I left the church behind me and walked back along Vicarage Close to what I supposed I had to call the main road. Certainly not the high street. Once or twice I thought I saw the grey curtains in the windows of the houses I passed twitch slightly, but I put it down to cats jumping down from the window sills, spooked by my presence.

At the junction I turned left and headed towards the coast, and the village hall. The pall of mist was still hanging overhead. I looked in vain for a tea shop or a café where I could get something to drink, and a bite to eat. Even a fish and chip shop would do. The drive had given me an appetite. Strangely, there was nothing. It used to be that English villages grew up around the local tavern and the local duck pond, but nowadays the heart of every one seems to be a delicatessen serving designer coffee with a variety of syrups, along with local fudge and hand-made soaps. More often than not it's situated next to a Chinese takeaway. With a bit of luck, I thought, there might be someone serving strong tea and flapjacks from a hatch in the village hall.

Before going inside I stopped at the top of the jetty and stared out to sea. The horizon was shrouded from view by the mist, but I could make out dark bulks of fishing boats bobbing up and down, their masts rising like the trunks of the trees in the woodland I had driven through, only thinner and straighter. Beyond them I thought I could see the shadowy outline of a string of rocks, almost invisible in the gloom. They looked like the half-submerged back of a prehistoric skeleton.

The expensive cars were still there, in the car park. Several of them were hire cars, I noticed – white paint jobs, a complete lack of clutter inside, and little barcodes attached to the dashboard that could be scanned by a clerk when they were booked in or out. What, I wondered, would so many hire cars be doing in a small, isolated village like Winterbourne Abase? I knew that the vicar had mentioned that the bring-and-buy sale dealt in 'specialised' items, but were those items unusual enough, and potentially worth so much, that people would be lured from far enough away that they would hire a car for the journey rather than take the bus? It occurred to me that perhaps the drivers had even flown in to Heathrow or Gatwick and picked up their hire cars there. I patted the pocket of my jacket to which I had returned the envelope when I left the church. There were American stamps on the front, after all. Maybe this bring-and-buy sale did have an international dimension – dealing in antiquities so particular that collectors would be prepared to travel long distances for them. I thought eBay had democratised and simplified the process of buying almost anything, these days.

I remembered the strange vegetables that I had seen lining the track into the village and in the churchyard. Perhaps they were some rare species that grew only in this area, and were prized by gourmets everywhere for their exquisite taste. They had to have something going for them – they were ugly things.

The door to the hall was closed, and I pushed it open against stiff and squeaking hinges.

Inside there were four rows of tables running down the length of the hall: one on each side with their vendors standing between the tables and the walls and two in the middle, with a space running down between them. There seemed to be more vendors than potential buyers – which, to be honest, was pretty much my experience of jumble sales and craft fairs across the south-west of England. The atmosphere was slightly hazy, which I put down to the mist outside creeping in through an open window, and it was hot enough that I felt a sweat break out across my forehead and scalp. I slipped my jacket off and held it over my arm as I moved forward to the nearest row.

The first table was covered in small statuettes. They had been carved from stone of various types and colours. I was used to craft fairs in particular having several stalls selling brightly painted cold-cast resin or porcelain dragons to people of the New Age persuasion, and for a moment I thought these were something similar, but as I looked at them more closely I realised that they were old, weather-beaten and chipped. They were also representing things that were considerably uglier than the usual dragons. Some of them were strange figures that mixed simian and octopoid characteristics, some looked like the opposite of mermaids – creatures with gaping fish-like heads and thick, stubby legs – and some had no recognisable shape at all, but were formed from ribbons of stone which twisted around and through each other.

The man behind the table noticed my approach and smiled at me. He was shorter than average, but he had a very wide mouth. His eyes were magnified by the pebble-like lenses of his glasses, and he didn't seem to blink.

'You see anything you like?' he asked.

I smiled. 'They're all very interesting,' I replied. 'How much are they? I can't see any prices.'

He stared at me with a disappointed expression on his face. 'What do you think they are worth?'

I wasn't sure what to make of the question. 'I'm sure to some people they are beyond price,' I replied.

He nodded, apparently satisfied. 'Beyond price, yes. Beyond gold or rubies. Beyond life itself.'

I nodded, and moved away.

'If you have anything similar,' he called after me, 'then an exchange could be arranged. I would be happy to assess anything you might possess.'

The next stall also had stone shapes on it, but these were not figurines. These were more like tablets – irregular blocks with writing carved into them. I presumed that the carvings were some kind of runes, based on the fact that I didn't recognise them as any language that I knew. Having said that, I'd seen stalls in other places selling things which had phrases carved into them in J.R.R. Tolkien's invented Elvish language or *Star Trek*'s Klingon. There was always someone who would buy an expensive knick-knack if it was associated with some fantasy or science fiction franchise.

A man was standing on my side of the table, holding one of the stone tablets. He wore a long black raincoat, despite the heat, and a black hat of the same kind that the author Terry Pratchett used to wear in interviews and at signings. His hands, which I almost expected to be gloved, were startlingly white, and his fingers were long and thin, like a pianist's. He turned his head slightly to acknowledge me, and smiled. His eyes were shielded by round glasses with dark lenses, reminding me of pictures I'd seen of John Lennon. He nodded his head. I nodded back.

Out of politeness more than anything else I picked up one of the blocks to examine it. The thing was heavier than I expected. The stone had a soapy texture to it, and it felt warm. Maybe, I thought, lots of people had been handling it, or maybe the stone was just picking up the heat in the hall.

I moved on to the next table. This one, I was excited to see, was stacked with books. Eagerly I picked up the first one. It was old – very old – bound in cracked black leather and held closed with iron hasps. It was the kind of thing that, if you'd found it in the British Museum, would have been readable only if you were wearing white cotton gloves and with the book held on a special stand, but here it was just lying around so that anybody could hold it and read it with no protection.

I opened it up and scanned the title page. It was in German, printed in blocky type. It appeared to be called *Von Unaussprechlichen Kulten*, which I translated as 'On Nameless Cults', or possibly 'On Unspeakable Cults'. My German is shaky. The author was one Friedrich Wilhelm von Junzt, and the publisher was a company I had never heard of in Düsseldorf. Reluctantly and carefully I put it down and moved to the next item – a pamphlet of faded paper bound in cardboard bearing the title: 'On the Sending of the Soul'. No author was listed.

There were so many antique items here that I had never seen before, never even heard of, that I felt dizzy. The heat wasn't helping. Visiting jumble sales and suchlike I was more used to riffling through piles of autobiographies of minor sports stars and faded celebrities in search of the unusual. Here they were stacked in abundance.

Scanning the table I saw, in quick succession, *An Investigation into Myth-Patterns of Latter-Day Primitives with Especial Reference to the R'lyeh Text* by Professor Laban Shrewsbury, *Clavis Alchemiae* by Robert Fludd (which, in the unlikely event that it was an original copy, was nearly five hundred years old) and Otto Dostmann's *Remnants of Lost Empires*. In amongst the old, cracked and dusty tomes I noticed a more recent book and a particular favourite of mine, one that I had in my own collection: *Off the Map* by Alastair Bonnett, which was subtitled *Lost Spaces, Invisible Cities, Forgotten Islands, Feral Places and What They Tell Us About the World*.

Sitting on one side was a maverick copy of Maeve Binchy's *Tara Road*. I can only presume that it had crept in by accident, although I'd seen the same book in my local surgery and two coffee shops near my house, as well as every single second-hand bookshop that I'd ever been in. I've suspected for a while that the damn thing is stalking me. Either that or the publishers had printed way too many copies and had dumped them on the charity market.

I glanced around the hall. There were several other tables there with books on, and even at a distance I could tell that they were old books. Very old books. With the exception of the Bonnett volume, and a few others that I noticed – including the Binchy – this place could have furnished the stock for an antiquarian bookshop that would have become legendary across the world – and yet the books were just stacked willy-nilly on folding tables. Unpriced.

Stunned, I turned back to the table that was pressing against my legs, and my gaze fell on a rust-red and ivory paper wrapper with tiny tears along the top edge. It was wrapped around a hardback book half-hidden beneath a yellowing 1930s magazine with the splendid title *Tales That Should Never Be Told*. I recognised the colour scheme immediately – it was one of the forty-six volumes of Pevsner's Buildings of England. More importantly, it was one of the Penguin first editions. I wondered which one it was – I had them all, of course, but some of them were in pretty poor condition and I liked to upgrade them whenever I could.

I slipped it out from beneath the magazine, and I could suddenly feel the hairs on the back of my neck and on my arms prickle, even before I saw the title. When I did see the title, I could suddenly feel my heartbeat thudding in my neck and my temples.

Buildings That Are Lost, and Buildings That Should Never Be Found was the title. I opened it cautiously, reverently, and saw the words Volume 47 on the inside front page.

There was no Volume 47 of Pevsner's Buildings of England. There never had been.

The smell of old paper rose up like some exotic perfume to make my nostrils tingle. Carefully I looked through the pages. From what I could see the text was authentically Pevsner, rather than one of the other writers who had written the Gloucestershire and Kent volumes and who had extended the series to include Buildings of Scotland, Buildings of Wales and Buildings of Ireland. The buildings actually described were, however, not ones that I knew – obscure chapels dedicated to unknown saints, castles that I'd never heard of, otherwise ordinary houses in which terrible things had occurred. The thought occurred to me that this might have been a proof copy of a volume that had never been printed, or perhaps a special limited edition of a few hundred copies. I checked the front pages, but there was no indication that the one I held was Copy X of Y, or that it had been signed by Nikolaus Pevsner himself.

I realised I was breathing heavily, and I needed to sit down. At the end of the row of tables I saw a small area with three round tables covered in cloth and set in a little group. Each table had several chairs around it. Nearby was a hatch in the wall, just as I had imagined, and old ladies were on the other side, serving teas and coffees. I put the book down, hiding it beneath the magazine again so nobody else could find it easily, and I quickly made my way in that direction, passing as I did so a table of strange little clocks and another table of fossil pendants on chains and leather thongs. I ordered a tea in a shaky voice from an elderly lady wearing too much lipstick and sat down.

I had to have that book. Or at least I had to make every reasonable attempt to get it.

I glanced around the hall, trying to work out how people were managing to buy things if there were no prices and none of the vendors – based on my limited experience, anyway – were inclined to talk about how much their wares cost. I noticed that the people there were an interesting cross-section of humanity – some were men in suits with silk ties and gold cufflinks, some were women in suits with silk scarves around their necks, some were obviously well-to-do locals in cardigans and corduroy trousers, or twinsets and pearls. There was also a smattering of children, and a few people who looked like beach bums or vagrants who had wandered in because of the cheap tea. I took a sip and realised that cheapness was the only thing the tea had going for it – the liquid was foul, with an oily, slightly rank aftertaste. Maybe the milk had gone off.

Looking around the hall again, trying to rub the taste off my teeth with my tongue, I noticed two things that had passed me by before. The first was that everybody there treated every item on the stalls with reverence – picking them up carefully and examining them with the eyes of experts. The second was that, on occasion, the potential buyers would put the items down, retrieve something wrapped in tissue paper from about their person – be it from an inside pocket, a briefcase or a Lidl carrier bag – and hold the item out to the vendors behind the stalls, who would unwrap it and take a careful, appraising look. Sometimes the vendors would shake their heads and hand the item back to the crestfallen customers, sometimes they took them happily as an exchange, but on occasions, when it looked as if some disagreement might flare up concerning the relative values of the things, the stall-holders would scurry out from behind their stalls and take both items across to the corner of the hall opposite where I was sitting, just behind a stall selling what, at a distance, looked like toiletries and perfumes in ornate glass bottles. A door there gave access to another room, attached to the hall. They would hand the items through a beaded screen to someone just inside the doorway, then wait for a few moments. The items would be handed back, and they would rush back to their stalls. The customers would stare intently at them, and they would either nod or shake their heads. If they nodded then an exchange took place and everyone was happy. If they shook their head then there was no appeal – the customers walked off, sadly, still clutching the items they had brought with them.

This wasn't a 'bring-and-buy' sale; this was a 'swap-meet'. There was no currency changing hands – it was entirely a system of barter, and someone in that side room was evaluating the items and authorising the deals.

And I had nothing to barter.

Or did I? Remembering the letter in my pocket, I slipped it out and stared at the stained envelope. Someone in America had sent it across the Atlantic to this village, to coincide with one of these gatherings. Was it too much to assume that they might not have been able to make it in person, but were attempting a remote bid via some agent they knew in the village? Either there was something in the envelope they were willing to exchange, or there was a description of something they could have shipped across, if the deal was acceptable to the experts in the side room. Maybe even photographs.

I knew I shouldn't do what I was thinking of doing. I knew I should just ask someone to point me in the direction of Mr and Mrs Cheadler of 7 Vicarage Close and hand the letter across. The trouble was that I'd just found a book that I had never even known existed, and I had to have it. And to have it, I needed something to swap.

I retrieved the key to my scooter from my pocket and slipped it through the gap between the flap and the rest of the envelope. With a quick movement I slid the key along the edge of the flap, breaking the bond between the adhesive and the paper. I may have been considering theft, but at least I was going to do it neatly.

The flap came open, and I slipped out the letter inside. It had been folded twice. When I carefully opened it up, I saw that several fragments of old parchment were held between the folds. Each one was in its own transparent plastic envelope. The fragments had brown ink markings on them, and I got the distinct impression that they were parts of a larger drawing.

My stomach chose just that moment to decide that it didn't like the tea I'd drunk any more than my taste buds had, and I felt a distinct sensation of nausea. I had to swallow several times to avoid throwing up. My hands were clammy with sweat.

I didn't read the letter. Somewhere in the back of my mind I knew that if I did then I would be personalising both the writer and the intended recipient. I needed them to be anonymous to quell my guilt. I tucked it back inside my jacket.

I stood up and walked back to the bookstall. Sliding the magazine to one side I retrieved the volume of Pevsner – the unknown volume of Pevsner – and held it up. The stall-holder – another little man with pebble-lensed glasses who could have been a brother of the first stall-holder I'd seen – stared at me. I held up the plastic envelopes in my other hand. The light in the hall seemed to glint suddenly off his lenses. He stepped forward, reached out across the haphazard pile of books and took them carefully from me. He held them up to the light and examined them. I held my breath. The heat and the humidity in the hall were causing me to sweat: I could feel drops trickling down my ribs and prickling in the small of my back.

'Do you know what this is?' he asked. His tongue moistened his lips.

'Of course I do,' I bluffed. 'It's obvious, surely?'

'And the rest? You have the rest of this document?'

I shook my head. 'Sadly, no. This is all I have.'

He thought for a moment, glanced at the parchment fragments again, and eventually made a small side-to-side motion with his head. 'I need to take guidance on this,' he said. 'I am not an expert in this area. Please, come with me.'

We crossed the hall diagonally, past the stall of liquids in ornate multi-coloured bottles, and up to the beaded curtain. I was about to walk through when he pulled me back, a hand clamping on my elbow. 'That is not the way we do things here,' he cautioned. 'There is a line we do not cross.'

He coughed loudly. A hand emerged through the curtain. There was something wrong with the skin, but I didn't have enough time to work out what it was before the bookseller handed the Pevsner volume over and it withdrew. Seconds later the hand was back, and the fragments of parchment in their plastic envelopes were snatched away.

We stood there, not making eye contact, waiting for the evaluation to take place. I glanced around the hall, trying to equate the relative normality of the people – well, some of the people – with the strange things they were handling.

I noticed, as I glanced around, that a couple of people were approaching us from the stall near to the tea hatch. I thought I recognised the woman in front as one of the stall-holders. She was holding an old wooden clock, but when I looked at it I saw that it had five hands, and the numbers had been replaced with odd symbols, irregularly spaced apart. The well-dressed man following her – obviously her customer – was steering a small child across the floor, but I couldn't immediately see what it was that he was proposing to tender in exchange for the clock. The kid looked completely bored – the way that children always looked when they were at craft fairs and antique fairs. He couldn't see the attraction. No stalls of toys or old computer games to look at. Judging by the colour of his hair and the shape of his face he was the man's son. He couldn't have been more than eight years old.

The three of them got to us. I nodded to the man, and my bookseller nodded to the woman. She made the same coughing sound as he had, a few minutes before, and the hand appeared through the beaded curtain again. In the brief moment I saw it again I realised that the thing that had bothered me was that it was swollen and white, and it glistened as if it was wet. She handed the clock across. The man stepped forward. He seemed nervous. The hand appeared through the curtain again and gestured impatiently.

The man pushed the kid forward. He grimaced, and shot an irritated glance at the man.

The white hand lunged, revealing a length of equally odd forearm emerging from the folds of a black sleeve. It grabbed the kid by the shoulder and pulled him through the curtain. He squealed, but the sound was choked off suddenly.

Despite the heat and the humidity in the hall, I felt a chill run right down my spine. My hands clenched. Surely the man couldn't be intending to exchange his own son for the clock? That would be madness!

I looked around the hall. Nobody was reacting. Nobody even seemed to have noticed. I glanced at the two stall-holders, but they were standing there like solitary passengers waiting for a bus, just staring into space.

I had to stop this.

Before anyone could stop me, I swept the bead curtain out of the way with my arm and I stepped through.

I was looking for the kid, and I found him just inside the doorway. I barely had time to look around as I grabbed him and pulled him back, but I saw enough to give me nightmares for the rest of my life.

The room was relatively small, with chairs stacked up against two walls. Five or six people were stood together in a group, but there was something very strange about them.

They were wearing long robes with hoods. They were shorter and yet wider than they should have been, and what I could see of their bodies through the gaps in the robes made them all look bow-legged. Their skins – at least, the bits I could see – were dead white, puffy and moist, like maggots. They were all staring at me out of eyes encased in swollen white flesh with the same shock and horror that must have been on my face.

That wasn't the worst, however. The worst was what was implied, rather than obvious. The centre of the room had a hole in it, large enough for a man to fall into… or climb up from. The hole was ragged around the edge, and the tiles of the floor had been pushed up, as if something from below had emerged into the room. Things like thick albino tree trunks, cracked with age, had emerged from the far side of the hole and covered the floor between it and the far wall. There I saw a cluster of the cauliflower-like vegetables, all piled up, but they were the size of pumpkins and the shape of squashed heads.

And they had eyes.

I know that what I saw had to have been a trick of the light – just areas of dirt or mould on the rough white surface – but it really did look like those things had eyes and were looking at me.

The worst thing was, they weren't staring in anger, or horror, or fear. The expression in those eyes was incurious. Uncaring. And yet, malign.

The kid was stiff with terror, staring at things that he really didn't understand. I grabbed him, snatched the plastic-covered fragments of parchment back from the hand of the nearest robed figure, and pulled them both back through the bead curtain, into the village hall.

Turning, I realised that the stall-holders had all left their tables and were heading towards me – all except for one who had grabbed a bell from somewhere and was ringing it furiously. It sounded discordant, as if it was cracked. Some of the approaching villagers were holding knives, some were swinging heavy sticks that they must have had stashed beneath their tables. Their customers were heading for the main door, their faces creased in worry and uncertainty.

I thrust the kid back at his father, who was already backing away. 'Take him and get out!' I shouted. 'Don't ever come back!' He took his son's shoulders automatically and pulled him close. His mouth moved, trying to form words, but either he couldn't find them or I couldn't hear them over the clanging of the bell and the growing shouts of the villagers.

The doorway was filled with retreating customers. I knew I'd never make it in time. Instead I turned and raced towards the serving hatch in the far corner. Jumping onto one of the chairs, I leaped through the hatch and into the kitchen, skidding and falling on the slippery tiled floor. The elderly servers were all clustered on one side, by a tea urn, but they had knives and cleavers in their hands and their expressions were changing from worried to outraged as I got to my feet.

There was a door on the other side of the kitchen. There had to be, otherwise nobody would have been able to get in and out of the kitchen. I ran for it, hauled it open, and bolted across a grassy path to the line of trees that marked the edge of the woods surrounding Winterbourne Abase.

Night had fallen. The vegetation clutched at my feet as I ran. My breath rasped in my throat, and I could feel my chest burning. From behind I heard the sounds of pursuit as scores of stall-holders and other villagers thrashed their way past bushes and chopped at obstructing twigs and branches with their weapons in order to catch up with me.

If they did, they would kill me. It was clear from their eyes, and their faces. I hoped it would be quick. I didn't like to consider what they might do to keep me alive, and in agony, as a punishment for the heresy I had unwittingly inflicted on them.

I didn't even know what I had intruded upon – that was the worst thing. I knew that some unnatural force had taken over the village, that things were being exchanged there for dark purposes, that the villagers – both the ones on the surface and the ones I suspected were living beneath the ground, and maybe beneath the waves as well – were amassing ancient knowledge that, like uranium or plutonium, was incredibly dangerous if it was stored in one place or one mind. But I didn't know why. I didn't know what it all *meant*.

Passing a clump of bushes I swerved left, heading towards the church. I hoped that my pursuers would keep on going in a straight line.

Surprised animals scattered in the undergrowth as I crashed through it. Maybe they were foxes and badgers, maybe they were something else. I couldn't see, and I didn't want to think about it.

Up ahead I caught sight of the ancient church walls through the trees, studded with the blunt ends of iron spikes. I veered towards where I knew the main door was located. Emerging into the open ground that surrounded the building I glanced left and right, looking for anyone who might have guessed where I was heading and taken the quicker road route, but there was nobody there.

I burst through the door and into the main body of the church. The vicar was still there, still in the pulpit, and she glanced up as I staggered down the aisle.

'Please – I need sanctuary!' I cried.

She shook her head sadly. 'You have come to the wrong place. There is no sanctuary for you here.'

'You're not part of this! You can help me!' I was approaching the pulpit as I shouted this, ready to pull her out and demand that she call the police, or confront the villagers in the name of God with a Bible in her hand, or something. Anything.

'I can't help you,' she said. As I came around the side of the pulpit and started to climb the few steps that led up to where she was standing, I saw why.

Thick white stems, glistening with moisture, had broken up through the flagstones at some stage in the past. They curled up the back of the stone platform on which the pulpit stood, twisting around the sides and pushing through any gap. They vanished beneath her cassock. As she turned her upper body to face me, her expression compassionate but sad, the cassock rode up and I saw that her feet, her ankles, her legs were all encased in the roots. No, not encased. I saw the way the cassock clung to her lower body, and I knew that everything from her hips down had been… overgrown. Replaced.

Absorbed.

'What happened?' I cried.

Incredibly, she smiled. 'There are things we are taught, in the seminary, that we never talk about to parishioners, and never preach about,' she said quietly. 'We say that God created Satan as an angel but that he was allowed to rebel against God's authority, and that daemons are either fallen angels or Satan's attempts at creating angels in his own image, but that's not what we believe. Not really. We are taught that there are older things than angels, and that there are things that God did not create. This village has fallen under their sway. I tried to help them find the Light, but they had fallen prey to the blandishments of the Old Gods. They had accepted the bargain that was offered without consideration of the ultimate price.'

'You... you should have left,' I said. 'You should have told someone!'

She shook her head. 'It creeps up on you, and by the time you are trapped it is too late. There was a time I could have bargained my way out. That letter you have – the one you said was for number 7 Vicarage Close? I think you'll find that the '7' is actually a '1', clumsily written. A friend of mine in America said he would send me something that I could use to make a deal, to assure my safety, but that was three months ago. The letter never arrived.'

'I only got it today,' I whispered, appalled.

'Nothing is accidental,' she said, smiling sadly. 'Everything happens for a reason. I was never meant to get out of here, but you are.'

'I tried!' I held up the plastic envelopes with the fragments of parchment inside. 'They weren't enough to exchange for a single book,' I shouted, 'let alone for my safety – or yours.'

Instead of answering, the vicar opened her Bible to a place which I saw was marked with a plastic envelope the size of a sheet of paper. She pulled it out from where it was caught in the Bible's spine.

'The Pnakotic Manuscripts,' she whispered. 'A part of them, at least.'

Inside the envelope were more fragments of a parchment sheet, like the ones I had, pieced together like a jigsaw puzzle. On them was a drawing in faded brown ink that my mind rebelled from. I couldn't take it in. I could, however, see the gaps in the jigsaw: gaps that the fragments I held would fit into perfectly.

'With the pieces that I assembled, during my time in the village, and the pieces that my friend was sending me, there would be enough to form a single page of a single volume of the Pnakotic Manuscripts. That would be enough for me to bargain my way out of here, but it arrived too late for me.' She reached out, handing the transparent envelope to me. 'But not too late for you.'

'Are you sure?' I whispered.

'Go,' she said in a suddenly commanding voice. 'Go from this place. Go in peace, but when you get to a place of safety… then start a war. Burn them all.'

I nodded, and took the envelope from her. I gazed into her soft brown eyes, at her benign, almost triumphant expression, and then I turned around and left. I walked down the central aisle towards the door of the church, and I didn't look back, but as I walked I took the fragments of parchment that had been in the letter and I pushed them into the gaps in the parchment that was held in the plastic envelope that the vicar had given me. They fitted perfectly, and they formed a whole.

Outside the door, in the darkness of the churchyard, they were waiting for me: the robed, shrouded figures with the sodden white skin, and behind them the more human inhabitants of Winterbourne Abase. They had knives, and curved metal weapons the like of which I had never seen before, and they had lit torches that flared in the darkness, casting shifting shadows everywhere.

I held the plastic envelope up where they could see it. Some of them fell to their knees. One of the robed elders reached out a trembling hand and took the envelope from me. He – or she, or even it, I couldn't tell – brought the envelope up close to where its eyes should have been, and examined it.

'What is the price?' it asked in a voice that sounded and smelled like it was bubbling up from beneath a swamp.

I touched my chest, and I gestured towards the road. 'My life,' I said.

After a moment that felt like eternity, it raised a hand. 'The offer is accepted,' it replied.

I left the village of Winterbourne Abase in the same way that I had arrived: on my Italjet Velocifero and along a rutted dirt track, but I wasn't the same person. I had seen things, and I knew things, that had changed me. I returned home, and I haven't had a full night's sleep since.

My interests have changed, as well. Yes, I'm still fascinated by lost spaces and ambiguous or forgotten locations, but it's not just an academic thing anymore. I know that these places exist, but I also know that they aren't barren. Things are living there, breeding there. Spreading their influence.

They have to be fought, and thanks to a misdirected letter and a vicar's sacrifice I appear to have been chosen to take part in that fight.

Was that letter really misdirected, I wonder, or was it meant to have landed on my mat? There are a lot of things that I suspect I will never really know, and that is probably the smallest of them.

ANDREW LANE

Andrew Lane has written over thirty books in fields as varied as science fiction, horror and crime, non-fiction, adult and young adult. Most recently he has been engaged on a series of YA novels concerning a fourteen-year-old Sherlock Holmes (eight to date) which attempt to be as faithful to history and to Arthur Conan Doyle as possible.

'Buyer's Remorse' is a story written against the fictional and nihilistic mythological background invented by 1930s pulp American horror author H.P. Lovecraft (generally known as the Cthulhu Mythos), but transplanted to the backwaters of England rather than its native New England. It only occurred to the writer afterwards that instead of the jumble sale in the story he could have had a Lovecraft Fayre...

GONE AWAY

MURIEL GRAY

It's always been a matter of curiosity to me why postmen persist in wearing shorts regardless of the viciously unpredictable seasons of England. Perhaps it's a badge of honour in an occupation so starved of appreciation. For a short while we had a postwoman who eschewed her small red van for a bike, and she was possibly the only one who dressed appropriately for the elements.

Last week, however, it was our usual bare-legged chap, and on account of the driving rain, and the fact I had taken shelter from it under the grandest of our sweet chestnut trees, I decided to save the poor wretch the business of continuing all the way up the drive to the house by relieving him of his deliveries.

Had I given it rational thought I would have stayed put and let him pass me by, since there is always a terrific amount of last-minute post before Grandfather's party. But having unburdened him from an armful of letters and small packages I found myself remaining under a dripping tree waiting for the shower to pass lest I should ruin the paper. There is no other reason than this that I would have found myself browsing idly through the pile of RSVPs, bills, catalogues and flyers that would have normally never attracted my attention, since our post is separated by Adam every morning and all items redistributed discreetly to their intended recipients, which judging by what I held in my arms, must often include the dustbin.

On coming across an opened and resealed letter amongst this most mundane pile of paper, my interest was stirred. The curious thing was that this piece of returned mail did not have our address on it.

We are not hard to find. The correct address is 'Bosmaine House, Fieldings, By Catscombury, Gloucester'. There is no need for anything as vulgar as a postcode, since the estate encompasses two villages in the area, including Catscombury itself, and its small, irritatingly but picturesquely inefficient post office. Hence Grandfather regards having to identify the family seat by numbers and letters an intolerable insult which is why no such thing is included on our writing sets.

But this envelope, a small affair, calling-card size, had merely the words 'Squire-966' scribbled on the back in pen, and yet had been delivered to our door. Since it clearly belonged to nobody at this address I pocketed it without conscience. I confess I was intrigued. The rain softened and I walked up the driveway, anticipating with pleasure a hot bath, and less so an evening of dull conversation.

Grandfather had three 'Amusantes' staying. One apparently presented a political late-night television programme that nobody watches but everybody admires. Another was an artist of some sort whose work involves decaying fruit, and the third was a female bullfighter and is now an architect of perfectly preposterous structures, admired and written about by people who live in Georgian townhouses. They were all terribly pleased with themselves, and adopted that easy posture that the lower classes care to affect to indicate they are not impressed by being entertained by the last remains of English aristocracy, but which in fact reveals they believe quite the contrary. We do not slump casually at dinner and undermine etiquette. We sit properly and attend to our manners. I judged them accordingly.

I know I am a plain woman, but unlike my ancestors, modern life affords me the freedom to enjoy my privilege without the intolerable pressure they suffered of marrying unattractive wretches who pitied them but required an increase in status.

Grandfather has often remarked on his relief at my genetic predisposition to clumsy, ungainly, sexual unattractiveness, as he says it 'brings less trouble to the door'. He may be right. Untroubled by suitors, I have a quiet, if splendid life.

Grandfather sits, of course, in the Lords, and I am titled, and when he dies I shall inherit Bosmaine, which, unlike the properties of many of our friends and family who are obliged to sell cream teas to obese people with tattoos and screaming children in fold-away buggies just to have the roof repairs done, remains an estate that more than earns its keep.

It's assisted, of course, by substantial investments Grandfather made in Africa via the great friends he made when his parents were mine owners, whom I know, though it's never discussed, he continues to assist in siphoning foreign aid into private bank accounts with a skill that would make him the greatest chancellor Great Britain never had.

The upshot is, we are a rarity. We are an aristocratic family that still has money.

Of course when I say family, we are certainly diminished in that respect. When mother and father and Hugo and James died in the Cessna plane crash off Antigua (the pilot was a drunk; Grandfather ensured his family were subsequently made destitute), Grandfather was apparently a broken man. But even though I was only three, and Grandfather is not the most emotionally demonstrative of human beings, he was all I had left, and indeed I was all he had left, and so we love each other in a cautious but unbreakable bond that is unspoken but ever present. It's admittedly lonely at times, but then I imagine, if called for, I would take a bullet for the old goat.

The dinner was as tedious as anticipated, with the architect and the TV presenter fighting for attention as they argued about politics in Europe and I saw my opportunity to slip away. Nobody, I imagine, mourned my leaving. My contribution to the evening was watching and listening, and despising these monkeys we have never met, and will never meet again, 'busy' people, yet not busy enough to turn down a weekend invitation from a stranger to dance to the tune of money. Before pudding was served the artist did at least turn to me and ask, 'And what is it you do then, Sarah?' I replied, 'I am currently a visiting professor at Harvard researching the outcomes of proto isolated genetics.' She nodded sagely, waiting, and when I added nothing further said, 'Very very cool,' and turned away again.

Grandfather loves this. Of course I am no such thing. I made it up. But I know he enjoys the discomfort of the Amusantes when they curse themselves for not having thoroughly googled me. There always follows a great deal of barely disguised regret that there might have been someone useful at the table whom they ignored, and they may have seemed foolish, and so with that triumph I chose that moment to leave.

I kissed Grandfather on the head and retired. I smiled, feeling their palpable uneasiness that they were the only ones there, and there was no A-list party other than themselves, no 'networking' opportunities, their sole chore being to amuse Grandfather over his pigeon pie. These are the people who write in the *Guardian* about refusing honours, and reforming the second chamber, yet they can all be summoned with merely the opening of a gold-trimmed invitation card. Anticipating their horror at reading the reports in all the society magazines of his summer solstice party only two weeks from their dinner, to which none of them would be invited, sealed the schadenfreude.

Tragedy, as I was taught by my ridiculously attractive drama tutor Miss Anderson in boarding school, is defined by the protagonist bringing the calamity upon themselves.

When I retired to my room I opened the letter expecting something mundane. It was not. It was perplexing. Several Post-its, from a high-end hotel chain, had been stuck with red pointing arrows to locations on a ragged map of our area.

On each Post-it, in a rough ring, in the centre of which appeared our estate, was a person's name, and a letter of the alphabet, either A or B. I confess to having felt a worm of excitement. Whether of pleasure or trepidation I can't decide.

My life is contented but it rarely has the extremes of dark and light that describe the thrill of being alive that I understand some other people experience, from having read accounts of their exploits. It was perhaps that the letter may have actually been connected to us in some way, and not just a delivery error, that ignited the part of my brain long buried from childhood, when I played solitary detective games in the grounds, picking up meaningless objects and constructing crimes and clues around their origins.

The addressee on the envelope was one 'Allun Carver'. A strange spelling of a common first name, but not a mistake as the hand was careful, by a nibbed pen.

I opened my laptop and googled the street name on the address, a street in London. Then disappointment. A shabby, empty corner shop next to a bookmakers.

In truth there was nothing remarkable about this. But it niggled sufficiently to puzzle me, and there had been little else to do this last while, except fend off the exasperation of the household staff who appear to become hysterical when dealing with catering and parking arrangements. I had not been in London for months, so resolved to go almost immediately. I would visit and investigate, just as I had done when aged seven, when I found the bare footprints before the party, just by the summer pavilion, that really had no business being there in the mud.

I resolved to pack lightly and head off in the early hours. If I timed it right I would be long gone before the Amusantes had eaten their sullen breakfast in a fog of their own failure.

* * *

It doesn't take long for a person of my standing to get what I want. Even before I arrived on the train the estate agents named on the To Let board had been alerted to my interest in the vacant shop and one of their representatives was waiting for me as I stepped out of the cab. He was a young man whose skin and features suggested an Arab origin, but with a personal grooming style currently fashionable in the less affluent boroughs of London. His hair was slicked down like a licked newborn calf and the sharp suit he wore was of a garish pastel powder blue that any decent tailor would pay to have removed from his workshop under cover of night.

He unlocked the security grating, pushed open the peeling front door and we entered. I'm not certain what I expected to find, but the dusty empty shop floor was a crushing disappointment. A quick glance told me this had been an electrical appliances store. Catalogues of fridges and TVs lay in untidy piles, and a few cardboard boxes still contained odd cables and plug attachments.

The empty shelves were fringed with Day-Glo labels proclaiming special offers on selected computers.

I quizzed the estate agent as to the previous owner, and he told me it had been a British Indian gentleman who had now gone out of business. I asked if the gentleman had perhaps had a business partner, but drew a blank and in addition a sideways glance of suspicion that perhaps I was not a straightforward businesswoman looking for a vacant shop let. I asked if I could survey the back premises. Having lost interest in me he opened the office behind the counter and then began tapping into his phone and staring out of the window.

I opened the door onto a grimy office, as dusty and empty

as the shop, but on the floor lay some in-trays. On the top to the left, the unopened mail, perhaps a dozen or more letters, of one Allun Carver.

How very disappointing. The answer straight away. No trail to follow. No secrets to uncover. Just a man who worked in a shop, who didn't open his mail and must have left before the last one arrived. Why it had come our way may be perfectly well explained, but it seemed as though I was to be thwarted in adventure. The child detective in me wilted but while my bored companion gesticulated at the sky with a loosely flapping hand as he droned in a monotone to someone on the phone, I nevertheless scooped up all the envelopes and slid them into my bag.

Since the occupants had taken everything of value it seemed no great crime. It would be something to read later in my room at the club.

The tiresome Wilkinson sisters were staying in town and so it was no hardship to leave the dining room, these days full of city women with flattened-end false fingernails, to their braying and take supper upstairs.

I started at the bottom of the pile, eleven letters in all, and began to open them in order, bottom to top. There is no point in dragging this out. Mr Allun Carver was clearly an invited guest to Grandfather's summer party. There was the invite, or should I say three of them, right at the bottom of the pile. There were the familiar bronze tissue-lined envelopes, gold-trimmed, finest hand-spun cards, and punch-stamped lettering, requesting the RSVPs by, well by next Wednesday as luck would have it. The most curious thing was they had been sent in the same packet, only one short month after last year's celebrations. Affording Mr Carver and his two mystery companions a good clear eleven months to respond seemed not only excessive, but highly unusual since our invites did not go into the post until May.

The other pieces of mail were an enigma. Three names. Callum Dale, Olive Channing, Shirley Fog. I looked at the postmarks. Each one had arrived within a month of the other. A piece of paper with three names, and a reminder that there was ten months to go, then nine and so on.

Only the one I had intercepted contained the map and the arrows and, as I realise now, the 'by Wednesday' note. It must surely only refer to the party itself. On reflection, the last returned letter had an unusual air of urgency about it, as though the sender had been perplexed at the others not having been acknowledged.

It suggested the sender had been staying at various outposts of this high-end hotel, posting out regular reminders, doing little else other than counting down to a date. Only this last missive conveyed a palpable sense of anxiety.

In fact on examination only the first one had the Squire-966 on it, and one can only surmise that it must be a postbox number for Bosmaine, otherwise how would it have arrived at our door?

So if I did not send this, then it can only have been Grandfather.

I realised that I had wished for some rare detective treat to unfold and found myself childishly disappointed that it had not led to something grisly and sinister. The dull part was that I simply had to go home now and ask Grandfather what it meant.

I had dreamt of trails of clues, secrets unfolding, but here I was once again, the solitary grandchild of a solitary man, dreaming of adventure in the musty bedroom of a gentlewoman's club in Bloomsbury, with nobody to share my dreams. Opening the mail of a stranger for thrills and receiving none.

What had I secretly hoped for? Perhaps that dear Grandfather was a serial killer or a Satanist? How very predictable. Slaughtered innocents? Secret cult members being invited to parties to perform rituals?

I almost yawned at the prospect. This was the stuff of the English tabloids. I would frankly be disappointed if none of Grandfather's cronies had dispatched the odd orphan or danced naked except for antlers and a cape. It took not the slightest flight of fancy to picture half the board of governors on his Trust engaged in such a thing at this very moment.

The horrible truth was that I had been excited at the prospect of a more intriguing mystery. It was my loneliness I suppose. There. I will admit to it. I am lonely.

It embarrassed me where this solitude-induced weakness had led. All that was left was to return to the country the next day and have Grandfather recount some dreary tale why a dreary man in London gets letters every month reminding him about the summer party. A caterer perhaps? The man who provides the generators for the marquees? He'd moved on a year ago and his mail was delivered while the shop stayed open, but since it had closed his letter came back.

I felt a fool. Looking for adventure when none was present.

I glanced down at the map again, and the letters written neatly under their names.

Olive Channing A-

Shirley Fog B-

Callum Dale AB+

Blood groups. Blood.

I had a good two hours before my direct train, and I used them to return to the shop on Caledonian Road. It was locked and shuttered again. I entered the bookmakers. It was not a smoky and squalid den, but had the feel of a dowdy airport lounge. Two men stood staring at a TV screen high on the wall, an older woman sat at a machine and a young man attended the screened-off counter.

I approached him.

'May I ask if you knew the gentleman who ran the shop next door?'

The young man stood up straight, and plucked at his tie. 'Nah. Sorry, love. I don' know 'bout that.'

'Do you know when it closed?'

'Nah. Was closed when I started.'

'Thank you.' I turned to go.

The woman looked up. 'You asking about Saheed's place?'

'The electrical shop. Next door.'

She nodded. 'Yeah. Saheed. Been gone two months now.'

I moved to her and sat down unbidden.

'Why you asking?'

'I had some mail for a man who may have worked there. A Mr Carver.'

She narrowed her eyes, thinking. 'Can't place him. Nah. Saheed was a nice man though. Nice and polite. Do anythin' for ya.'

'Do you know why he left?'

The woman rubbed at the back of her neck. She smelled faintly of rose water and urine. 'Kept gettin' visitors like.'

'Visitors?'

She nodded. 'I never saw 'em. But he said he didn't care for 'em.'

'Tax men? Gangs?'

She blinked up at me through smeared spectacles. 'Visitors. I just said, didn't I?'

The two men had turned to look at us, irritated that their concentration on a greyhound race was being disrupted.

'Thank you,' I said kindly.

I decided a coffee and cake in the station would be a more valuable use of my time than speaking further to a woman with mental health issues. I left as quietly as I'd entered.

We entertain in grand style only once a year. The summer party is everything. I have little involvement. I have a handful of friends, well acquaintances really, that I formed at Cambridge. I always ask them but they rarely attend. They are married with families and busy lives, or live abroad, and after years of being turned down I mostly leave the guest list to Grandfather, who enjoys the company of celebrities of every hue.

But what I have been accustomed to is the calmness of Grandfather's demeanour preceding these events. He is perturbed by very little.

However, on the occasion of my return from London this was far from the case. My sole living relative was pale, distracted, almost wringing his hands at every turn. His temper was short and his attention shorter.

In such a mood it was perhaps not wise to bother him with questions about the returned letter.

However, Grandfather's mood was so out of character, so tense, so tetchy, that he caught me short in the great hall.

'Sarah!' he bellowed. 'Are you completely at a loss?'

I was not quite sure what to make of this. At a loss? Did he mean idle? A tiny wound I had hitherto been unaware of opened in my heart, but small as it was it was sufficient to change my mood. I replied with ice in my voice.

'Something amiss, Tather?'

I should say at this point that we have pet names. When he is in my favour he is always Tather, an inheritance from my mispronunciation at toddler level. He in turn calls me Podge, which is exactly as it seems, an affectionately impolite reference to my build. That he had called me Sarah indicated he was annoyed.

'Everything.'

'Then perhaps we should have a whisky. It's not too early.'

He sat down heavily in the chess chair. I poured our drinks and sat opposite him.

He gulped his down.

'I have a question for you, Tather.'

He was barely paying attention, fidgeting and shifting.

'Do we know an Allun Carver?'

The crystal decanter set was a wedding present to my parents. I was sorry to have lost one of the six glasses as

Grandfather dropped it on the hearth, but I was sorrier still to see the raw, primordial fear that rendered his familiar face as unlovely as it was unrecognisable.

Adam had helped Grandfather to his room and he had been quietly resting for over an hour when he appeared at my door. He was still putty white, but there was a new, composed nature to the man.

'Sarah. Let's walk in the garden.'

We said nothing at all until we were well away from the house, through the laburnum walk and down to The Pearly Gates, the plot of meadow where all the family dogs have been buried over the years.

I am patient, and I waited for him to speak first. He continually glanced here and there, as if expecting company, but in such a secluded spot it was unlikely. He looked at me with rheumy eyes.

'We are not as small a family as you think.'

'What do you mean? Since Uncle Oswald and Lottie died there's only us.'

'No. No. They are legion.'

'Please, Tather, sit down.'

His madness was frightening me. I guided him to the stone bench we had carved for Meg, the insubordinate wire-haired fox terrier we had both loved, and he sat like a child.

Grandfather then took my hand, a gesture I had never experienced. It was awkward but the tightness of his grip let me no choice but to endure it.

'I shall keep this simple, Podge. We haven't much time.'

I shifted uneasily.

'My great-grandfather. A taste for the slaves we owned back then. Fathered many, many children.'

'Oh please,' I interrupted, 'that kind of historical behaviour isn't a family matter.'

He squeezed harder, and became stern. 'Listen. He kept one woman, some witch doctor's daughter. Brought her to England, kept her in a cottage right under the nose of Lady Bosmaine. They had seven children. Those children, born and bred in England, had many more.'

'Well I imagine that bloodline is well diluted by now, Tather. And illegitimacy is no concern of ours.'

He hissed a warning through his teeth to be quiet. 'They had a summer ball. The slave woman, having lost her mind in age and sickness, turned up at the house in a fine dress waiting to be admitted. Lady Bosmaine had her thrashed and thrown out of the grounds.

'When the staff arose in the morning the front steps were adorned with the skull of a baby, woven through with willow twigs and nightshade, smeared with blood, and burned in the sockets was the remains of an invitation to the ball. The woman was found dead by her own hand later that day.'

I sighed. My only living relative was beginning to go senile. 'What is this primitive nonsense? Who is Allun Carver? Tell me now.'

He dropped my hand. My ire had been noted. 'We have since held a summer ball now for 123 years at Bosmaine. Following some, shall we say, disturbances, at the balls following the slave woman's death, on the advice of her son it became the custom to invite those unrecognised family members to the party.'

'Then why have I never been introduced?'

'Only the relatives who have died in the year between balls are invited. They decline.'

I confess I snorted. 'Tather, I am telling you honestly now that we are going to see Dr Maston together as soon as we have done with this ridiculous party. But if I'm right you're informing me that for 123 years the family have been inviting dead people to Bosmaine.'

'Yes, Sarah.'

I stood up. 'And how, pray, do we deliver these invitations?'

'We lay them on their graves.'

'And Carver?'

'Not family. Merely the postman. He is informed by another who follows the bloodline, notes the births and deaths, and finds the graves. Carver delivers. We pay them well.'

He stood up, agitated again. 'Where is he, Sarah?'

'Gone away.'

He is a tall man, my grandfather, and as described a man of great personal power and standing. But he shrank before my eyes, diminished to a huddle.

'Then we are undone. We are undone.'

He wept.

I was unable to witness this and I paced as he sobbed. When I turned he was sitting again, his head in his hands.

'He left a map.'

Grandfather sat up straight. 'Oh, my dear girl. My love!'

I have never been embraced by him like that, and I hope never to be again.

* * *

I had little idea of how I would feel on approaching the grave. It was a modest affair in a tiny village churchyard south of Market Harborough. It was an unlovely place, a 19th-century church of no great merit bounded on both sides by unpleasant modern bungalows. Olive Channing had, by all accounts on her newly carved granite stone, been the beloved wife of Ernest, himself deceased, and mother to two loving children who missed her dearly.

There were some withered chrysanthemums on the grass and an ugly white plastic bowl of fake violets, still tied around with tattered purple ribbon. That this woman, this ordinary, unremarkable nobody of a person could in any way be connected to the Bosmaines seemed ridiculous.

What did any of these imposters even look like? Had the rogue gene survived the journey intact, or were my hundreds of dead relatives part of a giant human kaleidoscope?

I took the invitation out of my bag and looked at it with distaste. Had I not been foolish enough to have intercepted the postman that rainy day only a week ago, I would have been sheltered from this preposterous superstition that has blighted my otherwise robustly sane grandfather for his entire life.

But now I was drawn in. Curiously I found myself beginning to anger. By what right did these individuals deserve to have such cloak and dagger fuss made over their mere existence? They had their own families. Considerably more than I had. Husbands, wives, children, siblings, the company of warm, loving, living relatives.

And while I was playing on my own these people, who history claims share my blood, were being part of something I could never enjoy. Even in death they were joined, invited in some stupid ritual to still be part of the bigger picture, a piece in the jigsaw from which I still felt excluded.

Did Grandfather expect me to keep this going after his own death? Was I bound now to carry on paying our mysterious servants to follow this ritual until my own death when the Bosmaine line ends with me?

I am too old to bear children now even if I wished. On reflection, over the grave of this plain woman, it seemed all I had was our history. There is no future.

I felt hot tears prick my eyes and I bowed my head as I bent down to the grave.

Wednesday's grim trip to those gravesides seems a long time ago now that I am standing in the lily-bedecked library with a very fine glass of Médoc in my hand. Grandfather is quite himself again. He is dressed magnificently in white tie and is delighted that we have a minor young royal here for this year's event, with the young ladies going perfectly mad over him in the garden.

The party has become quite The Thing amongst smart sets over the last few years and I find myself as pleased about this as much as Grandfather. I am not in much demand at any party but I stare with quiet satisfaction out of the window down the lawn to the far woods. The weather has been a friend all day and the high summer sun is only now setting behind the tall beeches, throwing the great trunks into deep shade against the pinking sky.

As my eyes adjust I notice some guests have strayed into the trees. I smile at the state their party shoes will be in when they emerge. They have little idea how muddy it can be, even in the driest of weather. We have guests who, when shooting for pheasant in the season, often emerge from that same coppice, covered head to foot in muck as though from the trenches. It will be no less brutal to taffeta than to Harris tweeds.

I lower my glass a little and squint. There are three, I think, but I wonder at what they are doing. They're coming this way, back to the house, slowly. Their gait is unusual. Are they injured? I hope no incident has occurred. This is an important night for us both.

I feel my heart beat a little faster, though I'm not certain why. I put down my glass to go and find Grandfather. It takes some time to locate him, and the candles are being lit as it grows darker. For some reason I feel a little panic. Eventually I find him, standing in the entrance hall behind the great pillars, greeting some late evening arrivals with much slapping of backs. He sees me, and his face falls.

Do I look concerned? I walk slowly towards him, the desire to be at his side stronger than it has ever been. To be together. A family. I reach him and lift my hand to hold his.

The door knocker sounds. Instead of opening the door wide and standing back in greeting, Adam slips through the narrow gap so that we cannot see our new arrivals. Grandfather is looking at me.

Adam is talking to someone. We only hear his voice. It is rising in anxious agitation. It is loud enough for us all to hear: 'I'm very sorry, but I'm afraid I'm going to have to ask to see your invitations.'

Grandfather's eyes are black holes, of disappointment, accusation, and naked, visceral fear.

He knows what I have done.

MURIEL GRAY

Muriel Gray is a broadcaster and author of three horror novels, plus many short stories. She is chair of the board of Glasgow School of Art and a board member of The British Museum. She lives in Glasgow.

ASTRAY

NINA ALLAN

Here is something I remember: me and my friend Lynsey in the apartment in Wiesbaden, scaring ourselves senseless watching a video of a horror movie called *And Soon the Darkness*. We were ten years old, and we were watching it because it had Michele Dotrice in, who we both knew as Betty Spencer from *Some Mothers Do 'Ave 'Em*. We had no idea beforehand that it was a horror film. The movie was about two friends who go on a cycling holiday through northern France. The woman played by Michele Dotrice ends up being murdered by a local policeman. Not the kind of thing our parents would have wanted us watching, Lynsey's parents especially, but we were alone in the apartment and no one even knew we had the video. What frightened me most about the movie was the music, a French pop song they kept playing. It was so catchy, so happy-sounding. The music fooled you into thinking everything was going to be all right in the end, only it wasn't. I can see Michele Dotrice's bicycle lying on its side in the grass with its wheel spinning, even now.

* * *

It's an offence to open an item of mail that isn't addressed to you, did you know that? Even junk mail – credit card offers and mail order catalogues, the unsolicited nuisance letters that keep being delivered long after the person who they are addressed to has moved on. Most people just throw them away, I suppose – they're probably not aware that it's illegal to open them. I've sometimes wondered if anyone has ever been prosecuted for perusing a copy of the Next directory that wasn't addressed to them. It's unlikely, though it is theoretically possible. You're supposed to send them on, those dead letters, or mark them 'return to sender' and feed them back into the postal system without checking their contents.

The term 'dead letter office' was actually coined by the United States Postal Service in 1825. In the United Kingdom of Great Britain and Northern Ireland, all undeliverable mail – that's unaddressed mail, letters directed to an address that no longer exists, or with an address that has become indecipherable – ends up at the National Returns Centre in Belfast. Why Belfast, I have no idea. National Returns Centre is an ugly, obfuscatory term that could only have been invented by British bureaucracy. Dead letter office is semantically more accurate, and a lot more poetic.

I bought this flat because it is close to a bus stop, because it still has its original 1930s parquet floors and because the garden is enclosed by walls and completely private. Buses stop frequently – there is one every fifteen minutes or so – and reach the city centre in under twenty minutes. Also, the flat has a spacious entrance hall and the internal doorways and access corridors are wide enough to accommodate my wheelchair, on those infrequent occasions when I am forced to use it.

I used to collect stamps as a child. Not in that obnoxious Stanley-Gibbons-always-to-hand manner so beloved of public schoolboys and insane kings, although the rituals and motivations I attached to my own version of the hobby would probably seem just as arbitrary and obsessive from an outside point of view. It was not so much the stamps as the letters that were important to me, and I was less interested in rare New Zealand commemoratives or the Apollo-Soyuz First Day Cover than in the stamps that happened to come my way by chance. My mother and father were both in the army, which meant that one or the other of them was always away and we never got to live in the same place for more than three years. They argued over my schooling. Mum thought it would be better for me – more settled – if I went to boarding school. There were a lot of free scholarships for army kids, at least there were back then, and by Mum's reasoning a boarding school would have provided me with a stable community, somewhere I could call home, even when my actual home was in a state of flux. But Dad had hated his own boarding school experience so much he couldn't bear to consider it, so I went where they were based, a long catalogue of place names that included Wiesbaden and Salisbury and Cyprus, Northallerton and Northern Ireland, Paderborn and then Cyprus again. I attended twelve different schools in all. Kids are meant to hate that kind of disruption, aren't they? I'm sure

I pretended to hate it from time to time, just because I knew it was expected, but in reality it suited me just fine. Run up against a teacher you hated, or the school bully or the school molester or any other breed of tedious lowlife, and you would know from the very first moment that they had a limited shelf life. An expiration date. Which made it so much easier for you to tell them to go and stuff themselves. And any friends you happened to make that genuinely mattered? Well, you could always write to them.

The post office became my best friend. As I grew older and our house moves kept happening and my network of friends and ex-friends and hopeless crushes became larger and more complicated I began to see the post office almost as an organic entity, a kind of social insect colony with outriders and drones and workers, all of them buzzing away in the service of the divine office, carrying reason and delivering truth, defeating ignorance and honouring the queen. For there was a queen too, of course there was. Her head was on all the stamps, wasn't it?

My peripatetic childhood brought some bad times, moving away from the army base at Wiesbaden especially. Having to leave Lynsey behind – one of those rare instances where a hopeless crush actually became a lasting friendship. But even the bad times were made bearable by letters, and during the years between learning to read and returning to England permanently to attend university I wrote and received thousands of them. You think email is the same, but it really isn't. I know, because I use email all the time – I'm not one of those dinosaurs who refuse to own a computer. I use it enough to know that no email was ever invested with the same longing or the same anticipation or the same despair that is invested when you see or set actual handwriting on actual paper. You can hear a person's voice in their handwriting, don't you find that? You feel distance and closeness simultaneously – the distance that the letter has travelled, the closeness of fingers brushing against fingers, through pen marks on paper.

Stamps for me were talismanic, a guarantee of safe passage. The idea that a letter might go astray had never occurred to me. Not until that business with the Lucy Davis letters when we first moved to Salisbury.

I was eleven, a fraught, difficult age, or at least it was for me, a circumstance that was only partially assuaged by our new quarters. The Salisbury house was actually a bungalow, a peculiar 1920s white elephant the army had doubtless picked up cheap in a probate sale. It was exceptionally spacious, and positioned close to several extended bridleways that led right out into the countryside and as far as Salisbury Plain if you had the stamina. I loved that house, and in particular my own bedroom, which had a separate, smaller annexe room leading off it.

The first week in a new house is perplexing, exciting and disturbing in equal measure. Your home is not your own yet – a fact that is repeatedly borne in on you when you find odd items of post still turning up for the people who were there before you. The day after we moved into the Salisbury bungalow, a letter arrived for a Ms Lucy Davis, which was strange in the first place, because I had repeatedly heard both my mother and father refer to the family who had just moved out as the Buchanans. I think it was probably that fact, as much as my own pent-up resentment and anxiety about the move, which made me feel that it would be all right for me to open the letter. The Buchanans were the rightful ex-tenants – any items of mail addressed to them should be forwarded as quickly as possible and without undue tampering. This Lucy Davis on the other hand – who was she? Did she actually exist, even?

The envelope had been postmarked in Westbury the day before. What made things even odder was that the letter had originally been sent to a place called Tytherington, a made-up name if ever I'd heard one. When I looked it up later in our *Road Atlas of Great Britain* I was surprised to find it was a village less than ten miles from us, over towards Warminster. The address in Tytherington had been typed directly on to the envelope. Someone had crossed it through with a blue biro and written the Salisbury address – our address – to one side of it. The letter inside was written in a spiky, difficult-to-read script that I almost thought I recognised, and filled with strange, somehow threatening exhortations to 'stay calm' and 'not to say anything'. I could barely make out its meaning, but the letter filled me with a prickling unease nonetheless, mainly because I couldn't help wondering what might happen next. Lucy Davis did not live here – probably she never had – and so the letter would never arrive. I stopped reading halfway through and put the letter back inside the envelope. Then I did the only thing I could think of doing, which was to stick down the flap with some Gloy Gum and replace it on the doormat where I had found it. Luckily I had steamed it open, rather than tearing it, and unless you looked at it particularly closely you couldn't tell.

The next time I passed through the hallway it had disappeared.

Neither Mum nor Dad said anything about it, and I

supposed that was the end of the matter. It wasn't, though. Three days later another letter turned up, the same crossed-out address, the same Ms Lucy Davis. I only glimpsed it this time – Dad got to it first, and I remember being quite relieved about that, because it meant I wouldn't have to know anything, although what there was to know I had no idea. It was a full week before the next one arrived. This time I was alone in the house – Mum was up at the training ground, Dad was in town somewhere. I knew he'd be gone for a while – plenty of time to steam open the letter, if that was what I wanted to do.

I knew I shouldn't. Not only because the letter wasn't mine to open, but because of how reading the first one had made me feel. But I couldn't resist. It was almost as if there was a story going on, a story I had made myself a part of by opening the first letter, and now I had no choice but to see how it continued.

This third envelope felt thicker, as if there was money inside. In fact there were photographs, two of them, each showing a girl about five years old, dressed in denim dungarees and a yellow T-shirt.

There was a note with the photographs. It said: 'Sarah misses you'. Just that. No 'dear Lucy', nothing.

I felt flooded by the same uneasy prickling sensation, and a feeling of horror so strong that for a few moments I thought I might be physically sick. I told myself later that it was guilt I felt, guilt about opening the letter in the first place, which was partly true but by no means the whole of it. I stuffed the photographs and the note back in the envelope, almost tearing it in the process. The idea of looking at them again was impossible, like looking through a drawer of my father's underclothes. I smoothed down the flap then carefully resealed it with glue, as I'd done before. When Dad came back from town, I made a point of showing him the letter.

"It came while you were out," I said.

He went quiet for a moment, then picked the envelope up off the mat and turned it over to look at the back. "I don't know why these keep coming," he said. "Someone must have the wrong address, I suppose." He took the letter into his office. I never saw it again, and so far as I was aware there were no more. A week went by, then two, then I stopped wondering.

I remember about ten years ago, when I first purchased a computer, looking up 'Lucy Davis' on the Internet. There were millions of results, of course. It is a common name.

The person who owned the flat before me was a Dr Outhwaite. He went south when he retired, to be closer to his daughter, and I can only assume that like most people moving house these days he used a postal redirection service. For the first six months after taking possession of the flat I received no wrongly addressed mail at all. Afterwards, for a period of about a year or so, I received the odd bit of junk mail addressed to D. Outhwaite, or David Outhwaite, or Dr D. A. Outhwaite – credit card offers, mainly, and once a shoe catalogue. I did also receive a letter addressed to the daughter, Sonia Outhwaite. The letter looked vaguely official, so I sent it on. I didn't see the point of forwarding the credit card offers or the shoe catalogue, so I did what most people do and threw them away.

Dr Outhwaite lived here for ten years and eight months. I know that because he had the place rewired just after he moved in, and there was a dated guarantee certificate for the work that was forwarded to me by my solicitor. That's why when a letter arrived for someone who wasn't the doctor I knew that either the sender had the address completely muddled, or they were clutching at straws. The letter was addressed to a Selena Rouane, but I knew she couldn't have lived here for more than a decade, if at all.

The surname, Rouane, was unusual. The letter had a Manchester postmark, but no return address, so I either had to open it or throw it away. I felt awkward about throwing it away as it clearly wasn't junk mail. I thought that if I opened it I might find a return address, or some other clue as to how the letter might be redirected, either back to the sender or on to the intended recipient.

The envelope was a brown A5, the kind you send tax returns back in or whatever, sealed with that rubberised glue that comes so easily unstuck you don't even need to steam it. I unpeeled the flap, carefully, without tearing. There was another envelope inside the first, a long white one this time, folded near one end and slightly grubby. It was still addressed to Selena Rouane but at a different address, in Lymm, which is a village near Warrington. The writing on the envelope was in black biro, bunched together and vaguely chaotic, the kind you might call mad professor's writing. The brown envelope had been addressed in loose, even capitals.

The white envelope did have a return address, as I'd hoped – R. Rouane, c/o Blackthorn Ward, Thomas Walsey House, Blanchfort Rd, Manchester. The impossibility of this bore down on me at once: the Walsey was gone, shut down – it had been one of the last long-stay psychiatric hospitals in the area and there had been a lot of negative press about its closure.

How long ago had that been, exactly? Eight years? Nine? I glanced at the postmark and saw that the letter had first been posted in 1997, more than a decade ago. No wonder it looked grubby. Where had it been all this time? It occurred to me that whatever was in the letter, logic said it was well past its read-by date. There could be no harm in destroying it – and yet I knew I couldn't do that, not until I'd seen what was inside.

I steamed it open, always a tricky procedure to accomplish cleanly when the paper has become friable. I couldn't see that it mattered, really – who was ever going to know that I'd even received it? – but old habits die hard. Inside the envelope was a single sheet of ruled white paper, torn from a notebook it looked like, the spiral-bound kind, folded in three around what turned out to be a photograph. I felt a frisson of disquiet, fear even – this was so like the Lucy Davis business, and yet the photograph was not of a child, but of a landscape. A blurred, black-and-white snapshot of what looked like a lake, or some other wide stretch of water, with a range of low hills in the background. The sky above was cloudy, almost the same colour as the water. The whole scene had a sombre, rain-soaked ambience that reminded me of a half-term camping trip I'd been on, when I was at school in Northallerton. There were four of us to each tent, and it poured non-stop for almost the entire week. Who takes kids to Yorkshire in November, for goodness' sake?

The image was so indistinct it was impossible to make out any detail. The paper bore a short note, in the same handwriting as on the envelope:

Selena – this is the place, I think. It fits the description in Amanda's diary exactly. I know this is difficult for you, and for your mother, but I need to know the truth. Nothing seems to make sense otherwise, and at least this is something to go on. I'll let you know if I find out anything more. Would you at least think about coming to see me? I do miss you, you know.

All my love, Dad

I felt guilty, if I'm honest. The letter was so clearly private, intended to be read by the recipient and no one else. I now knew things I had no right to know, even if none of them made sense to me. Who was Amanda, and why had Selena's dad been reading her diary?

I remembered how I'd felt about the Lucy Davis letters, that the very action of reading them had made me part of her story. I felt the same way now.

None of my teachers had ever called me imaginative – at least, that word was never included in any of my school reports. I have the feeling most of them saw me as a boringly adult child, never brilliant but not a simpleton either, not exactly biddable but under control. But that's army kids for you – everything battened down and no loose ends, because every army kid knows loose ends can kill.

This letter was a loose end. Someone else's loose end. I folded the note carefully around the photograph and put them back in the envelope. Then I replaced the white envelope inside the brown envelope. Seeing everything back the way it had been made me feel better. At least I could think straight.

I wondered about the name, Rouane. There can't be too many of those, I thought, even in a city the size of Manchester.

In fact there was just one: Rouane, Selena, 145 Carferry Road, Chorlton. I searched the address on Google Maps and discovered that Selena's house was one of a row of small Victorian terraces facing directly on to the street opposite the park. Carferry Road was twenty minutes' walk away, half an hour at the most, five minutes by bus.

I could get rid of the letter today, if I wanted to. All I had to do was stick on another address label and drop it back in the postbox. I could even put the original letter inside a new envelope and post that instead. That way, Selena Rouane would most likely assume that the letter had been redirected straight from Lymm. If she had suspicions about it having been opened, she would blame the Lymm people, not me. Not that she knew I existed, but even so.

It is easy to fall into paranoia. All it takes is a tiny seed – opening an envelope that isn't addressed to you, for instance. I googled Selena Rouane because I was curious, and because I still had the computer on from looking up her street address. It was an offhand, perfunctory gesture, one I fully expected to be met with a barrage of irrelevant results, as had happened when I googled Lucy Davis. What I found instead was a missing girl. Amanda Rouane turned out to be Selena's sister. She went missing in the summer of 1994, when she was seventeen. Which made her the same age as me. In 1994 I had been in Cyprus, studying for my A Levels and secretly getting anxious about applying to universities and, for the first time in my life, not having the security of my insecure army-kid background to fall back on. If I hated the people in my hall of residence I would have to deal with it, because I was going to be stuck with them. I didn't read the British press much, or any press come to that, certainly not enough to have come across a story about a girl going missing from a village near Manchester. I'd never even been to Manchester, not then.

There was a big police search, two primary suspects, both later released with no charges. No body, no ransom demand, nothing. I clicked on as many articles as I could find, which wasn't nearly as many as there would be these days. Most papers only started going online in the mid 1990s, and even now their online archives are far from complete. There was a summary of Amanda Rouane's case in the Wikipedia article on famous unsolved disappearances, and also a few write-ups at sites devoted to UFO abductions and lesser spotted serial killers (was Amanda Rouane taken by aliens? Was she the unidentified fourth victim of the Barbershop Butcher?) but aside from that it was mainly just repostings of the Wiki piece and the odd mention under 1994 at various 'this happened then' listings. If I wanted the kind of detailed day-by-day, week-on-week coverage you would expect to find in any missing persons case now, I would have to go to the Manchester Media Archive and look through about ten tons of microfiche.

Photographs of Amanda Rouane showed her either in her school uniform – a long-faced, slightly toothy adolescent with her dark hair in a centre parting – or in a too-big windcheater with clip-on silver earrings in the shape of bumblebees. Didn't they have any better photographs of her, I wondered. I bet she hated the school uniform one.

I took the letter out of the envelope again. I couldn't help it. I wanted to read it in the light of what I now knew and see if that changed things – if the letter made more sense, in other words. I found that it did, quite a lot. Amanda's father – I now knew from my online researches that the 'R' in 'R. Rouane' stood for Raymond – clearly believed that the location shown in the blurry black-and-white photograph was somehow connected with his daughter's disappearance. He had read Amanda's diary not because he was some sort of perverted voyeur but because he was desperate and had nothing else to go on. Selena and her mother were against what he was doing – this was a full three years later, remember, they could be forgiven for believing it was time to move on – but Raymond was pursuing his investigations anyway. Perhaps he felt guilty for some reason, perhaps he felt he had no choice. His need of Selena's approval was palpable. It wasn't just that he wanted to be reconciled with her. Above all, he wanted her to understand what he was doing.

Was I reading too much into it? I looked again at the photograph, the cold-looking expanse of greyish water, the blurred line of trees. There was something unsettling about it, something inauspicious. If you saw this place pop up on your TV screen, and the person sitting next to you told you someone had died there, you wouldn't be surprised. I found myself thinking of that Japanese horror film about a group of teenagers on holiday in a lakeside cabin. One of them finds a video tape with an odd piece of film on it. Everyone who watches the film dies.

I never watch horror movies. Well, hardly ever. The Wikipedia article said that one of the suspects in the Amanda Rouane missing persons case had been walking his dogs in the vicinity of a local beauty spot called Hatchmere Lake. If it was Hatchmere Lake in the photograph, there certainly wasn't anything beautiful about it. Not that you could see from the photo, anyway.

Why would Amanda have written about such a place in her diary?

Met someone for a shag there, most likely. Could it have been the wrong person, someone who meant her harm?

It was hardly an original concept, not exactly Inspector Morse. I put the letter and the photo back in the envelope and resolved to put the lot in the post to Selena the following day. It was her business, not mine.

I wondered if Raymond Rouane was still alive. He wasn't in the telephone directory, but who was to say he was still in Manchester. People do get away from here, sometimes. I glanced again at the return address on the back of the envelope. Raymond Rouane had been writing to Selena from a mental hospital. Nothing in any of the articles I'd read said anything about him being a doctor, or a nurse, even a ward orderly or kitchen staff. I could only assume he'd been a patient.

That explains it then, I can hear you saying. I have to tell you I don't agree. There are people in mental hospitals who talk more sense than all the staff put together, more sense than anyone on the outside, either. Take it from one who knows.

The question was: if I rang her up, would she think I was crazy?

I was thinking about Selena, and of course she would. What would you think if someone telephoned you and said they'd been looking you up online, and by the way, they had an item of post for you which they just happened to have opened and read?

I knew that calling her was impossible, but I had to do something. It seemed that overnight I had become one of those freaks: people who develop a fixation with someone they've read about in the newspapers or seen on TV. I felt proprietorial about Selena's story, her situation, her relationship with her father (be he alive or be he dead). I knew already that her sister was still missing – the Wikipedia article would have been updated if Amanda had been found – but I wanted to know how Selena had been coping, how she was now.

And we really did share a connection, through the letter, and because I was living in her flat. Or what used to be her flat – you know what I mean.

I didn't phone her up, don't worry. I wrote her a note instead:

Dear Selena,

This letter was accidentally forwarded to my address in Chorlton. It looked important, so I took the liberty of finding out your current address from the online directory. I hope this finds you well. I have been wondering if you might be the same Selena Rouane whose sister went missing in the 1990s. I remember the case well, because your sister and I were almost exactly the same age.

With best wishes,
Aileen McConahey

This was about the tenth version of the note I'd written and I'd given up trying to second guess how deranged it sounded.

I was past caring, or at least that's what I tried to tell myself. I stuck a new address label on to a new A5 envelope then slipped the letter inside, together with my note. I'd included both my landline and my mobile numbers as well as my email address. I assumed she'd remember the street address. I stuck down the flap with extra Sellotape then posted it in the pillar box just down from the bus stop. This took a little longer than it sounds – I don't move at the speed of light, even on a good day – but my mission was accomplished. I leaned on the post box to catch my breath, wondering what my chances were of being able to fish the letter out again, with a piece of bamboo cane, for example, or a length of Matchbox car track (remember that?) which would at least be more flexible. I decided they were pretty remote. Not to mention that trying to inveigle a letter out of a post box with Matchbox car track would almost definitely be classed as an illegal act. Tampering with the Queen's mail, it's called. Even if it's your own letter you're trying to retrieve, fishing things out of post boxes is still a no-no.

I didn't really expect to hear from Selena, but I couldn't leave the subject alone, either. Two days after sending my note, I took the bus into town and went to the Manchester Media Archive. I reckoned on being there an hour, perhaps less. I ended up staying most of the day. They had a new facility installed, whereby you could transfer articles in the microfiche archive straight to a 'print' screen, which was a vast improvement over the old photocopy system and saved me no end of time and trouble. At no point during the exercise did I ask myself what I thought I was doing. My actions seemed to have passed beyond the realms of the rational and into compulsion.

There were photos, so many photos. Here at last was Amanda Rouane as I suspected she had really looked at the time: a straight-waisted, long-faced, rather awkward young woman an inch too tall for her own comfort. Would I have been friends with her at school? Probably not, probably I'd have recognised a fellow freak and avoided her accordingly.

Photographs of Selena – there were plenty of those, too – showed her as a prettier but less interesting-looking version of her sister, a prime example of that elusive creature, the normal teenage girl. That was how she seemed in the photos, anyway. I suspect the loss of Amanda and whatever came after soon changed all that.

Even in its inconclusiveness, the Wikipedia article had been about as bald a statement of finality as you could wish for: this is all we know, this is all we're ever going to know. Following the events of that summer through the newspapers day by day gave them the texture and the tempo of a story not yet completed. I couldn't help focussing particularly on the articles about Allison Gifford, the twenty-nine-year-old English teacher at Amanda's sixth form college who was suspended from her job on account of an 'intimate liaison' she was supposed to have had with Amanda three months prior to her disappearance. In their coverage of the second suspect, Brendan Conway, the press were less avidly prurient but there was decidedly more in the way of conventional witch-hunting. Conway was a social security claimant with a learning disability and a skin disorder. He adored his dogs though, the two Irish wolfhounds he took care to exercise every day, and that gained him brownie points with the tabloids in the end, once it was established that he hadn't abducted Amanda and that he wasn't even a common-or-garden pervert either, just a poor idiot with a bad rash who happened to be in the wrong place at the wrong time.

And everywhere, everywhere in the newspaper photographs, Hatchmere Lake, that anonymous expanse of greyish water I had pored over in the blurred snapshot, reproduced for me here on a larger scale and in focus, with an adornment of police tape, in colour, in double-page spreads three days running in the *Warrington Guardian*, with police dogs and without police dogs, above all and most incongruously with a blue July sky unravelled above it like a swathe of coloured cellophane. Amanda had apparently been sighted close to Hatchmere Lake once, twice, possibly three times on the day of her disappearance, hence the arrest of the dog-walker Brendan Conway as a suspect, hence the search of the perimeter, the dragging of the lake itself (twice), the carnival array of red-and-yellow 'Keep Out' notices.

Nothing was found, though. Nothing that related to Amanda, anyway. Six weeks from the date of Amanda's disappearance, the newspaper coverage had dropped away almost to nothing.

There was no mention, anywhere that I could find, of Amanda's diary.

I found myself thinking that I could, if I wanted to, take a taxi out to Lymm and walk along the high street, which was where the last definitive sighting of Amanda Rouane had taken place. (Leanne Beetham, who worked at the Spar shop in Lymm and who had been serving behind the counter that

Saturday afternoon, confirmed that Amanda had been into the shop at around two-thirty, when she purchased a can of Coke and a Twix bar.) I could even walk past her house if I wanted to. Lymm was not a large place, and by any normal standards it was not so far from the high street to what had once been the Rouane family home on Sandy Lane. But so far as I was concerned, we might as well have been talking about the distance from the Earth to the Moon. I would probably make it along the high street and back (on a good day) but getting from there to Sandy Lane would be an agony. I could always instruct the taxi to do a circuit, but how would I explain my movements? I couldn't face the look in the driver's eyes.

I made the trip on Street View instead. I could see at once that there had been changes. The Spar wasn't there, for a start. Amanda probably wouldn't recognise the place. The houses on Sandy Lane were a mix of Georgian and Victorian cottages with newer builds. The house that used to be the Rouanes' is a 1970s semi with an integral garage, nondescript but clean-looking; what you'd expect from the newspaper coverage, really.

There's something so dispiriting about houses like that. I bet Amanda hated it.

I think about her, and it's as if we're circling each other, casting each other sidelong looks. Can I trust you? When the chips are down, can I trust you with my story? Or are you just the same as everyone else?

I think about the dead letter, which is really a long-line communication between Amanda and me. Amanda hugs her father in 1994. Raymond Rouane picks up a pen in 1997, leaning the hand that touched his daughter's hair upon the paper as he writes his note. I touch the ink, the paper, the hand, Amanda. A bridge that spans a distance of twenty years.

This is the point in the story where you'd expect me to start talking about being haunted, about being pursued by Amanda's ghost, about losing the (already precarious) balance of my mind. But you can't be haunted by someone who's still alive. And Amanda is still alive, I can sense it.

"Is that Aileen?" said Selena. I knew it was Selena without her having to say. Her voice at the end of the phone: hesitant, embarrassed-sounding, a soft northern accent.

"Speaking," I said. I felt hot, and a little breathless. I was living through a moment I had anticipated a hundred times, a thousand, in my imagination, without ever truly believing it would actually happen.

"This is Selena Rouane. You posted on a letter to me. I wanted to say thanks."

There was something in the way her words came out that made me think she'd been rehearsing them, that she'd thought them up beforehand as an excuse for telephoning. We were on equal ground, it seemed. That knowledge should have made me feel less nervous, but it didn't. I knew that a single wrong word from me – a word that sounded too knowing or too raw – would end the conversation on the spot.

"That's no problem. I thought it might be important, so." I paused. "You don't see that many hand-written letters these days."

"That's true." She laughed, just a little, which I took as a good sign, even though I knew I couldn't count on her sharing my obsession with paper and envelopes. Amanda might, but not Selena. Selena would have learned to be more practical – she would have had to. "I'm sorry to bother you, but I was just wondering. Did you happen to notice the date on the postmark? From when the letter was mailed to you, I mean?"

"The beginning of last week, I think. I would check for you, only I threw the envelope away." I hadn't, but I thought it sounded more plausible that I would have done. "I'm sorry if it was important."

"Oh, no, that's all right." She spoke in a rush. She seemed anxious to reassure me that I'd done nothing wrong. "I don't need it. I just wondered, you know, how long the letter might have been in the system."

The better part of two decades, give or take. Now we both knew.

"It just seemed strange," she went on, "that the letter should turn up now, after so many years."

"Not as strange as you might think," I said. "I heard of one dead letter that resurfaced after eighty years, from a soldier in the First World War. He was killed at Ypres, I think it was. The letter was delivered around the year two thousand, to his great-granddaughter in Gravesend, with her morning mail. No one really knows what happened to it in between."

"My God," Selena said. "It must have been like seeing a ghost." She fell silent for a moment. "How did you get to hear about it? Do you work for the post office?"

"It was in a book I read, that's all. I'm interested."

"In soldiers?"

"In letters."

I pressed the phone tight to my ear. I heard a car go by,

though I wasn't sure if that was at my end or at hers. Her mention of soldiers had disconcerted me, then I remembered it was I, not her, who had brought up the subject. The story about the letter from the soldier at Ypres is perfectly true. It was forwarded fifteen times before it reached the great-granddaughter.

"The thing is, I haven't had a letter from my dad in years," Selena said. "He died in 1998."

"I'm sorry to hear that," I said, though I had suspected something of the sort, I don't know why. "It must have been a shock for you. Seeing the letter, I mean."

"Yes, it was." I thought she would say more, tell me the reason for his death, or why he had been in a mental hospital, but she didn't. "You asked if it was me who lost my sister," she said instead.

"That was rude of me," I said. "I apologise."

"No, it's fine. I am that Selena. I was surprised, that's all. Most people have forgotten. It was a long time ago."

"It was your name that made me remember. Rouane, I mean. It's quite unusual."

"My grandfather's family were from Normandy, a town called Lion-sur-Mer. He died before I was born but Dad used to spend holidays there when he was a kid. I think that's why Amanda got so interested in France."

"People always want to know where they're from, don't they? Did she ever go there?"

"She wanted to. She started collecting all these old postcards. And she was doing a Linguaphone course. She borrowed it from the library."

"You don't think…"

"Dad did. He tried to get the police interested, to get the French police involved and everything, but there wasn't any evidence, so they refused. Dad went to France on his own in the end. I don't think he found out anything. Mainly he just drove around. Driving was the one thing that settled his mind. At least it did for a while."

There was so much I wanted to ask her. About her father and Amanda's diary, about Amanda herself. I forced myself to keep silent. I knew if I sounded too interested, too eager, Selena would probably clam up. She would put down the phone and never speak to me again. The important thing was that contact had been established. She wouldn't find it so strange now if I contacted her again. I couldn't, at that moment, think of an adequate reason for doing so, but I felt sure I could come up with something, given time.

"I'm sorry about your dad," I said again. I thought it would be better to make it seem as if it was I who wanted to end the conversation.

"Thanks. And thanks again for posting on the letter." There was a catch in her voice, as if she was searching for an excuse to prolong the call. I don't know. Perhaps I imagined it.

"No problem. Take care, then."

"Goodbye."

I waited until I heard the click at her end, then lowered the receiver into the cradle.

I looked up Lion-sur-Mer online. A small, picturesque town on the Normandy coast: sandy beaches, historic castle, cobbled streets and pavement cafés. Not exactly a typical setting for adolescent rebellion. Whichever scenario you cared to imagine – religious cult, serial killer, dodgy boyfriend (or girlfriend) – you would have imagined it playing out in Manchester, rather than a sleepy resort town like Lion-sur-Mer. Who gets themselves murdered on the Normandy coast, outside of a low-budget horror movie, that is? How would Amanda even have got there in the first place? She was seventeen, so it was unlikely she would have had an independent passport. There was also the question of money. According to Raymond Rouane, Amanda didn't even have a bank account.

There was a theory going around at the time, that Amanda had hitched a ride with the murderer and sexual predator Steven Jimson, who was nicknamed the Barbershop Butcher on account of the logo – Barbershop Plumbing – on the side of his van. Jimson ran a tin-pot illegal courier operation, ferrying packages of cannabis and knocked-off stereos and occasionally exotic reptiles all over Europe. He also used his van as a mobile murder venue. Jimson was from Stockport originally, but he had friends in Warrington and was often in the area. He was apprehended in the November of 1994, initially for a stolen passport, although as the team investigating soon discovered, that was just the beginning. For the first two months of 1995, media interest in the Amanda Rouane case spiked again as speculation mounted and the newspapers vied with each other for a lead on the news they all now saw as inevitable: that Amanda had been the Butcher's final victim.

That news never came, though. Steven Jimson contended that he'd never spoken to Amanda, never so much as laid eyes on her, and there was no evidence to prove otherwise. The

Barbershop Butcher was sentenced to life imprisonment for three counts of murder and five counts of aggravated sexual assault, but Amanda Rouane was still missing and no one was any the wiser about what had happened to her.

I googled 'Lion-sur-Mer murder' and then 'Lion-sur-Mer Rouane', scrolled rapidly through a large number of articles without really finding anything. There had been a murder in Lion-sur-Mer in 2009, when a man shot his brother with a hunting rifle in the car park of a local brasserie, the culmination of a dispute over property that had been smouldering intermittently for twenty years. There were also Rouanes in Lion-sur-Mer, though none of them seemed to be connected with the property murder. Berenice Rouane was some sort of local government official. Marcel Rouane ran a computer consultancy business. Jeanne Rouane was a freelance photographer. Her website had a page listing her more recent exhibitions, as well as a gallery of photographs, which seemed to be mainly of derelict buildings and abandoned construction sites. The photograph on the 'About' page showed a woman whose appearance struck me initially as being so similar to Amanda's I almost closed the window by mistake. As I examined the image more closely I saw I'd been wrong about that; Jeanne Rouane bore a surface likeness to Amanda but that was all it was: surface, a family resemblance maybe, but nothing more.

I wished I'd thought to ask Selena for her email address, so I could send her the link. I wondered if the photo of the French photographer constituted enough of an excuse for me to call her, and decided it wasn't. If I was sensible I'd admit it was time to forget the whole thing.

Instead, I thought about the defunct Walsey hospital, the many hundreds of keepsakes and letters and postcards they must have had to dispose of when the place closed down. Boxes of them, probably, letters that had been written to or from ex-patients who were now either dead or recovered or absconded, living 'in the community' or lapsed so far into delusion they were different people. Letters that never arrived or were never sent.

I thought about the dead letters of the dead, the thousands of miniature worlds and paper castles, guarded secrets and confided dreams and ancient enmities. Letters burning on bonfires and forgotten in attics, mouldering in landfill or kept guiltily in a suitcase under the bed, eventually destroyed by an indifferent grandchild when the owner of the suitcase, also, gave up the ghost.

It was Selena who phoned me, in the end. "I know this must sound weird, but could we meet up?"

I took a few moments to answer, as I knew I should. "What's this about?"

"I looked you up on Google," Selena said. "I found that article about your dad and how he died.

"I just wanted to tell you that I understand. That I know what it's like to lose a father. I don't mean just generally, I mean when he's not... when he's not how he was."

Selena looks older than she did in the photographs. I don't just mean that she has aged – we have all done that. I mean she looks at ease with herself – at ease in her own body – in a way the snapshots of a pretty schoolgirl never hinted at. Her clothes – a closely fitting trouser suit and jersey top – are unobtrusive but flawlessly right for her. The ring she wears, a ruby, is especially stunning. She barely resembles Amanda at all now, and yet I feel convinced that if it were Amanda sitting opposite me in the café she would still look exactly as she did in all those old news photos: unmade and slightly scruffy, not properly of the world she was forced to inhabit.

She wouldn't hesitate with her words the way Selena does, either, not because she's more articulate but because she wouldn't be embarrassed and wondering what the hell she'd been thinking of, asking a perfect stranger to meet her for coffee.

I made sure to get there first, so as to be already seated when Selena arrived. I didn't want the whole of our meeting to be influenced by her inevitably faulty perception of my disability.

Disability! What a weasel word that is, and how I hate it. I was in a car accident. My girlfriend Anya was driving. My spine was injured. The upshot is that I can only be on my feet for about fifteen minutes before excruciating pain sets in. I sometimes have to use a wheelchair, but not too often. The doctors seem to agree that neither the effects of the injury nor the pain will get any worse, which makes me pretty lucky, all outcomes considered. Anya died at the scene, as the saying goes, but you'll forgive me if I don't feel like telling you what that actually entailed.

The cafe I suggested to Selena as our meeting place is just about the only venue that is close enough for me to feel confident of walking there and back without folding up on the pavement. Luckily the coffee is so good here it's almost criminal.

"What you mean is that my father went mad and blew himself up. Shit happens."

I can see she's blushing. "I wouldn't say mad."

"Wouldn't you? I would." I am about to start reeling off my litany of synonyms – crazy, barking, insane, batshit, mental, loonytunes, marble-deficient (there are plenty more; believe me, I've made lists); all those mordant-ugly-beautiful words I start spouting when I'm feeling defensive, or angry, or when I simply want whoever I'm talking to to shut-the-Jesus-fuck–up – when I remember that Selena is not just a bystander. Her father was in the Walsey. She probably knows the list of m-words as well as I do.

"I'm sorry," I say. It's a rare admission, though she can't know that yet. We are barely acquainted.

"Don't worry. I get it." She sips at her coffee, holding the cup between her hands in a manner that seems oddly out of keeping with her elegant appearance, a gesture that belongs to an earlier part of her life, when she sat side by side with Amanda on the living-room carpet drinking a mug of Horlicks and watching *Black Beauty* or *Dick Turpin* or *Tales of the Unexpected*.

There are parts of us that can never be eradicated. Not by ourselves, not by the world either.

"Dad lost track of himself after Amanda disappeared," Selena says. "At first it was just small things – never being able to miss a news bulletin, all that driving around he did. But in the end everything mounted up and he collapsed. The doctors said it was simple exhaustion, but Mum and I both knew it was more than that. You can't avoid knowing, can you? Not when you live with someone. He was supposed to be in the Walsey for a couple of weeks at the most – to give him a rest, the doctors said. To recharge his batteries."

"But they kept him in?"

Selena nods. "Mum and Dad had split up by then and Dad was too ill to manage by himself. And to be honest he seemed happier there, more stable. Less overwhelmed by things. Perhaps I'm kidding myself."

I don't answer. She hasn't come to me for platitudes. "His whole life became about finding her. Amanda, I mean. He refused to even consider the possibility that she was dead. He had a room at Mum's, you know, for when he came to visit, and it ended up crammed to the ceiling with all this stuff he was hoarding. Newspaper articles, magazine clippings, anything he could find about missing people and unsolved crimes. He couldn't let go."

"What did the doctors say?"

"They said that until he learned to accept that Amanda was gone, he would never be well again. Dad wasn't having any of it. He said that what they told you in hospitals and schools was a form of brainwashing, that the people in authority wanted you to accept their version of things because it was more convenient. For them, I mean. If you carried on believing something they didn't want you to believe, they said you were mad."

Well, he had a point, I think but don't say. I sense that Selena is eager to ask me about my own father. That's what this meeting is about for her, isn't it? Swapping stories? Comparing experiences? Tallying up the points to see whose dad was maddest? Her questions are so rankly present I can almost smell them. Imagine her disappointment if I were to tell her that no, Dad didn't go off the rails, not until that final second when he put his decision into practice, and even the decision itself would have been carefully arrived at. There were no outlandish, glorious delusions, no gradual slide into lunacy. He made a mistake, that's all. A bad one, granted. The guilt must have cannibalised his brain like cancer. But no one knew what he was going through, least of all me. An army man till the end, that was my father.

"My father was tired, I think. He let things get to him." This is a part of the truth at least, and I think Selena must realise this, because she nods to herself, just slightly, and then carries on speaking.

"Dad became obsessed with Hatchmere Lake. The police spent a lot of time searching around there. At the start, anyway. They didn't find anything, but Dad kept on at them, he wouldn't let up. He had this theory that Amanda had been abducted by aliens. He got the idea from Amanda's diary. She'd written something in there about someone called Cally, and a city of white buildings on the edge of a lake. The police were fairly certain that Cally was just Amanda's code name for Allison Gifford – that was the teacher she was friends with – but Dad wouldn't have it. He called the Detective Inspector an idiot, right to his face."

I have to hand it to her. In the mad dad delusion rankings alien abduction has to be the winner.

"Why do you think he thought it was aliens?" I am genuinely curious.

"Goodness knows. Because she'd just vanished, I suppose. There was nothing else, no other explanation that made sense. Not that aliens made sense." She laughed. "It was strange, though, even for Dad. He was never into UFOs before."

"How did he die?"

"Heart attack. He was sixty-five. The hospital said his body was worn out, basically."

"You must miss him."

"I do," Selena says. "I really do."

There are tears in her eyes, and I find myself wondering if it is not just her father she is mourning, but the possibility he seemed to offer, that her sister was still alive somewhere, and that the universe was not so small as everyone insisted.

We became friends after that, sort of. I learned that Selena worked as the manager of an upmarket jewellery store owned by a Russian businessman who claimed to be a direct descendent of Ivan the Terrible. "He is seriously temperamental but he has a good eye," Selena said when she told me. She smiled. I was beginning to suspect that Selena knew more about diamonds and precious metals than any amount of Russian oligarchs put together. We had nothing in common, not really, but that didn't stop us finding plenty to talk about.

I never told her that I'd steamed open her father's envelope. If you're going to admit to something like that you have to do so upfront. I'd chosen not to, and so I kept quiet. I didn't see that it mattered much anyway.

We started meeting at the coffee shop fairly regularly. We even went to the cinema now and then. About six months into this new period of our relationship, Selena told me the second half of the story she'd begun confiding to me the first time we met, namely that two years after her father died, a woman made contact with her by telephone, claiming to be Amanda.

"I met with her a few times," Selena said. "For a long time she refused to say what had happened to her. She said she couldn't remember. In the end she told me she'd been taken to another world. She didn't know how she'd ended up there, or how she got back, just that there was some kind of war going on, and that whatever had caused the war was coming here.

"She seemed really upset about that for a while. Eventually she stopped talking about it. It was like she'd given up. I had no idea what to say to her. It was like Dad all over again."

"What was she like?"

"I don't know. Normal, I suppose, apart from the whole other planet thing. She kept on at me to let her meet Mum. I didn't want her to – Mum had been through enough already. But she was determined and in the end there was nothing I could do to stop her. She found out Mum's address from the Internet and just turned up there. I thought Mum would throw her out but she didn't. She stared at her for a moment, then wrapped her up in her arms, hugged her really tight, as if she knew who she was without having to be told. The oddest thing about that was that Mum had never been a huggy person, not even when we were little. She and Amanda never got on all that well either. They were always rubbing each other up the wrong way. They were just so different, I suppose."

"Different how?"

"Mum's the most practical person on the face of the earth. She'll do anything for anyone but she has no time for bullshit. Amanda's moods got on her nerves."

She asked me if I'd been close to my parents and I said

no, not really. I preferred it that way, I could have added, but chose not to. I asked her what had happened with the Amanda woman.

"She's still around, as far as I know. I speak to Mum on the phone now and then but we don't really talk. Not any more."

I wanted to ask her if she thought there was even a chance that the woman claiming to be Amanda really was her sister, but I sensed the issue was still too raw. If she wanted to tell me more, she would. It would be wrong to press her. We moved on to other subjects – her job, my research – and then we paid the bill. "Would you like to see something she wrote?" Selena said as we were about to leave. "This woman, I mean." She reached into her handbag and drew out an envelope, a brown A5 envelope exactly like the one Raymond Rouane's letter had arrived in. The coincidence startled me. Of course such envelopes are sold in their millions, but even so. Inside the envelope was a letter, two sheets of typed A4, folded in half to fit. There was no address at the top, just the date, a year ago, more or less.

The address on the envelope – Selena's – had been written in loose block capitals, with a blue felt-tip.

I know you don't believe me, but I want to tell you again anyway. I was taken from Hatchmere Lake near Warrington to the city of Fiby, which is the smallest of the six great city-states on the planet of Toshimo, a thousand light years away on the fringes of the Aw galaxy. Cally says that our peoples are related, although the ancestral links between us are shrouded in billennia. Fiby is the coldest of the cities, situated on the northern shore of the

Marillienseet and the only one of the six in the southern hemisphere. I was brought to Fiby because that is where the transept lies. I don't properly understand the laws of the transept, but I know it was created by engineers of the Lyceum in Clarimond, and that places on either side of the transept are each a perfect mirror image of the other. Hatchmere Lake is identical in every way to the Shuubseet, the slipper-shaped, forest-fringed fishing lake at the city's eastern frontier. You could superimpose an aerial photograph of Hatchmere Lake on to a photograph of the Shuubseet and there would be no discrepancy. The volume of water from one lake would perfectly fill the other. The only difference is that the Shuubseet is far older. There are Wels catfish in Hatchmere Lake, only probably not the giant ones we used to scare ourselves with stories about when we were kids – the lake hasn't been around for long enough. The Shuubseet is as old as the Earth itself. Older, probably.

There was a lot more, all equally outlandish. What could I say? I had no idea. There was something beautiful about it, though. There is no limit to what the human mind can invent. I wondered who she was really, this woman, and what she wanted. What con artists normally want is money, but Selena's income was perfectly average and her mother didn't earn a fortune either, so far as I knew.

Could she be the real Amanda? The idea seemed almost as far-fetched as what she'd written in her letter.

"What do you think?" Selena said, when I'd finished reading.

I shook my head. "I don't believe in life on other planets."

"We can't know, though," Selena said. "Not for certain."

She's right about that, there's no denying it. We know as much about the universe we live in as a woodlouse under a paving stone in my back garden knows about Sierra Leone. "Are you going to see her again?" I asked.

"I don't know. I don't know if I can face it. She's got Mum now. I mostly think I'm better off leaving them to it. I've got my job, my house. I'm fine, really."

We made a date for the cinema the following Saturday, and I thought what I'd often thought since meeting her: thank goodness I didn't fancy her, not even a little bit. It's good to have someone in your life that you can spend time with, without it landing you in trouble.

My father, Peter McConahey, was an explosives technician with the British army. You would probably refer to him as a bomb disposal expert. He loved his job, and he was brilliant at it. But the problem with a job like Dad's is that if you cock up even slightly there's a better than even chance that people will die. Dad was defusing a device that had been placed inside a police compound in Kuwait during the aftermath of the American bombing of Libya. A section of flooring collapsed while he was working, triggering the bomb and killing three Kuwaiti police officers and five international aid workers on the floor below. By an outrageous fluke – several hardened soldiers called it a miracle – Dad was thrown clear. Everyone including the official investigators agreed he was blameless, but that didn't stop my father blaming himself. He killed himself on his next tour of duty, defusing a car bomb. His civilian friends were horrified, his army colleagues were saddened and greatly surprised. Dad was a career soldier, trained to deal with all eventualities. In the end though they came to terms and carried on, because what else could they do? Dad's death could not have been predicted, or prevented. You never know how someone will react to trauma until it happens.

I was at university when it happened, here in Manchester. I didn't tell anyone. There was a memorial service for my father, which I attended, but I let people think I was going home for a weekend visit, nothing more. That was shortly before the summer vacation, when I moved out of university accommodation and into private digs with three other women, including Anya. No doubt it was my change of address, almost at the moment of my father's death, that meant I didn't receive his letter until after I graduated. Someone in halls just happened to see me, and passed it on – apparently the letter had been kicking around the accommodation admin office for more than a year.

Seeing Dad's writing on the envelope, the tense, slightly messy black handwriting that always seemed so at odds with the coolness of his outward persona, the writing I'd recognised when I opened the Lucy Davis letters and tried so hard to forget, was, as Selena had put it, like seeing a phantom. I saw from the postmark that Dad had posted it about a week before he died – too late to reach me beforehand but long enough in advance to prevent the letter being intercepted and impounded as evidence. It had slipped through the net, perhaps more completely than Dad had intended, though it was clear to me that he had planned this, as he had always planned everything, down to the last detail.

In the letter, Dad told me the story of his relationship with an army translator named Lucy Davis, how Lucy had become pregnant and given birth to a child, a little girl called Sarah. *I couldn't be present at Sarah's birth*, my father wrote, *which is something I regret to this day*. Dad said he loved Lucy in a way he hadn't thought possible. *I loved your mother*, he wrote, *but we were too alike, so determined to be independent we never allowed ourselves to need each other, not properly, not even after you were born. I regret that, too.* Dad tried to persuade Lucy to be with him, but she didn't want to be responsible for his divorce. That's what she told him, anyway, although I suspect it was Dad she didn't want to be responsible for. Perhaps she realised how cold he could be sometimes, unreachable as the ocean floor and just as dark.

Whatever the truth of things, it seems that what he saw as Lucy's rejection caused Dad to lose his legendary self-control. He persuaded two of his army comrades – God knows how – to help him kidnap his daughter Sarah. *I wanted to give her a fright, that's all,* he wrote. (He meant Lucy.) *I wanted to show her how much she needed me. She must have known I would have died rather than hurt Sarah. I was such a fool, Aileen, and I am so, so sorry.*

Sarah Davis was five at the time. The soldiers kept her in an empty house on the north side of Salisbury Plain, about ten miles from the village of Tytherington and the cottage her mother rented from the army. They took it in turns to stay with her, making her sandwiches and reading her stories and watching cartoons. They were compassionate men, fathers themselves as well as soldiers. They told her it was a holiday. Was she frightened? I think she must have been. Children always know when something is wrong, no matter what they are told to the contrary by adults.

What my father hoped to achieve by this I have no idea. After five days he came to his senses and took Sarah home. He parked his car around the corner from Lucy's cottage and told Sarah to walk down the hill. Your mother will be waiting, he said. Walk, don't run.

But of course Sarah ran, as fast as she could. She wanted to see her mother. She wanted to get away from the tall man who'd been behaving so strangely. It was a quiet road, but even on a quiet road there will still be vehicles. Lucy saw her daughter running and dashed to meet her, afraid that in her excitement Sarah might accidentally step off the pavement. Lucy was struck by a passing car as she crossed the road. In her anxiety to get to Sarah she hadn't even noticed it, even though, as witnesses confirmed, it was going quite slowly.

Lucy Davis was not killed, but she suffered severe head injuries, and the resulting brain damage left her unable to look after or even recognise her daughter. Sarah Davis was put in the care of social services, who quickly placed her with foster parents. Eventually her foster parents were allowed to adopt her.

My father, Peter McConahey, drove away. Neither the car driver, nor the three bystanders who rushed to the scene saw him go. Because he was parked in the next street, he never saw exactly what happened, although he did hear Lucy scream.

I have dreaded having to tell you these things, Dad wrote. *But I thought you had the right to know you have a half-sister.*

He enclosed a photograph of Sarah, the same as the one I had seen before, with the letter to Lucy. Perhaps it was the only one he had. I wondered who had returned it to him, who had been redirecting the letters, all those years ago, to our home in Salisbury. One of his comrades, still watching his back? Or someone else, an enemy who wanted Dad to understand that his secret was known, that it was only a matter of time before the truth came out.

What torture that would have been, I can only imagine. I replaced the letter and the photograph in the envelope and hid them in my desk, under a mound of papers and other detritus. I have always kept them with me, but I have never again looked at the photograph, or taken the letter out of the envelope to read it. By the time that letter reached me, it was already old news. Sarah was two years older, Dad was two years dead. I had always thought of my father in a certain way. Now I had to learn to think of him in another way. Sarah must be in her twenties now. She knows nothing of me. Whether it is best to keep things like that or not, I have no idea.

Some letters aren't supposed to be read. Have you ever wondered if that's why they go astray?

I think about Amanda all the time. I cannot put away the knowledge that she is out there somewhere, just across the city from me, going shopping, visiting her mother, writing letters. I would like to ask her about her alien planet and what it was like. What trouble she believes is coming, and when it might get here.

NINA ALLAN

Nina Allan's stories have appeared in numerous magazines and anthologies, including *Best Horror of the Year #6*, *The Year's Best Science Fiction and Fantasy 2013*, and *The Mammoth Book of Ghost Stories by Women*. Her debut novel *The Race* was a finalist for the 2015 BSFA Award, the Kitschies Red Tentacle and the John W. Campbell Memorial Award. 'Astray' was written while Nina was working on her second novel, which has resulted in more than a few uncanny similarities in character and theme. Nina lives and works in North Devon. Find her blog, The Spider's House, at www.ninaallan.co.uk

THE DAYS OF OUR LIVES

ADAM LG NEVILL

The ticking was much louder on the first floor and soon after the ticking began I heard Lois moving upstairs. Floorboards groaned as she made unsteady progress through areas made murky by curtains not opened for a week. She must have come up inside our bedroom and staggered into the hall, passing herself along the walls with her thin hands. I hadn't seen her for six days but could easily imagine her aspect and mood: the sinewy neck, the fierce grey eyes, a mouth already downcast, and the lips atremble at grievances revived upon the very moment of her return. But I also wondered if her eyes and nails were painted. She had beautiful eyelashes. I went and stood at the foot of the stairs and looked up.

Even on the unlit walls of the stairwell a long and spiky shadow was cast by her antics above. Though I could not see Lois, the air was moving violently, as were parts of her shadow, and I knew she was already batting the side of her face with her hands and then throwing her arms into the air above her scruffy grey head. As expected, she'd woken furious.

The muttering began and was too quiet for me to clearly

hear all of what she was saying, but the voice was sharp, the words sibilant and near spat out, so I could only assume she had woken thinking of me. 'I told you... how many times!... and you wouldn't listen... for God's sake... what is wrong with you?... why must you be so difficult?... all the time... you have been told... time after time...'

I'd hoped for a better mood. I had cleaned the house over two days, thoroughly but hurriedly for when she next arose. I'd even washed the walls and ceilings, had moved all of the furniture to sweep, dust and vacuum. I had brought no food indoors but loaves of cheap white bread, eggs, plain biscuits, and baking materials that would never be used. I had scalded and boiled the house of dirt and rid the building of its pleasures, with the exception of the television that she enjoyed and the little ceramic radio in the kitchen that only picked up Radio Two from 1983. Ultimately, I had bleached our rented home of any overt signifier of joy, as well as those things she was not interested in, or anything that remained of myself that I forgot about as soon as it was gone.

The last handful of books that intrigued me, anything of any colour or imagination that enabled me to pass this great expanse of time, that burned my chest and internal organs as if my body was pressed against a hot radiator, I finally removed from the shelves yesterday and donated to charity shops along the seafront. Only the ancient knitting patterns, gardening books, antique baking encyclopaedias, religious pamphlets, old socialist diatribes, completely out-of-date versions of imperial history, and indigestible things of that nature, remained now. Faded spines, heavy paper smelling of unventilated rooms, leprous-spotted, migraine-inducing reminders of what, her time? Though Lois never looked at them, I'm pretty sure those books never had anything to do with me.

I retreated from the stairs and moved to the window of the living room. I opened the curtains for the first time in a week. Without any interest in the flowers, I looked down at the artificial iris in the green glass vase to distract my eyes from the small, square garden. Others had also come up since the ticking began, and I didn't want to look at them. A mere glance out back had been sufficient and had revealed the presence of a mostly rotten, brownish snake; one still writhing and showing its paler underbelly on the lawn beneath the washing line. Two wooden birds with ferocious eyes pecked at the snake. Inside the sideboard beside me, the ornaments of the little black warriors that we bought from a charity shop began to beat their leather drums with their wooden hands. On the patio and inside the old kennel, that had not seen a dog in years, I glimpsed the pale back of a young woman. I knew it was the girl with the bespectacled face that suited newsprint and a garish headline above a picture of a dismal, wet field beside an A road. I'd seen this young woman last week from a bus window and looked away from her quickly to feign interest in the plastic banner strung across the front of a pub. Too late, though, because Lois had been sat beside me and had noticed my leering. She angrily ripped away the foil from a tube of Polo mints and I knew that girl by the side of the road was in trouble deep.

'I saw you,' was all that Lois said. She'd not even turned her head.

I wanted to say, 'Saw what?' but it would do me no good

and I couldn't speak for the terrible, cold remorse that seemed to fill my throat like a potato swallowed whole. But I could now see that the girl had been strangled with her own ivory-toned tights and stuffed inside the kennel in our garden. The incident must have been the cause of Lois's distress and the reason why she'd withdrawn from me to lie down for a week.

But Lois was coming down the stairs now, on her front, and making the sound of a large cat coughing out fur because she was eager to confront me with those displeasures lingering from the last time she was around.

The ticking filled the living room, slipping inside my ears and inducing the smell of a linoleum floor in a preschool that I had attended in the nineteen seventies. In my memory, a lollipop lady smiled as I crossed a road with a leather satchel banging against my side. I saw the faces of four children I'd not thought of in decades. For a moment, I remembered all of their names before forgetting them again.

Reflected upon the glass of the window, Lois's tall, thin silhouette with the messy head swayed from side to side as she entered the living room. When Lois saw me she stopped moving and said, 'You,' in a voice exhausted by despair and panted out with disgust. And then she rushed in quickly and flared up behind me.

I flinched.

In the café on the pier I cut a small dry cake in half, a morsel that would have failed to satisfy a child. I carefully placed half of the cake on a saucer before Lois. One of her eyelids flickered as if in acknowledgement, but more from displeasure, as if

I was trying to win her over and make her grateful. What I could see of her eyes still expressed detachment, anger and a morbid loathing. Tense and uncomfortable, I continued to mess with the tea things.

We were the only customers. The sea beyond the windows was grey and the wind flapped the pennants and the plastic coverings on idle bumper cars. Our mugs held watery, unsweetened tea. I made sure that I did not enjoy mine.

Inside her vinyl, crab-coloured handbag the ticking was near idle, not so persistent, but far below the pier, in the water, I was distracted by a large, dark shape that might have been a cloud shadow. It appeared to flow beneath the water before disappearing under the pier, and for a moment I could smell the briny wet wood under the café and hear the slop of thick waves against the uprights. A swift episode of vertigo followed and I remembered a Christmas tree on red and green carpet that reminded me of chameleons, and a lace cloth on a wooden coffee table with pointy legs similar to the fins on old American cars, and a wooden bowl of nuts and raisins, a glass of sherry, and a babysitter's long shins in sheer, dark tights that had a wet sheen by the light of a gas fire. Legs that I couldn't stop peeking at, even at that age, and I must have been around four years old. I'd tried to use the babysitter's shiny legs as a bridge for a Matchbox car to pass under, so that I could get my face closer. The babysitter's pale skin was freckled under her tights. And right up close her legs smelled of a woman's underwear drawer and the material of her tights was just lots of little fabric squares that transformed into a smooth, second skin as I moved my face away again. One thing then another thing. So many ways to see everything. One skin and then another skin. It had made me squirm and squirt.

Across the table, in the café on the pier, Lois smiled and her eyes glittered with amusement. 'You'll never learn,' she said, and I knew that she wanted to hit me hard. I shivered in the draught that came under the door from off the windswept pier, and my old hands looked so veiny and bluish upon the laminate table top.

Slipping the gauzy scarf around her head, she indicated that she wanted to leave. As she rose her spectacles caught the light from the fluorescent strip, a shimmer of fire above sharp ice.

There was no one outside the café, or on the pier, or the grassy area behind the esplanade, so she hit me full in the face with a closed fist and left me dazed and leaning against a closed ice-cream concession. Blood came into my mouth.

I followed her for ten minutes, sulking, then pulled up alongside her and we trudged up and down the near-empty grey streets of the town and looked in shop windows. We bought some Christmas cards, a pound of potatoes we'd boil fluffy and eat later with tasteless fish, and carrots from a tin. From the pound shop we picked up a small box of Scottish shortbread. In a charity shop she bought a pencil skirt without trying it on, and two satin blouses. 'I have no idea when I'll be able to wear anything nice again.'

As we passed Bay Electrics I saw a girl's face on two big television screens. Local news too, showing a pretty girl with black-framed glasses who never made it to work one morning just over a week ago. It was the girl inside the kennel.

'Is that what you like?' Lois whispered in a breathless voice beside me. 'Is that what you fancy?'

Increasing her pace, she walked in front of me, head down,

all the way back to the car, and she never spoke during the drive home. At our place, she sat and watched a television quiz show that I hadn't seen since the seventies. It could not have been scheduled, possibly never even recorded by ITV either, but it's what she wanted and so it appeared and she watched it.

She couldn't bear the sight of me, I could tell, and she didn't want me watching her quiz show either, so I removed my clothes and went and lay in the basket under the kitchen table. I tried to remember if we'd ever had a dog, or if it was my teeth that had made those marks on the rubber bone.

An hour after I lay down and curled up, Lois began screaming in the lounge. I think she was on the telephone and had called a number she'd recalled from years, or even decades, long gone. 'Is Mr Price there? What do you mean I have the wrong number? Put him on immediately!' God knows what they made of the call at the other end of the line. I just stayed very still and kept my eyes clenched shut until she hung up and began to sob.

Inside the kitchen the ticking lulled me to sleep amongst vague odours of lemon disinfectant, the dog blanket and cooker gas.

Lois was doing a one-thousand-piece jigsaw puzzle; the one with the painting of a mill beside a pond. The puzzle was spread across a card table and her legs passed beneath the table. I sat before her, naked, and stayed quiet. Her toes were no more than a few inches from my knees and I dared not shuffle any closer. She was wearing her black brassiere, a nylon slip, and very fine tights. She had painted her toenails red and her legs whisked when she rubbed them together. The rollers had come out of her hair now too and her silver hair shimmered beside the fairy lights. Her eye makeup was pink and gloriously alluring around her cold iron-coloured eyes. When she wore makeup she looked younger. A thin gold bracelet circled her slender wrist and the watch attached to the metal strap ticked quietly. The watch face was so tiny I could not see what the time was. Gone midnight, I guessed.

Until she'd finished the puzzle she only spoke to me once, in a quiet, hard voice. 'If you touch it, I'll have it straight off.'

I let my limp hands fall back to the floor. My whole body was aching from sitting still for so long.

She mostly remained calm and disinterested for the remainder of the time it took her to finish her puzzle, so I didn't have many memories. I only recall things when she is agitated and I forget them when she calms down. When she is enraged I am flooded.

Lois began to drink sherry from a long glass and to share unflattering reminiscences and observations about our courtship. Things like, 'I don't know what I was thinking back then? And now I'm stuck. Ha! Look at me now, ha! Hardly The Ritz. Promises, promises. I'd have been much better off with that American chappy. That one you were friendly with...' Increasingly roused, she padded back and forth through the living room, so long, thin and silky with her thighs susurrating together. I could smell her lipstick, perfume and hairspray, which usually excited me, particularly as her mood changed to something ugly and volatile. And as I sensed the vinegar of spite rising up through her I began to remember... I think... a package that arrived in a small room where I had lived, years before. Yes, I've remembered this before, and many times, I think.

The padded envelope had once been addressed to a doctor, but someone had written NO LONGER AT THIS ADDRESS on the front, and then written my address as the correct postal address. Only it wasn't addressed to me, or anyone specifically, but was instead addressed to 'You', and then 'A Man', and 'Him', and all on the same line above my postal address. There were no details of the sender, so I'd opened the parcel. And it had contained an old watch, a ladies wristwatch, with a thin, scuffed bracelet that smelled of perfume, and so strongly that I received an impression of slim white wrists when I held the watch. Within the cotton wool was a mass-produced paper flier advertising a 'literary walk', organised by something called 'The Movement'.

I went along to this walk, but only, I think, to return the watch to the sender. It was a themed walk on a wet Sunday: something to do with three gruesome paintings in a tiny church. The triptych of paintings featured an ugly antique wooden cabinet as their subject. There was some kind of connection between the cabinet and a local poet who had gone mad. I think. There were drinks after the tedious walk too, I am sure, in a community centre. I'd asked around the group on the walk, trying to establish to whom the watch belonged. Everyone I asked had said, 'Ask Lois. That looks like one of hers.' Or, 'Speak to Lois. That's a Lois.' Maybe even, 'Lois, she's looking. She's due.'

I'd eventually identified and approached this Lois, spoken to her, and complemented her on her fabulous eye makeup. She'd looked wary, but appreciated the remark with a nod and tight smile that never extended to her eyes. She said, 'You're from that building where the down-and-outs live? I was hoping you were going to be that other chap that I've seen going inside.' And she'd taken the watch from me, and sighed resignedly. 'But all right then,' as if accepting an invitation from me. 'At least you returned it. But it's not going to be what you think, I'm afraid.' I remember being confused.

That afternoon I'd not been able to stop staring at her beautiful hands either, or the idea of her wearing nothing but the tight leather boots she'd worn on the walk. So I was glad that the watch had a connection to this woman called Lois. I think my attentions made her feel special but also irritable, as if I were a pest. I wasn't sure how old she was, but she had clearly tried to look older with the grey coat and headscarf and A-line tweed skirts.

From a first sighting she had made me feel uncomfortable, but intrigued and aroused also, and at the time I had been lonely and unable to get the cold, unfriendly woman out of my mind, so I had gone to the community centre again knowing that is where the strange group of people, The Movement, met monthly. This dowdy, plain and depressing building was the centre of their organisation, and had pictures painted by children covering the walls. On my second visit plastic chairs had been set out in rows. They were red. There was a silver urn with tea and biscuits on a paper plate too: Garibaldis, Lemon Puffs and stale Iced Gems. I was nervous and didn't really know anyone well, and those that I thought might recognise me from the walk seemed unwilling to converse.

When something was about to occur on the stage, I sat in the row behind Lois. She was wearing a grey coat that she didn't take off indoors. Her head was covered by a scarf again, but her eyes were concealed by red-tinted glasses. She'd worn those boots again too, but had seemed indifferent to me, even after I'd returned the watch and she'd suggested some kind of enigmatic agreement had been made between us the first time we met. I did suspect that she was unstable, but I was lonely and desperate. I found it all very bewildering too, but my bafflement was only destined to increase.

To replicate the image in one of the hideous paintings that I had seen on the literary walk, a picture responsible for sending a local poet mad, a motionless elderly woman had sat in a chair on the low stage. She was draped in black and wore a veil. One of her legs was contained inside a large wooden boot. Beside her chair was a curtained cabinet, the size of a wardrobe but deeper, the sort of thing budget magicians used. On the other side of her was a piece of navigational equipment; naval, I had assumed, and all made from brass with what looked like a clock face on the front. A loud ticking had issued from the brass device.

Another woman with curly black hair, who was overweight and dressed like a little girl, came onto the stage too... I think she wore very high heels that were red. When the woman in the red shoes read poems from a book, I felt uneasy and thought that I should go; just get up and leave the hall quickly. But I lingered for fear of drawing attention to myself by scraping a chair leg across the floor, while everyone else at the meeting was so enraptured by the performance on the stage.

After the reading, the woman dressed like a little girl withdrew from the stage and the hall darkened until the building was solely lit by two red stage lights.

Something inside the cupboard on the stage began to croak and the sound made me think of a bullfrog. It must have been a recording, or so I had thought at the time. The ticking from the brass clock grew louder and louder too. Some people stood up and shouted things at the box. I felt horrified, embarrassed for the shouters, uncomfortable, and eventually I panicked and made to leave.

Lois had turned round then and said, 'Sit back down!' It was the first time she'd even acknowledged me that evening and I returned to my seat, though I wasn't sure why I obeyed her. And the others near me in the hall had looked at me too, expectantly. I had shrugged and cleared my throat and asked, 'What?'

Lois had said, 'It's not what, it's who and when?'

I didn't understand.

On the stage, the elderly woman with the false leg spoke for the first time. 'One can go,' she'd said, her frail voice amplified through some old plastic speakers above the stage.

Chairs were knocked aside or even upturned in the undignified scrabble toward the stage that was made by at least four female members of the group. They'd all held pocket watches in the air too, as they stumbled to the stage. Lois got there first, her posture tense with a childlike excitement, and had looked up at the elderly woman expectantly.

The old veiled head above her had nodded and Lois had risen up the stairs to the stage. On her hands and knees, with her head bowed, she then crawled inside the curtained cabinet. As she moved inside, kind of giggling, or maybe it was whimpering, the elderly woman in the chair had beaten Lois on the back, buttocks and legs, quite mercilessly, with a walking stick.

The stage lights went out, or failed, and the congregation fell silent in the darkness. All I could hear was the clock ticking loudly until a sound like a melon being split apart came wetly from the direction of the stage.

'That time is over,' the amplified voice of the elderly woman announced.

The lights came on and the people in the hall started to talk to each other in quiet voices. I couldn't see Lois and wondered if she was still inside the cabinet. But I'd seen enough of a nonsensical and unpleasant tradition, or ritual, connected to those paintings, and some kind of deeper belief system that I cannot remember much about, and couldn't even grasp back then, and so I left hurriedly. No one tried to stop me.

I think… that's what might have happened. It might have been a dream, though, or a remembered dream. I never really know if I can trust what appears in my head like memories. But I've recalled that scene before, I am sure, on another evening like this one as Lois bemoaned our coming together. Maybe this was as recent as last month? I don't know, but all of this feels so familiar.

Lois began calling me after the night she entered the cabinet on the stage of the community hall. On the telephone she would be abusive. I remember standing by the communal phone, to receive the calls in the hallway of the building in which I had rented a bedsit. Her voice had sounded as if it were many miles away and struggling to be heard in a high wind. I then told the other residents of the lodging to tell all callers that I was not home and the phone calls soon stopped.

I met someone else not long after my brush with Lois and The Movement… Yes, a very sweet woman with red hair. But

I didn't know her for long because she was murdered; she was found strangled and her remains had been put inside a rubbish skip.

Not long after that Lois came for me in person.

I think…

Yes, and there was a brief ceremony soon after, in the back of a charity shop. I remember wearing a suit that was too small for me. It had smelled of someone else's sweat. And I was on my knees beside a pile of old clothes that needed sorting, while Lois stood beside me in a smart suit and her lovely boots, with her fabulous eye makeup, and her silver hair freshly permed.

We had been positioned before the wooden cabinet that I had seen at the community centre, and in the odd paintings inside the chapel on the literary walk. And someone had been struggling to breathe inside the box, like they were asthmatic. We could all hear them on the other side of the purple curtain.

A man, and I think he was the postman in that town, held a pair of dressmaker's scissors under my chin, to make sure I said the words that were asked of me. But there had been no need of the scissors because even though our courtship was short, by that time I was so involved with Lois that I was actually beside myself with excitement whenever I saw her, or heard her voice on the phone. At the charity shop wedding service, as we all recited a poem from the poet that went mad, Lois held up the ladies wristwatch with the very loud tick that had once been sent to my address, though intended for someone else.

We were married.

She was given a garish bouquet of artificial flowers, and I

had a long wooden rule broken over my shoulders. The pain had been withering.

There was a wedding breakfast too, with Babycham and cheese footballs, salmon sandwiches, round lettuces, sausage rolls. And there was a lot of sex on the wedding night too; the kind of thing I had never imagined possible. At least I think it was sex, but I can only remember a lot of screaming in the darkness around a bed, while someone kind of coughed and hiccupped in between lowing like a bullock. I know I was beaten severely with a belt by the witnesses, who were also in the bedroom at a Travelodge that had been rented for the occasion.

Or was that Christmas?

I'm not sure she's ever allowed me to touch her since, though she takes her pleasures upstairs with what I can only assume was inside that box in the community centre and at our wedding. I may be her spouse, but I believe she is wedded to another who barks with a throat full of catarrh, and she cries out with pleasure, or grunts, and finally she weeps.

The betrayals used to upset me and I would cry in the dog basket downstairs, but in time you can get used to anything.

On Thursday Lois killed another young woman, this time with a house brick, and I knew we'd have to move on again.

The disagreement culminated in a lot of hair pulling and kicking behind some beach huts because I had said hello to the attractive woman who'd been walking her dogs past our picnic blanket. Lois went after the dogs too and I had to look away and out to sea when she caught up with the spaniel.

I got Lois home, up through the trees when it was dark,

wrapped in our picnic blanket. Shivering, all stained down the front, she talked to herself the whole way home, and she had to lie down the following day with a mask over her face. The episode had been building for days and Lois detested younger women.

While she convalesced I watched Ceefax alone – I had no idea that channel was still on the telly – and I thought about where we should go next.

When Lois came downstairs two days later, she wore lots of eye makeup and her tight, shiny boots and was nice to me, but I remained subdued. I was unable to get the sound of the frightened dog on the beach out of my mind; the yelp and the coconut sound and then the splashing.

'We'll have to move again. That's two in one place,' I'd said wearily.

'I never liked this house,' was her only response.

She relieved me into a thick bath towel, using both of her hands, kissed me and then spat in my face.

I didn't see her again for three weeks. By then I had found a terraced house two hundred miles away from where she'd done the killing of two fine girls. And in the new place I'd begun to hope that she'd never return to me. Vain and futile to wish for such a thing, I know, because before Lois vanished at the seaside, she'd slowly and provocatively wound up her golden wristwatch while staring into my eyes, so that my hopes for a separation would be wishful thinking and nothing else. The only possible severance between me and Lois would involve my throat being placed over an ordinary washbasin in a terraced house and her getting busy with the dressmaker's scissors as I masturbated. That's how she rid herself of the last two: some painter in Soho in the sixties and a surgeon she'd been with for years. Either a quick divorce with the scissors over vintage porcelain, or I could be slaughtered communally in a charity shop on a Sunday afternoon. Neither option particularly appealed to me.

In the new town there is evidence of The Movement. They've set themselves up in two rival organisations: a migratory bird society that meets above a legal high shop only open on a Wednesday, and an M. L. Hazzard study group that meets in an old Methodist church. No one in their right mind would want an involvement in either group, and I suspected each would convulse with schisms until they faded away. There are a few weddings, though, and far too many young people are already missing in the town. But I hoped the proximity of the others of Lois's faith would calm her down or distract her.

Lois eventually came up in the spare bedroom of the new house, naked save for the gold watch, bald and pinching her thin arms. It took me hours with the help of a hot bath and lots of watery tea to bring her round and to make the ticking in the house slow down and quieten, and for the leathery snakes with dog faces to melt into shitty stains on the carpet. She'd been through torments while away from me, I could see that, and she just wanted to hurt herself on arrival. But across several days I brought Lois back to a semblance of what we could recall of her, and she began to use a bit of lippy and do her hair and wear underwear beneath her housecoat.

Eventually we went out, just to the end of the road, then to the local shops to treat her to new clothes, then down and along the seafront, where we'd eat child-size vanilla ice creams and sit on the benches to watch the misty grey horizon. We'd not been down to the sea much before a drunken, unkempt man asked her to do something rude and frightened her, and then another dirty youth in a grimy tracksuit on a bike followed us for half a mile and tried to tug her hair from behind.

That second time, while I pumped two-pence pieces into an arcade machine to win some Swan Vesta matches and Super King cigarettes tied up in a five-pound note, Lois got away from me. I ran the length of the pier and shore looking for her and only found her after following the sound of what I thought was someone stamping in a puddle in the public toilets. And then I saw the bicycle outside.

She'd lured the lad who'd yanked her hair on the promenade inside the ladies toilets and been thorough with him in the end cubicle. When I finally dragged her out of there, little was left of his face, that I could see, and the top of his head had come off like pie crust. When I got her home I had to put her best boots in a dustbin and her tights were ruined.

Two people from The Movement came and saw us at home after the incident and told me not to worry because hardly anything like that was investigated anymore, and besides the police had already charged two men. Apparently, the smashed-up lad was always knocking about with them and they had form for stamping on people in the grimy streets. The visitors from The Movement also invited us to be witnesses at a wedding, which I instantly dreaded despite hungering to see Lois all dressed up again.

The wedding was held in the storeroom of a Sea Scout hut that smelled of bilge and in there, within minutes, Lois met someone else: a fat, bald man who did little but leer at her and sneer at me. She also did her best to lose me in the crowd, and there were a lot of people there to whip the bridegroom with leather belts, but I kept my eyes on her. At the wedding breakfast I saw the fat man feeding her the crisps that come with a sachet of salt inside the bag. He wasn't married and wasn't in The Movement either, so I was appalled by the fact that they let single men attend an event like that. At one point, as I hid below Lois's eyeline, I even caught her slipping the fat man our telephone number. All of the other women felt sorry for me.

I barely recognised Lois after the wedding in the Sea Scout hut. For days she was euphoric and acted as if I wasn't even there, and then she was enraged because I was there and clearly preventing her from pursuing another opportunity.

The fat man even approached me in the street when I was out shopping and spoke down to me and said that I may as well give up on Lois, as our relationship was dead, and that he intended to marry her within weeks.

'Is that what you think?' I said, and he slapped my face.

I writhed beneath the kitchen table for three days after the incident with the fat man, before getting up and dressing in Lois's clothes, which made me giddy. When I got the eye-shadow just right, my knees nearly gave way. But I still managed to leave the house in the early hours to pay a visit to the fat man. Lois ran into the street after me, shouting, 'Don't you touch him! Don't you touch my Richey!' When some of the neighbours started looking out of windows, she retreated indoors, sobbing.

Well aware that Lois was absolutely forbidden from making such an overture to a new partner, without my voluntary participation in a divorce, Richey hadn't been able to restrain himself from making a move on her. Through the spyhole in the door of his flat he saw me with my face all made up and he thought that I was Lois. He couldn't get the door open fast enough. Then he stood in the doorway smiling, with his gut pushing out his dressing gown like a big shiny pouch, and I went into that bulb of guts with a pair of sharp scissors, my arm going really fast. He didn't even have a chance to get his hairy hands up, and into his tubes and tripes I cut deep.

We cannot have oafs in The Movement. Everyone knows that. I found out later that he'd only been let in because the woman in the bird migrating group, the one who always wore her raincoat hood up indoors, had her eye on 'Richey' and had believed that she was in with a chance. She was only one week from crossing over too, but I think I saved her a few decades of grief. Later, for sorting out Richey, she even sent me a packet of Viscount biscuits and a card meant for a nine-year-old boy with a racing car on the front.

Anyway, right along the length of the hall of his flat, I went through Richey like a sewing machine and I made him bleat. I'd worn rubber washing-up gloves because I knew my hands would get all slippery on the plastic handles of the scissors. In and out, in and out, in and out! And as he slowed and half collapsed down the wall of the hall, before falling into his modest living room, I put the scissors deep into his neck from the side, and then closed the door of the lounge until he stopped coughing and wheezing.

Heavy, stinky bastard, covered in coarse black hair on the back like a goat, with a big, plastic, bully face that had once bobbed and grinned, but I took him apart to get him out of his flat piecemeal. Unbelievably, as I de-jointed his carcase in the bath, he came alive for a bit and scared me half to death. He didn't last for long, though, and I finished up with some secateurs that were good on meat. I found them under the sink in the kitchen.

Took me three trips: one to the old zoo that should have been closed years ago where I threw bits into the overgrown cassowary enclosure (they had three birds); one trip to where the sea gulls fight by the drainage pipe; and one trip to the Sea Scout hall with the head, which I buried beside the war memorial so that Richey could always look upon the place where he got the ball rolling.

When I got home, I shut Lois in the loft and took down the smoke alarms and burned all of her clothes, except for the best party tights, in the kitchen sink with the windows open. I went through the house and collected up all of her things and what I didn't dump in the council rubbish bins I gave to charity.

Before I left her growling like a cat, up in the loft amongst our old Christmas decorations, I told Lois that I might see her in our new place when I found it. I went downstairs and put her ladies' watch on my wrist and listened to it tick rapidly, like a heart fit to burst. Inside the sideboard, the little black warriors began to beat their leather drums with their wooden hands.

Lois was still clawing at the plywood loft hatch when I left the house with only one suitcase.

ADAM LG NEVILL

Adam LG Nevill was born in Birmingham, England, in 1969 and grew up in England and New Zealand. He is the author of the supernatural horror novels *Banquet for the Damned*, *Apartment 16*, *The Ritual*, *Last Days*, *House of Small Shadows*, *No One Gets Out Alive* and *Lost Girl*. In 2012, 2013 and 2015 his novels were the winners of The August Derleth Award for Best Horror Novel. *The Ritual* and *Last Days* were also awarded Best in Category: Horror, by R.U.S.A. Adam lives in Devon and can be contacted through www.adamlgnevill.com.

THE HUNGRY HOTEL

LISA TUTTLE

I never told anyone I knew him, and in fact I hardly knew him at all.

It happened more than twenty years ago, when I was twenty-two and engaged to Marshall, who was away all summer, doing an internship out of state. Our impending separation had pushed him to propose. We loved each other and all that, three months wasn't going to make any difference to our feelings, but the formality of an engagement was better, it left no room for doubt.

I never even thought about being unfaithful, and didn't imagine I could be tempted. So I can't explain why, when this cute but short and dark and scruffy character (he couldn't have been more different from Marshall) looked at me, and our eyes met for a moment, I responded as if I'd gone into that bar desperate to hook up with some guy. In fact, I was only there because I was supposed to be meeting a girlfriend – she was the one who wanted to hear the band – but she bailed at the last minute.

When he came over, I let him buy me my low-alcohol

289

beer, and we talked as best we could in that noisy place – I could hardly hear a word he said – but it didn't matter because our bodies were having their own conversation. When he indicated the crumpled pack of cigarettes in his shirt pocket, although I didn't smoke, I went outside with him. We sat in my car and made out for about an hour. We didn't do more than kiss, but that was a lot.

He had to go – his band was doing the second set – and asked if I would wait for him. Could we get together after the show?

Breathless, dizzy, drunk on his kisses, I agreed.

But I did not follow him inside. I got behind the wheel and drove away. There was no light on in our apartment, and as I drew in, I remembered: Lauren was spending the night with her boyfriend. So I kept on driving. I don't know how long I drove, past familiar landmarks and around the campus where I used to be a student, before entering neighbourhoods unknown to me, where dark, winding roads doubled back on themselves or turned into dead-ends.

I drove without aim or destination until I finally ended up back in the parking lot behind the bar and he was standing there, smoking. His face lit up when he saw me.

'I thought you must have changed your mind,' he said, getting into the car. 'I told myself, I'll give it one more cigarette.'

I said, 'I must be crazy. I have a boyfriend; I mean, my fiancé.'

'But he's not here, and I am.' He put his hand on my leg. 'We don't have to do anything. I'd like to get to know you, and spend some time with you. Just – whatever you want. I'm going away in a couple of days. I sure don't want to mess up your life.'

I asked him if he had a hotel room. No. The band had been put up in a borrowed house, sharing bedrooms. It might be empty now, but the others would turn up sooner or later; there would be no privacy. But if I didn't mind, if I only wanted to hang out…

I told him again that I was engaged. I said I couldn't risk it; I couldn't stand it if somehow word got back to Marshall that I'd been hanging out with some strange guys. Would I have been so worried about how it would look if it was an innocent friendship? Of course not. But I already knew – we both did – that it wasn't innocent. Those kisses.

So I took him to my place. This would be a very different story if my roomie had been home that night. But I knew she wouldn't be, just like I knew we would do more than talk.

It's funny, though, because while you might think sex was the main thing – it was what our encounter was all about, this unexpected, inconvenient, undeniable physical desire that had drawn us together, and it was certainly the aspect of our time together that Marshall might have considered unforgivable – it isn't what I remember.

Of course I don't mean I've forgotten the things we did that night in my bed; I remember his lips and his hands and his skin, how smooth it was, and how good it felt against mine, in places I hadn't thought of before as erogenous zones – and yes the erotic details would come back to me for a long time afterwards. That's not the point. He wasn't a better lover than Marshall, just different.

What I remember most about that night is how much we talked, and that we never slept. We were each too excited and disturbed by the presence of the other to finally let go and fall asleep. So you could say that we made love or had sex, but we never slept together.

When I was little, before I knew what were called then 'the facts of life', I was told that to make a baby, two people must love each other very much, and be married. But then it became clear that the teenager next door had a baby in her tummy, and she wasn't married; there was no loving father anywhere in sight. Someone said she had slept with a boy... and from that I came to believe that lovers created a baby in their dreams. If the baby was meant to be (already at the age of five I knew, from observing the miserable girl next door, that what the potential parents wanted was irrelevant), then by sleeping together in one bed, at the same time, they would each dream the same thing, and that dream would somehow get into the tummy of the mother-to-be, and grow into a baby.

'So people are dreams made flesh,' he said. 'I love it!'

Our talk was not like a normal conversation, at least, not like one I'd ever had before. We weren't on a date or planning a life together. We didn't have to impress each other, or assess each other for suitability, or lay down the beginnings of a lasting relationship. We were strangers, free to say anything. I didn't tell any lies about myself; I don't know if he lied to me – he fantasised and made up stories, but I knew that was what he was doing: he wrote songs. He made up one just for me; it was kind of silly, forcing unlikely words to rhyme with my name, but I was charmed. I wish I could remember it now. I'd sing it to cheer myself up.

No one had ever been impressed by my creativity, and I thought of myself as practical and unimaginative, down-to-earth. He didn't know that; he had no particular expectations, and it didn't matter if I disappointed him. The situation set me free.

* * *

When I heard Lauren coming in the next morning, I made him leave by the window. It was easy to do, perfectly safe, and I gave him directions to a nearby cafe where I said I'd meet him for breakfast in half an hour, but seeing him clamber out of my bedroom window added an element of old-fashioned farce, as if it was happening in a black-and-white movie, or an old cartoon, certainly not part of my real life.

I regretted having suggested breakfast as soon as he'd gone. What if someone I knew saw us together? I stopped by the cafe to order coffee and bagels to go, and greeted him like a casual acquaintance – 'Hey, good set last night!'

We exchanged a secret, conspiratorial grin. He looked wrecked, but happy, telling me he was about to go crawl into bed to sleep for the rest of the day. I said, 'Thank God it's Saturday!' so I could do the same. He told me he'd leave a comp ticket, if I wanted to come to the show that night, and I said I would.

When I got to the venue, I was immediately hailed by some friends of Marshall's, so there was no chance for us to talk. When the band began to play, I was surprised to learn that he was the drummer. When we'd first stood together talking in the noisy, crowded bar the previous night, when I had let him buy me a beer, he had told me a couple of drummer jokes, so I knew that the drummer was to the musician what the blonde or the aggie was in a similar context, but I hadn't realised he was making fun of himself.

Getting away from Marshall's friends was not easy. Eventually I left, drove off, feeling sick at the thought that I might never see him again. But the unspoken bond between us held; when I drove back some time later, he was waiting for me in the parking lot, like before; he crushed out his cigarette under his heel and got into the car.

Lauren was at home, so I couldn't take him there. Feeling like a teenager again, I drove west, towards the lake, until I found a sufficiently secluded spot to park. We got into the backseat and started making out, but it was cramped and uncomfortable and soon unbearably hot. There wasn't a breath of wind, and the open windows invited flies and mosquitoes, and added to my fear that someone unseen in the darkness could be spying on us.

For the first time I asked myself what I thought I was doing.

I didn't want to linger. As soon as I could, I scrambled back into the driver's seat, hastily adjusting my clothes.

'What's wrong?'

'Nothing.'

He didn't ask again. We drove back into town, and the only voices in the car came from the radio, the songs either wildly inappropriate, or offering ironic counterpoint to our sordid little affair.

I dropped him off at an intersection he said was near the house where he was staying. For years afterward, whenever I chanced to stop at the lights there, I remembered that moment, watching him walk away from me, not looking back, thinking that was the end.

It should have been, but when I finally went out the next morning, an envelope that had been wedged between the door and frame fell at my feet.

Inside the plain white letter envelope was a sheet of paper

folded in thirds. The handwriting was unfamiliar, but I knew who it had to be from.

It was his last day in town, the band was driving down to Houston – late tonight, to miss the worst of the traffic and the heat – and he hoped he could see me before they left. Could he take me out to lunch and/or dinner? Would I take him sight-seeing? He hoped he hadn't missed me already. He was just going off to have a late breakfast in the café I had suggested to him before. If he got to the bottom of his bottomless cup of coffee before I showed up, he would probably smoke a couple of cigarettes before he wandered off and tried to find something else to do. He would be sorry not to see me to say goodbye.

I had woken up that morning with the sad, empty feeling of having done something irrevocable. His letter offered what I thought I wanted: the chance to part as friends.

But it was already past noon, getting close on to one o'clock. I had no idea what time he'd stopped by with the note. Would he still be drinking his coffee, or smoking his cigarettes, or had he given up on me?

I was wearing my usual outfit for a weekend laundry run – ragged cut-offs, a promotional T-shirt, and flip-flops. I thought of going inside to change, at least to put on eye make-up. But what if that five-minute delay meant I missed him? Did it matter what I looked like, even if this would be his last memory of me? After all, I wasn't out to seduce him – quite the opposite.

Deciding that speed was of the essence, I hurried to my car just as I was, threw my bag of dirty clothes into the trunk, and headed for the café.

Being a Sunday, the place was packed. I recognised a

couple of cars belonging to people I knew before I saw him, grinding a cigarette out under his heel and giving me a shy, crooked grin.

'You got my letter. What's the plan?' he said, opening the door on the passenger side.

I drove off as soon as he was buckled in, thinking that it would be just like Fate to have one of Marshall's friends – or maybe the ex-girlfriend who carried a grudge – see me giving a lift to a strange guy, a musician I shouldn't even know.

My plan was to get out of town. 'You said something about sight-seeing. I thought we'd head for the hills. There's a state park, and some cute little towns, markets, a German bakery, good barbecue… I'm just going to stop off at home first to change my shoes.'

'A lot of walking?'

'Could be.' Mostly I wanted my make-up.

Those cute little towns, and the state park, attracted a lot of visitors, especially on the weekends, but it was a very different crowd from the people Marshall and I knew. The last time I'd taken this route I had been with my parents, when they came to visit me during my first year of college.

Going there with him felt strange; it made me feel different, like I was playing a part. I *was* playing a part, and like an actor who can't get to grips with it, I kept wondering, 'What's my motivation?'

Why had I agreed to meet him? Why were we here? Before, at night, it had been like a shared dream. In daylight, part of the crowds strolling around the quaint town square, walking into the pottery, or investigating the dim recesses of a room stuffed with old junk optimistically described as 'Collectibles and Antiques', our being together was all wrong. I tried to think up an explanation, in case I was asked. He could be my cousin from out of state… but not if it got back to Marshall, who knew the names and ages of all my cousins… The safest thing would be to connect it to work. If my boss had asked me to entertain a visitor for her… It was unlikely, but as Marshall knew, she had once asked me to take her mother to a doctor's appointment.

Soon I was treating him as if we'd met for the first time that day. I 'made conversation', asking him about the band, their touring schedule, and he obliged with answers and anecdotes. He tried to take my hand, and I flinched.

We had a late, heavy lunch in an ostentatiously German restaurant, and talked about food, our favourite dishes, the fact that neither of us knew how to cook. Then we talked about recent movies we had seen.

Driving back to the city, the sun going down behind us, we were silent, exhausted by the effort of working through every possible subject for conversation. I noticed, as we drove through the practically deserted back road leading into town, that there was a new development on this western outskirt. In addition to the houses, town-homes and a shopping mall still under construction there was a brand new hotel, towering over the landscape from its hilltop perch, its multitude of windows glittering like faceted gems in the last rays of the sun.

'Turn here,' he said suddenly and I did; off the highway, onto an empty access road which wound around and around and brought us into the parking lot in front of the hotel. Although the building looked finished, and there had been a sign advertising it, I wondered if it was actually open yet, as there were only four cars in the vast concrete expanse of parking lot around it, and no one to be seen. I stopped the car and gave him a quizzical look.

'Why here?'

'From the top floor, we can look down and see the whole world spread out before us.'

I was slow; not getting it, I craned back my head and looked up. 'You think there's a restaurant up there?'

'Let's spend the night together.'

My heart lurched. 'You're going to Houston.'

'They are. I don't have to. I could get on a bus tomorrow… unless you want me to stay. We could have one more night – or forever. What do you say?'

It had taken Marshall three years to decide he wanted to marry me, and this guy, who hadn't even set eyes on me three days ago, was talking about 'forever'.

I didn't say anything. I took my foot off the brake and steered the car around to drive back onto the highway.

He sighed deeply. 'I mean it. I want to spend my life with you. But if that's too much – I know you've got a man, you love him and he loves you, and you'd probably have a better life with him than I could ever give you – he's—'

'Don't you talk about him,' I growled, feeling my face flame.

'I'm sorry. I didn't mean… Of course. It's nothing to do with him.'

'That's right.'

'I was just going to say – if you don't want me for all the time, I'm happy to be your wayfarin' stranger, see you when I'm passing through. If you're lonely—'

'I won't be. And it would be wrong, when I'm married.'

'Okay.'

We went for a little way in silence before he said, 'Can we be friends?'

I wanted to say yes, and I wanted it to be true, but I didn't see how that would work.

'If I came back…'

'Then I'd have to make up some story about how we met. I'd have to lie… I'm not good at that.'

'Leave it to me. I'm good at making up stories. Stories and songs,' he said cheerfully. 'You know, it's just as well we didn't go into that hotel. It had a hungry look about it. I have a feeling that if we went in, we might never have come out again.'

I was happy to let him change the subject, and to listen to something that was not about us. The fanciful story he began to tell turned into a song. I wondered if he was making it up as he went along, like he did with his song for me, although it seemed so much more polished and clever, it must have been something he'd already written. But I think I was the first, and maybe the only person to hear it.

I wish I could remember the words now, or even the tune.

All I can recall is the title – 'The Hungry Hotel' – and that it was somehow both whimsical and sinister, scary and sweet at the same time. But how did it end?

It cheered me up, it wiped out the whole estranging experience of the afternoon and the unhappiness we both felt at what was a necessary, unavoidable final parting, and it also filled most of what remained of our journey, down into the city, and back to the parking lot of the bar where we had first met. There was nothing going on, and only a couple of cars parked out back at that hour on a Sunday evening.

'You sure this is where you want me to leave you?'

'I don't want you to leave me.'

'Stop it.' I was only annoyed with myself for that unfortunate turn of phrase.

He sighed. 'I know you don't want to hear it, but I have to say it—'

We spoke at the same time, our voices overlapping:

'No you don't.'

'I love you.'

Tears started in my eyes. I had to bite my lip not to say it back to him.

One last time we kissed, and then we parted.

A year later he was touring Europe with his new band and I was honeymooning with Marshall in Mexico.

A few years after that, when I was a wife and mother, juggling work and family life, too busy and too happy to have any regrets or even think about the past, I would have forgotten all about him if he hadn't suddenly gotten famous.

Fame is relative, of course; he was already well-known in certain circles, as a performer and a songwriter, and he'd written a couple of hits that had made him rich. I'd sung along to one of them in the car never knowing, or even wondering, who had written it. It was only when he married a real celebrity – the mega-talented, sexy young singer who'd made hits of two of his songs – that his face as well as his name began to appear all over the place.

I saw him on TV very late one night, as I was trying to feed the baby, my dull eyes fixed on the screen where a music video flashed hypnotically. At first I thought I'd fallen asleep and only dreamed it was him I saw playing the keyboards, dancing (badly) with the singer, dressed like Charlie Chaplin, doing the funny, cane-twirling walk as the music swelled and the singer laughed, and finally in a clinch with the beautiful, sexy singer, the camera zooming in on their lips as they kissed.

And after that – he was with his wife on the red carpet at some event; snapped by the paparazzi; bounding onto the stage with a big grin to accept an award; speaking earnestly to a popular talk-show host; his picture in magazines like *Heat* and *People*; on the Internet, popping up, usually with her, whether I wanted to know or not.

I wanted to say that I had known him – that it was me he had picked before he met her. But if I could not tell Marshall (and I couldn't; more than ever, now, I did not dare) I could not tell anyone. It had to stay my secret.

That was probably just as well. Even if I had confessed all to Marshall before we were married, and if he had admitted in turn to some small infidelity of his own, and we had agreed to forgive and forget, and truly had – even if I could now, in good conscience, talk to others about this famous person I'd bedded – well, how could I? What price reflected glory? I was no groupie, to brag about the notches on my bed-post.

Anyway, his stardom was fleeting. The marriage ended; he moved to Berlin to be with his new girlfriend, a designer of bizarre and expensive footwear, and although he continued to write songs and published a book of whimsical short stories, his fame now encompassed a smaller, or at least a different, sphere, and made no impact on the world I lived in.

The club where we had first met was demolished to make way for a towering bank building, and after we moved to

Montana, I no longer drove past it, or the intersection where I'd watched him walk away. Before long, there was nothing to remind me of that particular weekend so long ago.

The kids grew up so fast. It had seemed like a lifetime before they started school, but after that, the years went by like months. And then Jesse went away to college. Sarah was still at home, but it would not be long before she moved out, and then Marshall and I would be left alone, to finally have that long-delayed conversation about our marriage. I knew things were going to change, one way or another.

One day I got a letter.

A letter! Who wrote letters anymore? Sometimes charities would try to fool you with an envelope that looked hand-addressed, but this one really was. My name and address were written in blue ink, in a looping casual hand that was naggingly familiar.

Inside, though, there was no note, no explanation, nothing but a grey plastic card with a magnetic strip on one side and an arrow on the other. A hotel room key, offering no clue as to what room in which hotel it belonged.

I looked again at my name on the front of the envelope, and suddenly remembered the letter left in my apartment door twenty-two years ago, and – and I thought of the hotel on the western edge of the city where he had wanted me to stay with him.

But how had he found me now? We had no friends in common; I didn't think he even knew my married name.

But it should be easy enough to find him. I had not heard anything of him for years, but when I entered his name in a search engine, right below his Wikipedia entry (which read to me as if it had been hacked by a malicious joker) was his own website. It had not been updated in over a year. He did not blog or tweet. The most recent 'news' I could find was a three-year-old interview: he had moved to Brooklyn following his divorce and was writing a novel. I could find no clue to why he should have gone to the trouble to find me.

I returned my attention to the envelope, stretching it open and peering inside, as if somehow I could have missed an enclosure. But the only thing I had missed was the number pencilled in a bottom corner; a number, it now occurred to me, that might be a room number.

In what hotel? Surely not the one we'd stopped outside twenty-two years ago, the one that had inspired a song I might think of as his gift to me, if I could actually remember it. But that was in another state, and besides… he knew where I lived.

The postmark on the envelope was local.

He had sent me his room key.

I was sure of it. I still didn't know why, but the idea that he still thought of me after so long was balm to my soul. And I knew where to find him.

There weren't that many hotels near where I lived. In fact, until recently, I would have said there were none within thirty miles. The area had been still pretty wild and unspoiled when we bought the land to build our house, but since then, the surrounding acres had gradually filled up with houses, and with the expanded population had come restaurants and banks, a big store, a new school, a church, offices and boutiques, and most recently the ground had been broken for an upscale shopping mall. And near the mall-to-be – I had noticed the sign for it just the other day – a hotel.

He was waiting for me there.

How unlikely; but I so wanted it to be true!

Like the impulsive, thoughtless kid I'd been two decades before, when I had imagined the whole universe conspired to bring us together, I responded to his desire. I left without so much as a note to tell my family where I had gone.

I parked near the entrance and went in boldly, hoping to look like a registered guest, clutching my key in case anyone asked, but the woman behind the desk didn't even look up as I marched past to the elevators.

It was only when I stepped out on the top floor that I had second thoughts. I should have called him from the lobby. We'd have lunch. What did I care if the woman at reception, who looked almost young enough to be my daughter, saw us together?

I turned around, but it was too late, the elevator had gone. I pressed the button to recall it. I would start this story over. Maybe I'd meet him in the lobby as he came in from smoking a cigarette – hotel rooms were all no-smoking now. Maybe he'd given up smoking, like everyone else I knew, but even if he didn't want a smoke, he wasn't going to sit alone in a hotel room all day, waiting for someone who might never arrive. I'd ask the receptionist to call his room. If he was in, he would come down. If he was out, I'd leave a note. And if he wasn't here at all, and I had been completely wrong about what the card had meant – I'd go home and forget about it. No one else would ever know.

My stomach growled. Where was that elevator? I strained to hear any sound of it, and stabbed the button several times with no result. I was hungry and impatient. Since I was here, I might as well try the room.

Immediately outside the elevator niche a sign on the wall showed the numbering system and indicated which way to turn. The number I was looking for was on the right, about halfway along the long, curving hallway. I stopped outside the door and listened. The silence was undisturbed. I held my breath and knocked: timidly at first, then more assertively.

Nothing happened.

Then I looked at the brass-colored door handle, set into a brass square with a slot at the top. He had sent me the key so I could let myself in – but suddenly I didn't want to.

What kind of game was this? Sending an anonymous plastic key card did not constitute getting in touch. What made him think that after twenty-two years without a word, he only had to whistle? No, not even whistle; make me guess and seek for him. But what made me think this was his game?

The back of my neck prickled. Was somebody watching me, silently, through the fish-eye lens of the spy-hole?

I hurried away, back to the elevators, and slapped the button, my breath coming fast and anxious. I imagined Marshall waiting behind that closed door, waiting to humiliate me. But even if, somehow, he knew – that was not his style. I imagined a psychotic, murdering stranger, or him, horribly changed.

'Come on, come on!'

But the elevator would not be summoned. How long had I been waiting? I shouldn't even be here. I was wasting time. I charged away down the other curving arm of the corridor, the branch I had not taken. But I saw no sign for Emergency Exit or Stairs, although I went to the very end and then walked slowly back, checking each door as I passed.

There must be a staircase, if only for use in case of fire.

It was surely illegal to erect a multi-story building without fire escapes. Most big hotels had more than one. Yet I found no doors that could be opened without a key, and I couldn't remember seeing any kind of exit sign on the other side, either.

Returning to the elevator niche, looking down the other half of the long, curving corridor, I remembered his song about the hungry hotel, 'built in the shape of a smile'.

I knew then that the elevator was never going to come, no matter how long I waited. I wasn't really surprised to find I couldn't get a signal on my phone. I can take pictures with it, and record this message, but how is that going to help?

Eventually I will have to use the key, because that's the only thing left to try.

Maybe I'm dreaming, and when I use the key, I will wake up. Maybe it will open an ordinary room, with a window looking down onto the parking lot, and a telephone that works. But I don't think this is that kind of dream.

I've been thinking about my childish belief that babies got made by people dreaming together, and I've been thinking about that song he made up for me, and now I seem to be inside it. (I wish I could remember how it ended!)

Maybe we dreamed this hotel together, and maybe the key will open the door to a room where he's waiting for me, and it will be like the one night we spent together, only it will last forever.

Or maybe it will just be the end.

LISA TUTTLE

Lisa Tuttle lived in Austin in the 1970s, in London in the 1980s, and since 1990, has stayed in a remote, rural part of Scotland. Her short stories have won awards and been widely anthologised. Her first novel, *Windhaven*, was written in collaboration with George R.R. Martin, first published in 1981, and has since been translated into many languages and frequently re-printed. Her eighth novel, *The Curious Affair of the Somnambulist and the Psychic Thief*, is a new departure, the first in a series of fantastical mysteries set in the 1890s, and is scheduled for publication in 2016.

LONDON

NICHOLAS ROYLE

Ian is one of those names, isn't it? I know half a dozen Ians. One or two in their thirties, two or three around my age, and a couple well into their seventies. It's one of those names that's neither fashionable, nor unfashionable.

At that time I was working mainly as an editor for a small publisher and I was very aware that editors (and agents) took to social media at their own risk, since it had become one of the best ways for new writers to make their acquaintance. I was being stalked on Twitter by a guy called Ian. Haunted might even be *le mot juste*, and I don't know why I say that, rather than 'the right word', because, as a self-identifying chippy northerner, I have nothing but scorn for people who pepper their newspaper columns and Facebook posts with French and Latin expressions suggesting the kind of relaxed confidence only an Oxbridge education can instil.

Ian, who I guessed would be in his twenties or thirties – his thirties as it turned out – followed me one bright, chilly autumn morning when I was sitting at my improvised desk checking Twitter every five minutes because I couldn't settle to any of the various jobs I was meant to be getting on with. I examined his profile. I liked his photograph. A lilac-tinted head-and-shoulders with severe parting and blurred face, it reminded me of something, but I couldn't think what. In addition, the mini biog attracted me. Like most people who followed me on Twitter in those days, he was writing a novel, but his sounded interesting. He didn't say much about it, but the title – and I was struck by the boldness both of the title itself and of his announcing it in a public medium while the novel was, apparently, still some way off being finished – was *L0ND0N*, with zeroes for Os. I didn't immediately follow him back, but was for some reason prompted to get up from my desk and grab my jacket.

There was a small pile of post on the floor in the hall. I sorted through it. A circular from the council. A couple of fast-food menus. A brown envelope addressed to someone I'd never heard of. A former resident, I presumed. Jane seemed to get a lot of these and hardly any post for herself.

I was staying at my girlfriend's place between Stoke Newington and Dalston. She always said she lived in Stoke Newington, a claim that was backed up by her postcode, but her front door was just five minutes' brisk walk from Dalston Kingsland. I skirted the station and walked west on Balls Pond Road for a few minutes before turning left and then left again into a residential street that would ultimately lead me onto an unusual diagonal back towards Kingsland Road. Jane and I had often walked up and down this street to admire the houses. They had windows that went down almost to the ground, protected by retractable security grilles. We would fantasise about buying one of these houses, a fantasy that required us to believe we had a million and a half in the bank, a million and a half more than we actually had, and then console ourselves that at least we were spared the inconvenience and indignity of living with a retractable security grille.

I walked on down to the canal and then along it for a short stretch and back up the main drag, calling into the supermarket opposite Dalston Kingsland. I found myself standing in the tinned soup aisle holding a basket containing a bunch of spring onions and a lemon. I looked at the Heinz soup cans and thought about Andy Warhol's soup cans, their endless repetition, and realised that I liked these soup cans better than Warhol's, because Warhol's were all the same, whereas these were the same but different – different flavours and, therefore, different text, type and illustrations. I had always liked definitive postage stamps for the same reason – the identical image of the Queen's head, but a different price, a different colour – and immediately I realised why I had liked Ian's profile picture on Twitter: because it reminded me of the Belgian definitive stamps of the 1960s that I had collected as a child, with the repeated picture of the Belgian king in various pastel shades.

When I came out of the supermarket I got my phone out and went on to Twitter and followed Ian back, but then a moment later unfollowed him. It was too soon; I didn't want to appear eager.

I became aware of him keeping an eye on my tweets and interjecting from time to time in some conversation I might be having with a writer or an agent or another editor. He judged those interruptions just right – respectful, but not overly so, confident without appearing arrogant – so that they didn't feel like interruptions. It was exactly the kind of perfectly judged approach that gives the impression of being effortless and is probably far from it. I daresay he spent hours composing those witty rejoinders and cutting remarks, which were never at my expense, of course. (Oh, how well behaved he was in the beginning.) They were minor masterpieces of irony and concision. After one particularly funny, apparently offhand tweet, I followed him back, and his first direct message arrived later that day. I knew what it would say.

The publisher I worked for had posted a line on their website stating clearly that they were closed to submissions. At the time I was receiving at least two emails a day that would begin, *Hi Nick…* My friend, the writer Joe Cross, once told me what he thought of people who began emails with *Hi Joe*. It wasn't people assuming they could call him Joe that bothered him, but the use of *Hi* instead of *Dear*. So, *Hi Nick*, these emails would begin. *I know you're closed to submissions…* But would I make an exception to consider their 100,000-word historical saga? Would I please find time to have a quick look at their dystopian fable? Would I perhaps be able to cast an eye over their series of so-called flash fictions disguised as a novel?

They were remarkably similar, these emails, as if the writers had bought a template from a subscription service or done a module on a creative writing MA about how to charm overworked editors. Mainly they'd had an agent, who had taken them on, raving about their novel, then submitted it to all the major houses, where it had been knocked back, and the writers had then suggested they send it to one of the smaller places, but the agents had said they didn't deal with those places. Of course not; there was nothing in it for them. So, the agents were fired and were probably delighted to be fired and the writers could submit to people like me, only to find we weren't open to submissions, but we'd make an exception, wouldn't we? For them? Even though none of them seemed to have gone to the trouble to assess my taste by checking out the books I had actually acquired.

Ian's approach, via direct messages on Twitter, was different. He was serious, but it was like he didn't really care. I guessed it was a front and he cared a great deal. But the thing was, when he told me a bit about the novel, it was like it had been written just for me. It was about London, he said. That was the first and most important thing. It was also about despair. And it was about holes in the fabric of reality that may or may not exist. And maps, he said. And spies. Spies? Yes, spies, but they weren't that important. OK, I said. I was hooked. The question, for me, then, was could he write? There was only one way to find out. So I said he could email it to me and I'd have a quick look.

A quick look turned into me reading the whole thing in two days. Be suspicious of those people who claim to read entire novels, even short novels, in a single sitting. That's not reading; that's turning the pages. Just as writing a novel in a month isn't writing; it's typing. A couple of chapters in, I started making notes – corrections, editorial suggestions. That was how confident I was I would be telling him I wanted to publish it. It was so good, he was going to have to fuck it up quite badly for me to change my mind. He didn't fuck it up.

Having decided I wanted to publish it, I found myself on edge, not sure if I *should* publish it. I walked around Jane's flat, weighing up the pros and cons. In one corner of her bedroom a glass-eyed mannequin with a red wig balanced on a stand. I called her Jane.

'What do you think, Jane?' I asked her. 'I've never met Ian. His novel is extremely bleak. It's claustrophobic with existential despair and the narrator is deeply unsympathetic.'

I paused.

'No, you're right,' I said. 'I do always insist that characters don't have to be likable, just believable.'

I straightened the mannequin's wig, studying her glassy-eyed stare. She was wearing a summer dress of Jane's, blue, which matched her eyes, unlike Jane's, which were green.

I wasn't questioning my view about the likability or otherwise of characters, but I was concerned about what I might be getting into. A widely held opinion is that it is a mistake to conflate narrator and author, yet a convergence of Ian and his narrator was precisely what I feared.

What if Ian was like his narrator? Did it even matter? Well, yes, I tended to believe it did. Not in general, but in this particular case. I kept a Wankers Shelf – a section of my library reserved for authors so narcissistic they asked their publisher to stick their author photo on the front cover of their book, or they wrote a piece for publication constructed around extracts from their fan mail; for authors so convinced of their own greatness they refused to 'get out of bed for less than a grand' when invited to contribute to an anthology; for authors who were just wankers – wankers to their editors, wankers to their publicists, wankers to booksellers, wankers to their readers. Just wankers.

Was Ian's narrator a wanker? I wasn't sure, but he was the kind of guy who would fuck someone over without a second's thought. He was amoral, but was he immoral? He was almost certainly bipolar or perhaps suffering from a personality disorder, which maybe explained some of his behaviour, but did it excuse it? Was I being a dick by worrying that Ian might be a wanker? That he might be writing about himself? Not that there's anything wrong with that; I do it all the time.

I wandered into Jane's kitchen and stood at the sink for a minute looking across into her neighbours' kitchen. I removed the half-full compostable bag from the waste food caddy and took it outside. On my way back in I picked up the post, dropping the fliers for prayer meetings and club nights and cards for taxi firms straight in the recycling box in the hall. I carried the rest back up to the kitchen and dropped it on the table. I flicked through the letters while the kettle was boiling. Nothing for me, nothing for Jane. Where were these people now, I wondered. Would HMRC and the banks, power companies and credit card companies who sent this stuff carry on doing so, to these people at this address, until someone told them to stop? I poured the tea, but left it cooling on the worktop. I stood at the window in what I called the front room, watching mothers walk past with their children, having collected them from the primary school at the end of the road. I went into the second bedroom, where Jane had encouraged me to set up a work station – the little table that had become my desk and a typing chair rescued from a skip. I came out again. On the chest of drawers on the landing (Jane had cleared the bottom drawer for my use) was an asymmetrical red glass vase about a foot high that happened, right then, to be catching the light from the window. I took my phone out to take a picture of it. While the light continued to favour the vase, I moved it around to find its best position, taking numerous photographs as I did so.

I drifted back to my desk and thought about Ian. When I thought of him now I tended to picture him, because of the link with the Belgian stamps, as looking like King Baudouin. Severe side parting, glasses. Pastel colouring.

I created a new email.

Hi Ian…

I backspaced over that.

Dear Ian…

I deleted that too.

Ian…

I leaned back in my typing chair and took my phone out of my pocket. I opened my photos. The screen filled with thumbnails of the red vase. I touched one to expand it and then navigated through the series, deleting some, keeping others. When I had chosen the one I liked best I emailed it to myself and opened the email on my laptop, then saved the picture to a memory stick. I ejected the memory stick, closed the laptop and removed it from the desk. I had a hiding place for it in Jane's bedroom.

As I knelt down to slide the laptop between the wardrobe and the wall, I looked at Jane in her red wig and blue dress and put my finger to my lips – *Shhh*.

I walked up to the main road and turned right. In among the Turkish restaurants – the artists Gilbert and George ate at a particular one at the same time every night – and the cafés and bars where ownership of a MacBook Pro earned you a seat in the window, I eventually found a print shop and went in. It would take an hour, they said, so I left it with them and walked on down Stoke Newington Road. When I had last frequented the area as a student in the 1980s making repeat visits to the Rio cinema, it had felt like the edge of nowhere, half deserted, forgotten; in the last few years young men with RAF moustaches and full beards, dressed in plus fours and waistcoats, had started to appear. Just as they had in the 1980s, many of the women wore boilersuits, but now they were made of cotton drill, not polyester, and they were paint-spattered. You were as likely to hear French as Turkish or Jamaican-accented English. Late in the evening, young people from all over London stood in long lines outside anonymous doorways leading down to basement clubs.

An hour later I was back in Jane's kitchen unpacking beer from Dalston Wines and vegetables from the market. I also had a ten-by-eight colour print of the red vase and a cheap clip frame from the print shop. I located Jane's hammer and a nail and I hung the framed photograph on the wall above the chest of drawers on the landing, in other words behind the red vase itself. I don't know if you can picture that: a picture of a thing, *in situ*, behind the thing itself. Not *right* behind it, so it couldn't be seen, but up on the wall above and behind it.

I didn't tell Jane about it, preferring to wait and see how long it would take her to notice it. She came home that night and didn't immediately spot it. I poured her a glass of wine and suggested she relax in the front room while I served up dinner.

'If you mean the sitting room...' she said.

As I was coming through with the food, I saw that Jane had got up from the sofa and was looking at herself in the mirror over the fireplace with rapt attention. I waited in the doorway, partly concealed, and watched her pull and prod at the skin under her chin, which she habitually described to me as her 'turkey neck'. I always told her I didn't know what she was talking about, and I didn't. She had beautiful skin, unlined, just like that of the mannequin, but she worried disproportionately about the appearance of signs of ageing.

I didn't care about looking my age. I cared instead, not about getting older as such, but about its ultimate consequence. Death was not so far away and getting closer. It wasn't so much the inevitability of it, at some point in the future, as the possibility of an early death, especially a preventable one, so I maintained a constant vigil for danger signs. I couldn't bear the thought that death might make a fool of me, creeping up on me when I had my back turned.

So that Jane wouldn't think I was doing exactly that to her, I cleared my throat to announce my presence. I looked down at the bowls I was carrying, but not before I noticed her fingers move quickly up to her face to brush away some imaginary crumb of mascara.

Who in their early fifties hasn't known loss? I had lost my father, Jane her mother, who had died very young from a progressive disease when Jane had been barely out of her teens. I sometimes wondered if Jane's preoccupation with ageing was part of a specific worry about the same or a similar progressive, incurable condition. She had watched her mother deteriorate, at first slowly, over several years, then rapidly. What worried me was what she might do if she actually found the evidence she was looking for.

'This looks delicious, darling,' she said as I handed her one of the bowls.

We ate in comfortable silence.

More alarming perhaps was the loss of friends. Breast cancer had taken one of Jane's oldest friends. A brain tumour had curtailed the life of a friend of mine, but she had already been terminally ill when I had made her acquaintance, which had somehow, in retrospect at least, made it easier to bear, as a loss, as if it had been written into the T&Cs of the friendship from the start.

Jane took the dirty bowls through to the kitchen and returned with dessert, twice passing the chest of drawers on the landing. If hanging the picture of the red vase behind the red vase was an experiment, it was not one concerned with measuring Jane's powers of observation, but one more to do with the phenomenon of doubling, of repetition. I wondered if there might be circumstances in which we fail to notice a picture within a picture, or a story within a story.

'What shall we cook for Joe?' Jane asked me.

As I gazed blankly into the deep-sea green of Jane's eyes, I experienced a sickening sensation as if I was falling into some kind of abyss. I pressed my hand on the arm of the sofa as if to steady myself.

'What's the matter, darling?' I heard Jane's voice asking me.

'I don't know,' I said. 'I mean, I'd forgotten Joe was coming.'

'That's all right, isn't it? You must have asked him.'

Joe Cross and I had been friends for twenty years. We met after I wrote to him about his stories, which were always the same but different, by which I mean they were always recognisably his and they were always not only set in London but very much about London, although each one told a different story with different characters. Well, characters with different names, but a lot of them were a lot like Joe. And the stories tended to feature similarly weird stuff that happened to characters like him. He was my kind of writer, using a lot of real experience, then twisting his material so you didn't really know where his story ended and his narrator's began.

When a small press had offered to publish Joe's first novel, I said we needed to get him an author photograph sorted out. We went for long walks around the East End and in Docklands and along the river, touring his locations, trying to get a decent picture. The trouble was he always looked like he was being shot by firing squad rather than by me, with a camera. He stood as straight as a post, hands by his sides.

'I don't know what we should cook for him,' I said to Jane. 'It's funny I've never had him round to eat wherever I've been living – or staying.'

I glanced at Jane and she smiled at me. She asked what Joe and I tended to have when we ate out, which we didn't do that often, and I said curry, down Brick Lane and around there, so that was that.

Later that night I emailed Ian to tell him I wanted to publish his novel.

When Joe arrived, I was in the kitchen at a crucial stage. I heard Jane let him in and take him straight into the front room. I turned down the heat, grabbed drinks and glasses and made my way through.

'You two have met, haven't you?' I said, once I'd said hello to Joe.

'Several times,' Jane said, rolling her eyes, 'and you say that every time.'

'I know,' I said, smiling at Joe, who chuckled obligingly.

I glanced at the mannequin, which had been moved into the front room and was standing in the corner, still wearing the blue dress and the red wig.

After we'd been chatting for a few minutes, I said the food would be about ready and Joe asked for the bathroom. Jane told him where it was and I watched as he left the room, his body briefly framed in the doorway. His head was as distinctive from the back as from any other angle. He'd worn a short back and sides since the eighties, the kind of short you can only get with clippers, either your own or the barber's, and his skull stuck out above the neck, creating a somewhat pronounced overhang.

When he returned, he looked at each of us in turn and I noticed that his hairline – he'd always kept his hair longer at the front, not quite Stray Cats style but getting there – had perhaps receded a little since I had last seen him. 'Love the vase,' he said.

Jane looked momentarily puzzled, then smiled. 'Thank you! It's just an old thing I got... I can't remember where I got it.'

Joe turned to me, frowning. I looked between him and Jane.

'He means...' I started to say, but tailed off.

'I mean what you've done with it. Classic *mise en abîme*.'

Jane wore an air of bafflement.

'Thanks,' I said, beginning to regret my initiative.

'I'm so sorry, Joe,' Jane said, accessing another level of politeness as she tended to do if she felt herself backed into a corner. 'I'm not quite following. I wonder if it might be because of some clever thing Nick has done, maybe?' This with a little pointed look at me.

'I'd better go and serve up,' I said.

As I left, I heard Joe start to explain the term *mise en abîme* and Jane step out on to the landing to take a look at the vase.

'How could I have missed that?' she said, then, louder and with a slight edge: 'I wonder why Nick didn't tell me?'

We ate around the coffee table, scooping up chicken chana and Bombay aloo with poppadoms and naan bread.

'So, how long has that picture been there?' Jane asked.

'Only since yesterday.'

'I don't know how I could have missed it. You should have told me!' she said, digging me playfully in the ribs. Well, playfully enough to give Joe the impression it was playful.

'So,' Joe said, looking up at me from his clean plate and clearly keen to change the subject, 'how're things with you?'

'Good,' I said. 'I've just taken on this really great novel. It's a first novel but the author doesn't want me to describe it as a debut. He's from the north, but doesn't want to be categorised as a northern writer. Keeps changing his mind about his date of birth.'

'Sounds like hard work,' said Jane.

'It should be worth it,' I said.

'What's it about?' Joe asked.

'London. Holes in the fabric of reality. A crisis. A personal crisis. Also espionage, but that's kind of in the background. And maps. Lots of stuff about maps.'

'Another one for the Richard and Judy Book Club,' Jane said, straight-faced.

I reached over and wiped her plate with my last bit of naan.

'Hey!'

'More drinks?' I suggested, standing up.

I returned with two more beers and the rest of the bottle of wine. They were talking about Joe's high blood pressure.

'I suppose I could cut down,' he was saying, 'but it's not like I drink that much anyway.'

'Shall I take this away again?' I said, withdrawing the beer I had been about to offer him.

'Ha ha, no. Give it here.'

'Good health,' I said and we clinked bottles.

When Joe had left, we carried the dirty pots through to the kitchen.

'I'll do this. You relax,' I said.

'It's my place. I should clean up,' Jane said.

We worked together in silence for a few minutes. Jane washed a pan and stood it upside down on the draining board. I picked it up to dry it.

'You can leave things to drain,' she said.

'Actually...' I began, reaching for a piece of kitchen towel and wiping some dirt from the inside of the pan. I was aware of both wanting Jane to know she had left the pan dirty and not wanting her to know at the same time.

She stopped what she was doing and turned her sharpest gaze on me. I carried on wiping at the inside of the pan. The residue was stuck on and more effort was required. I reached for another piece of kitchen towel and Jane grabbed at the paper unspooling between my hand and the roll, tearing it, then moving the roll away from me, taking hold of the pan in my hands, but I didn't let go, so that we briefly engaged in a tug-of-war. Eventually I surrendered and she dropped the pan back in the sink whence came the barely discernible but unmistakably muffled sound of glass breaking under water.

We both stared at the dirty water.

'Shit,' I said. 'Sorry. That's my fault.'

'It doesn't matter,' she said, turning her face to the window. In the neighbours' kitchen across the way, a woman finished cleaning a saucepan and passed it to the man by her side, who took it off her and started to dry it. 'They're old glasses.'

'But I seem to break one a week.'

'Never mind.'

We both stood for a moment, as still as dummies, staring at the neighbours as they peacefully shared the washing-up.

'Look,' I said, 'I'm sorry I didn't tell you about that picture. Or even ask you. I should have asked you, never mind told you.'

'It's not a big deal,' she said.

I wanted to ask if it wasn't a big deal why it had started to seem like it was.

On a bright, cloudless afternoon, I arrived by train at a small town in Surrey best known for its famous boarding school. Although I had never been there before and there was no immediate sign of the school outside the station, I started walking and just when I was starting to think I might have gone the wrong way, I rounded a bend and there on my left was a Victorian fantasia of Gothic towers, spires and gargoyles in light-hued sandstone that glowed with surprising warmth on a cold day.

A teacher from the English department, Mr Wakeling, met me and took me to the library and thence to a high-ceilinged room with dark wood panelling and tables arranged in a square. At three sides of this square sat two dozen smart-looking pupils who were perhaps 14 or 15. Mr Wakeling introduced me, reminding them that after the workshop they would need to gather in the Mary Olive Room, where he would be introducing the writers of the shortlisted entries in the ghost story competition that I had judged for the school and I would be announcing the winner.

After Mr Wakeling's departure I asked the youngsters a few questions and discovered that two of the shortlisted writers were in the room, but that all would be present in the Mary Olive Room for the readings later. Once I had them working on an exercise, I opened my laptop. That morning I had been back on Ian's novel, having had to work on other projects for a couple of weeks. I had reached the point where the narrator, Whitehead (we never learn his first name, only that it begins with R), confesses to having sexual fantasies about a teenager he sees at dog-training classes. I say 'confesses', but in Ian's novel there's no sense of confession about it. It's just another detail in the narrator's sordid and depressing life. Sordid and depressing in a way, but utterly compelling for the reader. This was the striking thing about Ian's novel – the material was unpleasant, but you didn't want to stop reading, partly, perhaps, because of the absence of a moral dimension.

I had made a note to ask Ian if he wanted to specify the age of the teenager, to make it at least legal, were the narrator to have sex with her, but as I went on I realised that he wanted it to be uncertain. The uncertainty was part of it.

I looked up from my screen at the pupils in the room. A mix of boys and girls, they were about the age I imagined the teenager in Ian's novel to be.

When you attend conventions for writers and editors and agents and illustrators – and fans – and you sit on a panel discussing topics from the world of literature, one question crops up with predictable regularity: 'Is there anything you wouldn't write?' As in – are there any taboos? What is taboo for you? For me the suggestion of sex with kids is somewhere I wouldn't go as a writer, but for some reason I had been quite happy to go there as an editor.

Noticing that most of the young people around the room had stopped writing, I announced that there were just two minutes remaining and then we would move on to the next part of the exercise.

The Mary Olive Room was an intimate space in dark wood, with two baronial-style high-backed wooden chairs (I was invited to sit in one) facing several rows of folding chairs. These were occupied by boys, girls and members of staff, more of whom stood at the back and along the sides. This was the kind of event that, when I had been starting out, would have had me on edge for days prior to its taking place.

Having noticed that five of the shortlisted entrants were Year 9 boys and one was a Year 13 girl, I had suggested to Mr Wakeling that it might be an idea to give two prizes, since one would expect a seventeen-year-old girl to write better than boys four years her junior. In the event we gave a prize for the most effective ghost story and a prize for the most original story. I talked about all the stories and heard myself going on and on, as I invariably do, going into too much detail, getting sidetracked, looping back on myself, making little jokes that didn't quite come off, which staff laughed at out of politeness. I even heard myself start to talk, for some tangential reason, about Ian's novel, and as I did I realised I hadn't yet taken care of one of the most important jobs in the whole process, which was to find someone to do a cover quote. I didn't know what made me think of that at that moment, but think of it I did. I moved the subject back to more relevant matters and, probably rather abruptly after such a rambling speech, wound things up.

The event was over. The librarian offered to drop me off at the station and I accepted. It was an extremely cold evening and I wanted to get back to London as soon as possible, raising the likelihood of a late dinner with Jane.

As I stepped on to the station and started walking towards the subway that would take me to the platform from where the London train would depart I felt a vibration in my pocket. I reached for my phone and saw that I was being called by Steve, a close friend, with whom I would normally communicate by email or text, so I was surprised, but I didn't immediately think of bad news. I answered the call and Steve said hello and asked how I was and then asked if I had heard about Joe. He hadn't wanted me to hear about it on Facebook, he said.

I thought later about the difficulty Steve must have faced making that call and perhaps other similar ones to other mutual friends. At what stage would he have said what it was he had called to say? Whenever he said it, it would have been too early in the conversation. It was such an absurd thing to say, delaying by another two or three sentences would not have made it more reasonable, would not have lessened in any way the effect of it. *Joe is dead.* Was that what he said? Probably not. Certainly not. *Joe died.* More likely. It seems to suggest some agency of Joe's. He wasn't just dead; he died. It's OK. *Joe died last night.* Or: *Joe died in the night.* No, he was telling me this in the evening of the following day. *In the night* wouldn't have made sense. The night had been too long gone. *Joe died in the night last night.* Too many nights. Keep it simple. *Joe died last night. Joe died.* Maybe, after all: *Joe is dead.*

How do you end a call like that? How do you have the balls to make it in the first place? Do you have all the necessary information? You call someone and tell them that, they're going to be thrown by what you tell them. They're going to ask questions. You're going to be expected to have answers.

I walked around the platform in tight little circles as I asked Steve the questions to which he had no answers. I told him when I'd last seen Joe and he told me when he had last seen him. We talked about strokes, heart attacks, sudden death syndrome. Neither of us mentioned suicide, not because we didn't have the guts, but because we both knew, we just knew, it wasn't, it couldn't be, the truth. At some point during the conversation I checked the train times on a screen above my head and saw that I had fifteen minutes before the next train to London. Enough time to conclude this call, surely? Did I really think that? I knew I didn't want to have this conversation on a train. I knew also that I wanted to stay on this platform – the wrong platform – until the call was over, in case entering the subway caused me to lose the signal.

Somehow we did end the call and I walked towards the

subway. I still had five minutes before the train. Joe had sometimes written about trains and stations. He had never driven, so he had relied on trains. Tube trains, the Overground, suburban lines. As I started walking down the steps to the subway that would take me under the tracks, I noticed the details of the wall ahead of me at the bottom of the steps. Something compelled me to study the wall, as if it held a clue to how I felt at that moment, as if it would help me to make sense of what I had been told. The colours – silver, orange, white, green – and textures both dry and damp. The white wall and the patches of green moss and mould. The rust-coloured traces of running water. The orange hand rails, which matched the frame surrounding a fish-eye mirror mounted in the corner, a useful view of which was denied to anyone descending the steps, such as myself, by a strange electrical box attached to the adjacent wall. The single grey cable running out of the top of this box and into a steel cable concealer that ran across the top of the two adjacent walls, then turned through ninety degrees to drop vertically until it reached a level where it could turn through ninety degrees again and run into the section of the subway that passed under the tracks.

Go ahead. Skim. I'm just telling you what I saw. It might be important. It might not.

I hurried through this part of the subway, dodging the water that dripped from the ceiling. The walls were spoilt in many places, render coming away in leprous patches as if something was trying to force a way through. When I reached the other end and climbed the steps to the platform, the train was arriving. I waited for it to come to a stop. The doors opened to let passengers off. I boarded and walked through to the end of the carriage. I looked at the narrow shape made by the interconnecting passageway, the width of a man, and I had a sudden flickering image of Joe standing in that frame with his back to me, like the view I'd had of him leaving Jane's front room a few short weeks earlier. I hadn't seen him since. I hadn't even spoken to him on the phone. Had we emailed? I wasn't sure. Was it possible he had emailed me and I hadn't replied? It was possible. I found a seat and took out my phone and accessed my mail, trying to find the last email I had received from Joe, but I often had difficulty finding particular emails on my phone. I tried the sent box to see if I could find the last one from me to him, but I couldn't find any of those either, and within a couple of minutes of pulling out of the station my signal had vanished. Either I turned my face towards the window and saw myself staring in at me from the country dark or I looked forward to the narrow frame of the interconnecting passageway. I didn't want to look forward to that. I *didn't* look forward to that. The shape of it. The narrowness. When the signal returned I texted Jane and at Waterloo she was there to meet me. We went to a restaurant close by where we had had good times, but for all the kindness she showed me and the support she offered me it didn't feel right. I didn't know what we were supposed to do or how I was supposed to act.

I tried to avoid Facebook for the first two days and work solidly on my editing of Ian's novel. I was behind anyway. The publisher needed the manuscript for typesetting in a few days and I was still on chapter two of my second go round. His chapters were quite long and I had no notes on the first two chapters from my first reading. That was my excuse. Plus, although I was steering clear of the Internet, I checked emails as they came in and I answered any about Joe, including one from the editor of a magazine, who asked me to write a piece about him. The fact was I wanted to know what had happened. We all did, all Joe's friends.

Towards midday I headed out to get something for lunch. At Dalston Kingsland I considered my options, detecting a whiff of something sweet and hot from the market across the road. As I was crossing at the lights, the turn of a head caught my eye. Razored back and sides, pronounced overhang of the back of the skull. He disappeared into the market and I changed direction without checking to see if anything was coming. A bike swerved around me, its rider trying to blow his whistle at the same time as giving me a mouthful of abuse. By the time I looked back towards the market, Joe had disappeared.

I went in the shopping centre and entered the supermarket and immediately forgot what I had gone in for, so I wandered, waiting for it to come back to me. I ended up, like Freud's man in a strange city always winding up in the red light district, in the tinned soup aisle.

Back at Jane's, I opened the front door and stepped on the post. I picked it up without checking the envelopes and dropped it all in the recycling box. In the kitchen I emptied a can of Heinz Vegetable Soup into a saucepan, adding black pepper and Worcester sauce and chilli flakes and curry powder as it cooked. I poured the soup into a bowl, dumped the pan in the sink and ate at my desk while staring at Ian's novel and thinking about Joe. Those thoughts just kept coming back to the same one: that it didn't make sense, it wasn't actually believable, it was too baffling. Maybe that's three thoughts, but they all felt like one to me. It was as if life was a story and the author had fucked up with a plotline that didn't quite work, that prevented the suspension of disbelief.

Halfway through the afternoon I emailed Ian. A puzzle I had enjoyed on my first pass through the novel, but hadn't tried too hard to figure out, now seemed to need addressing. I had hoped that on my second reading I would decide the mystery could remain unsolved. An espionage subplot revolved around a fake map-making company called Geographia that operated out of several addresses up and down Fleet Street.

Geographia was a real company, I wrote to him. *It actually did have offices, at various times, at numbers 55, 63, 111 and 167 Fleet Street. I'm not sure I understand why – or how – you're using this stuff. Is it important?*

I sent the email before I could delete it. I could imagine Ian objecting to it, perhaps just to the last question, to the use of the word 'important'.

I closed the laptop, telling myself I needed to wait for Ian's response before I could carry on. In Jane's bedroom, after hiding the laptop and glancing at the mannequin and noticing that she was wearing a different dress, a grey one from Phase Eight that I remembered buying, I looked at the books on her shelves, then wished I hadn't. I pulled out a copy of Joe's second novel, which I had lent to Jane. I opened it to the title page and saw that Joe had signed it to me.

With thanks for your help and support. All the best xxx

That slightly uncertain sign-off – *All the best* – followed by three kisses. I had to sit down on the edge of Jane's bed. I stared at the book in my hands and then lifted my head. My gaze met Jane's for a moment before I looked away.

* * *

Ian didn't reply that day, or the next. I put a mental bookmark in place and carried on editing. I also finally looked at Facebook and lost an entire afternoon. I read every post and every comment. I noticed how many people had posted and who had posted and how many likes they had. I didn't want to post, because I didn't want to feel I was entering into some competition to reveal the closest connection to Joe or the greatest sense of loss, or to win the most likes. I generally felt uncomfortable reading people's posts about the loss of their parents, or their dog (actually, I didn't read those ones. Fuck them and their self-pity and fuck their dogs), and never commented. Had my father died twenty years later, there was no way I would have posted on Facebook about it. It was a matter of taste. And judgment. But I wasn't judging the mutual friends who had written about Joe, and it was inevitable that I would follow suit, albeit awkwardly. So I wrote something quickly and quit the browser because the last thing I wanted to see was somebody liking it.

Walking by the canal in Hackney had become neither relaxing nor an opportunity to think things through, but I was determined not to be crowded off the tow path by the constant stream of bikes, runners and walkers two-abreast. There should still be room for the determined *flâneur*. Approaching Broadway Market I could see people crossing the bridge over the canal and among them I caught a glimpse of a man with a bit of a receding quiff and hair shaved up the side of his head. Then someone passed in front of him and when they had gone, he had gone also, or he had become invisible from my vantage point. To leave the canal at that point you had to double back up a ramp fifteen or twenty yards and then turn back through 180 degrees. I ran up the ramp, but by the time I got to street level, Joe – or the man who looked like Joe – was lost in the crowds of early-evening strollers and post-work drinkers gathering, in spite of the winter chill, outside the many pubs.

I poked my head around doorways and into the fringes of loitering groups – outside restaurants, spilling out of the off-licence, drawn to a roast chestnut seller. Just when I was about to give up I saw a familiar-shaped head moving away from me between a dog walker and a man pushing a bike down a side street towards the bus garage.

'Ian,' I shouted, but he didn't turn round.

I ran a few steps and he started to turn at the sound of my pursuit. This man's hair was short all over. Not even the suggestion of a quiff. He squared up to me.

I stopped short. 'I'm sorry,' I said. 'I thought you were my friend Joe.'

'Make your fucking mind up,' he said. 'You said Ian.'

'Did I?' I said.

'Yeah.'

'I'm sorry. I meant Joe. You're not Joe. You look like my friend Joe. Or you do from the back. I'm sorry. Look, I made a mistake.'

The man curled his lip, baring tiny teeth, and shook his head, dismissing me.

I saw my hand reach out and touch his shoulder.

'Fuck off, mate,' he said, more casually now, yet I felt his shoulder tense under my touch and my arm fell to my side.

'I'm sorry,' I said again.

His eyes flashed. 'Look, mate,' he said, leaning in close and lowering his voice in a way that made it more threatening. He smelled of smoke and something sweet. 'You don't exist and your boyfriend doesn't exist.' Then he placed both hands on my chest, pushed me backwards with surprising force and walked away.

I got to my feet and watched him go, shock and adrenaline making me unsteady.

Ian had finally replied to my email earlier that day, cryptically, his email containing no message but a link to an article about disagreements between Raymond Carver and his editor Gordon Lish. The lack of a message allowed me to make my own inference, which seemed pretty clear. Carver had thought Lish too interfering. Ian wanted me to lay off his prose, stop trying to tie up his loose ends.

They were all within a couple of minutes' walk of each other, the four former Fleet Street addresses of Geographia Limited. First I found No.167, a large, anonymous-looking office block on the north side of the street, home to numerous businesses of various types. Addresses on Fleet Street are numbered sequentially, eschewing the convention of odds and evens occupying different sides of the street. Right across the street from No.167 were Nos.55 and 63, the former an upmarket pawnbroker with a downmarket email address printed on its fascia (when I checked this on the Internet it transferred to a somewhat smarter-looking jewellery business based in Colchester) and the latter an optician's. Less than a minute's walk east, and back on the north side, was No.111, or where No.111 should have been. A grand doorway topped with a frieze depicting a pair of cherubs either side of a garlanded globe and carved figures – 110/111 – was now filled with a picture window belonging to an espresso bar. To the right of this was a chain sandwich shop that the Internet told me occupied No.109, while on the left of 110/111 was a branch of a Japanese restaurant chain confusingly also resident at No.109, again according to my research. The espresso bar, meanwhile, located between the sandwich place and the Japanese chain, was, supposedly, No.110.

All of which, unsatisfactory and contradictory as it was, assuming either EAT had eaten Wagamama or vice versa, giving them the right to share an address, left No.111 still unaccounted for.

To the right of EAT, I'd already checked, was Vision Express at No.108. Clearly, on that side, then, the numbers were counting down in the right order.

I rested my back against a narrow section of wall between two mobile phone shops on the south side of the street and checked my email. Still nothing useful from Ian.

I tried a different approach and searched the Internet for 111 Fleet Street. The answer, when it came, was mundane: serviced offices. But the north side remained a puzzle. Between Wagamama and Boots, at No.120, there was an alleyway, Poppins Court, blocked off with three bollards. So where was No.111? Not to mention Nos.112 to 119.

My phone buzzed faintly in my pocket. A red blob had appeared on the Mail icon. I tapped the icon. An email from Ian. I felt a tightening of my scalp, tiny hairs rising on the back of my neck. I opened the inbox and tapped his incoming email, which said, simply but totally mystifyingly:

DL-CCC

I stared at my phone, trying to make sense of Ian's message. In a daze I raised my head and looked straight in front of me. People streamed past in both directions, a blur of colour and a murmur of countless conversations leaking smells of burgers and sandwich fillings and astringent perfumes and cigarettes and Lynx and exhaust fumes and drifting from somewhere nearby the sweet aroma of roasting chestnuts. It seemed impossible to me that I should be able to see through all of this and all the red buses and black cabs and white vans and all the cycle couriers and motorbikes and the corresponding streams of people on the far side of the street to make out that distinctive shape of the back of the head ducking into Poppins Court and walking north away from me.

The human sea parted and I stepped into the road.

The medics told me I was lucky – no shit – and the police said that witnesses had reported hearing the cyclist blow a short blast on a whistle. Yes, my ears pricked up at that, too. Some cyclists use whistles, like a horn, but not that many. The cyclist hadn't stopped. Well, he'd stopped – I'd stopped him – but he got back on again and rode off. The police said they hoped looking for a damaged bike would make it easier to catch him, but I decided they were either being kind or taking the piss.

Somehow I had managed not to break anything. Even my phone just had a little crack across the lens of the camera.

But there were lacerations, a dislocated shoulder and the possibility of concussion. I was kept in for observation. A psych report was mentioned. I asked if that was because I'd insisted I'd seen angels, because all I'd meant was the cherubs, which were the last thing I remembered seeing, upside down, as I recall, before everything went dark. They said it was because I had walked straight out in front of a bus. The bus had been a couple of cars' length away, but still.

I asked them to contact Jane, but they couldn't get hold of her. They said the number was dead. I said I needed my work, and could someone go to my girlfriend's place and pick up my laptop. They said they might be able to rustle up an iPhone charger.

I emailed Ian and suggested we meet. I told him where to find me. I didn't expect a reply and I didn't get one.

I used my newly charged phone to look into Geographia a bit more and came across a forum for collectors and map enthusiasts on which a user had posted a question about an undated map and one of the replies had explained that, if Geographia dated their maps at all, they did so in code. The code required you to number the letters in CUMBERLAND from one to ten. So, if you saw, for instance, M.RM in the bottom left corner it meant March 1963.

This got me thinking – I had a lot of time for thinking – and I looked again at the email from Ian that I'd been puzzling over just before I'd stepped into the road.

DL-CCC

I checked that out and decided Ian probably hadn't been alerting me to the existence of the Detroit Lakes Community & Cultural Center.

Instead, applying the CUMBERLAND code in reverse produced 107–111 and when I looked up 107–111 Fleet Street, I discovered that the serviced offices at No.111 were actually serviced offices at Nos.107–111, and I knew without looking that there would be a perfectly ordinary-looking entrance to these at No.107.

The other thing I found out using my phone was that Joe had died from a subarachnoid haemorrhage. The kind of random event you can't anticipate.

There was a lot of post in the hall at Jane's. Some of it became squashed against the wall when I opened the front door. The flat was cold and the milk in the fridge had gone off. I whacked the boiler on and made some green tea.

I retrieved my laptop from the bedroom, pausing a moment to check Jane out. She was still wearing the grey dress from Phase Eight. The wig was slightly askew – again. I straightened it and smiled at her.

I opened Jane's wardrobe. Everything looked normal. The upper drawers in the chest of drawers on the landing were still full of tops and tights and underwear.

I'd lost a lot of time. I worked on the edit. When I felt a headache coming on I took a handful of pills and kept going. I left all Ian's mysteries unresolved and, in the spirit of cartographers who introduce deliberate errors into their maps to catch out plagiarists, I allowed three different spellings for one particular term – ghost writer, ghost-writer and, finally, the correct term, ghostwriter.

I emailed the edited manuscript to the publisher and they got back to me within five minutes, asking if I would be long with the cover copy. I sent them the blurb I'd written some weeks earlier and had been waiting for Ian to approve. Fuck him.

They got back to me again. *Just waiting for a cover quote now,* they said.

I sent them the following: '*This ghostly tale of death, desire and delusion will keep you guessing right to the end – and beyond*' *– Joe Cross.*

I closed the laptop and got up and stretched, which was a bad idea. My shoulder was still painful. The pipes and radiators were making encouraging noises, but the flat didn't seem to be getting any warmer. I tried Jane's number, but couldn't even get it to ring. I went down to the hall and scooped up all the post and carried it back upstairs. I took it into Jane's bedroom and dropped it on one side of the bed. I lay down on the other.

I turned on to my side and propped myself up on an elbow.

'I think it's just you and me now, Jane,' I said.

Her glass eyes glinted in the light from the window.

'Maybe,' I said. 'Maybe you're right.'

I shuffled through the post. Letters for dead men.

'Maybe there'll be something here for me,' I said.

NICHOLAS ROYLE

Nicholas Royle is the author of *First Novel*, as well as six earlier novels including *The Director's Cut* and *Antwerp*, and a short story collection, *Mortality*. In addition he has published more than a hundred short stories. He has edited nineteen anthologies and is series editor of *Best British Short Stories* (Salt). A senior lecturer in creative writing at MMU, he also runs Nightjar Press, which publishes new short stories as signed, limited-edition chapbooks, and is an editor at Salt Publishing.

'Like most of my stories, it's eighty percent true, and the difficulty for me – hopefully the fun for the reader – is working out which is the twenty percent that's made up. It's not always, or even often, the strangest part.'

CHANGE MANAGEMENT

ANGELA SLATTER

'Mail Redistribution Centre' was what Eva was supposed to call it now. She hated the way it looked on the labels she printed out in the back office. 'Change is the only constant,' her father liked to intone on those rare occasions when he decided wisdom was necessary. On those rare occasions when he was home.

Eva preferred the old name.

'Dead Letter Office' seemed more exciting, poetic, essential. As if she was dealing with artefacts, fossils, things that had once pulsed with the energy of their allotted task: to carry messages from one person to another. And she was a link in the chain that took care of them, even if only a little link. A caretaker, a pathologist, trying to work out why they'd failed to do their job, if any got a second chance (perhaps a number transposed, a missed connection with an address redirection, unpaid postage), silly little things that might be easily remedied if she did a little investigation. Mr Burstock kept pointing out it wasn't her job: 'Just send 'em to the specialists.'

Anything she had to send to the Belfast MRC made her feel defeated; that she was an undertaker because she couldn't be anything else. It always felt like failure, but she'd learned to live with it. Sometimes there was simply nothing to be done.

Change was the only constant, yes, but it didn't mean she had to like it. Since the restructure, though, she still spent a chunk of her day in the same building, swiping in with the same keycard in the same slot as she had for ten years, so much was different. The biggest, and worst, of those adjustments was Mr Burstock, brought in two months ago to replace Mrs Arrowsmith, the old supervisor, hired to rationalise things.

Eva was fairly sure rationalising things didn't include his coming to her desk twice a day, sometimes more, to lean over so close his chest touched the back of her head and shifted the soft brown curls about. It didn't include touching her hand or shoulder or knee every chance he got (when they were alone, always alone). It certainly didn't include asking her to come for a drink at the end of each day. She told him, every time, that she didn't drink, which was true. When he persisted she said she had to be home on time to relieve the carer who looked after her infirm mother.

It didn't stop him asking.

It wasn't quite a lie. It wouldn't have been three years ago when Beth was still alive, but no one who worked with her knew that her mother had died. The crotchety old woman remained Eva's go-to excuse when she wanted to get out of anything social with her work colleagues.

She was, as far as they were concerned, a solitary little mouse; lived with her mother, did her job well, troubled no one, although she could be a little obdurate on the matter of dead letters. They were uninterested in her, thought they had her pegged. No one knew how stubborn she'd had to be in order to remain at work when Beth became bedridden, bitching and moaning about the carer, demanding to know why Eva wasn't looking after her.

Beth had had every expectation, based on long history, that Eva would give in to her. Eva hadn't gone to university but found a job instead. She'd not accepted Teddy's invitation to the final year prom, but stayed safely home. She'd cut her hair short as instructed so it wouldn't get caught in the vacuum cleaner filter. Eva had crumbled in every battle of wills – except this one. She'd firmly refused to give up work, defiantly hiring a home nurse who took Beth's insults and complaints with a smile and an extra five pounds an hour.

It had been a matter of intense pride to Eva that she'd held her ground. She kept her job, got out of the house just enough to stay sane, to not put a pillow over her mother's face while the bitter old woman slept – at least not until the very end. It meant she got to stay with the poor dead letters, the failures, the missives and parcels that were never quite good enough. The things she understood, the things with which she felt a kinship.

It gave her the chance to be among people without being one of them. Pretty Alice on the front desk who flirted with Scott, the delivery driver, while her fiancé, Huw, was out back unloading the trucks, hefting the heavier things into piles and stacks that Megan and Toby and Lou would sort through later. They'd bring the smaller items to Eva's hidey hole, give her a smile, ask 'All right, Evie?' and she'd nod and never say, *I hate being called Evie, that's what my father called me when he did terrible things.* She thought it, she felt it, but she didn't say it.

And that had been enough for a long time, until change came.

She looked at the flexi-box on the bench and began to flick through the top layer of its contents: a padded bag with no postage; a mid-sized parcel with the address label half gone; a plain C6 envelope marred by disapproving red lettering. NOT KNOWN AT THIS ADDRESS on the front. RETURN TO SENDER on the back. In black (but equally disapproving) POSTAGE UNPAID, with lines drawn through the address: Jonathan Oaks, 12 Lodge Lane, Seaton, Branscombe, Devon EX12 ???!!

Not helpful, thought Eva, pursing her lips, *but not too hard to fix.* She turned it over and a small wad of tightly folded pages fell out through the slit in the top. Filofax inserts, held together with a black paper clip; a tiny blue Post-it read: *Jon – found this in a junk shop Filofax. You're into this kind of found shit, no? LOL. Kind of creepy, sad. Love, Steph oxox.* Little red-brown dots spattered the back page.

Honestly, how hard was it to finish a string of numbers? Eva was about to grab the postcodes reference list when she was distracted by a noise from out the front. Voices, two, yelling. The female louder and angrier than the male. It was irresistible, and she padded along to stand just back from the doorway so she could watch but remain inconspicuous in the dim corridor.

Mr Burstock, monolithic in his grey suit and highly polished shoes, was turning a wonderful shade of red, even his scalp under the close-shaved black stubble. But the woman who was yelling at him: oh! Thin, thinner even than Alice, dressed in black jeans and a black tee-shirt under a battered red leather jacket, her skin so pale it had almost a blue translucence. Her hair, long and oil-slick ebony, drank in light and held on to it. Her mouth was a crimson slash, narrowed in anger, and her eyes dark as dark could be. She was beautiful and frightening all at once, and Eva could barely breathe for the sight of her.

'I'm telling you,' said the woman in jagged tones, 'it was sent to my brother, Jonathan Oaks. It's not arrived, so it should have come *here*.'

'Well, where is he?' asked Mr Burstock.

'He's sick. He sent me.'

'Where's your ID then? Show me proof of who you are. Where's your brother's authority letter, then?'

The woman remained silent.

'I thought not,' rumbled Mr Burstock, his petty satisfaction at sanctioned unhelpfulness evident. 'You'll not be going through Royal Mail property like it's a jumble sale table. Off with you.'

The woman could have been anywhere between nineteen and forty for she had a way, as if she carried a shell around her, to hide as many truths as she could. She lifted one hand and pointed a long, thin crooked finger at the supervisor. That was all she did but the gesture said everything it needed to.

Eva gasped and though Burstock didn't seem to hear, the woman did. She flicked her gaze to where Eva hid, sought her, caught her in the shadows. Stared at her for long moments, then backed away, never once changing the direction of the accusing digit from Mr Burstock's fat red face, not until she backed out the front door and walked off.

Eva remained, hands clasped to chest, feeling the thud of her heart as if it was trying to follow the girl, the woman. As if… as if… as if…

Then Mr Burstock began to turn and Eva skipped away from the threshold, down the corridor, and into the little room. She picked up the letter meant for Jonathan Oaks and stuffed the Filofax pages inside. Hearing the thud of Mr Burstock's footsteps she slipped the envelope into the pocket of her cardigan. Eva took a deep breath and focused on the other items in the tub, waiting for her supervisor to arrive for his morning visit.

On her way home, Eva felt herself watched.

Don't be silly, she thought, *that's just guilt.* Low-level guilt; it was easy to distinguish from the real thing. The letter still in her pocket seemed to be burning a hole against her hip. *You nicked Royal Mail property.*

As she headed towards the train station the sensation grew too strong and she looked over her shoulder. In the late afternoon sunshine a silhouetted figure drifted behind her, not too close, but not too far. It made her heart pause, then the figure passed into the shadow thrown by the off-licence, the bright corona dissipating, and resolved itself into a woman wearing black and red, with a wave of hair floating behind her.

Eva faced forward, quickened her step, and heard the other's pace pick up too. Not enough to say *I'm taking you seriously,* but rather teasing, tormenting, warning *I can catch you any time I fucking well please.* She could make it to the station, but what if no one was around? It happened sometimes, admittedly not often, but still. On her right, a pub appeared, the same pub she'd walked past every day for ten years, the same pub Mr Burstock asked her to meet him in, the same pub she'd never set foot in before.

She pushed the door open and stepped into the Hart and Hounds. It was ill-lit and smelled like beer, but her shoes didn't adhere to the wooden floor and the seat she chose was neither damp nor sticky. The woman behind the bar smiled, a bleach-blonde spider in a web of glass and metal and mirrors.

'What can I get you, love?'

'Gin and tonic, please,' said Eva, though she'd never had one in her life. Her mother used to talk about Great-Aunt Agatha who went to clubs and drank such things and, inevitably according to Beth, did things with the men there that got her into trouble. Eva repeated, as if to make sure her mother, wherever she was, heard: 'Gin and tonic.'

She paid and stared at the clear liquid, fascinated by the way the ice bobbed against the wedge of lime, shifted and shuffled by the tiny bubbles making their way to pop on the surface. The barmaid wandered off to attend to the two old chaps at the other end of the bar who looked like regular fixtures. Eva sensed as much as saw someone sit beside her. It took long moments to turn her head and meet those dark, dark eyes, take note of the sheen on those red, red lips.

The tips of a tattoo peeped from the neck of the woman's tee-shirt and Eva wondered about the design even as her hand itched to pull at the fabric and see what lay beneath. She made a fist, then two, and laid one on either side of her glass.

'Hello, hen,' said the woman. 'I'm Lucy.'

'I saw you.'

'I know you did, that's why I followed you.' She leaned in. 'What's your name?'

'Eva.' It was out before she could stop herself.

'I'm hoping you might help me, Eva.' Lucy said the name beautifully, in a grown-up way that rolled shivers through Eva; she didn't shorten it or make it sound like a little girl's silly nickname.

'I can't. It's against the rules,' Eva poured out in a high voice that attracted the attention of the barmaid, who called, 'All right, love?'

Eva nodded quickly, not wanting to cause a scene. And she had to admit she wasn't entirely sure whether her nerves came of fear or arousal. Other women had interested her, yes, but never enough to risk doing something about it. But this one… Eva wondered if her drink had been spiked, then remembered she'd watched it being made, and she'd not taken even a sip yet. But she was giddy, dizzy at this woman's proximity, her smell that was lavender and sweat.

'I'm looking for a letter—'

'I know.' The envelope, still in her pocket, felt much heavier than it should. But she wasn't going to surrender it; she had the same feeling as when she'd refused to give up her job, as when she refused to meet Mr Burstock for a drink. It was sheer stubbornness, she knew, sheer bloody-mindedness, but she clung to it.

'And as I said to that man made of seven varieties of shit, it's *mine.*'

'You said it was your brother's. Jonathan Oaks in Branscombe, Devon. I heard you.'

Lucy smiled like a cat who sees a mouse out in the open, too far from its hole. 'Ah, but I didn't say where he lived.'

'You must have.' A tremble rippled her tone.

'You've seen it then. You know my name's in it. I've done all sorts of things to get it back, and will continue to do so. It's *mine.*' Lucy slipped off the stool, rested her hand on Eva's arm, leaned in. 'Bring it to me. Or else.'

'I could take it to the police.' Eva's voice rose again, panicked, and Lucy's teeth showed. The barmaid began to walk back towards them.

With their faces so close, their breath mingling, Eva saw, or thought she did, a flicker in the other woman's eyes: uncertainty, hope, surprise, desire, then the gaze was hooded so quickly she couldn't be sure. Lucy ran thin, soft fingers down Eva's cheek, tapped her under the chin. 'You won't though, will you, hen?'

When she'd stopped trembling, when she'd four gin and tonics under her belt, when she'd slipped out the door just as Mr Burstock thundered in, when she'd tottered to the station and managed to get the right line, when she'd made it up the stairs to the two-bedroom flat she'd shared with her mother for too many years, when she'd locked herself inside, then and only then did she manage a deep, ragged sigh. She'd been panting, sharp and shallow gasps that didn't get enough oxygen in and made her light-headed. *Perhaps it had as much to do with the alcohol as anything else,* she thought and gave a hiccup that became a burp, and she had to run to the bathroom.

At last her stomach stopped heaving, and she felt able to stand. Eva made a pot of tea and took it over to the sofa. She curled in her favourite spot, and took the envelope from her pocket, tipping out the contents.

The dates ran from August 1 to September 18; the handwriting was neat and assured, entirely different from that on the small blue Post-it, which looked childish by comparison. She read the entries, all the strange little pauses in a person's life, the events, the reminders, the things that were important to them if to no one else.

A letter from Lucy.

Mark 8pm

A letter from Lucy.

A shopping list.

A movie date with Kev.

Letter from Lucy. Photos!

Kensal Green. Amanda – lunch.

A white scrap of paper Scotch-taped in, something about street photography.

Visiting Lucy!

Then almost two weeks of blank pages until Friday 13: an unhappy face and *OVER* underscored three times.

'Oh, Liar-Lucy! It's not yours at all. Why would you make diary entries about meeting yourself?' Eva said aloud. She pondered the writer, imagined she could feel her or his excitement in the Lucy notations, the anticipation. Everything else in there was unimportant, but Lucy, oh Lucy was a beacon, someone invested with the hope of another's heart.

Lucy.

What would it be like to be loved, to be wooed, by someone like Lucy?

Dangerous. Uncertain. Different. Oh, so exciting. There would be no ordinariness, nothing banal or commonplace – no status quo, only constant change. The idea threw a frisson down Eva's spine that was part terror, part elation. What on earth was happening to her?

She examined the last page, with the red-brown dots – the reason, Eva was certain, the woman wanted the letter. Little stains that, when sniffed, touched to her tongue, smelled and tasted ever so faintly of old iron.

Blood.

Eva knew blood; there'd been so much when her mother had found her beneath her father, in the kitchen, on the table, when he'd thought Beth out of it. But his wife had used the sleeping pills for so long their effect wasn't anywhere near as strong. Eva knew blood, how hard it was to clean up, how much bleach you needed to make it go away, or at least render it unidentifiable. Traces were still caught, she was sure, in the grooves of the cupboards, seeped beneath the linoleum. Her father died grunting over her, too busy to notice the knife being drawn across his throat before it was too late, before the red-black splashed across his daughter's back, before he collapsed on top of her. Eva knew blood; she knew evidence when she saw it.

Then again, what would she do with it?

Eva booted up the ancient desktop in the corner of the dining room and googled 'Jonathan Oaks, Branscombe'. She was utterly unsurprised to find that gentleman reported as deceased a few weeks ago, his killer uncaught. She searched for 'Steph' and 'Murder' together and found thirty-seven recent reports containing those words or fragments of them; none seemed quite right, yet none could really be dismissed.

How had Lucy tracked the pages? Had she panicked, overlooked things, when she'd killed their writer – Eva had no doubt the diarist was dead – then recalled only later that she'd left traces of her relationship? Had the victim's flat or house been cleared out by family or friends or a landlord who'd shuffled as many unwanted possessions as they could to a junk shop? The death must have been cunningly disguised as a suicide otherwise she didn't imagine the police would have let anything go. Perhaps it was someone like Eva's own father, who'd drifted in and out of their lives as and when he wished, arriving and abandoning with the same rhythm as the ships he claimed to crew, so that the neighbours who'd long ceased to ask after him didn't even notice when he was gone for good. Had Lucy gone back, traced whoever had cleared out the place, then gone to the shop, been told who'd bought that lot, then found Steph, and so on? Only Lucy knew for sure, but Eva could imagine the train of events.

She was pulled from her reverie by something hitting the window. Her flat looked out over the back garden. Standing in the moonlight so she could be seen, close to the stone wall that ran where, rumour had it, a corpse road once lay, was Lucy in her black and red. On the spot, almost, where Eva and Beth had buried their father and husband, deep, deep, deep, though it took them most of the night and all of their strength.

Lucy stood there and smiled. She stood there as if she knew what lay beneath. She stood there as if she'd never go away.

Eva remained at the window, palms pressed against the glass, for so long that she lost the feeling in them, either because the evening's cold had crept through the double glazing or her circulation protested the angle of her arms. Lucy didn't move either. Lucy stayed, never shifting, never fidgeting; she hardly even seemed to breathe.

At last, though, Eva drew away, a tiny act of defiance so hard won it almost hurt. She was filled with pride but regret, too, as if it might result in a loss. As if she might never see Lucy again.

Nevertheless, before she went to bed she took a paring knife from the magnetic strip above the kitchen sink, and slid it under her pillow. She kept the curtains closed so she wasn't tempted to peek out at the garden and its inhabitant. And, surprisingly, she slept almost as soon as she was horizontal, one hand curled around the knife's black plastic handle as if it were a favoured toy.

'I don't feel well,' Eva said into the phone. 'I don't know, Alice, maybe something I ate, or just a tummy bug. Yes, yes, I'll take care.'

When she woke she felt rested, no trace of the hangover she deserved; her slumber had been dreamless and deep. When she woke, Eva couldn't have cared less if she never entered the old red brick building, if she never sat within its four grey walls, if she never saw her colleagues ever again.

When she woke she felt… energised. Different. She, who'd always clung to a sense of repeated order just as a drowning woman does to a scrap of floating debris. She, who never bought brand-new clothes because their difference was too much to take in. She who always shopped second-hand for things whose age gave them a familiarity so it seemed she was stepping into an old skin, not yet hers, but something she could redefine. Today, however, she felt change was brewing, coming, liable to break at any moment; she didn't need to seek it, it would arrive all on its own. Even more strangely, it was something to be desired.

She spent the day wandering between couch and bed. She watched television shows she could feel numbing her brain as surely as a shard of ice. She read her mother's beloved Dickens' collected works. After five, the dark had already crept into the flat but she didn't turn on any lights; when there was a knock at the door, and she wondered if she might ignore it, dared play dead. In spite of everything, she felt the old fear of change rear its head, threatening to overwhelm her.

But the knocking didn't stop, and in the end she drew her dressing gown tightly around her, retying the frayed belt so it wouldn't slip. She half-expected Lucy's pale face and razor-sharp smile, but it was Mr Burstock, worse for wear, tie hanging loose and the top three shirt buttons undone. He swayed, the scent of stale hops wafting from him.

'Evie,' he half-sang.

'Don't call me that,' she said, surprised by the firmness of tone, the determination. *Change.* Yes. Things were going to change. This was just the start: correcting people when they spoke to her in a way she didn't like or appreciate. Showing that what she wanted counted for something. 'Don't *ever* call me that.'

He shouldered the door, and she was too small to give much resistance. She backed along the hall and he followed, one hand reaching for her. 'Came to check on you. See if you're all right.' He leered and pressed on. 'See if you were really ill or just pretending.'

He sniggered, staggered, sniggered again; tripped and almost fell, almost took them both down, but Eva slipped away, scampering on bare feet. Burstock caught himself, steadied, then nodded as if to say, *All right now, sotally tober.*

'I want you to leave now. Or I'll report you.'

'To who?' he boomed and laughed.

'To management,' she said. 'And the police.'

'You won't say anything, little mouse,' he said, low-pitched. 'We're friends and I choose my friends very carefully – friends not brave enough to tattle.'

He closed in and began to croon, 'Evie. Evie, Eeeeeevieeee.'

Eva stared at Mr Burstock, but she couldn't see him. Not his face, any road. It had been replaced by her father's, sing-songing 'Eeeeeevieeee' as he always did, trying to convince her to cooperate, before he gave up any hope of collusion and chose force instead.

And Eva surprised herself yet again, by not merely standing her ground, but meeting his onrush. By reaching into her pocket where she'd put the paring knife when she got out of bed. By bringing up the not terribly sharp but sharp enough blade, and slicing across Mr Burstock's throat.

The spray of red was warm, its pressure surprisingly firm, at least on the first few spurts. The man's fall was strangely slow, the noise of his landing strangely loud. His face was his own again with no trace of her father in it, except the stupid expression of surprise. At last he stopped moving, stopped moaning, stopped hissing air from the wound, stopped trying to pull himself onward, then Eva considered how to manage the mess. She should have waited, played it out, and led him into the kitchen. The linoleum and the paint were easier to wash down. The carpet would have to go.

The sticky hand that held the knife was rock steady. Eva

began to make a mental list of the things she'd need: new carpet, spray cleanser, more bleach certainly, heavy-duty garbage bags. He'd be hard to get down the stairs, but the Franklins in the bottom flat were away for another three weeks. She could drag him to the lounge window and toss him out, then set about digging him a place beside her father on the corpse road.

She nodded: *yes.*

Now that she had a plan, her field of vision expanded beyond the remains of her supervisor and she noticed, at last, that the front door was still open, and Lucy stood there. They stared at each other for what seemed a long time until Lucy stepped inside and closed the door. That was when Eva's hand – indeed all of Eva – began to shake, but it wasn't fear.

It was excitement, the sense that change had arrived, for better or for worse. It had been summoned. It was not going away.

Lucy stepped across Mr Burstock until they were close enough to touch if they so chose. Her voice was gentle when she said, 'Every hunter must be blooded, Eva,' and Eva thought she'd been very careful not to say Evie. Then Lucy held out her hand, expectant, confident.

Eva didn't hesitate; she laughed, a short snarl of a thing.

She ran one hand up Lucy's neck, cupped her ear, caressed her crow's-wing hair. She leaned forward and kissed Lucy, who seemed untroubled by the gouts of blood still adhering to the other's skin and hair. Eva felt the firmness of lips that returned her own voracious demand. She tasted saliva and the sweetness of the lemon sherbet candy the other woman had been sucking on, and the iron that she kissed into Lucy's mouth. Hands moved at her waist, her shoulder, her breasts.

The letter was safe, it was hidden. One day she might hand it over. One day, and she had no doubt she'd feel lighter for the loss. But for now everything was going to change: life would be about what *Eva* wanted, not what others demanded.

ANGELA SLATTER

Angela Slatter has won a World Fantasy Award, five Aurealis Awards, and is the only Australian to win a British Fantasy Award. She's published six story collections (including *Sourdough and Other Stories* and *The Bitterwood Bible and Other Recountings*), has a PhD, was an inaugural Queensland Writers Fellow, is a freelance editor, and occasionally teaches creative writing. Her novellas, *Of Sorrow and Such* (Tor.com) and *Ripper* (in *Horrorology*, Jo Fletcher Books), were published in 2015, and Jo Fletcher Books will publish her debut novel, *Vigil*, in 2016, with its sequel, *Corpselight*, coming in 2017. She blogs about shiny things that catch her eye here www.angelaslatter.com and she can be found on Twitter @AngelaSlatter.

"I must admit that when Conrad asked me if I'd contribute to *Dead Letters* he caught me at the perfect time. I'd just realised that a parcel containing a rather expensive pair of earrings that I'd sent as a gift to my best friend had not arrived, and indeed was never going to arrive. I was suitably enraged. *Yes*, I thought at the time, *I'll bloody well write a story about lost mail. Bastards.* When I received my story-starter 'dead letter', I must also admit, I'd forgotten what I'd agreed to and it took a few moments to remember. But in the end the ideas that stuck with me were about identity, our own and the ones others impose on us; the things we cling to whether unhealthily or otherwise; how little things can have big and unexpected impacts; how the secrets people keep can be utterly unexpected and unsuspected; and also how love might occur in the strangest places. I'm not sure too much of my original rage made it into 'Change Management'... although maybe it did and it just morphed from mine to Eva's. She's probably got more to be furious about, in all honesty."

LEDGE BANTS

MARIA DAHVANA HEADLEY & CHINA MIÉVILLE

It's mid-morning on this, the hundred and thirteenth day of my eighty-seventh year of employment at this shabby shitter of an office.

I wait patiently for Adam, the new and rather-too-inquisitive mail sorter, to nip off for tea. Then I busy myself at the forty-year shelves. I don't even have to sigh or steel myself anymore. I'm inured. I just get on with it, pulling out the letter opener I keep with me, slicing open a few packets in quick succession, taking out what's inside, and eating it. A rainbow decal in the shape of a peace sign; a damaged letter from a great uncle disowning a nameless great niece for bra-burning; six bent paper clips; a ten-pound note.

No results beyond the usual: ulcerous pangs and gastric distress.

I gobble a stale biscuit in an attempt to quiet my miserable stomach. Would I had any other means of comfort, but no, no – she's taken them all from me. I knew when I met her that she was trouble, and yet I still fell for her, a foolish youth dropping from a rope swing and directly into a lake full of piranha.

To be clear, when I say I knew she was trouble, I don't mean I had a bad feeling about this one. I mean I knew I'd end up here. I knew which shirt I'd be wearing. (It's a grubby one.) I knew I'd be damaging my teeth on forgotten tchotchkes.

All too quickly, Adam's back. He's as chipper as a monk drunk on root tonic.

'Here's for you, Old Man,' he says, and passes me a soggy cardboard cup with too much milk in. It's time to drink my tea, then. I have the sharp point of a clip stuck in my craw, but I can ignore that. I'm well used to that sort of misery by now. The last time I found any part of what I'm hunting, it was 1989.

Am I miserable, though? Or is misery intrinsically pathological? Is it still misery if it's the new normal? (I started ruminating on questions of qualia a few decades back, after I ate a philosophical pamphlet. Phenomenology and ontology are uniquely tangled in my own head, I suppose.)

Yes, I'd say I was miserable. I'd definitely say that. I give a few envelopes a shake as if my fingers might still be aerials, sensitive to contents. They aren't. My belly hurts. More of the new normal. Gnaw. Nibble. Choke.

There's official work to do too, technically, so when I need a break from painful swallowing I move things from one place to another, and scribble stuff in the log. My managers appreciate this little charade and it's no skin off my business to indulge them. The log contains a journal of my years of woeful paperchase.

When Adam repairs to the loo, I swallow down a misaddressed love letter written in rhyming couplets, along with its accompanying plastic ring, a set of collectible Balinese stamps, and a tin knight on a warhorse. That's the kind of joke I'm hopeful she might make, but it has nothing to do with her. The knight stabs at my oesophagus, and the horse's hooves kick all the way down.

'Fuck's sake, Old Man, is that your stomach rumbling, then?' says Adam. I didn't hear him come back in. 'Your gut's legendary, mate.'

I was thrilled when he first called me this. I thought an acolyte had found me. Since then I have learned quite what a range of dull phenomena he describes as legendary, and the thrill has palled. He has not yet called me 'ledge', as he does other things, but it cannot be long.

I look at him without expression until he has to look away. I pull out the particular icy blue glare I use in such moments. Occasionally I coil my beard into a white knob, which discomfits everyone, including me. I caught a glimpse of myself in the mirror recently. What can I say? I never meant to get this old. It's her fault.

Everyone has a lover they regret, and she is mine. She'd say I did this to myself. She'd say I gave her everything I now regret losing, indeed, that I gave it to her on bended knee.

She's got a point. But still, what I say is, beware young women. They're thieves.

I belch, tasting tin and what's most likely lead paint. Adam looks at me in disgust. I know he's cultivated a soft spot for me by now, but in his first days, I heard him asking management why I'm not removed.

As if management can manage me. I can exactly imagine the expression they wore when he asked: a sort of evasive queasiness. Give him enough time – if he lasts, which most of the staff here don't – he'll understand what the old-timers do: that I'm just here. That, as far as they're concerned, I've always been here. Ancient when they turned up on their first day, still ancient now, poking about in the room of the misdirected, announcing myself with epically rumbling stomach. That no one quite knows what, officially, I do; that my records and paperwork have always been less than precise. That the line to my line manager always gets too tangled to unpick, so it's not clear who'd have the power to give me the heave if they wanted to. They can just leave me be.

You wouldn't ask a beefeater to sack a Tower of London raven, would you? I am an institution and institutions do not retire.

Of course, they would if they could. Indeed, they'd flee these premises with a hop and a skip and never look back. But at least two pieces of mail are still missing. Without them? I can accomplish nothing, and there's a big something, coming fast, right at the centre of everything. It urgently needs accomplishing. I need the mail.

I use my last monogrammed hankie to clean the blade of my letter opener, besmirched by something sticky and pink. I try to keep it clean; it's not ostentatious like some letter openers but it's quality, I've had it a long time, and in the office of dead letters, there's an astonishing quantity of muck.

I've been at this for centuries now. I've sorted through nonsense in a lot of places, done plenty of different jobs by way of searching, but this is about the worst of them. Time was I'd get wind of a clue, set off, and I'd end up fighting a monster, or rattling up a tower's foundations. I even found a couple of my missing pieces that way, but there were a lot of fallow years of digesting little nugget traces of what I used to be, during which I chased after false trails and went artefact-hunting. The world did all manner of jiggery-pokery, changing into this peculiar shiny dirty thing through which I trudge, as I tracked the last few here.

Long story. A chain of informants, an overheard swaggering curse, and what I originally dismissed as sheer bloody silliness – with the swallowing of one la-la ripped from a scrunched-up envelope pilfered from its shelf in this tallying house of the lost, the swallowed la-la dissipating in a blissful spread of my own bloody quiddity up and down from my gut – turned out to be true. The rest of me was misdirected, stalled on its way to no-known-addresses.

Since then I've been on this dread postal quest, forced to chew my way through decades of lost mail, trying to get my teeth into the things that were stolen from me.

They've no outer indication of their character. The only way to find them is to chew. Dentistry, while vastly better than it was at my beginnings, is now the NHS, and my teeth are nubs. I've eaten sonnets and collection notices, pornographic Polaroids, political screeds. I've eaten a set of medieval illuminations, each panel depicting historical events inaccurately – I know from having been there at the time. I've gnawed comic books. Once, because I thought it would be like her to make me eat socks, I swallowed a set of lady's woollen stockings patterned with clock faces, gagging them down.

And indeed, that was the meal, consumed in late 1989, with which I regained a significant portion of my abilities, and heard the faint echo of her laughter as well. With an edge of desperation: she could never fool me, even about how she'd go about fooling me. Since then the eating's been in vain. And I despair. Because construction is well underway on the Crossrail, and London's guts are being ransacked. I've seen the route, and I remember enough topography to deduce where things are heading; I know it's a matter of time, and not a lot of it, before that wyrm-sized screw spinning under the city smashes into Albion's soul. I must recover my belongings – by which I mean my me – before a platform opens onto that apple seed-strewn cavern. There must be no happy ending.

Adam – bless his curious soul – insists me into a pub after work. I can see management watching us, aghast, as he tries to persuade me. I'm vaguely charmed. I come with him to throw him off the scent of my oddity, and to scandalise them. We have a pint each.

'Trouble with the missus?' asks Adam. Lord but I feel grim.

'She was a witch,' I say. I don't mention that I was a wizard.

'Oh, mate!' Adam laughs. 'Bants! Don't I know it! But you can't let it keep ruining your digestion, man. What was your lady's name?'

'Viviane, or so some called her,' I say. I can hear the note of the bloody balladeer in my voice, and try to banish it. It tempts.

'Some did, did some? Yeah? But… what did you call her, mate?' Adam reminds me of fools in my future, and in my past as well.

I twist my beard into a monkey's paw, then out again. There's a bit of a banned edition of *Ulysses* stuck in my gullet. My beloved always liked the transgressive texts. A few days ago, I choked down Episode 4, 'Calypso', and Episode 15, 'Circe', because I just knew she'd like to madden me by compacting all the last of my magic into the witches. Never into the Molly Bloom finale. My lover was no Penelope. She'd never kick her heels at home for anyone's return; instead she Peneloped me and quested her way around England. Until her last overreach. There was nothing hidden in that tome, only ink and paper. My tongue is still smudged, and everything tastes of iodine.

'Nimue,' I say, and sigh. I still love her, of course, no matter the encyclopedia of wrongs she's done me. I spent a century at the top of a pine tree convinced I was in a tower, another century wandering Rome dressed in a wolfskin. For a while, I was a lovely maiden, which was not as lovely as I'd thought it might be, and for another time I was napping in the middle of a public square for three hundred years, shat on by pigeons and sat on by everyone whose feet ached.

Soon as I started spooning after her I knew all this would happen. That's prophecy for you: it's an utter bugger. Point, of course, being you know it; as in, it's a done deal. If you knew it might happen, you'd try to do something about it.

'My sympathies, man,' says Adam. He leans over and drinks the rest of my pint. I don't mind terribly. Beer in this century is like water. I prefer water. Its ingredients are more interesting.

Her problem was that she had to get creative. I still don't think it was in her nature to be a real shit, though she could be as petulant as the rest of us. When I eventually got out of the tower, or the tree, or whatever it was, the trower, where she'd ensconced me, I set off on her tail. She got wind of it, naturally; even depleted, she must've felt me coming. I could still pull a few rabbits out of a few hats then, as it were.

'She's fearful of your power,' one soothsayer told me. 'She cannot control nor kill you.'

'Control the watcher of Albion's protection?' I said while he cowered. 'She dares?'

I thundered my wrath. I did a fair bit of that at the time.

'She seeks a spell,' he said. 'To disperse you, lord. To disperse your powers, exile them from the world. To impossible places, by lost ways. Also, she's bent out of shape by your romantic perfidy. There's something in the sooth about someone's handmaiden, someone else's fateweaver, and a passel of false promises.'

I gave him my blank look. He sprouted donkey ears, and a pig's snout, though only briefly. I was merciful.

And I should be fair. I've never doubted that a bit of what she did, she did out of anxiety for England. Whatever her own questionable genealogy she never thought it was healthy for cambions, half-succubi, to walk the earth. Fair play. I'd say what she did was forty percent strategy to dissipate the most dangerous magic in that age of its ebbing, and sixty percent to annoy me.

She found her spell, too. A Ward of the Shattering and Scattering, and she let fly with it, aimed it foresquare at the target. I was in Wolverhampton. I heard it howling through the air at me.

And then it hit, and I was diminished.

Scores of aspects of my memories, my strength, my powers, were exiled from the world. Which turned out to mean that they were hidden, camouflaged in matter, in lost places, fabled gulleys, reachable only by impossible ways. Hence those years of monster-hunting.

You should never underestimate the magic of magic's passing. The strength of the death of that strength. Eventually, I came to clock that the things I found – eggs and jewels and chains and trinkets that were, in part, me – I found in more and more quotidian places and forms. Protected by forces that would have raised fewer eyebrows, less high, among populace by now utterly sceptical of the sort of mythic shenanigans with which I used to divert myself. Each piece shifting with the epochs, each still some snide material joke, a pun or a prod from my missing ex, but now camouflaged not in the hearts of dragons, but in shapes and places appropriate to the age. All without breaching the terms of the spell.

I hunted them, and I hunted her too, but of my Nyneve, there was no word or sign. I was convinced that I couldn't find her because I'd lost my powers.

It was early in the 20th century, with only a handful of bits of me left to scarf down, that I realised that the impossible place had become a storeroom for misdirected mail. That the last of me lay in that ever-refilling warehouse of packaged junk, those shelves and shelves of brown paper and misspent memories and lost chances.

I applied for the caretaker's job.

I still can't help feeling sorry for my lady, despite my years of rumbling guts. She underestimated herself.

A few days after that beer, I'm sorting painstakingly through the dead letters of the past three months – if anyone asks I'm scanning for powdered poisons – when among the handfuls of these accursed packages I happen upon a lumpy, semi-squashed parcel on which for no particular reason my hands linger.

It's wrapped in that ubiquitous brown paper, marked 'Fragile', addressed to someone in Bristol. I have my superstitions on this search. At the moment I'm avoiding reading names. I cover the supposedly intended recipient with my hand and give the thing an unhelpful shake.

No sign of Adam. I slice it open and take out a little box from the Victoria and Albert Museum. Inside of which something's wrapped in white paper and topped with a tiny typewritten (typewritten!) note.

'Just a little reminder of what you come from... hahaha a ahah G.'

Hahaha?

I've eaten a comic book, so understand the aetiology, but I may never recover from the present moment's tendency toward the ha, ha, ha. It causes severe indigestion.

Still. Adam's back, so I put the box in my pocket and ply him with three cups of strong tea. Hahaha? Ha ha ha? Ha, ha, ha. However you render it, it doesn't get any better. Ha-ha-ha.

When at last he departs for his morning micturition, I wield my letter opener and pour the box's contents into my hand.

It's a ring box. In the ring box is a tiny skull.

With those teeth it's definitely rodent, mouse, I think, and I should know. It's no longer than my thumbnail, which isn't even that long today. It's less enticing than the magical gemstone I'd briefly, excitedly imagined. The thing is, though, that this skull doesn't feel like a skull. It doesn't feel like what it seems to be. I couldn't even tell you what that means. It has the right weight and heft, it looks like bone, which makes me imagine this is a skull carved from a bigger skull.

It reminds me of a gobstopper. With a nub of gum in the centre. I first tried gum in the 1950s – that was a humiliating education. At that time my beard was a luxuriant spiral stretching to my navel. Gum forced me to reveal my chin, and I have never forgiven it. It took years, sans spellcraft, to regrow my whiskers, and they were never the same.

I open my mouth wide and hold up the skull, just as Adam returns.

'Snacks, bruv?' he asks. And without warning, with the sort of laboured twinkle with which he accompanies what he likes to think of as horseplay and the braying idiocies he announces to be 'banter', that expression he imagines is winning, he reaches out, snatches what he thinks is a sweet, pops it into his own mouth, and chews.

'Easy, geezer!' He laughs at the sight of my face. 'It's jokes, mate. I'll buy you another.' And then I see him taste it.

And then I see the first of its effects.

Adam's eyes bulge. His nostrils flare. His face lurches sideways and then lengthwise into yawning maw, which becomes a pinched moue. I leap at him, feeling my own spells swirling out of the bone and straining to return to my body, and some of them even make it through his pores to me. I can feel myself opening like a bud, I can, but too much, too much is in him. I'll swallow down his spitty cud – I'm not proud – if I can make him retch it up. But he's already swallowed.

I pound his back but oh, I am too late, and he transforms into a stoat. He's eaten my precious magic.

* * *

Witch. She always was. I think of the first time I saw her, and as I watch a portion of my soul wrench the body of my colleague down into a little furred, fanged mouse-eater, I still can't regret our love affair. There was something about her, the apprentice who took over the business. Even now, I find her irritatingly enticing. Enticingly irritating. You know.

'Adam,' I tell the stoat, sadly. 'Cough up that skull, or I'll have to cut it out of you.'

The stoat blinks. 'What's the difference between a stoat and a weasel?' it says in a whispery stoat voice. I'm not surprised that Adam can speak.

'One eats another person's magical skull!' I shout. 'One steals another person's ancient magic, smashed into a wee skull by that person's ex-girlfriend, a long, long time ago, that same ex-girlfriend who banished him behind the mist, who dwelled in a lake with Excalibur clenched in her fist!'

There's a silence. Adam blinks again, this time more rapidly, his eyes pinkish and watery.

'One is weaselly recognised, the other is stoatally different,' whimpers Adam. 'That's all I've got. Something's the matter with me. I've a tail.'

Witch.

I crouch on my heels and regard the ermine that is Adam. That the transformative power of my bones is in his, not my, bones, is a grave annoyance.

'Just a little reminder of what you come from…'

Certainly, I've been a mouse. Fuck's sake, I've even been a stoat, but never for very long. I tested the world's possibilities. I've been a blue whale and an eagle as well. What's her point?

'Hahaha a ahah G.'

Why G? There was a rumour once that she had a son called Guivret, but I doubt he's still knocking around, if he ever was. And what has he to do with anything? 'A ahah' sounds like someone having a stroke. What is with this absurd cod-chilling message? Hahaha? Why not just write mwah-hah-hah and have at it? I begrudge no one a taste for theatre. Let's not go into the costumes in which a certain wizard has been seen in his earlier, shall we call them Proto-New Romantic Days (very Proto – 14th century) but this is just camp. It's as though the world's most powerful witch, cousin to selkies, embodied woman-water-spirit of the lake's fury, is taking lessons in Gothic from a children's television programme. A not-great one.

Adam forages for snacks. Actual snacks. I have a bit more of my magic back. Not enough. And something very important is still missing. Something that I've reason to believe is still in this room. What am I supposed to do now. Eat Adam? Is that the great plan?

I look at his stoat self, his pale fur, his tipped tail. I don't want to eat him. Over the years I've become increasingly vegetarian. This is what happens when you've been a variety of earth's creatures and you don't know what's coming for you.

Beneath London, the drill named Elizabeth still propels itself relentlessly across the city, west to east. I can always feel it, and now I feel it more vividly than ever. It's approaching the apocalypse.

'There's more in here,' says Adam, nose trembling. 'I smell it, me. Magic in a packet. Smells like crisps.'

He sniffs about and, miserable, in a non-new normal way, I watch him. His magic stoat nose twitches.

And as he goes foraging ferociously, I realise, with a slow burgeoning I think for a moment is more indigestion of some unusual kind, then identify as the thing called hope, that what's twitching in that nose is both the stoatness and the magic.

'Go forth, Adam!' I bellow. 'Sniff! Hunt! Find!'

Adam ransacks the office of dead letters. He roams with tooth and claw, slavering, growling. He shreds dull correspondence, tears into circulars, slashes postcards. He pisses upon a stack of the 1970s. I can't say as I blame him. I've been in that shelf myself. Once I ate some blotter acid and I thought I'd gotten all my magic back, before coming down a day later and realising my powers were imaginary.

'Dig, Adam, dig!'

He digs. I don't much like using Adam this way but he might even be enjoying himself a bit, I suppose. He is rampaging through a land of packaging.

When I met her, I was all over smitten – and, too, I thought I'd found someone to do my dull bits, the piecemeal fill-in tidying spells. An assistant. A stunning spell-maker who'd deal with the bits of the court I found tedious: the love philtres and the yammer-stoppers, the powdered items requested by various knights for use in week-long orgies, the herbal birth control fizzies requested by ladies for use after same. I'd grown weary of mushroom foraging and unicorn coaxing. I'd had a couple of run-ins with an aggressive manatee, and one with a white rhino that saw through my charms. I had a vision of a more alchemical period in my magic, and perhaps even a small beach vacation, leaving Nimue capably in charge of the court. Instead? She blasted me.

The first time she and I travelled together, it was by fish.

We were at the bottom of the river, and she was nothing grey and mottled. She was a parrotfish in freshwater, not proper, not correct. That was when I noticed she'd taken some lessons from me. Lady of the Lake indeed! My love was a lady of the sky, the sea, the wilderness. The all of it.

She was right: she didn't steal my magic. I gave it to her, willingly, and now I'm here, in a postal office, my mouth tasting of lost objects, following a co-worker I might have to eat.

Adam flies up at last from a heap of ravaged packages. He has a small envelope in his teeth. He shakes his head ferociously, and presents me with his find.

'Will I be a stole?' he asks, forlorn.

I give him a pat on the head. It's the sort of pat that guarantees nothing.

Still – something about this envelope attracted his magic stoat attention. It has a dragon sticker on it. Really? I slash open the packet with my trusted opener, my fingers trembling.

What's inside is a mermaid made of bone.

Could she really be so on the nose? Though of course it wasn't her choice.

There's no slogan here, no silly statement of her victory-that-was-and-wasn't. I haven't seen her in hundreds of years. I feel my heart beginning to pound. Nimue was like nothing anyone had ever seen. She had no qualms.

'Merlin,' she said. 'Don't be a fool. You're an old man, and you'll die one day. Do you not think you should teach someone the things you know?'

'I'll live forever,' I said, and though I could clearly see this miserable century of post office in my future, I didn't know what it meant then.

'Forever alone,' she said, and started to walk away, at which point I decided in lovesick desperation to teach her everything I knew.

I bring the cheap-looking mermaid to my lips. In her is the rest of my magic, all the secrets I gave to Nimue, all the transformation spells, all the subtleties, the things I learned of my mother the mortal, and my father the devil. Inside her is the history of Arthur and his reign, the knowledge of his future kingdom.

I've entertained myself imagining the words of the hex.

> *Scatter all you spells like seed,*
> *You powers to hold the world in thrall.*
> *I shatter that we do not need*
> *Soul of the mightiest mage of all.*

I don't know.

> *Magus Prime spreads o'er the map,*
> *Turned into tons of stupid crap.*

Whatever the doggerel, both parts of the spell worked perfectly. And it was aimed at the greatest magician in the world.

It took me a long time to guess what had happened. A lot of leads. A certain trail of insinuation.

I taught her well. It turned out there was no way to choose between us anymore.

Magic is good for many things, but fuzzy logic is not one of them. Faced with two exactly equal greater powers, maybe the spell could've shrugged and dissipated. But it didn't. It worked on both of us. I was scattered, and she was scattered too.

I bite into the mermaid's tail and taste the apples of Avalon. I taste the pitch of the tree I lived atop just after Nimue and I were parted. She dove, and I rose, her hand full of the sword, and my hands full of air. I lived in a crystal cage, and my love lived at the bottom of a lake until she took Arthur to his hiding place.

My teeth part the mermaid's flesh, and I taste my memory, my magic, and the divine bitterness of foolish love.

And then, wrenching free of my teeth, hauling backwards in a storm of spirit, Nimue stands before me.

I stare. She shines. Her gown shimmers like a beetle's wing. A sword glows in her girdle. Oh, I know that sword.

She looks at me with sea-green eyes, holds Adam in her arms, and pets his face. The stoat nuzzles traitorously into her bosom.

'That took forever,' she says. 'My neck's all cramped.'

'It took less than a thousand years,' I say, offended. 'That's nothing when it comes to forever, as you should know.'

I soften. I can't help it.

'So,' I say. 'You're looking well.'

'You have gum in your beard,' Nimue says.

Liar! I'm about to shout, but she snaps her fingers and shears my chin. Six feet of white braids fall to the floor. She grins. 'Old goat.'

As ever, I am quite lost. 'Is that all of my magic back?' I ask her, after some panting and uncertainty. I can feel the answer.

I'm surging. She had the last of it in with her, packed tight like it was provisions for a trip through the underworld. I've got it all back in me now. Except for the stuff in that bloody animal.

'I have my own,' she says, and gives me a dose of her wicked eyes, her silken skin, her curling upper lip, the one that has never caused me anything but problems. 'Your spells are out of date. I was only keeping them safe for you. And then I got into a little trouble and had to make myself scarce.'

'Right,' I say.

Adam burrows into her cloak. He looks to be making himself a nest.

'That,' I say, with dignity, 'is my mate you're holding.'

'Your tastes have changed,' she says, eyebrow up.

I can feel myself turning colors. 'My colleague. Kindly return him to his own form.'

'Do it yourself,' says Nimue. She passes him to me. 'You have your spells. I have more important things to do. Surely you've seen the news. They're getting close to you-know-where.'

I'm left holding the stoat, like a magician's assistant.

'So you've been keeping up, then,' I say to her back. 'Despite...'

'I was keeping my head down,' she says. 'I wasn't ignoring what was happening.'

'Right,' I say. She's so annoying. What I want to say is, you were just about to ride to the rescue of the world, as soon as you'd decided to stop being a gimcrack mermaid, right?

'So. We're agreed?' she says.

'Yep,' I say stiffly.

'Well come on then,' she says. She glances me up and

down. 'You're not going to get far, fast, like that. Take shape.'

Adam looks up at me with a particular blankness, one I recognise from my own arsenal of expressions. There is no option. I'm allowing myself one snip, however, before the inevitable.

'Do you wonder,' I say to her, hating my whiny voice, 'why my powers were scattered in parts and you were scattered into one part? One of those parts, even, you might say. I mean, I did teach you everything you know... so it's almost as if all your powers combined are just one single aspect of mine, isn't it?'

And with that I chant a single powerful word, and my body shrinks. I wriggle up from a heap of jacket and trousers, flipping myself through the cloth. I rather can't breathe, and my skin hurts, and my eyes are bulging, to my alarm. I look out from my man clothes, and discover Adam staring at me, his stoat teeth bared.

'Fishie?' croons Adam, with savage longing.

I can feel my scales. Errors! I shout another word, before he leaps. Panic subsides: I'm ermined.

Nimue bends and points at us, one hand to each mustelid. She whispers to me.

'That did occur to me, yes,' she says. 'As did what I considered significantly more likely: that my defences are stronger than yours, my reflexes quicker, my soul more coherent.'

Damn it. I'm still thinking of a blistering retort when she turns and rushes away. Frankly, that sounds more likely to me too.

I whip out of the door behind her, and Adam chases after me.

'She's your wife?' he shouts.

'My witch,' I tell him over my stoat shoulder. 'The only witch for me, the worst and best of them all.'

When we reach the street – how long since I have smelt the night with animal nose and nerves! – Nimue is striking a manhole cover with the hilt of Excalibur, drawing green sparks. We leap into the void after her, and land heavily beside her in London's sewers. I hear Adam cough something up—

—and with a rush, as he vomits, a jolt of my newly returned powers are gone. I can't bear it. The chewed-up-and-swallowed skull containing grots of my magic has dropped into the darkness and washed away, and Adam is back, in confused human form.

I rush off with the sewage after it, but it's dissipated, in a new, even more humiliating way. I rage impotently. Adam is pale and disheveled. I see Nimue pat him, with the same sort of no-guarantees pat I used earlier. She bends down and does the same to me. I'm still a stoat.

'Carry me, knave,' I shout from ankle level. To Adam. She's already gone.

Adam dazedly obeys. I direct him into the dark.

There must still be some uncanny calories in him, the way he follows her glowing self, passes through tunnels and sewers, past the scent of bones buried in Roman times, skeletons of saints, skeletons of paupers. I yearn for a gnaw, of anything in tooth-reach, but restrain myself. From inside his pocket, I can feel Adam's quick breathing and his clammy skin.

His reaction to Nimue is typical. He's sweating, and it's sheer temperature, as well as quickened blood. Ladies of Lakes live in lakes for reasons.

Back when I first met her, I once saw Nimue turn a loch into a steam bath, and an iceberg into a mammoth-filled mist. I never expected any lake to withstand her temperature.

When I'd managed to wrench myself out of my first tranche of various punishments and begun the process of reclaiming my magic, I heard the stories of her later doings.

Mortally wounded, Arthur had Excalibur thrown into her lake, they said, and it was her hand that rose out of the water to catch it. Then she carried him, and his court, wife, knights, and tables, off to Avalon. Which wasn't an island. It was an apple orchard. Arthur liked apples, and so did Nimue. Anyone who's been existent since time began likes apples. Just as that little gumball of a skull contained my knowledge, apples contain the magic of millennia. Orchards are useful places.

The orchards towards which we're descending lie beneath Britain. There are the roots of trees that lived and thrived a thousand years ago still here, twined in the soil. Under the hill, over the wood.

For a long time now I've been watching the Crossrail's progress, tracking its route, and feeling increasingly urgent. No happy ending. This is not the foretold future. The future I, among others, foretold. I once had a deal more skill. Lately, though, in my still-scattered state, I've been resorting to tarot. There's a tattooed card reader in a hotel lobby in Shoreditch who's got a bit of old magic inherited from a great-grandmother, I heard. She works Saturday nights, while all the noble children dance. On the prescribed day I came to her. I brought in the paper, showed her tarot deck the photo of the drill, and asked when the drill would break through.

'To the other end of the line?' she said.

'To what sleeps below,' I said, in my best voice. 'And bring the end of everything.'

'Dunno, nutter,' she said. 'I get my news online. You have an Instagram, Granddad? I could tag you. That beard is a piece of work. You got a bird's nest in there?'

'Just ask the bloody cards for the answer,' I said, requiring, to my embarrassment, their magical boost. I, the legendary wizard of Britannia. Even the legendary, the ledge, can fail when they fall. My love story is not the one they've made films about. Mine was nothing so scandalous as that of Guinevere, and Lancelot, Arthur and his heartbreak. I've seen those films. My story was just that of a wizard and his witch, the knowledge of centuries passed onto one younger and wiser. If it knew the truth of what we got up to, though, England would blush.

The reader held out her palm, asking that she be crossed with silver, which she rejected, then paper, which I'd accumulated over the decades of foraging through dead letters. Plenty of notes stuffed into lost birthday cards.

I drew The Magician, reversed. That's all I ever draw with tarot. Decks convert themselves. An old joke of Nimue's I assume.

Imagine, for a moment, a wizard standing at the top of a pine tree, looking around in rapture, seeing the walls of his crystalline tower, imagining that all he will have to do, for centuries, is enjoy the silence, read the books he hasn't read, and learn the spells he hasn't learned. I was happy in my 'punishment', at first. Imagine a wizard feeling himself loved by a witch. It took a hundred years before this wizard stepped off the platform he'd imagined, and tumbled head over heels through pine cones and owl nests, not in a shining tower after all, but only abandoned.

From Adam's pocket, I can see the glowing hilt of Excalibur. I've never felt that magical swords should glow. Enemies can see you coming – it's stupid. Plus it overinvests a person in the mere fact of glow: I remember the first torch I saw and then procured in a shop. I did so because I was briefly and shamefully delighted by the possibility that it possessed powers beyond the normal; I don't know, the capacity to cut through steel, for example. I was swiftly disabused. Its glow was just glow, from a battery. Still, I wish we had a torch now. I do not feel Nimue is to be trusted with Excalibur. She smells of mermaid and pine tar. She's been cooped up much too long to be a reliable sorceress, and in any case I don't know what sort of sorcery she practices these days.

We pass what's clearly a hoard of gold and bronze buried in just a skip's worth of dirt. Little lizards in there too. My stoat self is inclined to dig, and again, I deny myself. This is an inconveniently appetite-driven body.

Nimue rams the point of Excalibur into a wall and stops our descent. We are in a cathedral-sized hole. I see several flights of stairs, with startled workers on them, trying to convince themselves they aren't seeing us. A tremendous passage yawns below us, and within it is that draconic drill they've named in questionable honour for the queen. Tunnel walls are being girded with steel. I glance up at the witch.

'You plan to stay stoat, then?' she says. Even a bit demagicked, still, I realise I don't have to. I chant to shift myself into something new. Nimue gives me a look that says my new form is not appropriate. I prod the wall of the tunnel with my antlers.

Nimue waves her fingers and changes me into a lovely

maiden, which is fair play, and a palpable hit. Those years were worse than the ones in which I was a prophetic stag, which was at least a form respected by other wizards. Being a lovely maiden and thus assumed to be intellectless was, as Nimue knew it would be, perfectly maddening.

Adam jolts, trying to keep his footing.

'Old Man,' he asks, his voice shaking. 'You still in there? You're pretty as a lady. What're we at, mate? What's going on?' He shifts sadly. 'I've still got a tail,' he whispers. 'It's bunched up in my arse.'

What might I transform him into. A mouse? My subtleties feel coarse. All this magic newly returned to me, and I should be readying magics for Arthur, but I fear I do not remember what to do. I have been preparing myself for failure.

'Can you swing a sword?' Nimue asks Adam. 'They may wake spoiling for a fight.'

'I've played rugby,' he says, bigging himself up. I doubt he's done any such.

'That'll do,' says Nimue.

She leaps, and takes us thistledown light onto the drill itself, while the drillers gawp. Nimue sniffs the air and takes off, running as fast as a river off a cliff. She's a water witch, and I'm a lady in waiting, chasing after her. Adam stumbles after us both. I feel Elizabeth spinning beneath my feet, and I feel the desire for magic, forgetting then remembering that I have it.

I'm horribly confused after all this time. Still not sure what I can do, I transform back into my Merlin self, with capes and celestial robes and all that, with the lovely pointed hat she always mocked. Adam snickers and I don't care.

I go horizontal and fly.

Halfway down the tunnel, I realise Adam's hanging from my ankle.

'Old Man!' he cries.

'Release me!' I shout.

I can barely see Nimue. She's springing ahead, lit by the flicking glow of Excalibur, soundtracked by the grinding of the drill.

'I'll stay a stoat, if I'm only her stoat,' Adam wails. 'Swear down!'

'Bigger fish!' I shout furiously. Then I, fellow-sufferer, relent, and allow him onto my back as though I'm a fucking broomstick.

God help us, I can smell the apples of Avalon, as the tip of Elizabeth pierces the wall of the cave where the king of England sleeps. I hear Nimue bursting through the rock and magic, into the orchard where Arthur and his court wait.

'What're we doing?' howls Adam.

'We have to stop King Arthur waking!' I shout in what I realise is terror. 'He's there to protect us all, and with his waking comes Albion's happy ending!'

I keep flying.

'That,' says Adam carefully after a moment, 'doesn't sound so bad?'

Poor Adam. Perhaps someone told him stories, once. Perhaps he reads and loves stories still. Perhaps it takes someone from inside a story to explain to someone from without them, that even a happy ending is an apocalypse.

I burst through the rock behind Nimue. She stands before the point of the encroaching drill, Excalibur raised high, confronting the Crossrail.

Behind her I can definitely see Arthur in his own crystal cave. He's twitching, stirring, coming out of his rest, roots all around him, apple cores covering the ground. I can see Guinevere and Lancelot, one on either side of him, each holding his hands. And yes, Arthur's crown still gleams, as the story lurches towards a finish.

'BEND!' shouts Nimue, sword trembling, magic surging from her fingertips. 'BEND, ELIZABETH!'

The drill considers. It decides to shrug off magic, and whirrs forward at Nimue.

Adam rolls off my back, and charges the drill. He flings himself between Nimue and Elizabeth, his pale chest bared to the diamond-tipped point, offering his heart to be impaled by progress.

I fumble for my own magic, patting the pockets I have again with the habits of magicless centuries, and find my letter opener instead.

I pull it from my robes, sliding it out as smoothly as it was once, under my guidance, pulled from a stone.

'FLEA!' I shout, waving my own sword.

I never lost everything I had; I knew I'd find use for that neglected sword. Never as flashy as Excalibur, no, but that long marinading in the stone didn't leave it entirely useless, you might say. I wave the nameless – and, I might add, sensibly unglowing – sword my ward tugged out of the rock. It was always the poor relation – I felt sorry for it, is the truth, when Nimue's own blingy Excalibur turned up and turned heads. It was a bugger to find: no one ever seemed quite sure where they'd left it. So when I finally found it, I made sure to keep it close, discreetly. Now at last I can let it stretch. I imagine that old iron must be luxuriating. It is not without power.

'Flee! Flea!' My magic is a bit of a mess and I'm not sure if I'm trying to transmogrify the drill into an insect or to send it packing. Not without power notwithstanding, and either way, nothing happens.

All, apparently, is lost. Or won. Same thing.

Nimue calmly picks up an Avalonian apple, and tosses it into the path of the drill.

The apple slams Adam aside and is split in two, cored by a tunnel never to be.

I wave King Arthur's original sword again, this time in conjunction with Nimue and Excalibur, and the startled drill seems to hesitate, and waits in time stretched out – until at last and with a pneumatic sigh it surrenders to these ancient obstacles, shying away in a mechanical motion that could be displacement by magic, or could be a sensibly altered route. I swear you can't tell.

It sends sad surveys back to its operators.

You always have to take account of such archaeological finds. Elizabeth adjusts her course and tilts away from Avalon.

Behind Nimue, Arthur rolls on his rock, and takes Guinevere in his arms, and Lancelot holds Arthur in their cosy napping threesome. All the court of the King beneath the hill settles down again and gets back to dreaming.

I turn to my witch. She's eating one half of the apple. She offers me the other. As I take the fruit, sweet as the future, sour as the past, filled with old, dirty magic, I look at her, the Lady of the Lake. I drop my sword, a letter opener again, back in my pocket.

'Would you like to go skinnydipping?' says Nimue. 'There's

an underground lake somewhere down here as I recall.'

'Roman baths too,' I say.

'That pine,' she says, and glitters at me.

'That shining tower,' I say.

'Old Man,' Adam says. He stumbles to his feet and looks groggy. 'Is this Camelot?'

MARIA DAHVANA HEADLEY

Maria Dahvana Headley is a *New York Times*-bestselling author whose books include *Magonia*, *Aerie*, *Queen of Kings*, the memoir *The Year of Yes*, and with Kat Howard, *The End of the Sentence*. With Neil Gaiman, she is the #1 *New York Times*-bestselling editor of the anthology *Unnatural Creatures*. Upcoming is the novel *The Mere Wife*, with Farrar, Straus & Giroux, as well as a short story collection. Her Nebula and Shirley Jackson Award-nominated short fiction has been anthologised in many year's bests. Her work has been supported by The MacDowell Colony, and Arte Studio Ginestrelle, among others.

"We work on each other's stories and longform all the time, editing, structuring, mucking about in each other's sentences, but we've never formally collaborated, so *Dead Letters* seemed like a good opportunity. The skull (China) and the mermaid (Maria) looked like two pieces of the same universe to us. The idea of a much reduced Merlin hunting his scattered magic in the Office of Dead Letters comes from a mutual interest in the snarled lovesick relationship between Merlin and his (clearly brilliant) apprentice witch Nimue, though neither of us remembers where the idea of eating the dead letters came from. From there, the parts that look like one of us wrote them were probably written by the other, in nearly all cases. One of us had a great deal of fun writing a ridiculous verse spell, and the other had an appalling amount of fun writing the line 'I go horizontal and fly.'"

CHINA MIÉVILLE

China Miéville is a writer of fiction and non-fiction who lives and works in London.

AND WE, SPECTATORS ALWAYS, EVERYWHERE

KIRSTEN KASCHOCK

The mother is an older mother, historically speaking. There is a streak of grey she does not dye. Her adoration of the child is like too much make-up. Her attentiveness to his every stumble in the park makes me feel nervous for him, and rushed. Will the child fall today? Irrevocably? This is the worry of her posture, as she leans forward off the bench ready to spring to him across the woodchips. Astounding – given her disquiet – that she allows the child, called Gibb, to risk splinter on the shifting ground.

I sit alone, under a tree. I do my best not to haunt the area by keeping an open book on my lap. It is Rilke.

The next day they come again. She is petite, slightly dishevelled, and has strapped him against her as if they were nomads. They are not. He is calmer than most toddlers who roam this half-acre with their nannies and blood mothers. The needless gadgets she must undo before he can be let down to join the fray frustrate me, whose job is to watch. His swinging limbs have the look of the unliving. I am familiar. When she packs him up to leave an hour later, he is more vivid, the bloom on the centre of his forehead visible even from here. She sticks a bottle in his face. He drops into a milk-fed stupor, and she re-secures the latches and belts.

Against the bark, my lower back begins to ache – an injury recalling itself. An old attachment.

To leave, she walks north through the grass. He is old enough to walk. He should be walking. Situations like this one grow only more and more untenable. He is three, it should be noted, despite the bottle. The talent for manipulation can manifest as early as eight months. Passivity, a strategy.

On the third day, they do not arrive at their usual time.

It is raining. I wander to Main Street for a poncho and a sandwich at Ipp's, which I cannot eat. I return to find her struggling to push a stroller through muck at the far edge of the park. Her umbrella is fighting her. The wind keeps yanking the large red nylon off to the side. She is an aging matador, less bravado than pathos. The boy's face is whipped with stinging spray, as mine almost certainly is, and his complaints cut across the field, clear as keys on glass. Why aren't they home yet? Her apology is muffled, but it is an apology, and, to accomplish it, she hunches – her spine suddenly a dowager's. Simultaneously, the umbrella springs upright as if sprouted from the earth. A battlefield poppy, wound-fed. As I have observed it, much of mothering involves contortion.

* * *

On the fourth day I am not there. I offer my initial report, which is incomplete.

When I see them again, something has shifted. She has had her hair cut, expensively. The boy – left longer than usual with sitter or Nana or friend – still seethes. The layering at the back is coquettish. Her neck, exposed. Someone convinced her to do this, probably citing ease. The boy requires time. Of course she should remove parts of herself to make room for that time: mothering is also truncation. How often does she shower? Whatever the frequency, it is more Victorian than her prior habit. The homes of small ones have ever received their taint from hidden food and sour female smells.

It has been a month. My tree is not as welcoming as it was at first, but I am not done with my watch. We are sentries, the tree and I. No thing must falter from the plan God has for all things. Sometimes, that means we are asked to steward one another. To cultivate, to prune. I climb up into its branches to oversee. A maple. Its red glow is buds. They are tight with their spring blood, jealously gripping it in a futile withholding of gush.

When they finally come back to the playground, the boy is in pain. He does not say so, but affects a slight limp. His left foot makes less viable connection with the balance beam than the right. She holds his hand, failing to register this new asymmetry. The boy's gait is his first test for her and she fails.

The mother clearly prides herself on attention to minutiae – so says the unnatural lift of her brow. The boy has a bruise on his heel, but it might be bone cancer. After the initial fever, polio can look like this, in other boys. In other times and countries.

Distraction is written all over. The blue sky scrawls with plane sign, and worms are fingering bottle caps and butts near the exposed roots at my feet, covered in boot. My book, soaked through days before, is illegible – each page polluted with the next, warped, stuck, tearing if turned. A buzz emanates from the mother's purse. She checks it, smiles, and puts him down. She is no longer beside him. She is somewhere else.

The next week, she untethers the boy from her gaze. He is both upset and freed. Curious, drawn, he wanders close. He has faint freckles, a thing I did not see before. Has she applied protection? It is March, but he is truly fair and the atmosphere is not what it was. I try to detect either coconut or cocoa in the breeze that wafts past him, but cannot. The imitations smear together in a chemical blur.

"Gibb, don't bother the nice lady."

She has seen him seeing me. She has ascribed me a gender. She hurries towards us, to remove him from danger even as she attempts to paint me harmless.

The boy stares. It is the first time he has allowed himself this directness. They can retain some feeling of what we are, especially the ones we have been assigned.

"Give me that."

That is the ruined book. He has spoken very clearly, and I feel compelled to reward his lack of fear. I hold it out, though not very far. She is close enough now to see my face, to see that it is not, in fact, nice.

She takes his hand as he reaches it towards me. He is still leaning out, listing towards the book with his small body, unsteady. She tugs. He makes an unpleasant but effective sound. She lets go immediately. Ashamed of her capacity for even this minor harm, she sweeps him up and away, cooing, acknowledging me no further. Except with her back.

I have ever wondered at the permutations of mothers – how they differ in discipline, training, expectation. Their samenesses are even more mystifying: the tensile strength of enveloping arms, the stamina it must take to toss the ache of a child from hip to hip, season upon season, and to love it.

The tedium.

I do not wear this body again.

She is giving birth. The boy is out in the hall with her mother, his grandmother. There are no fathers here. Not hers, not his, not his soon-sister's. Only nurses. Even the doctor is a woman. The last time I saw the boy he was a beast – all small boys are beasts. Now he is a thief. He has taken a dollar and three quarters from his grandmother's wallet. He is at the vending machine.

My voice comes from behind.

"What's your poison?"

He turns to look up at me. I see a glimmer of recognition, but he shakes it off.

"Chocolate isn't poison," he says as he retrieves the M&Ms.

"That wasn't your money."

He isn't seven yet. He flushes. He is good at sneaking but

not at lying, not when he doesn't know he's going to have to.

"Nana always gives me money."

"Nanas like pleases. They like thank yous. They like to be asked."

Authority is a trigger, and mine is great. He shoots past me back through the hall to his grandmother in the waiting room. Its beige tile transforms everything that bounces off it into hollow clicks and whispers.

I sit down across from them and he pretends not to see me.

"Your grandson?" I ask her. She is smaller than her daughter, frail beneath jewellery designed for a more regal frame and bearing than she has. She must know this. Her eyes, not pointed this way, are sharp.

"It is." She smiles through thin lips, unnaturally wet, and ruffles his hair absently, her focus on the double door.

The maternity ward. I come here, or to places like here, often. "A delivery?"

"My daughter's second child. This one –" and she squeezes the boy's arm with nails like polished talons "– is about to become a big brother."

He does not look at me. Instead, Gibb shoves an M&M deep into the pocket of each cheek – first one and then the other. He takes grave time. He is sucking off the candy shell. The smell of American chocolate in the mouth of a child is similar to vomit.

I am allowed an occasional half-truth. "What a lucky sister you're going to have."

In discussions of the unborn, gender is often prematurely assumed. Nana's eyes flicker this way. She decides my gaffe is innocent, or beneath mention.

The boy knows what is what. "I want a brother."

"A girl will bring your mother more comfort," I say and stand. This is known. Nana frowns. I am a man, overbearing and insensitive. Leaving.

As I pass, I brush her hand with my hand. I am able to do this quite tenderly. The old woman startles like a virgin. I can steal as well as anyone, although we don't call it that. We call it calling home.

Nana is dead within two weeks' time. The boy knows what is what. He does not want to envy me my power. He wants to hate me. He speaks to no one of this.

Lucy is two. Gibb, nine.

The mother is making preparations to marry Lucy's father, a musician. All the preparations. He is younger, in most ways. The family is living in Nana's brownstone. The mother has inherited everything. Gibb does not like Lucy's father. Gibb does not like Lucy.

Gibb has begun to limp.

My post in the alley across is adjacent to a dumpster. My olfactory judgments are unbecoming, deemed worldly. Adjustments are underway.

This body both hurts and reeks. Its joints are beyond repair – I must stretch incessantly. The boy walks past with friends on the way to school. Lucy's father has insisted. No coddling. Gibb's hobble is more pronounced on the way home each afternoon. As is his hatred for the sack of flesh he has been told to call father.

The mother has moved from freelance to firm.

Lucy has a nanny. They spend hours at the park when Gibb is gone so Lucy's father can sleep. It is hard to day-sleep. While waiting for the boy, I pretend unconsciousness, resisting assault on the senses. I curl among newspapers, eyes slitted. Quiet helps Lucy's father. From the bags he tosses over me with a sound louder than clink and an odour its own brand of sour, I gather whiskey helps also.

My stay on the corner is brief. I kill another cat.

Such minor infractions are frowned upon but not verboten. We are presented with certain valves for our energies, which – to wield – take an intense will we are not free to wholly master. Beside my knobby spine, the slots of pain sear.

Lucy's father leaves the mother a week before the wedding.

She told him to go. But in an endless string of abandonments, any loss is perceived as desertion. She tells herself she told him to go. She tells herself of course she did and she was right to. She wanted this, she tells herself – respect. The mother buries her face in Lucy's belly. He left me.

During the next few months, she will take small but constant comfort in Lucy's laughter, needs, squeals. The boy and I will not.

I am renting the third floor.

Gibb is not an able-bodied boy. It is difficult to see, but he is torqueing in upon himself. The crooked mile requires the crooked man: the rhyme misunderstands causality. One by one, friends have their parents refuse the mother's invitations.

Some game he played too rough. His loneliness is like a gun in the mother's bedside table. He has been in there. There is no gun. He has asked me, the woman upstairs, do I carry.

The mother acts like a mother. She worries for me more than for Gibb. I do not eat with them though invited. I leave briefly every day, but she does not know where I go. If I work. She wants to ask. She has her job, but the nanny is expensive. Lucy's father gambled so much of Nana's egg.

My job is watching and, now, to listen. I appear, for once, as I would choose to. We don't choose. I look genderless, although the mother thinks lesbian. The misapprehension allows me to stare at her, and the boy, unimpeded by decorum. Outsiders are given tremendous leeway, seen as they are as renouncers of all things the devout have secretly forsaken.

Lucy, a wet muffin, is heavier than bread should be. Yeasty. I do not volunteer to hold her but sometimes must. The mother and I are friends. This is a word women use when someone sits with them, more than once.

Disaster rots Gibb's whole world, or he would pin his bad feeling on me, especially as he has attached to this body his first stirrings. He leers around corners. A pencil skirt I wear has lace that emerges below the hem like a mistake. I have watched him watching. For him – it is legs.

When Lucy's father left, the boy thought things would be made right. This has not happened. His pain increases. He is my charge – it is up to me to reduce his extremity.

* * *

I go to him. We are advised to remain corporeal in these moments. The alternative can be devastating.

The mother and I share a bottle of wine she doesn't notice that I do not share. I retire. After she goes down with her television on, I return to the second floor and enter Gibb's room.

It is nightlit. A lava lamp. The walls swim in rose.

I wear the silken whites that have ever supported nocturnal visions.

I am an emissary. I lower myself onto the bed beside him. He is small in the bed.

"Do you know me?" I ask.

"Yes." Remarkably clear, the boy's elocution. Even in sleep.

"Would you like to feel better, Gibb? Because I can make you feel better." I pause. "Even good."

He is awake now, pretending not to be, squinting to peer between thick lashes, breathing shallowly. "Yes."

This is a whisper.

The yes he has given me is a secret, as are the instructions I pass on. A deeper secret I have not told.

So close do I lean in that my lip grazes the red shell of his ear. I can feel his pulse there, and the words I expel, in whorl. I tell him what he will do. I give this information to him in fine detail. In smoke and filigree. He is barely breathing. His whole small body strains to listen. Were he like me, he might leave it there on the mattress. Behind him.

And then, as we do, I kiss him.

I lean over the boy. His eyes are wide. I kiss him on the mark so faint only the mother remembers it. It is at the very centre of his forehead. The birthbloom – the one I gave to him nine years before – trembles in kindling against my mouth.

"Sometimes we have to take back a thing that has been given," I say to him. "Sometimes God asks us to undo God's work, and we must ask for your help."

Children find delegation deeply unfair. Why must they slave for those who know how and better? Nevertheless, they ache to be obedient. Especially the most awful ones long to be part of something greater, filled as they are inexplicably with awe.

It is this internal conflict that makes them such remarkable, friable pawns.

Gibb looks up at me. My request is too big. It is not actually a request, and I let this knowledge settle hotly upon his chest like a nesting alley cat. I knead my fingers into his ribcage to remind him of his Nana. Of what I did to her.

Of what I could yet do.

I see him thinking of her. The mother. It shocks me, his love. How it manifests even in this child. Even towards this mother. The softening at the jaw, the release of fisting muscles around the eyes. The intensity of Gibb's love begins to darken the room.

It is getting darker. Darker. I turn away from the boy. The lava is stuck. A congealed layer has turned black and, watched, flakes away from the amorphous body imprisoned in the tube.

The substance begins to flow again, only now shot through with scabs. I look at the boy.

He cannot say his yes this time. He nods.

I envy this – what he is able to do in this moment – a thing he does not even recognise as choice.

* * *

The six-inch butcher blade was Nana's pride and joy. A small woman requires precision instruments. She has no leverage.

Gibb leaves for school when the mother leaves. He meets his remaining friend on the corner and walks two blocks before turning to run back for a forgotten worksheet. The friend continues on. Inside the brownstone, the nanny is warming a bottle in a pan on the stove. I am waiting in my room, hands folded in this lap.

When I hear her scream, I discorporate. He is young. It may take him some time and I have never grown accustomed to these sounds, familiar as they are in the factory of my work.

I appreciate Mozart, and Motown. Certain Gregorian chants. Ive Mendes. Thelonious Monk.

I get the details as one must. I read the files.

He stabs her first just above the waist. Nicking her spine, not severing it. The blade dips deeper into her thighs than forensics might expect, given his size and weight. She grabs for the boiling water but it rains down on her. Welts. The blood, pooling thickly on the tile, likely causes her fall. She flails as she slips. Spatter. Once she is prone, he moves to the throat, and, again, the efficiency of the cut is technically remarkable. The defensive wounds – minimal. She does not grab the blade. He manages the carotid quickly. The team thinks this either lucky or studied.

Lucy was strapped into her high chair, during.

After.

Because he is a smart boy with a good memory, the twisted school-tie tourniquet holds, and Lucy lives.

Studied then.

Once he has gotten through the ankle, not easily, he takes the still-stockinged foot and inserts the blade up through the arch, between the third and fourth metatarsals, transpiercing it. He then walks with slow ceremony through dining and living rooms, leaving a trail of blood. Soon, I suppose, weddings will have flower boys. He places the foot on the sill while he opens the window. He hurls out the vanquished rose, with the blade inside. Lucy's foot makes it, improbably, past the wrought iron and ivy and onto the sidewalk.

In the original instructions, before our game of telephone, Gibb's excision ended Lucy.

I am allowed certain valves, half-truths, improvisations. Although they are minor, I am always punished.

There was nothing to do for the nanny.

On his eighteenth birthday, Gibb is transferred to a private institution. The mother pays with what remains of Nana's egg but never visits. The mother and Lucy are inseparable, and Lucy would never think to come. With state-of-the-art prostheses, Lucy grows into a noted tennis player, a spokesperson for the disabled, a differently bodied model. In interviews she and the mother do not speak of Gibb. In interviews, if pressed, they leave.

They think the worst. They think him without a soul. But his soul is intact. It twists in him, like a dish towel, wringing.

Once every year or so, Lucy's father drives upstate to see him. He is barred from Lucy's life, blamed somehow. He never liked the boy, but knows what it is to be stricken. He talks to himself, and the boy sits close by as if listening. Over years the Dixie-cup cocktails have drained Gibb of much, yet not all, of his speech. Lucy's father's whiskey loosens his tongue, and blurs the sharp corners of the four-hour trip.

The man has sent Lucy a bouquet of single socks on each birthday since she turned three. He likes to shop for them, despite the eyes of clerks. She must have, by now, every color and pattern that exists. Plaids, stripes, polka dots, rainbows, skulls and butterflies, flowers and barbed wire, tie-dye and argyle and angels. She keeps them too. He has seen her wearing them at matches. He goes when he can – sits in the back and leaves early. "Not red, Gibb," he says to the boy. "Never seen her dress that foot in red." And then he laughs. "I believe that's on you." Lucy's father is still a musician. He still plays jazz violin. Beautifully.

And he has kept all of the half-pairs.

At the end of this particular visit, his last, nearly incoherent at the end of the hour, he sticks his finger in Gibb's chest. "You. You should have'm. I'll tell you what – I'm gonna sendem to you."

Gibb spends all the time outside that he is given. Once, in one of the rare lucid moments of his later years, he asks me about the book in the park – the one I nearly handed him.

I tell him the truth. That, like the bodies, it was a prop. A crutch.

And that I read it anyway.

The boy walks slowly these days, shambling, but he is no cripple, and he does not hate me for what I am – orderly, doctor, patient, or thrush on the fence – or for what God had me have him do.

He does not know he was my greatest disobedience.

The mercy I had him show was never God's.

I was given Gibb to protect and to love – in the ways accessible to us – as a punishment.

As I will be given my next, more severe charge in censure for my handling of this case.

And so on.

Each spring, the owners hire a team of groundskeepers to tend the hedges. They all soon know Gibb. His interest is keen.

Until the boy dies, aged forty-seven, all but forgotten, I collect the socks. I intercept them, parcel by parcel, from the thick must of the mailroom. Lucy's father does not mean to be cruel. No. Cruel is not what he means to be.

KIRSTEN KASCHOCK

Kirsten Kaschock has authored three books of poetry: *Unfathoms*, *A Beautiful Name for a Girl*, and *The Dottery* – winner of the Donald Hall Prize for poetry. Her debut novel, *Sleight*, is a work of speculative fiction about performance. She has earned a PhD in English from the University of Georgia and another in dance from Temple University. Recent work can be read at *American Poetry Review*, *BOAAT*, and *Liminalities*. She is on faculty at Drexel University and serves as editor-in-chief for *thINKing DANCE*, a consortium of Philadelphia dance artists and writers.

"I have always been drawn to stories and films of children who were somehow off or wrong – like *The Bad Seed*, *The Fifth Child*, etc. When I received in the mail a toddler-sized sock with a skull pattern, I began thinking about such a child's caretakers. I wondered, was it possible to write a bad-child story and have blame NOT fall primarily on the mother? What kind of presence was necessary to shift that trope? I began writing from there, from inside that presence. It felt… odd."